PENGUIN CL. _ _ _

PARTITIONS

Kamleshwar (1932–2007) was born in Mainpuri, Uttar Pradesh. He did his master's in Hindi from Allahabad University in 1954 and soon afterwards started working as a scriptwriter for Doordarshan. In the course of a glorious career as a writer, he wrote ten collections of short stories, ten novels and over thirty books in genres as diverse as literary criticism, travelogue and memoir. As a journalist he was associated with the *Dainik Jagaran* (1990–92) and the *Dainik Bhaskar* (1996–2002) among other important assignments. He served as the additional director general of Doordarshan and wrote scripts for TV serials like *Darpan*, *Ek Kahani*, *Chandrakanta* and *Yug*, apart from producing and directing various TV programmes and documentaries. A prolific scriptwriter, he had such acclaimed and popular films as *Sara Aakash*, *Aandhi*, *Mausam*, *Rajanigandha*, *Choti Si Baat* and *Mr Natwarlal* to his credit. He was the recipient of various awards including the Sahitya Akademi Award in 2003.

Ameena Kazi Ansari teaches English at the Department of English and Modern European Languages, Jamia Millia Islamia, New Delhi.

PARTITIONS

KAMLESHWAR

Translated from the Hindi by
AMEENA KAZI ANSARI

PENGUIN BOOKS

PENGUIN BOOKS
Published by the Penguin Group
Penguin Books India Pvt. Ltd, 11 Community Centre, Panchsheel Park, New
Delhi 110 017, India
Penguin Group (USA) Inc., 375 Hudson Street, New York, New York 10014,
USA
Penguin Group (Canada), 90 Eglinton Avenue East, Suite 700, Toronto,
Ontario, M4P 2Y3, Canada (a division of Pearson Penguin Canada Inc.)
Penguin Books Ltd, 80 Strand, London WC2R 0RL, England
Penguin Ireland, 25 St Stephen's Green, Dublin 2, Ireland (a division of Penguin
Books Ltd)
Penguin Group (Australia), 250 Camberwell Road, Camberwell, Victoria
3124, Australia (a division of Pearson Australia Group Pty Ltd)
Penguin Group (NZ), 67 Apollo Drive, Rosedale, North Shore 0632, New
Zealand (a division of Pearson New Zealand Ltd)
Penguin Group (South Africa) (Pty) Ltd, 24 Sturdee Avenue, Rosebank,
Johannesburg 2196, South Africa

Penguin Books Ltd, Registered Offices: 80 Strand, London WC2R 0RL,
England

Originally published in Hindi as *Kitne Pakistan,* by Rajpal and Sons 2000
First published in English by Penguin Books India 2006

Copyright © Kamleshwar

All rights reserved

10 9 8 7 6 5 4 3 2 1

ISBN 9780143063704

Typeset in *Perpetua* by SÜRYA, New Delhi
Printed at Saurabh Printers Pvt. Ltd, Noida

Author's Note

This novel was born out of a constant ferment within my mind. For decades, I had done various things like writing stories and columns, taking up jobs and then leaving them, making TV films on terrorism in Kashmir and on the Babri Masjid dispute in Ayodhya. The social scenario traumatized me, and so I got caught up in producing programmes like *The Burning Question* on the Shalini burning case, and *Closed File* on the suicide of three sisters in Kanpur. During this period, I also wrote a couple of film scripts besides writing the screenplay for protracted serials like *Chandrakanta*, *Yug*, *Betaal* and *Viraat*.

It was during those days that I got an opportunity to write a serial on India's agricultural history. The power of my reading glasses changed as I perused histories and studied the development of world civilizations. In the course of penning down twenty-seven hour-long episodes, my mind mulled over the beginnings of time and the advent of the Aryans. It constantly opposed the dynamics of war evolved by the Mohenjodaro and Harappa civilizations, and also the Aryans. Many a time, I wrote and rewrote the episode on this issue. Once, in a fit of weariness, to finish this work at hand, I even incorporated the ideological tilt of Western intellectuals in my writing. I also juggled with Lokmanya Tilak's conceptualization and theory that the Aryans were the original inhabitants of India. Taking this into account, I rewrote the episode. But, somehow, I was not quite convinced by what I had written. All the while I felt that I had failed to reach the core of truth in my composition. If one preconceives and predetermines the truth, it can only give one ephemeral insight; it rarely accords inner harmony. That is why, perhaps, a composition always seeks its own possible truth. It was this seeking which revealed to me that the Aryans had no reason to be aggressive. They had not been attacked. These Aryans were just nomadic tribes familiar with agricultural techniques, and they sought the benevolence of nature and fertile soil. The Indus Valley had no dearth of either.

So, there was no need for aggression and warfare. The Aryans just came and randomly settled down.

Echoes of warfare resound in the Vedas' account of the demonic Asuras. These are assuredly sagas that describe the dynamics of the social system, the power and grandeur of a society that had gradually stabilized. In all the histories of the world's civilizations, there is no evidence to suggest that a community, which had faced invasion, had composed anything that could match the constructive charm of the Vedas. Such works can only be written during times of peace, faith and forbearance; not during times of war. This emergent truth gave me much solace and made it possible for me to write *The Story of Agriculture*.

Kitne Pakistan was intermittently written in the midst of these stories, articles, fictionalized histories and other impediments. From this variety of compositions, I was able to enhance my creative skills and learn the art of controlled expression.

I began writing this novel in May 1990. In the midst of dense forests, Subhash Pant had made arrangements for me at the Jhajra Forest Rest House near Dehradun. For provisions, one had to walk downhill. Gayatri was there with me. We had also taken along with us our four-year-old grandchild, Anant. He had made friends with a dog that visited us. Anant had named him Moti. Sometimes, we got to see multicoloured wild pheasants and Anant would walk long distances just to see them.

Occasionally, adivasi woodcutters would pass by. One day, Anant disappeared from sight while in pursuit of a pheasant. Gayatri was alarmed. We searched all over, ran around calling out to him, but he was not to be found. An old man passing by told us that a short distance away, he had seen a little boy walking with a woodcutter. Hearing this, Gayatri felt faint with fear. Having read about the tradition of human sacrifice amongst tribal people, she was terrified. Even I was alarmed. After reassuring Gayatri and giving her some water to drink, I left her in the care of a servant and set out. I walked swiftly in the direction indicated by the old man. I had gone some distance when I saw Anant sitting on the shoulders of a woodcutter, feet dangling, and hands resting on the man's turban.

The child was bubbling with joy. In his left hand, the man held an axe and he was walking towards me. I heaved a sigh of relief. It turned out that the woodcutter had taken Anant to show him deer and bears.

This incident provided me a new perception on tribal people. It was a perspective based on experience, far removed from what books had to say. Seven or eight years later, this experience inspired me when I wrote about the Maya civilization in this novel. Anyhow...

Two compulsions are associated with this novel. One is that in my mind there was no hero or villain, so I made Time the protagonist. The second is that, while writing the novel, I constantly felt as if this was my maiden literary venture. I was all the while beset by an unvoiced restlessness and a perception of inadequacy. Like all novels, this one, too, had to culminate somewhere. So it ended. Yet, in my mind, the debate carries on...

Kamleshwar

Translator's Note

When Charles Dickens wrote the first sentence in *The Tale of Two Cities*—'It was the best of times, it was the worst of times'—little did he know that that these words would poignantly sum up the state of affairs that prevailed in the wake of India's independence. Sadly, the euphoria of independence was dampened by the trauma of massacres that marked the partition of the country. *Kitne Pakistan* is the voice of a man who happened to live through, and keenly felt those troubled times.

It is a novel that fictionalizes mythologies and histories. All along, it underscores the unnatural division of a people and a land along lines of religion. It subtly bemoans the fact that, in 1947, the people who mattered allowed the fragmentation of land, society and psyche, all of which resulted in one of the most horrific bloodbaths in human history. This event forms the backdrop of the novel and informs the consciousness of the protagonist—a nameless *adeeb* or littérateur.

Giving the protagonist a name would perhaps limit him to specific confines of name and place, both of which he is made to transcend in the course of the narrative. He is a contemporary Everyman, a man of many parts and personae. He is introduced as a writer who has lived through India's partition, experiencing the trauma of hearts and minds being divided as the contours of Pakistan are drawn up by the British. As the plot unfolds, the adeeb plays many roles—that of a journalist who questions the establishment, of an unrequited lover whose mistress lives across a volatile border, of a historian who questions pantheons of divinity as well as civilizational myths and history, and an activist who rails against massacres, imperialism and nuclear proliferation. In each of these roles, the adeeb comes across as a person with an extremely sensitive conscience which makes him take a position of critical moderation. He is an articulate voice of the common man's concerns which have gone largely unheard in history's relentless march of time. It is this man who embodies the people's court which sets out to judge human as well as divine acts of omission and commission down the trajectory of history.

Sweeping over vast tracts of time and space, the narrator summons Father Time to assist him in his judgement. And, it is this Time which emerges as the protagonist, presenting before the reader a tableau of men and matters that await the adeeb's judgement. In the carnival of historical personages who march through the pages of *Kitne Pakistan*, the adeeb's court questions, cross-examines and passes strictures. Slices of past, present and future appear before the bench but, ironically, it is a blind beggar who is made to show the way to a subcontinent's troubled populace.

Kitne Pakistan is about people—people all over the globe—who have suffered injustice, oppression and dislocation of various kinds. It is the voice of a man who has lived through a crucial epoch of the world's history and seen both the best and the worst of times. The work externalizes and puts on paper a gut-wrenching debate that went on in the author's mind (and which continues in a reader's mind) as one peruses the novel. Its power and appeal lie in addressing and impacting contemporary audiences.

For me, as for many others like me, *Kitne Pakistan* has a special personal relevance. Born as I was a dozen years after India's independence, I grew up hearing my nani talk of how complete her family's 'partition' had been—three children in India, the other three in Pakistan. We all lived through war and peace, always hoping for the best. It was my ten-year-old son who so succinctly summed it all up some years back when I visited relatives in Lahore: 'Amma, the people here look the *same* as us.'

Translating *Kitne Pakistan* has been an experience of a very different kind. To me, the novel reads as a work encompassing many texts, co-texts and subtexts that represent a multiplicity of perspectives. In translating it, I have tried to negotiate with and evolve a mode of expression that captures its imaginative, cultural, and philosophical nuances.

Besides juggling with the academic intricacies of translation, *Kitne Pakistan* for me has been both a purgation and an assertion. It is purgation because the hopelessness of my nani's generation has been redeemed through a creative work that looks to the future after learning from the past. It is an assertion as it echoes my belief that, despite the bitterness of Partition, there are people who look to the future with hope and confidence. I imagine this novel would make great sense to the readers of my generation, as it would to those of the generations before and after me.

Ameena Kazi Ansari

In band kamron mein meri saans ghut jaati hai
Khidkiyan kholta hoon toh zahrili hawa aati hai

Suffocation overwhelms me in these closed rooms
When I throw open the windows, miasma engulfs me

1

He recalls a long-forgotten tale.

He came from a desolate land, a world of silent allure, where nothing was ever said, aspirations tossed and turned within the mind, yearnings surfaced only to be eclipsed, and dreams were gathered and taken away like garments from the clothes line at dusk. Obscure, discrete reflections often remained entangled in memories, neither crystallizing nor fading into oblivion. These thoughts left their imprints on the fabric of his life in uneven patterns.

It seemed almost as if his entire kasbah with its many windows gazed at him in silent supplication. Sometimes, the impressions of retraced steps could be made out in the dust after a light shower; heavy rains filled up these little depressions with water as though they were tear-laden eyes that would dry up with time and disappear forever. Some eyes longed to say so much; but not a word did they utter. Here, a kajal-rimmed eye beckoned; there, a silhouette stood framed by a window; a gesturing finger or shamefaced yearnings, homeward-bound, driven by a tale born of despair.

Those were strange times.

Days passed like neem flowers drifting to the ground.

Days that resembled the yellow kaner blossoms.

Days that seemed like endless afternoons.

And then came days bereft of any direction.

Days, when a bleak present strained to move into the future. Independence was imminent, its dawn about to break. The facility of railway reservations did not exist in those days. He couldn't quite remember...perhaps, Vidya had been a student of science...but as their holidays coincided, they always met at the Allahabad railway station. She came from Fatehgarh, but it was at Allahabad station that they had run into each other. A strange affinity between them always made one wait for the other, and it became an unspoken habit for both to board the first passenger train on the morning the vacations began. Though express trains plied this route, they preferred to travel on the passenger train which meandered along, halting at every station on the way.

Travelling together so often, they had committed to memory the names of the various stations through which their train passed. First came Bamrouli, then Manori, Syed Sarawan, Bharwari, Sirathu, Fatehpur and then...Kanpur. Along the way, they read not only the names of the places they passed through, but also remembered, by rote, the capacity of each of the mushroom-like overhead tanks that supplied water to the platforms. They could even recall particular stations at which the water tanks of the train engine would be replenished. Sharing as they did a strange bond forged from unvoiced yearnings that fused, suddenly, into a silence born of tacit understanding, he offered Vidya sour chutney to go with the samosas they ate at Bharwari, or added sweet chutney to the pakoris they had at Fatehpur. Though she had never actually said so, he instinctively knew that she liked these condiments. Sometimes, their gaze tried to pick out the sharp silhouette of a solitary tree from the blur of greenery that whizzed past the train.

A few more stations, a few more moments of togetherness, both of them wishing the journey would never end. But in the end, they always reached Kanpur. Here, Vidya would get off to board the metre-gauge train bound for Fatehgarh. Crossing over from one platform to the next, she would reach the one where her train waited for passengers from incoming trains. In those days, the convention of saying 'bye-bye' did not exist; flying kisses were unheard of. Only the deepest silence served as the true measure of affection. She would alight wordlessly. He would hand over her jhola along with her small tin trunk and her bag of books. 'Achha,' she would murmur and walk across to the overbridge that led to her platform. He never escorted her there, as he risked missing his own train.

He would travel on to Shikohabad Junction and then take a branch line to Mainpuri, where his mother lived. He knew the names of all the stations that lay between Shikohabad and Mainpuri; yet, he could never remember anything about the water tanks or the trees that grew beside the tracks along this stretch. Perhaps, if Vidya had been there, he would have.

*

Through unspoken words did they decide on the day they would undertake the return journey, after the vacations were over, and the passenger train they would board for travelling to Allahabad. On that day, he would take the main-line train to Kanpur, where he would change trains to board the Allahabad passenger train. Having arrived before him, Vidya would be waiting at the platform.

Two years went by. They met, waited for each other and travelled together. Then came a year when things seemed different. Summer vacations, Allahabad station and the passenger train remained the same, but the atmosphere had changed perceptibly. Passengers appeared to be strangely silent. Syed Sarawan was unusually crowded, more so than any other station. Many of the passengers were women and children, a departure from the earlier predominance of men. There was also an uncommon assortment of luggage—tin trunks, sacks and roughly tied bundles, large and small. When the train steamed out, no one on the platform was heard crying out 'Khuda hafiz'. Conversations between the passengers revealed that most belonged to rural families bound for Aligarh on their way to Pakistan.

Passing through the railway yard at Kanpur, the train started to slow down. Vidya had to get off here. The platform appeared and she stepped off. As always, he gave her a hand with the luggage. Then Vidya spoke: 'I don't think I shall be returning to continue my studies next term.'

'Why not?' he asked.

'My family isn't keen that I should.'

A feeling of profound disquiet hung over this exchange. Sharing the depths of unwritten, unexpressed passion, they had not felt the need for coaxing answers out of each other.

Vidya started climbing the overbridge that led to her waiting train; it was almost time for his own train to depart. And so their saga ended. From the overbridge, Vidya let fall her handkerchief. At that very instant, his train sounded its final whistle. From his carriage, far away, he watched the handkerchief wafting down. For a moment, he even thought of retrieving it, but was unable to leap off the moving train. After all, a journey was a serious affair. It could not be abandoned midway, leaving books and baggage behind. So her handkerchief lay unclaimed, as he continued on his way. His destination lay ahead, as it did for all passengers, even those bound for Pakistan via Aligarh. Even Vidya travelled on, her train rattling towards Fatehgarh. He was convinced she would not return. He had a hunch she was getting married that very summer.

He got off at Shikohabad to board the train to Mainpuri. Passengers going to Pakistan continued their onward journey. He never met Vidya again, but he often wondered what direction her life's journey had taken. The one certainty in his life was the handkerchief he invariably saw, sailing down to settle on the platform, whenever he passed the station at Kanpur. It's a vision he has, even today.

*

Years later, after changing many jobs and cities, he would settle down in Bombay. It was there that he received a mysterious, even puzzling letter. The envelope told the tale of its long journey. It had been redirected—as many as five times. While the addresses marked on it had been struck out, his name remained untouched, intact. Unknown, kindly hands had written down his changed addresses. It had dawned on him then that letters inspired by genuine feeling and concern always reached their destination, even if it took them ages to do so.

He opened the envelope with painstaking care. As he read the contents, he was overwhelmed by a deep sense of mystery:

O Littérateur par excellence!
Why should I lament, if I have given my heart away?
When the heart throbs no longer, why should the tongue
    complain?

You brought me disrepute, may you be consumed by
    flames!
Why be my confidant, if you cannot brook my pain?

What is trust, what love? If I have to beat my breast

Then why, O stone-hearted one, should it be at your
    threshold?
—Khuda hafiz.

The writer's name and address were conspicuously absent.
Particularly disturbing was the salutation. The letter's unusual contents
suddenly brought back memories of Vidya. Perhaps, she had written
to him after all these years, relying on her power of recall for his
address. Sympathetic souls had contributed their mite by redirecting
the letter and ensuring that it reached the addressee. What was most
astounding, however, was the fact that Vidya had been a student of
science. Her knowledge of Hindi was rather limited. Of Urdu, she
knew not a word. He was struck by the great incongruity of the
'Khuda hafiz' with which the letter ended. Oh, no, he thought, it
could not be Vidya...it had to be someone else. The underlying
mystery of the letter deepened further; it became extraordinary,
incredible, and it so happened that...

2

Oh, no, that was not the way it happened...
    'Sir, please let me tell you how it happened...'
    With a start, he looked in the direction of the voice. Mahmood
Ali, his assistant, steno and peon, all rolled into one, stood before
him. In his hands, he held the rough paper that bore the news from
the teleprinter.
    'What happened?' he asked.
    Mahmood set down the paper in front of him. With a cursory
glance at the news, he looked out of his cabin and saw the evening-
shift reporters crowding around the long desk in the hall outside.
They were engrossed in an animated discussion. Then he noticed the
two news editors walking rapidly towards his cabin. The first city
edition was about to go to press; he could hear the muffled
reverberations of the printing machines in the basement. The news
editors entered his cabin.
    'Sir, we need a front-page editorial from you today.'

'If you could dictate it now, sir, it would appear in the first edition.'

'All right. Tell them to be ready in the computer room. Get me a cup of coffee in the meantime.'

Mahmood left to do his bidding, but the buzzer summoned him back. A quick perusal of the desk page reminded him of what had happened in 1948, 1965 and 1972. An undeclared war had now erupted in Kargil where Pakistani soldiers, disguised as civilians, had intruded into Indian territory and attacked defence positions. Advancing quite a few kilometres into India, they had also set up bunkers. They had crossed the Line of Control at Kargil, Batalik, Drass, Mushkoh, Turtuk, Zojila, Kaksar, Chilindiyal and Hotapal. Pakistani officers claimed that this was the work of the mujahideen, but, in truth, the troops were their own—in disguise.

'That is not all, sir. By acting in this manner, the Pakistanis have violated the 1972 Treaty. They have also flouted the terms of the Lahore Declaration which upheld the principles of friendship, brotherhood and trade. The movement of their troops must have started well before our prime minister's trip to Lahore. They have now taken over the higher peaks, with the result that we have ended up paying a heavy price in terms of casualties and equipment.'

'Connect me to Najam Sethi.'

'Najam Sethi?'

'Yes, Najam Sethi, the editor of the *Friday Times* in Lahore, Pakistan. Why are you gaping at me...don't you know that Lahore is in Pakistan?'

'Yes, I do. But what can Najam Sethi do in the circumstances?'

'He can ask Pakistan's prime minister, Nawaz Sharif, what exactly is going on and why.'

'Sir, the Pakistani prime minister and foreign minister have issued statements categorically denying any links between their army and the infiltrators. They also claim that this is a situation created entirely by the Indians themselves.'

'Even if we do accept their contention, there is no denying the fact that these intruders are Pakistanis.'

'That is the crux of the matter, sir. If Pakistan honours the terms of the Lahore Declaration, it is their responsibility to prevent infiltrators from crossing over into India.'

'Sir, if this attack leads to full-scale war, the consequences will be disastrous.'

'The common people of both countries will bear the brunt of any hostilities that break out. That is why I must speak to Najam Sethi. It is perceptive and liberal journalists like him who mould public opinion against bloodshed...'

At this point, another news editor arrived, carrying a list of the casualties in Kargil. 'Sir,' he announced, 'here are the names of the soldiers and airmen who have sacrificed their lives for their country. They come from all over India—Nagaland, Rajasthan, Bihar, Karnataka, Kanyakumari, Maharashtra, Uttar Pradesh, Andhra, Punjab, Haryana...'

He called Mahmood and began dictating, 'Dear Prime Minister and Defence Minister...'

3

Dear Prime Minister and Defence Minister,

It is with a heavy heart that I address this open letter to you.

Last week, newspapers carried horrifying reports of the dire situation in Kargil while you feigned ignorance. They condemned your stance as self-destructive and informed Indian citizens about the real state of affairs in the country.

While the Congress is embroiled in the native–foreigner issue that revolves around the question of Sonia Gandhi's Indian citizenship, the BJP and its allies are caught up in their respective agendas of self-promotion. The caretaker prime minister, A.B. Vajpayee, is busy releasing *Marasim*, a music cassette brought out by Jagjit Singh and Gulzar. Newspapers are choc-a-bloc with detailed accounts of the World Cup. News that needs to be disseminated speedily is put on hold as the Information and Broadcasting Minister Pramod Mahajan is engaged in formulating strategies that will hasten the dissolution of Prasar Bharati. Oblivious to the ongoing border skirmishes at Kargil, Foreign Minister Jaswant Singh is touring Central Asian countries with a view to forging new ties with them. Defence Minister George Fernandes is involved in organizing an international conference to discuss the ramifications of the joint air attack on Yugoslavia by NATO and the United States. No politician, national figure or political party has either voiced concern or issued a statement on the explosive state of affairs in the country.

In the Kargil–Drass sector, Pakistani guns are constantly making their presence felt from across the border. Infiltrators breaching the Line of Control can be effectively dealt with only after the elected government makes its political intentions clear. Indifference in this regard could cost us dearly.

Mr Prime Minister, it was after this note of caution was published that your advisor Shri Brajesh Mishra appeared for the first time on Star News. Among other things, his statement acknowledged the failure of state intelligence agencies in identifying and dealing with the problem of enemy infiltration across the border. Mishra went so far as to say that he held military intelligence responsible for this lapse. To instil confidence in the public, Air Commodore Subhash Bhojwani, Director of Offensive Operations, and Brigadier Mohun Bhandari, Deputy Director General of Army Operations, addressed a press conference in Delhi. They were briefed to issue statements about air raids that had been carried out that very morning on infiltrator hideouts in Indian territory. This was to warn Pakistan that any intervention on its part would invite an appropriate response from India. The two army spokesmen declared, moreover, that as a result of the air offensive, the infiltrators had been hemmed in from all sides by the Indian Army. They had been deprived of all possible sources of help (in the form of arms, ammunition and medical supplies) from their Pakistani mentors. Their escape routes had been cut off and a hundred and sixty of them had, reportedly, been killed. This information was received, according to the two spokesmen, from unidentified military sources.

So, Mr Prime Minister, the moment for testing the strength of your moral fibre is at hand. When your government collapsed, you had appeared on state television the very next day to address the nation. Yet, you did not feel the necessity of a national telecast to stand by your grieving countrymen when they learnt of Squadron Leader Ajay Kumar Ahuja's martyrdom, Flight Lieutenant Nachiketa's courageous ejection from his damaged aircraft behind enemy lines, the death of four soldiers in a helicopter crash in Kargil and the government's questionable casualty figures: only twenty-nine dead, a hundred and twenty-eight injured, and twelve missing. It all adds up to extreme insensitivity on your part.

Your defence minister is a past master at issuing callous statements. He justified the nuclear blasts at Pokhran. Quoting intelligence reports, he accused China of targeting India by deploying its missiles in Tibet, and pronounced it to be the country's arch enemy. This time, however, his intelligence network failed to detect the Pakistan-backed infiltration in Kargil after the snows had melted on the mountains. To cap it all, the defence minister issued another outrageous statement, claiming that neither the Pakistani prime minister nor the Inter Services Intelligence, backed by the Pakistani army, had any hand in the Kargil incursions. These infiltrations were, apparently, the handiwork of the Pakistani army. The Indian defence minister needs to be told that his statement is an absurd one, betraying the extent to which his mental faculties have been impaired.

If it is indeed true that there is a complete absence of coordination between Pakistan's executive body, its army and its other state agencies and that they all operate independently, the situation is fraught with still greater danger. At a moment when both countries have atomic weapons at their disposal, is our mentally inept defence minister trying to suggest that if war (opposed by the common people of both countries) breaks out, it is Pakistan's army, rather than its government, which will make the crucial decision? Going by the minister's argument, it logically follows that in the eventuality of a nuclear confrontation, decisions will be taken by the Pakistani military rather than by the democratically elected government of Nawaz Sharif.

If our nation's defence minister is given to issuing such irresponsible statements, only Bhagwan or Allah can save the peace-loving peoples of both countries. The defence minister's words not only dishearten those citizens of Pakistan who believe in peace and democratic values, they also sow the seeds of doubt in the minds of India's liberals. Viewed from any perspective, his statement undermines the cause of democracy. It smacks of devilish cunning and foments discord. It seeks to ridicule the Pakistani army and implies that this vexatious issue can only be resolved through a show of military might, as the present Pakistani government has little influence over its armed forces. Seemingly innocuous statements like this hamper the process of dialogue and become handy weapons in the hands of hardliners and warmongers. It is obvious that only an insane defence minister is capable of issuing such statements. If not entirely deranged, he is surely mentally incompetent. The least you can do is support our armed forces, so that the jawans posted on the border and the courageous pilots of the air force, bound by duty to defend the nation, are not made to pay with their lives for your irresponsibility.

Politicians like you are used to getting your minor ailments treated abroad at state expense. It is not possible to provide the same facility to each of our soldiers wounded in battle. But the least you could do for them would be to arrange for the best possible medical treatment at the country's premier hospitals.

The last rites of Squadron Leader Ajay Ahuja have been performed at Bhatinda. Given your hectic schedules, neither you, nor your defence minister, were there to share his family's grief. The defence minister has taken a flight out to Kargil as if he were a seasoned defence strategist. Send for him, so that the two of you can proceed to Kota, Rajasthan, to offer your condolences to the martyred Ajay Ahuja's bereaved family. You and your ilk do not hesitate to commiserate in person with people and politicians with dubious associations and criminal antecedents. In this case, a soldier has died defending the country.

The members of Flight Lieutenant Nachiketa's family have suffered sleepless nights. Arrange for him to be released and brought back from Pakistan and reunite him with his family. Ask their forgiveness for your failure to demonstrate any sense of political responsibility. Arrange to locate the twelve soldiers declared missing in action and apologize to the nation for the needless death of twenty-nine of their comrades.

It is hoped that you have not lost all compassion for your fellow countrymen. This is the least you can do to compensate for your heinous crimes—political opportunism and sheer callousness.

> —A writer, journalist and adeeb
> who shares this moment of national grief.

4

Having dispatched his letter, the writer agonized over its consequences. He wondered whether his views and suggestions were about to be turned into harbingers of death for others in the name of national security. Was it necessary for some to die so that others might live?

Death! All wars, great or minor, bear witness to the fact that death alone is the arbiter of victory or defeat. How many deaths can one endure or inflict on another? Victory can never be conclusive, until the last enemy soldier has been killed. This has always been true of all conflict, be it the Aryan war of Kurukshetra or the battle fought on the plains of Marathon between Darius and Melidiades.

The writer was lost in these thoughts when a tremor shook the earth and a severe dust storm darkened the sky. Clamping his hands over his ears to shut out the reverberations of the fearful tumult outside, he yelled for Mahmood. When there was no answer, he called again. Then he saw Mahmood, panting and staggering towards him.

'Where were you?' he asked.

'Lost in the mists of time,' Mahmood replied.

'Lost in time...why?'

'I had gone to visit my ancestors.'

'Ancestors?'

'My dear sir, why this great consternation?' asked Mahmood. 'True, Islam is the most nascent of all religions. I find it more relevant than others and have chosen to embrace it. But I do have ancestors and whatever their state—fallen or upright—they are my blood, after all.'

'This is not the moment to debate over such issues. First go and find out why such a violent storm rages, maddening even the beasts with its eerie echoes.'

'Perhaps, the reason lies in the assassination of Shambuk.'

'Shambuk?' asked the writer.

'Yes, sir. I have seen for myself that whenever religion is desecrated, these violent storms invade the earth. I have also seen Raja Ramchandra...sir, it was morning. The royal court of Ayodhya echoed with the chant of sacred texts. The raja had just emerged to declare the Ashwamedha Yagna, when he heard a Brahmin weeping. Greatly surprised by the sight, he wanted to know what had caused the man such grief. A courtier had stepped forward and pushed the Brahmin before the king with the words, "This man alone can explain the reason for his tears."

'Clasping his son's lifeless body to his breast, the Brahmin berated him. "Ruler of Ayodhya!" he exclaimed. "What kind of Ramrajya is this, where a father must witness the death of his son? You are his murderer! You!"

'A hum of conversation was audible as people whispered among themselves, debating over the grave injustice of a Brahmin boy's death and the disturbing implications of a Kshatriya king's helplessness in preventing it, the impossibility of such a deed being perpetrated in Satyug, the epoch of truth, and there having to be a plausible reason for it.

'It was then that Naradji came forward as usual. He told Raja Ramchandra that only Brahmins, Kshatriyas and Vaishyas could aspire for moksh after they had committed themselves to the rigorous study of the sacred texts, taken up meditation and observed penance. When Shambuk, the Shudra, dreamt of achieving moksh, he committed a grave heresy in the kingdom. And now, the Brahmin's son had had to pay for the Shudra's unpardonable sin. So, learned sir, Raja Ramchandra chose to pursue Kshatriya tradition and protect the honour of the Brahmin cult by instantly having the pious and learned Shambuk beheaded. The raging storm and the enveloping darkness are the aftermath of such a sin.'

'Which era are you talking about, Mahmood?'

'Sir, I refer to Satyug which I have just visited. On my way back, I ran into the Vedic age which was beating its breast in despair.'

'Why? What led it to do so?'

'Sir, each era repents for its sins. The Vedic age was only trying to forewarn its successor by its gesture of lament.'

'True, Mahmood. Cultures that are capable of remorse are the ones to survive the rigours of time and perpetuate themselves in timeless traditions. It is no easy task to establish the parameters of sin and piety. But why was the Vedic age so filled with despair?'

'Sir, it has to do with a tale of lust and debauchery. Ahilya, the wife of Rishi Gautam, is a woman of such incomparable beauty that even the apsaras are overshadowed by her presence. So enamoured of her was the god Indra that he assumed the form of her spouse Gautam and seduced her, while his accomplice, the Moon, guarded the entrance to the rishi's ashram.'

The adeeb was momentarily lost in contemplation before anger roused him and he thundered, 'Where is that debauch Indra? Bring him before me!'

'Sir, you cannot assume the powers of a court of justice to try Indra for a crime of lust!'

'Don't forget, Mahmood, that in every era, there has always been someone or the other to assume the role of a court so that judgment could be passed on crimes involving injustice and oppression.'

'But, sir, Rishi Gautam has already punished the perpetrators of this act. He laid a curse on Indra, condemning him to the humiliation of defeat and eternal shame.'

'And what form of punishment was meted out to the Moon?'

'Rishi Gautam cursed him as well with disfiguring spots that would forever mar his face. Only on one day of the month would the Moon attain the fullness of his existence; on all others, he would only be partially visible. Then the rishi cursed his wife Ahilya...'

'Why was Ahilya punished?'

'The reason lies in the way the materialistic Aryans always regarded women—as chattel. The very sight of Ahilya had aroused the rishi's fury and driven him to accuse her of infidelity and arrogance. He had chastised her for failing to see through Indra's subterfuge. Repeatedly proclaiming her innocence, she had begged his forgiveness. Unrelenting, he had cast a spell on her, turning her into stone. The spell would only be broken, he told her, when Lord Ram stepped on that stone.'

'This is gross injustice! Not only have these Brahmins degraded their fellow human beings to the status of Shudras, they have also reduced womankind to the same level of lowly existence.'

'This is why I keep repeating, sir, that whenever a man's conscience is overwhelmed by injustice, oppression and evil deeds, severe storms lash the earth.'

'But the world is not passing through such a phase today. Why, then, this terrible tumult, this earth-shattering din, this inexplicable flight of frightened animals?'

'Sir, these are merely the echoes of the battle described in the Mahabharata. It is the sound of the Kauravas of Hastinapur moving towards the battlefield. To the north-west, on the other side of the Jamuna river, their army is preparing for war; in the south-east, the

Pandava army has advanced beyond Matsya Pradesh, Alwar, Viraat
and Jind to set up new camps.'

'Mahmood, I would like to have a vivid description of this great
battle.'

*

Exactly eighteen days later, Mahmood returned with the following
account: 'The Kauravas have lost. Not one of them has managed to
escape with his life. With Bhishm Pitamah as their commander-in-
chief, their army had returned victorious on the first day of battle.
On that very day, Uttamkumar, the brave Pandava warrior, was
slain. On the third day, Arjun defeated valorous Kauravas like
Bhishm, Drona, Ambashtpati, Chitrasena, Shrutayu, Jayadratha,
Krupa, Bhurishrava, Shala and Shalya. And...'

'I don't need a daily account. Just tell me how many brave
soldiers lost their lives.'

'I did not keep a tally, sir. Perhaps, Yamraj or King Chitragupta
could tell us, since they keep an account of the deaths that take place
every moment.'

'I am not keen on meeting Yamraj, but ask King Chitragupta to
report to me immediately with the records in his ledgers.'

It did not take long for Chitragupta to present himself. As he
could not carry the heavy ledgers with him, he had brought along a
convenient miniature device that would serve just as well. In the
blink of an eye, this gadget could perform the most complicated of
mathematical tasks.

'Tell me the exact casualty figures in the battle of Mahabharata,'
said the adeeb.

'Countless,' came the reply. 'Except for Krishna and the five
Pandavas, no one escaped alive. So many died that it would take
aeons to compute the exact figures. Suffice it to know that eighteen
divisions of soldiers fought each other. Each division had one lakh
nine thousand and fifty foot soldiers and sixty-five thousand one
hundred cavalrymen. Multiply these figures by eighteen and you
get...' Chitragupta paused, looking wistfully at his machine.

'That's enough! Stop it!' exclaimed the adeeb. 'My head reels
with the effort of gauging the magnitude of death.'

Clutching his forehead, he sat down. Tears moistened his palms. Chitragupta vanished because his time was up. The dark storm raged, unabated. The frightened cries of beasts would not be stilled.

Suddenly, an old peasant materialized before the adeeb's tearful eyes. 'You...who are you?' the adeeb asked.

'I am an ordinary man like you,' came the reply. 'You write for a living. I don't. But I too have to work.'

'What kind of work do you do?'

'I have a laboratory,' replied the old man. 'There, I collect the tears of the dispossessed, the oppressed and the tormented and of those caught in the tentacles of death.'

'What do you want from me?'

'Your tears.'

'My tears!' exclaimed the adeeb.

'Yes. In this world, there is nothing more sacred than tears. I carry them away, cupped in my palm. I analyse them, seeking to understand the suffering, sorrow and despair from which they sprang.'

'You are involved in a strange mission indeed! Have you drawn any conclusions from it?'

'Yes, I have, but no one seems to give any serious thought to them. Neither pain nor its causes ever fade away. No one gives me a hearing. I simply carry on collecting and depositing tears.'

'Where?'

'In the ocean of tears.'

The adeeb gave a start. The old man continued with his tale. 'For centuries, I have ploughed the same furrow. I have seen man ravage nature. When that was done, he created weapons to destroy mankind, unleashing the tidal wave of tears. The Divine Hand of the universe had created death so that the spirit could seek its release from the body. But ever since man became the purveyor of destruction, wars have caused an untold number of unnatural deaths. Horrifying massacres have taken place. I have remained a helpless, mute spectator, dying many deaths and enduring countless others as a witness to this macabre dance of destruction. I have died on the plains of Marathon, in the battle of Abela and during the manoeuvres at Jhelum, Canae, Somnath, Tarain, Crecy and Panipat. Because of the myriad ways of slaughter man has devised, I have had to bear the burden of these many deaths.'

'So, Baba, how do you propose to put a stop to your recurring pain?' asked the scholar.

'We have to find a way of making life take precedence over death. Your tears are needed to help achieve this end. Tears alone can breathe life into mere existence.'

Having uttered these words, the old man drew tears from the adeeb's eyes and continued: 'I will study these tears by extracting their essence and storing it. I am well aware that no one will pay me any attention. When I am not gathering tears every time someone sheds them, I sit on the shores by the ocean of tears, listening to the sounds of weeping, sounds that reveal the unnatural manner in which people have met their end. The time has come for someone to embark on a quest, so that this onslaught of needless, unrelenting death may be challenged. Gilgamesh of the Hittite civilization has already set out on a mission through which he swears not only to overcome pain and privation, but also to vanquish death itself.'

5

Meanwhile, Gilgamesh, ruler of Yuruk, announced his intention to challenge suffering, endure privation, and defeat death by seeking his release from its bondage. His words echoed around the world and made the deities of Babylonia, Mesopotamia, Sumeria–Akkad and the Indus Valley tremble in fear. The ramparts of Yuruk, constructed by Gilgamesh for his household deities, shook in terror. Even the temples that housed a goddess like Ena, along with the supreme god Anu and the supreme goddess Ishtar, quaked in fear. Gilgamesh merely repeated his resolve, causing pandemonium among the divinities of the various pantheons.

Yavnik, a Sumerian god, yelled, 'Have you heard what Gilgamesh plans to do?'

Another Sumerian deity, Vapun, blamed his own brethren for this state of affairs. 'By never opposing Parashakti, the Supreme

Power, when it bestowed on mankind the gifts of life, happiness and discretion, we have undermined our own cause,' he declared.

The frightened Babylonius intervened. 'Then Parashakti should be held accountable for sustaining a creation that allows man to aspire for eternal life,' he countered. 'Wallowing in wretchedness and sin, man has sunk to the depths of despair. If he triumphs over death, he will pollute the pristine environs of our abode.' The Babylonian deity urged the different pantheons of gods to compel the Supreme Power to address this vexatious issue. He further demanded that Indra, the most powerful of the Aryan gods, be entrusted with the responsibility of bringing back an answer.

At this moment, the apparitions of three messengers presented themselves before the assembled gods. One of them had news to disclose. 'Gilgamesh is a man utterly devoid of moral values who craves the luxuries of life,' he told them. 'If he sets out to conquer the world, no warrior will be able to beat him. A monarch driven by uncontrollable carnal urges, he has celebrated each of his victories by defiling countless virgins and taking as concubines the wives of the men he vanquished in battle. And now, he is bent on breaking the shackles of death by his newfound claims to a higher spirituality.'

The other messengers had similar revelations to offer. Then Babylonius spoke again. 'Gilgamesh is capable of anything,' he cautioned. 'We must locate the dispersed Aryan pantheon because it is only their god Indra who can challenge him.'

'My lord, centuries ago, these Aryans had set out from the Vindija region of Croatia. Overcome by weariness, some of them settled down in the Russian steppes. Others made Egypt their home. For most, however, the sun held a great fascination. Following the direction in which the sun rose, they moved further east. After crossing the mighty Euphrates and Tigris rivers and travelling through Tabrez and Tehran, they settled down in the Indus Valley.'

'This means that the Aryans are scattered all over the world...'

'Yes, my lord. One of their caravans travelled through Mashhad, Herat, Balkh and Bolan Darra to reach the Indus. They eventually settled down in Mohenjodaro and Harappa. Their ruler is, perhaps, the leisure-loving Indra who closely resembles Gilgamesh.'

'How are we concerned with leisure?' asked the deities. 'All we ask Parashakti is to tell us whether it is appropriate for mankind to be granted unlimited discretionary powers.'

Then the booming voice of the Aryan Indra from the Indus Valley was heard to declare, 'O hear! Parashakti is mute, the elemental configuration of the smallest atom. It is the universal power that knows neither beginning nor end. Its energy creates, sustains and is capable of destroying the universe. It is unknown, unknowable. It defies all confines. Being eternal and immortal, it challenges the parameters of definition. It is more radiant than a thousand suns. It creates all matter, just as it dissipates it all. It presides over the realms of the earth, the sky and the heavens. Beyond it, there is nothing; from the primordial to the present, this power alone represents all consciousness, energy and creativity. Our pantheon calls it Brahma. But what it is, in reality, none can tell. Having no visible form, it cannot be explained, compared or measured. Defying all questions, it offers no answers...'

Listening to these words, a silent pall of gloom descended on the assembly of gods. They knew that no pantheon had ever undertaken the kind of spiritual endeavours that the Indus Valley gods had. It would be difficult to ignore them. Only one question remained unanswered: Who would stop the Sumerian ruler Gilgamesh?

At that moment, Anu, the powerful Sumerian deity, appeared before them from the rocky mountains and said in reassuring tones, 'You have nothing to fear. Although Gilgamesh has had many temples built and dedicated to me, Goddess Ishtar and other deities, his misdeeds, sins and acts of injustice have provoked outrage. I had heard of his people's woes and was determined to either transform this extraordinarily cunning ruler into a nobody or to destroy him altogether.

'I have sent Enkidu to earth in the guise of a human. A brutal and barbaric creature who was made to live with wild animals, he resembles a long-haired beast himself. A carnivore by nature, he becomes herbivorous when circumstances so dictate. A hunter once caught sight of Enkidu and was so overcome by terror that he dashed home to his father and stammered out an account of the peculiar and

fearsome beast he had seen in the forest. Though it kept the
company of other animals, reported the hunter, the beast seemed to
be an incarnation of man.

'On hearing his story, the father advised his son: "Hasten to
Yuruk and inform Gilgamesh about your encounter. The gods fear
our king and must have sent this creature down to earth to challenge
him. Mere words are not enough to praise the intelligent, powerful
and wise Gilgamesh! Apart from his knowledge of the many secrets
the earth holds, he is well aware of the hostile and indolent ways of
the gods. In the divine hierarchy, these gods occupy the region
between high divinity and the human, and they conspire to destroy
our monarch. Waste not a single moment. Go and tell Gilgamesh
about the strange being you have seen in the forest. And yes, in
order to tame this creature, go to the love-temple of Ena and
procure the most charming of her damsels. Go! Don't waste any
time."

'On reaching Yuruk,' continued Anu, 'the hunter narrated his
tale to the king. "Your father is right," Gilgamesh told him. "The
gods have conspired against me. Take the beautiful devdasi Runa
with you to the forest. I am familiar with the ways of the gods; they
fall prey to feminine charms. Their lust overpowers their imagination
and resolve. My enemy too will be irresistibly drawn by such charms
and, subsequently, find himself cast out by the animal fraternity.
Even Aryan tradition relies on apsaras to keep its gods in line. Go,
fetch Runa and proceed to the forest. Ask her to charm the beast—
man you have seen."

'The hunter faithfully obeyed Gilgamesh's orders. He fetched
Runa and waited with her for Enkidu on the shores of a lake. Three
days later, Enkidu appeared at the lakeside with a herd of animals to
quench his thirst. The sight of him filled the hunter with both fear
and elation. He pointed Enkidu out to Runa and exhorted her to cast
aside her veil of shyness and disrobe herself. Her beauty, the hunter
promised, would draw the beast—man to her and turn him into her
slave. Runa followed the hunter's suggestion and lured Enkidu to
her.'

Here, Anu paused to reflect. 'The amazing thing,' he remarked, 'was that even after Enkidu had slaked his lust, he could not bring himself to let Runa go. He would take her in his arms and stare intensely at her, as if in search of something he could not describe. Such is the bond of passion that draws men and women together. Pondering over it, I had been disturbed by a sense of foreboding at the time. Swept away by this river of passion, Enkidu had even become oblivious to his divine lineage and human incarnation. And I was powerless to help him.

'When Enkidu and Runa had spent a week together, she said to him, "How wise and clever you are, Enkidu! Though you are of divine descent, I shall love you in your human form. Leave the company of these animals and come away with me. I will show you my beloved Yuruk, its ramparts and its temples, where Anu and Ishtar reside. There also dwells the powerful Gilgamesh, who strives to create a better world for his people."

'Eventually, Runa was successful in transforming Enkidu into an ordinary human being. She bathed him, offered him a part of her own garment to cover himself and taught him to eat cooked food. Then, she took him to Yuruk. When they entered the kingdom, a sea of people turned up to gaze at her. And at the gates, Enkidu met Gilgamesh, face to face. With seething hatred, the two glared at each other. An angry snort escaped Enkidu's nostrils, Gilgamesh gave a battle cry and the two closed in on each other like a pair of angry bulls. The earth shook. The gateways of the temples collapsed.'

Anu narrated how he witnessed this fierce confrontation and how incredible it was to watch Enkidu writhing in Gilgamesh's grip: 'Enkidu was hurled into the air, where he floated as helplessly as a leaf. Gilgamesh caught him as he fell and asked, "Tell me, who has sent you to annihilate me?"

'Unversed in the devious ways of mankind, Enkidu revealed the secret of my conspiracy to Gilgamesh. The latter was incensed by the revelation and turned abusive. "So Anu has sent you to kill me!" he exclaimed. "The god to whom I have dedicated temples and ramparts, on whom I have showered my devotion! I had urged my subjects to worship him, but now, I cannot imagine a being more corrupt, more devoid of principles. He seems to have forgotten that gods like him owe their very existence to me."'

Gilgamesh's words incensed the gods. Vapun's anger knew no bounds and he roared, 'This king's arrogance has to be curbed!'

'That is impossible now,' Anu declared. 'After Gilgamesh defeated Enkidu, they have become the best of friends.'

Suru, the deity from Akkad, said nervously, 'This is, indeed, disturbing news!'

Anu retorted, 'That is precisely the problem! An earthly king has discovered the unknown boon of friendship.'

At this, the assembly of gods was weighed down by despondency. Alvonious, a Mesopotamian deity, tensely declared, 'Anu, our weakness lies in our failure to cultivate the spirit of love and friendship amongst ourselves. The goddesses only exist to satisfy our lust; no god can call himself another's friend. This is a serious shortcoming that threatens our future. The situation is dire indeed.'

Alvonious's peers shared his concern. It was the goddess Tanya who voiced a further note of caution. 'Ye gods of Dajla, Farat and Danube,' she declaimed, 'mankind's discovery of friendship and love has evidently left you deeply perturbed. But what has prevented you from cultivating the same virtues yourselves? You are the epitome of arrogance. You have allowed yourselves to forget that it is to mankind's worship that we owe our very existence and our privileged status. Every one of you is self-centred and utterly devoid of sentiments. In your arrogance, you band together to outrage a woman's modesty and father illegitimate offspring. Your selfishness knows no bounds and you cannot fathom the value of friendship. Lacking the spirit of unity, you perpetuate rivalries. Your immoral conduct renders you incapable of creating either a culture or a civilization. You forget that besides love and friendship, mankind has also established the pious rituals of childbirth. All you are capable of is unbridled passion, not love. You have fostered malice, not camaraderie. In your abode reside your illegitimate offsprings who are ignorant of traditions and values.'

The assembled gods and most of the goddesses voiced their displeasure at these words. 'Tanya!' they exclaimed, 'you are insulting your own kind with such words.'

'My intention was not to insult, only to caution,' Tanya replied.

'The store of values that man has discovered for himself will be enriched with time and sound the death knell of our existence.' With that, Tanya vanished, leaving the gods dumbstruck and overcome by feelings of inadequacy.

It was Anu who spoke up. 'In this hour of distress and anxiety over our future,' he suggested, 'we should get in touch with the Aryan gods dwelling in the plains alongside the seven rivers—the Indus, Vitasta, Asiki, Parushani, Vipashu, Shudradi and Saraswati. Our realm enjoys the bounty of only three rivers: the Dajla, Farat and Danube.'

With head bowed in humility, a messenger intervened, 'Not these alone—' but was interrupted by another god who demanded to know who he was.

'My lord, I'm just a roving herdsman who occasionally acts as your messenger. I wander across the vast expanses ranging from the Indus Valley to the Bosphorus, traversing deserts and rocky plains through which the Aryan gods travelled to reach the river valley. Some of them settled down in Ariana; others moved on to inhabit the plains of the Jamuna after crossing the rivers Indus, Saraswati and Drashdwanti. They now call this place Brahmavart. It has the river Ganga as its eastern boundary. The Aryan gods have established their domain there and four rivers lie to the north-west of this region.'

'Have the Aryans given names to these rivers?'

'Yes, my lord, they have. By naming their rivers, they have consolidated their claims to the area. They call these four rivers the Kabul-kuma, Krumu-kuram, Gomti-gomal and Swat-suvastu. The Ariana tribes lost their rights because they had not established the tradition of naming rivers.'

'Such convoluted names!'

'Yes, my lord. Along with the rivers, they also named their territory. We are nomads. Whenever we go to the Aryan lands, we bring back animal skins. We relish their delectable liquor and obtain the finest grain from their provinces. This grain is unrivalled by any other. Apart from their water resources, the Aryan gods enjoy the matchless beauty of dawn breaking over their mountains and the electrifying cadence of their rains. Their society is divided into categories. They have domesticated animals and have mastered the techniques of agriculture.'

'Do the gods perform all these tasks themselves?' Anu asked.

'No, my lord, they shun work like the rest of you. They have no need to work; their work is carried out by humankind.'

'Divine Anu,' interrupted a deity, 'we should not allow this messenger's account to divert us from the matter at hand. We are here to address the issue of King Gilgamesh's announcement that he seeks a weapon that will empower man to defy death itself.'

'My lord,' answered the messenger, 'I have given you my account to help you gain an insight into the subtleties of the situation. Enkidu no longer remembers his divine lineage. He sought and found love in his human incarnation. Gilgamesh has discovered the invaluable bond of friendship. The human Aryan has learnt to mine the treasures of the earth by dint of hard labour, going to the extent of pacifying the destructive forces of nature by harnessing the power of peace. Having achievements of such magnitude to his credit, the only goal that remains for man to seek is the antidote for death. In these circumstances, my lords, your annihilation is inevitable.'

Fury blazed across the gods' faces at these words. The messenger continued, 'Do not be angry, my lords. Learn to face the truth. Man has powers that are not at your disposal. He has succeeded in evolving the concepts of life, love, friendship, peace and performance. His yearning for immortality, therefore, is not entirely misplaced.'

'No!' the gods exclaimed in unison. 'We cannot grant it to him.' A clamour of voices rose, each proclaiming its owner's intention to destroy those very human qualities that the gods themselves had been unable to cultivate. At that moment, there appeared before the gathering a trio of goddesses: Ena, Susoti and Kalpa. The assembly looked at them in surprise.

'Why are you here?' Anu asked them.

'We rush from the abode of the gods to the portal of death. We goddesses are distressed by the injustice meted out to us by gods like you. You have always victimized us. You are utterly devoid of the love that mankind has found and nurtured. You are either adulterous or effeminate. Your peers in the Indus Valley follow in your footsteps. Their self-restraint evaporates at the sight of the apsaras. They derive pleasure from annihilating valiant warriors. At this very moment, your friend Zeus sports with Ishta, a devdasi in a temple. By the banks of the Danube, the god Suvog lies in the arms of goddess Paranti. For centuries now, Brahma, the god of the Indus Valley, has been consorting with his daughter Shataroopa. You and your Aryan counterparts worship the Sun whose consort Sangya happens to be his own niece and the daughter of his brother Vishwakarma.

'All of you worship the Moon. In the Aryan myths, Chandrama, the Moon, presides over the stars and the Brahmins and holds the key to medicinal cures. Did you know that he conducted the royal rites to celebrate the victory of Tribhuvan? Also present on that occasion was Tara, the wife of the guru to one of the gods. Chandrama was so smitten by her that he abducted her. Unmoved by her husband's humble pleas, he continued to force himself on her. Eventually, after a terrible battle, a pregnant Tara was restored to her spouse. Chandrama was not held accountable for the indignities he had inflicted on her. The list of such misdemeanours is endless. You gods are shameless sinners—every one of you!'

Dumbstruck by these words, the gods could not muster the courage to address a single question to any of the three goddesses. After some hesitation, Anu spoke up. 'You have all been born from divine wombs,' he observed. 'You are immortal. How long, and with how many men do you propose to spend your eternal life?'

'The question does not arise. You are unaware of it, but Ishtar, your favourite goddess and queen of the heavens, had approached Gilgamesh on her own to seek his love. Do you know how he responded to her invitation? He told her that he could not reciprocate her feelings, because he would not be able to safeguard her modesty. Can any of you lay claim to either the moral courage or the sense of justice that comes through in Gilgamesh's words?'

Cringing with embarrassment, the gods exchanged glances. Then Susoti said, 'Even now, Anu cannot bring himself to offer a truthful account of what transpired during Ishtar's visit. She could not bear the humiliation of Gilgamesh's rejection. Returning to Anu, she accused the king of having insulted her. She lashed out against the other goddesses, vilifying us as depraved and debased creatures. No one has any idea of the number of gods she has consorted with. Speak, Anu! Let everyone know whether I speak the truth!'

As the gods gazed at Anu with suspicion, Kalpa levelled another charge at him: 'Following Enkidu's change of heart, you had sent a fearsome bull down to earth to destroy Gilgamesh. It was then that the bond of friendship between the two was put to the test for the first time. As soon as this ferocious beast attacked Gilgamesh, Enkidu seized it by the horns to protect his friend and thereby repay his debt of friendship. During the fierce combat that ensued, the bull breathed fire on Enkidu and asked, "Have you forgotten that it was the same god who sent us both down to earth, that we shared a common goal—to kill Gilgamesh?"

'On hearing these words, Enkidu shook the bull by its horns and replied, "Neither a brute like you nor even a god like Anu can ever comprehend the fundamental values of friendship. As long as I live, no one can kill my friend Gilgamesh."

'His words provoked the bull into attacking him yet again. This time, it was Gilgamesh who struck at the animal's neck and flanks. In the end, the bull succumbed to its injuries, but Enkidu was fatally wounded. Gilgamesh sent for the best Greek physicians to cure his friend and ceaselessly endeavoured to raise Enkidu's spirits. Runa, who loved the beast–man, nursed him with devotion. To help him rally around, Gilgamesh urged him: "You must live. There shall be no more burials in the cemeteries of Ur and Keish. Man will be immortal!" Observing his friend's increasingly inert body, the king cried out in desperation, "My friend, how are you feeling? What kind of sleep has overtaken you? Enkidu, why have you turned ashen? Why do you not answer me?"

'Despite his best efforts, Gilgamesh was unable to bring his friend back to life. Realizing that Enkidu was dead, the king broke down in tears and recalled how his friend's selfless efforts had saved his own life. "You took on my torment for the sake of friendship, Enkidu!" Gilgamesh wept. "You sacrificed your life!" Then, wiping away his tears, the king announced, "Hear me, O Deities! This is the second time I am addressing you. It is not the cry of a man who seeks to honour the gods. Rather, it is the collective expression of mankind's yearning to transcend pain, suffering, torment, labour and death." While Ena cried out in fear, Gilgamesh continued, "No matter what pain or torment I must endure for the sake of my friend and my fellow humans, my endeavour shall henceforth be to defeat death. Now, all I seek is its antidote.'"

Gilgamesh's words left the gods distraught. Ena announced that a water nymph of the Aryan pantheon had disclosed the secret of immortality to the king. 'Gilgamesh survived the Flood,' she explained, 'by hiding in his navel all that death cannot touch. The water nymph had informed him about the wise man of Shurupak who knew about the antidote for death. No one knows where this wise man had taken shelter during the Flood. So listen, ye gods of Sumer! Gilgamesh will not rest till he has sought out this man and extracted from him the secret of immortality. We leave the heavens to go to the region beneath the waves. Gilgamesh has already reached the ocean whose bottomless depths hide the wise man he seeks.'

The gods were shaken by her words. Pandemonium broke out. Then Anu suggested that Gilgamesh be seized and imprisoned before he could descend to the depths of the sea.

'It is now too late even to imprison his shadow,' Ena commented.

Anu then called upon all the venomous creatures of his realm to surface and prevent Gilgamesh from reaching his destination. 'Take him into your sinuous embrace!' he exhorted. 'Let your poison course through his veins so that he perishes!'

The three goddesses watched as Gilgamesh was enmeshed in the coils of countless snakes and stung by hundreds of scorpions. Moments later, they noticed him flexing his muscles, oblivious to his assailants, and plunging into the sea. The waves warmly welcomed him with the words, 'Son of the earth, as long as your limbs function, no poison has the power to subdue you. The water of this ocean is the antidote for all the earth's venom. Go forth on your voyage to the underworld.'

Thus, Gilgamesh proceeded to the fathomless depths of the ocean. Lower and lower did he descend, and the centuries went by. To this day, his quest continues.

6

Centuries have elapsed, but Gilgamesh is yet to return with the antidote. However, the bond of love that united Runa and Enkidu, took firm root in the sensibilities of man and lives on forever. It remains an inviolable part of his being, impervious to the vagaries of death, fire, water, wind and weapon. It was accepted as an eternal truth when someone carved the following words on the walls of an ancient Egyptian temple: 'I wait for you.' The words are symbolic of the world's first love story. The pyramids came much later. More ancient than the history of the pyramids is the saga of human love. It was born when Runa and Enkidu, having gratified their carnal instincts, looked into each other's eyes and discovered their souls.

7

Here is yet another love story, featuring Buta Singh and *retpari*, a sand nymph.

The sweltering deserts of Rajasthan...

A voice screamed, 'That wretched Pakistan has seen the light of day!'

Heaven gazed down with parched eyes, robbed dry of every single teardrop. The experts at the meteorological department had declared that there was no chance of rain. The blood of humankind would quench the thirsting land instead.

In the midst of these dire forecasts, the middle-aged Buta Singh walked back from his barren fields. To circumvent the division of their land into separate plots, his three brothers had ensured that Buta remain a bachelor, as unfulfilled as the arid land craving for moisture. As Buta walked along, he heard a babel of voices.

'That wretched Pakistan has been created!'

'Jo bole so nihal, sat sri akal!'

'Nara-e-Takbir...Allahu Akbar!'

'Har har Mahadev!'

Buta Singh had no inkling of the weatherman's forecasts. Little did he know that, in this year marking the country's independence, showers of blood would sweep over the land instead of rain. As on every other day, his feet left their imprints in the sand. He was in no hurry to get home. No expectant gaze awaited his return. At that moment, a youthful voice cried out for help.

He turned in its direction. He saw a young girl, no more than eighteen years old, running towards him. Her clothes were threadbare, her hair a tangled mess. She was gasping for breath. A savage-looking young man pursued her. The scantily clad girl fell at Buta Singh's feet and beseeched him, 'Save me! Save me from this brute! He is trying to molest me.' Having uttered these words, she hauled herself up and clung to Buta.

'Do you think you can escape from me?' asked her pursuer and, turning to Buta Singh, demanded that the girl be handed over to him.

'I refuse to do that,' Buta said firmly.

'You had better! She is part of my share.'

Buta stared at the man and asked, 'Your share?'

'Yes, my share! Pakistan has been created. Hindus and Muslims are now divided.'

'Where has Pakistan been created?'

'Beyond the fringes of the third village from this spot,' the man replied. 'After Pakistan's borders were established, this Mussalman girl became a part of my spoils. I wrenched her away from a caravan that was heading there. Hand her over to me.'

'No,' retorted Buta, protectively stepping in front of the half-clad girl. 'So what if the borders of Hindustan and Pakistan have been demarcated? The honour of women cannot be apportioned to any particular side because of the Hindu–Mussalman divide!'

The young man's cruel gaze appraised Buta before he offered, 'You can buy her honour if you wish!'

'Buy her!' exclaimed Buta. 'You are willing to sell her?'

'Yes, I am.'

'For how much?'

'Fifteen hundred in cash,' the man replied after closely assessing Buta's worth.

'All right. You'll get your money, but you'll have to come to my house to fetch it.'

The trio set off for Buta's house. The two men walked ahead, while the girl followed them with downcast eyes. On arriving home, Buta dipped his hand into the numerous old earthenware pots he kept there, hoping to find some money. All the while, the ferocious young man remained standing. The half-naked girl sat cowering in a corner, her arms clasped around herself, hiding her body from view. Eventually, Buta dug an earthen pitcher out of the sandy floor. He extricated a dirty bundle from its depths, undid its knot and began to count the soiled notes and coins it contained. At last, he held in his hands the sum he needed for the transaction.

After counting the money, the fierce-looking young man tucked it inside his turban. He glanced at the girl and pondered: 'He's an old man...she will have an easy life.'

The girl sat huddled all through the proceedings. When the man left, all she asked was, 'Why did you choose to part with so much money for my sake?'

Buta remained silent.

*

Dusk was descending. The girl had managed all day with her threadbare clothes that barely concealed her nakedness. But spending the night in that state was a different matter altogether. Buta suggested that she wrap his loincloth around herself. In a tone of helplesslessness she replied that he himself would be almost naked without it. Embarrassed, Buta conceded, 'You're right...I have a solution.' He then set about digging a hole in the sand. The girl grasped the import of what he was about and watched him in silence.

'Would you like to stand inside this pit or would you prefer to sit on your haunches?' he asked.

'If I keep standing, I shall get no sleep at all.'

At this, Buta inspected the depth to which he had dug the pit and said, 'In that case, this should be deep enough. Come along here.'

Crouching on her haunches, the girl moved slowly towards the pit he had dug. Climbing into it, she lay down in a half-reclining position. Buta then refilled the pit with the sand he had excavated and declared, 'That's fine, now.'

The girl shot him an intense look. Buta returned it while pretending to scratch his beard. The flicker of a smile touched the girl's lips and she lowered her eyes. Buried in the sand, she resembled a retpari.

'Arrey, I forgot to ask you...what's your name?' Buta inquired.

'Zainab.'

'Your village?'

'Marhiyar Dhani.'

'Caste?'

'Hindu Rajput.'

'Religion?'

'Mussalman.'

'How did you fall into that man's clutches?'

'We had left our home to go to Pakistan...before Partition, we had wanted for nothing. We were comfortably off. Abba would let out his fields to sharecroppers. We owned bullocks, buffaloes and cows. We never touched their meat. Life was so good. And then, the borders of Pakistan were demarcated. Life became really difficult in the village. The Mussalman villagers set out in a caravan to cross the border...we could not understand why we were leaving behind our village...we had lived through disagreements, conflicts and upheavals in the past. Somehow, I got left behind, as my fellow travellers proceeded onwards. It was then that he waylaid me. He tore at my clothes, but somehow I managed to struggle free and run away. Then I saw you,' said Zainab, looking gratefully at Buta.

*

When morning came, Buta's brothers learnt that there was a girl in his house. The village elders advised Buta to marry the girl, given the situation. Buta had to go to a bazaar, a short distance away, to buy Zainab something to wear. While leaving, he told the elders, 'First, I must get her some clothes.'

8

By the time Buta left to buy clothes for Zainab, the borders of Pakistan had already been laid out. The weatherman's forecast had been accurate—it was, indeed, raining blood!

Zainab, the retpari, remains buried up to her neck in sand.

Buta Singh has gone to a bazaar, a short distance away, to buy some clothes for her.

King Gilgamesh is still on his way to the murky depths of the ocean.

A vulture perched on the shoulders of Prometheus continues to gorge on his flesh.

Till Gilgamesh returns, the hands of death will snatch life away from many a man who bequeaths to his progeny his aspirations, his promises and his dreams. Since time immemorial, this has been the way of life, because Gilgamesh has yet to return. Spanning countless centuries, rapt in great dreams, cleaving through immense depths of water, he moves swiftly towards the world's nethermost regions. Occasionally, he calls out to mankind: 'Do not lose hope. Venomous creatures continue to entangle me in their embrace, poisoning my blood. Like a true friend, however, the ocean comes to my aid, honouring the tradition of friendship born out of Enkidu's sacrifice. The corrupt gods have cursed the ocean, turning its water to brine, rendering it useless for mankind. But don't let this dishearten you. Even if it takes me centuries, I will continue to descend to the depths of the ocean to acquire the antidote from Shurupak. I don't know how long it will take. Till then, keep resisting death. Continue to nurture your bond with the earth. Die when you must, but live on in your children. I shall return only when I have obtained the antidote for death. Till then, wait for me...'

'Wait...wait for you?' echoed a voice in the universe.

'I will return only when I have the antidote. Wait for me till then.'

Once again, the gods worked themselves into a frenzy. The Babylonian deity Zibanithu, along with his Mesopotamian counterpart Cronos and Sumerian Anu, was enraged. Aphrodite's son Eros emerged from his abode, trying to locate the source of the voice. Zeus stepped out from his palace, as did the twin deities Castor and Polux. Europa, Leda and Hera arrived, fear writ large on their faces. Astra and Philira lost their composure and the Egyptian deity Hapi was in a fury.

Belonging to various pantheons, they had gathered together to search for Gilgamesh's voice. Their messengers and minions were commanded to join in the pursuit, but all their efforts were in vain. Zeus tried, once again, to urge them on by impressing upon them the dire need for silencing Gilgamesh's voice. Their survival was at stake, he pointed out. 'We have to capture and imprison his voice.'

'Act with discretion,' moaned another voice. It came from Prometheus who had dared to commit the offence of stealing from the very hearth of Zeus's palace, the object that was, once, the sole monopoly of the gods—fire. In a voice quavering with pain, he repeated, 'Don't stifle Gilgamesh's voice.'

Zeus, along with all the other gods, turned to look at him. Prometheus had, for centuries, stood shackled in chains as punishment for conspiring to steal fire. Zeus's vulture continued to feast on his flesh. Some of its shredded pieces writhed on the floor of his prison house. Overcome by fear and loathing, the gods spoke in unison: 'You deserve to be cursed, you wretched thief.'

'You arrogant and debauched gods!' Prometheus thundered, wiping the blood from his gaping wounds. 'You will be held accountable for your sins! Every one of you is the epitome of wickedness! In the guise of divinity, you have appointed yourselves the sole guardians of nature's limitless potential. Now no longer your slave, nature itself is laying bare its secrets to mankind.'

'Death! Condemn him to death!' the gods clamoured in one voice.

'Come off your raving and ranting!' came the rejoinder. 'No matter what you do to me, you cannot silence Gilgamesh. His voice has broken free of your chains. The devdasi Runa has fled with it, taking along with her, love and friendship, peace and progress. You cannot catch her. You saw no worth in these values. So, Runa has taken them away to the netherworld. Behold! She reaches her destination!'

9

Stunned and fearful, the gods looked down to see Runa being carried away by the white-winged swans of heaven. As she descended, she was joined by all manner of winged creatures, some dark as the night, others white as moonlight; some as beautiful as the peacock and the kingfisher, others as melodious as the koel. Creation seemed to sway to their lilting calls. Alighting from the wings of the swans, Runa quickly made her way to the abode of the adeeb. Standing at his door, she raised her hand to knock, but realized that many knocks had preceded hers. The adeeb sat with his head in his hands, while a peon loudly summoned each of his visitors. On noticing Runa, the adeeb asked who she was.

'O Adeeb, I am an echo from the vile world of the gods! For mankind I have brought love, friendship, peace and progress, along with King Gilgamesh's voice. When the gods tried to suppress this voice, I hid it in my navel. This is mankind's greatest gift, this fearless and eternal voice. I have come to entrust it to your care. Please accept it, because only a man of knowledge and integrity can keep it alive for centuries to come.'

Accepting Runa's gift, the adeeb infused it into his bloodstream. When she had seated herself at his invitation, the din created by the incessant knocking rose dramatically. Addressing one such summons, the adeeb loudly asked where it had come from.

The reply came: 'Sir, I come from Kosovo in Serbia that lies along the Danube. Centuries ago, you migrated from there to settle by the Indus. Even now, the Danube nurtures fond memories of you. Today, despite their torment, the restless spirits of those who died there still remember you.'

'What has transpired there to make my descendants think of me?' asked the adeeb.

'In this ancient cradle of civilization, there rages today, a fierce, one-sided battle.'

'One-sided battle?'

'Yes, sir,' replied the summons, 'a despicable monster called NATO has taken birth in our land. Its chief is a demon who lives across the ocean. Working in unison, the demon and the monster have made a graveyard of Serbia and Yugoslavia. They are bent on dividing our nation and keeping Kosovo under their yoke.'

'Why...what gives rise to these oppressive conditions?' asked the adeeb.

'Sir, the spirit is easily broken by oppression. Once that is accomplished, nations can be dismembered and cultural bonds severed. Later, market forces feed like leeches on the blood of divided peoples. In the graveyards of destroyed civilizations are born carnivals that celebrate the perversion of religion and the distortion of history. Civilizations have been held to ransom and, subsequently, sundered by the brute force brought to bear on them by primitive cultures. The latter amass weapons of destruction. Kosovo has witnessed the deaths and forced exodus of thousands of its sons. It now stands deserted, as its refugees flee from NATO's missile bombing. Thunderous explosions can be heard, as fuel and chemical-storage facilities go up in flames. Air and water in the region have been polluted. Death relentlessly pursues life and innumerable innocents in Kosovo meet an untimely end.'

'Why has no one tried to stop these barbarians?' the adeeb asked angrily. 'Where is Kofi Annan, the Secretary-General of the United Nations? Let him be brought before me!'

The peon left to execute his order.

'Sir,' called out another voice, 'the same story was enacted in the Dajla-Farat Valley.'

'Kofi Annan will also have to answer for that,' the adeeb declared. 'We are waiting for him.'

The profusion of knocks reached a crescendo. The adeeb calmed them down and turned to Runa. 'I am grateful to you for entrusting me with the voice of Gilgamesh,' he said. 'By infusing it into my blood, I have ensured its protection. As long as mankind survives and blood courses through its veins, this voice shall live on.'

'Be careful,' Runa warned, 'forces opposed to man will now embark on missions of bloodletting and slaughter. The gods have become dissolute, self-centred and corrupt. That cowardly lot will do anything to snatch back the voice, so beware.'

At that moment, the peon returned. Kofi Annan was not with him. This infuriated the adeeb who asked, 'Didn't you bring Kofi Annan with you?'

'Sir,' replied the peon, 'on hearing of your summons, Mr Annan complained of severe chest pain and breathing difficulty. He was admitted to hospital and, given his condition, it would have been neither possible nor proper to insist on asking him to accompany me.'

'Go straight down to Kofi Annan's hospital and tell him that excruciating pain frequently occurs in the thoracic cavity of the world. The world finds it difficult to breathe. He had been assigned the duty of attending to these global maladies, but it seems that he has surrendered to a malevolent power and laid down his moral weapons. As a result, we are passing through an epoch of unrestrained repression. In case he has forgotten, remind Mr Annan that the world is a witness to the conflicts that take place in the name of global economic enterprise and threaten to destroy the common man in every country and culture. A dark chapter, based on blind faith, has opened in history and is leading to genocide. So long as these conflicts are perpetuated, dysfunctional communities will emerge, giving birth to an unjust and unprincipled world. Fish will continue to perish in the Danube. Man will never cease to reap harvests of thorn from fields irrigated with human blood. Women will remain perennial victims of rape and assault. Their offspring will be afflicted by mental illness. Tornadoes of bigotry will sweep the planet. Inept rulers will continue to hold the reins of power. Go and ask Kofi Annan if he was installed at the United Nations to preside over such misery.'

'My dear sir, I will carry your impassioned words to Kofi Annan, but I doubt if I'll succeed in making him understand the subtle import of your message. It would be better if you could explain it to him yourself when he stands before you.'

'I know only too well that he will never make an appearance here. For this is the eternal court, representing the will of the people. Those who trade in the name of religion and law can never summon the courage to face it.'

At this point, Runa sought permission to leave. Bidding her farewell, the adeeb cautioned her, 'Take care, Runa. The gods are merciless. For stealing fire, Prometheus continues to endure punishment. I shudder at the thought of the divine punishment that awaits you for stealing Gilgamesh's voice for the betterment of mankind. I pray for your well-being.'

There was no let-up in the intensity of the knocking after Runa's departure. The adeeb felt as if his eardrums would burst. Clamping his hands over his ears, he told the peon, 'Let's go away somewhere...take me away from here...take me anywhere!'

'Where shall I take you, O Adeeb? Predators prowl everywhere. Tremors set off by chaos, plunder, genocide, abduction and rape reverberate around us. Hyenas, dogs and vultures feast on rotting carcasses and aborted foetuses. Horrific sights of bloodletting abound—more horrific than the Flood that swept away mankind, aeons ago.'

'Just take me away from here,' the adeeb repeated, and this time the peon had to comply. He put the adeeb in a boat and rowed it through an endless ocean of blood. The thickness of the blood made the going extremely tough. When they had sailed some distance ahead, a mountain of corpses rose before the peon's eyes. Tired of rowing across the bloody waves, he anchored the boat to a cliff of rotting corpses. The adeeb sought its shade.

Suddenly, he heard echoes. Gesturing to the peon, he asked, 'Do you hear something?'

'No, sir.'

'But the echoes of Jaishankar Prasad's words resound in my ears. On the highest peak of the Himgiris, in the icy shade of its summit, a man with limpid eyes surveys the scene of devastation. I can also hear the Sumerian goddess Inna's wrathful words: "Does my lineage have to be obliterated? Does it have to die an unnatural death?"'

The peon looked at him closely, as he continued: 'The pronouncements of the Greek divinities also reverberate in my ears as they congregate on Mount Olympus to escape the Flood. The Holy Father of Christianity speaks out. "Noah," He says, "evil prevails on earth. I will destroy not only man, but every other species, because the world is overrun by brutality. With you, I am pleased, Noah, because you alone remain untainted. I will protect you. Build yourself an ark and enter it. You alone shall escape the Flood.'"

The peon now looked with concern at the adeeb who continued, unmindful of the effect his words were having on his companion. 'Do you remember how Zeus had opened the heavens for the clouds to wipe out mankind? Then Yu of China channelized the floodwaters into the ocean. He gathered the soil of the Chi river in his palms and waited for the waters to recede, so that mankind could, once again, sow seeds. Do you remember?'

'No, sir, I remember no such thing,' the peon replied indifferently.

'Even if you can't recollect, it doesn't matter. Can't we have a man like China's Yu today, who would put a stop to the spate of bloodshed?'

'Sir, Gandhiji had strived to do so, but found himself alienated...'

'Yes,' came the reply, 'after this cycle of blood will come the phase of fire. Then we shall yearn for Gandhi's ahimsa and Einstein's penance.'

'Einstein?'

'The same man who discovered the link between the mysteries of nature and the explosive possibilities of energy. Mahmood Ali, I cannot understand why every great man's life ends like a dirge, why we see the ascent of malefactors after witnessing the birth of great inventions and new philosophies. During the great Flood, the demon Hygreev had stolen the Vedas. The horned fish had given King Satyavrat the magic spell for ensuring eternal life, restored the knowledge of the Vedas after killing Hygreev and protected its sacred words. And as a result, once the waters of the Flood receded, Satyavrat was venerated and the universe was born anew. While all divine pantheons witnessed the Flood, only mankind bears testimony to its cycle of blood. Earth alone has levelled out this ocean of blood, absorbing its overflow into its soil. The waves of blood are receding. Yet, no one knows if the universe will ever again be rejuvenated. Could it possibly happen?'

'Why worry, O Adeeb? After Satyavrat, Buta Singh and Zainab have taken on the challenge...'

10

Buta Singh placed the garments he had bought near Zainab and asked, 'Shall I help you out of the sandpit?'

'Please go outside. I'll manage to climb out myself.'

Slowly, Zainab emerged. She took off her threadbare kurta and put it away carefully, thinking that she might need it sometime. She tossed away her old ghagra that had hardly any remnants of cloth left to speak of, except for the narrow strip through which the cord was drawn. Then she inspected the new one Buta Singh had bought for her and put it on, tightening the cord at her waist. She heard his question, yelled out to her from outside: 'Does it take so long to get dressed?'

'Just wait outside!' she replied, adjusting her undergarment, then putting on her kurta over it. Draping her chunni over her shoulders, she called, 'Come in, now.'

Buta entered and sat down. Driven by habit, he mumbled, 'Onkar...Onkar...Satnam.' Though hardly a sound escaped his lips, Zainab guessed that he was invoking the name of Vahe Guru and asked him about it.

'I am,' he replied, 'but how did you know?'

'Sometimes, Nanakis from Sindh province stayed over at our place. I heard of Vahe Guru from them. Occasionally, congregational prayers were held on our veranda.'

'Then it is fine,' said Buta with relief. 'Mind if I ask you a question?'

'You have given me the clothes on my back. You have the right to ask me anything you want,' came the reply, though her tone lacked conviction.

'No, I don't. Any man can disrobe a woman. Some of the elders of the hamlet have advised me to marry you. Living together outside marriage isn't right, somehow.'

'Whatever you and the elders decide,' Zainab acquiesced.

'But there's just one thing.'

'What is it?'

'My own brothers don't want me to marry.'

'Are you married?'

'No, never have been. My brothers rejected all the proposals that came my way. Actually, they just could not tolerate the idea of my marrying.'

'Why not?'

'Our fields have a low yield which just about allows them to make ends meet for their families. If I had married, there would have been children...poverty...the land would have had to be divided and apportioned. The struggle for existence might have been bitter. That's why they are against us marrying,' said Buta, sifting the sand through his fingers.

'Don't worry. This is Zainab's promise to you—I will spend my entire life with you without the blessings of marriage. The question of children does not arise right now. I am willing to live with you, even if you don't want to marry me because of the objection raised by your brothers.'

'No, Zainab, marry you I shall. Or else, for the rest of my life, I will have to bury you in the sandpit at night and keep you company.'

'Amen,' said Zainab, holding her palms against her eyes.

Dushali Singh, one of the elders, felt it was necessary to unite Buta and Zainab in matrimony. The news greatly disturbed Buta's brothers and their wives and they banded together to oppose the event. Dushali Singh reprimanded them. 'What kind of brothers and sisters-in-law are you?' he asked. 'You want him to remain unmarried so that your own interests are protected? Now that a woman has come to live with him, it is only right that they should be married. After all, it is a matter of propriety...'

Vahe Guru showered his benediction on the couple. In due course, Zainab presented Buta with a bonny baby girl. They named her Tanvir Kaur. The year Tanvir was born, thousands of migratory birds from the north arrived in the hamlet.

11

At about the same time that Zainab was making the decision of her life in the desert village, Lord Mountbatten, the last viceroy of India, was addressing his wife Edwina in their official residence in New Delhi. In a voice that could barely contain his anger, he admonished her: 'Do stop defending a people broken by partition, massacres and death. In the history of nations, these are but trifles. Listen, Edwina. You are no longer Edwina Ashley. You happen to be the lawfully wedded wife of India's viceroy and Governor-General. You are expected to honour the traditions of the British Empire. So, it's quite useless wasting your tears on the suffering of refugees and the massacres on the borders of Pakistan. The British Empire does not take kindly to such tears.'

'The British Empire has no tears...don't I know it?' Edwina replied. 'But Louis, even the summits of the Alps and the Pyrenees would be reduced to tears witnessing this horrifying human tragedy. Have you lost all your capacity for Christian compassion?'

'Stop this talk of compassion, Edwina, and listen to me! The tears that well up in your eyes for these dead Indians are a blot on British royalty and the English race. And I absolutely refuse to condone the manner in which you cried on Jawaharlal Nehru's shoulder! How you leant against the Indian prime minister, expressing regret on behalf of the Empire!'

'Dicky, what are you trying to imply?' Edwina retorted, addressing Mountbatten by the nickname given to him by his royal British grandmother.

Mountbatten composed himself, but Edwina continued caustically, 'When confronting heart-rending tragedies of such magnitude, one cannot wipe away tears with handkerchiefs provided by the state...one needs the shoulders of friends, even strangers, to cry on. Don't you understand, Dicky?'

As he looked remorsefully at Edwina, he felt he had not handled the situation with finesse. She returned his gaze. Then he spoke. 'The truth, Edwina,' he said, 'is that even I am perturbed by the genocide. Such bloodshed had not taken place even on the Burmese front after World War II...so much blood, shed now, after Partition...so much blood that is bound to be spilled in the future. I wanted to keep India united. Gandhi, Nehru, Patel, Ghaffar Khan and even Jinnah were despondent about the proposal for Partition.'

'Even Jinnah?' Edwina asked incredulously. 'Are you serious?'

'Yes, Edwina, I am.'

'But during the meeting on 2 June, Jinnah had rejected the Cabinet Mission Plan, thereby nullifying the possibility of a united India. He wanted Partition, nothing but Partition.'

'Therein lies the irony. Due to compulsions arising out of the consequences of World War I, imperialism has had to present a liberal face and a façade of accountability, and peoples' movements, led by Gandhi, have radically shifted the axis of power. Gandhi's planned resolve has, for the first time, snatched power away from the political dynasties and entrusted it to the masses. It is from this juncture that the face of the world has begun to undergo a transformation.'

Edwina gave Mountbatten an inquiring look and he continued, 'It is from this point onwards that the ironies become manifest. Monarchs can go back on their decisions in many ways and on various pretexts. They can save their skins by blaming prime ministers, senates or advisors. But the newly emerging crop of peoples' leaders cannot retract statements they have made in public. This is Mohammed Ali Jinnah's tragedy. Having openly demanded the partition of India, he cannot take back his words, no matter how much he regrets them now. If he does, he will lose all credibility and no politician can bear to do so. This is the strength as well as the weakness of movements that are born from stirred passions. A statement, once issued, cannot be retracted even if, in hindsight, it is discovered to be incorrect or inappropriate. Whenever this happens, brute forces, opposed to change, rear their ugly heads. Edwina, as a witness, I can vouch for this...this is precisely what happened to Jinnah. He had made an impassioned appeal for the creation of Pakistan. When I had run through all possible options and finally presented the proposal for Pakistan and Partition to him, he became dejected and withdrew into silence. He wouldn't commit himself to either a yes or a no.'

'Go on.'

'I told him then that I had given him exactly what he wanted and that Pandit Nehru, Sardar Patel and Acharya Kripalani all felt that Partition was imperative and had voiced their approval for it to go ahead. Moreover, I had also obtained the consent of Sardar Baldev Singh, the Sikh leader, knowing quite well that it was the Sikhs who would pay the heaviest price for Partition. I told Jinnah that he should now lend his support to the historic occasion—the creation of Pakistan.'

'So...what did he have to say to that?'

'He was silent for a moment before asking me, "Does Gandhi accept Partition?" I replied that I did not think it likely, as he had been the biggest obstacle all through the deliberations. I told Jinnah that if he accepted Partition, along with Liaquat Ali Khan and Abdul Rab Nishtar, the issue of India's independence could be resolved there and then.'

'What was his reaction?'

'He replied that he was not in a position to commit himself without consulting his party, the Muslim League. Exasperated, I had to remind him that *he* was the Muslim League, that without him, the Muslim League did not exist. To that he had no answer.'

*

History waited, untroubled by regret. Regret is exclusively the lot of mankind, never of history.

Sattar sat in Gali Qasimjan, revelling in destiny: 'Pakistan has already been created—it hardly matters now whether Jinnah speaks up or remains silent. The foundation of Pakistan was laid on the very day that Ramdayal ignored my greeting and slipped away.'

'That's all very well,' replied Najmul, 'but these English bastards should remember that centuries ago, they wormed their way into this country in the guise of obsequious traders. What profit they earned, they are welcome to keep. But now they should keep their hands off what is ours...'

'Absolutely! Our rulers were squabbling with each other even before the British arrived, but what gives the latter the right to bully us into accepting their solutions? Arrey bhai, leave us to God's mercy and go your way.'

'Sometimes, Mahatma Gandhi of the Congress Party is brutally frank. This is exactly what he has been saying all along,' said Najmul.

'I've heard that Pakistan will be created only after a referendum. Mahatma Gandhi's words are heeded not only by Hindus, but by a number of Muslims as well. It would be wonderful if the Mahatma could get all the Hindus to vote for Pakistan. What would Jinnah do then?'

'He'd forsake politics and go back to being a lawyer in Bombay, what else?'

'I'm thinking of going back to Gangauli,' mused Sattar. 'The situation is fast deteriorating. We may be compelled to part with whatever we have here, but no one can forcibly usurp our land in Gangauli. There's no telling what Jinnah Sahib is up to!'

The next day, Sattar boarded the train for Gangauli Ghazipur.

*

Time rose from the midst of the distressed masses and entered the luxurious study of Viceroy House where Viceroy Mountbatten and Mohammed Ali Jinnah were present. Mountbatten said, 'Consult your Muslim League by tomorrow.'

'I'll need at least a week for these consultations with the Muslim League.'

'Look here, Mr Jinnah. We don't have time to waste over such a decision.'

'It seems you're in more of a hurry than we are.'

'You can say what you like, but today is 2 June 1947, and I wish to declare the partition of India tomorrow, 3 June. You had asked for Pakistan and we are giving it to you. The world thinks and knows that Pakistan will never come into existence, but the British Crown is handing it to you on a platter. What, then, makes you so hesitant now?'

Jinnah uttered not a word and Mountbatten continued: 'At the meeting tomorrow, the Congress will be represented by Pandit Nehru, Sardar Patel and Acharya Kripalani. Baldev Singh, the spokesman for the Sikhs, will also be there. Along with Liaquat Ali Khan and Abdul Rab Nishtar, you will speak for the Muslim League. They will not have the guts to defy you. If your newly awakened conscience stops you from taking a stand and giving your assent when I present the plan for India's partition, just move your head imperceptibly. Leave it to me to interpret the message your gesture conveys.'

Jinnah gazed at Mountbatten, only too aware that in the game of political chess, he was a mere pawn in the hands of the British. He was being paid back in his own coin—Pakistan! History stood witness—the Indian blood coursing through his veins froze at the realization that mutual obstinacy, minor acts of discourtesy and overriding arrogance had given birth to never-ending hostility. Fostered by hidden personal rivalries, such animosity had shattered the dreams of the masses, leaving in its wake bigots handicapped by illusions of religious superiority.

At this moment, Jinnah's spirit left his body and went to stand by his wife Rati's grave.

The spirit said not a word, but its silence was eloquent. It was here that the spirits of Jinnah and Gopal Krishna Gokhale met and gazed at each other. The compulsions of history on 3 June 1947 drove Jinnah's spirit back to his body. When Mountbatten presented before the concerned parties his proposal for the partition of India, Jinnah Sahib seemed non-committal. He merely tucked in his chin by half an inch and continued to sit there in that manner.

*

At that very moment, the adeeb noticed a visibly disturbed Rahi Masoom Raza from Gangauli storming towards him. Embracing him, the adeeb wanted to know what had happened. It took sometime before the panting Rahi could reply. 'Listen to that boy who has entered the house mouthing slogans!' he said. 'That Dullan who is hardly eight or nine years old...he says, "We will not rest till we have Pakistan."'

'From whom will you wrest Pakistan?' asked Phunnan Miyan, his eyes blazing with anger.

'From the Aligarhwalas,' Dullan replied.

Then Kulsum reported: 'Arrey, that man who has arrived from Aligarh, the one who wears a black sherwani and...brandishes a cigarette...he referred to the number of times in the Koransharif that Allah has exhorted the mians to vote for the Muslim League.'

'And what was happening in the mango orchard?' asked Najjo Bua, a widow who had converted to Islam three years ago.

The pandit with the tilak marking his forehead told of how the god Krishna had declared, 'O Arjun, I am the Supreme Power. There is none but I. Today, beloved Bharat of the Gita sends forth a clarion call to each Hindu, exhorting him to rise and banish these vile Muslims from the sacred banks of the Ganga and the Jamuna.'

'But where would we go?' Bafati, a middle-aged Muslim, asked his dear childhood friend Kanhaiyya, a Hindu. The latter replied, 'Go wherever you can lead a comfortable life. Now that Bhagwan Krishna has commanded us to do so, we must drive you away. Besides, Jinnah Sahib's Pakistan is in the making. You can make your way there and lead a life of ease.'

'You've told me to go away. Even if I manage to scrape together the money for the fare, how do I take my fields to Pakistan?'

'This is, indeed, a problematic issue. If Pakistan comes into being, how is Bafati going to transport his fields there?'

'Hmm,' mused Bafati, 'just reflect on the situation! I've lived here all my life and now I'm supposed to go to Pakistan to die, am I? Well, I'm not going to Pakistan, whether the Koransharif or your Kishan Bhagwan in the Gita says so.'

*

In the meantime, Tannu, now Major Hasan, was on his way back to Gangauli after the Armistice had been declared at the end of World War II. He too had heard that if the partition of India became a reality, the Indian Army would be split in two. Actually, he had been taken prisoner in Italy just before the war ended. And quite some time had elapsed before he was released and allowed to return home. He turned tearfully nostalgic when he saw the indigo warehouse once more. Unable to sit in the horse-drawn ekka any longer, he jumped down. The ekka came to a halt.

'You go on ahead,' Tannu told the ekka driver, relishing the breeze that wafted through the sugar-cane fields. He walked on.

Before him stood Fussu Miyan's shrine. Light from the petromax lamp peeped out through the cracks in the closed doors of the building's zenana quarters. On the veranda lay a pair of cots and a couple of easy chairs. Once he had set eyes on the veranda, it was impossible for Tannu to walk along at a leisurely pace.

'Fussu-cha, adaab!' he called loudly from afar.

'May you live long,' came the reply, as he was passionately embraced.

Then together, they travelled down memory lane. They reminisced about Tannu's late father...how happy he would have been. Sallo was mentioned. Jawad Miyan, his paternal grandfather, appeared, stroking his long beard. When he went inside, he was enfolded in a hug by Da Rabban. Sallo's mother Sakina cracked her knuckles to ward off the evil eye. Then he was greeted by Salma, Kubra, Sayyeda, Umme Laila, Kaniz, Rubab and Mehjabeen. Finally, Chhoti Dadda asked him, 'All right, now tell me if the war is really over or something still remains to be done?'

'The war is well and truly over,' he assured her.

After getting up next morning, Tannu had breakfast, washed his hands and went outside. Near the bamboo thicket, he came across a crowd of youngsters, vociferously chanting, 'Muslim League, zindabad!' A smile flitted across his face. He could also see some Hindu boys in the crowd. In the same enthusiastic manner as the others, they were seeking benediction for the League.

'What kind of Pakistan is in the making?' he asked the boys, but they moved on without replying. They continued shouting slogans.

'Nara-e-Takbir, Allah-o-Akbar!'

'Quaid-e-Azam, zindabad!'

'Muslim League, zindabad!'

Suddenly, he found himself standing before the Hakim Sahib's huge gates. He quickly greeted the gentleman. It seemed as if everyone from the northern strip of the town had congregated here. A couple of sherwani-clad men from Aligarh stood in their midst. One of them was speaking: '...and the most significant point is that

another Islamic government will find its place on the world map. It
is also possible that the green flag of Islam will flutter, once again,
aloft the Red Fort in Delhi.'

Tannu was least interested in the fate of Pakistan, so he sat down
on the edge of a charpai.

Someone said, 'I hear that Jinnah Sahib is a Shia.'

'But he is a Muslim,' retorted the black sherwani.

The other black sherwani joined in, 'Listen, my dear sir. We
should firmly grip the rope Allah has provided us. Today, that rope
is Mohammed Ali Jinnah. All of you are Allah's strength. Rise and
assert your claim to Pakistan.'

Tannu laughed and the black sherwanis regarded him with
irritation.

'Look here,' he said, 'I am not a politician. This is a locality of
Muslims who support the government. Their votes will naturally be
cast in favour of the League. But you cannot claim the vote of an
illiterate Muslim like Kulsum, who cannot even spell "Mumtaz", her
son's name, and mispronounces it as "Muntaj". What an upright
fellow he was! What do you know of him? He took part in the
farmers' agitation led by Swami Sahajanand and Rahul Sankrityayan
and died of gunshot wounds at the Qasimabad police station. I was
away at the time, a soldier in the British Army. But I've heard that
he died like a man. When fatally shot, he did not beg to be taken
to the hospital. He just caught hold of a man in the stampede and
asked him to tell his amma in Gangauli that he had died. You cannot
truly appreciate this farmer's selfless martyrdom; you cannot fathom
the pain hidden in his message, "Tell Amma that I died." Your Jinnah
Sahib can get a mansion built in Pakistan that will be even more
imposing than the one he leaves behind on Malabar Hill in Bombay.
If he so desires, he can exhume his wife Rati's remains from her
grave here and carry them to Pakistan, because he has no bond with
the soil. But Kulsum can neither take away her ancestors' graves nor
that of her dead son "Muntaj" to Pakistan. If all the graves of
Hindustan are carried away, the country's very soul will be ravaged.
Muslims will certainly get a fragmented state to themselves, but they
will leave behind the essence of their hearths and homes. Is this what

you seek? Speak up! Is this what you people desire?'

His words left the black sherwanis speechless.

'You deliberately instil fear in others,' Tannu continued angrily. 'It's we who will be left to reap its bitter harvest. The prospect fills me with dread.'

Black sherwani then resorted to rhetoric. 'Why should you be afraid? After all, you are the descendant of Mohammed bin Qasim.'

'I am not a voter,' Tannu interrupted. 'I am a Muslim and I love this village because I *am* this village. I cherish its indigo warehouse, its pond and its untarred streets.'

The expressions of the onlookers seemed to indicate a feeling of empathy for Tannu who continued: 'I have witnessed the macabre dance of death in the battlefield. When death came close, I remembered Allah and was reminded not of Mecca or Karbala, but of Gangauli. I would seethe with anger or weep when I thought I might never again be able to sit in the warehouse and eat sugar cane, or that I would never get to taste the halwa made on the eighth day of the Majlis. If Allah is everywhere, what is the difference between Gangauli and Mecca, the indigo warehouse and Kaaba, the waters of Zamzam and that of our pond?'

'It's people like you who will sell off the Hindustani Muslims to the Hindus,' came the angry retort from a sherwani. 'Aren't you ashamed of yourself? You actually dare to compare the sacred city of Mecca with this desolate village?'

'Yes, sir, indeed I do. And I am not ashamed of it. Why should I be? Gangauli is my home town; Mecca is not my city. This is my home and the Kaaba is Allah's. If God—glory be to Him—loves His abode, won't He understand that we too cherish our homes?'

'Listen, my boy, what you say is blasphemous,' Hakim Sahib reprimanded him. 'What the hell do you think you're up to, you bastard? The Kaaba is, after all, the Kaaba.'

'I don't deny the Kaaba. I only ask: can Lahore ever become the Kaaba? Look, Chacha! You have not seen the wide world the way I have. So, you cannot understand things as I do. Anything built on the foundations of hatred and fear can never flourish.'

12

'Congratulations,' said Abdul Rab Nishtar. In a celebratory gesture, he picked out some grains from the sugar bowl on the conference table in the viceroy's room and popped them into Liaquat Ali Khan's mouth.

Jinnah Sahib silently drew out his jade cigarette holder, fitted in a Caravan-A cigarette, and began to smoke.

*

Bhangi colony—the locality of untouchables. Dusk was settling in. Gandhiji had returned from his walk in time for the prayer meeting. A swayamsevika or assistant was cleaning his feet with a pumice stone. A middle-aged individual, clad in khadi, entered and announced, 'Bapu, Partition is now a reality.'

Gandhiji sighed deeply and drew back his tired feet. Swallowing, he said softly, 'I wish they'd partitioned my body. May God grant them wisdom.' Then he looked up at the heavens and reflected, 'Ill-considered decisions give birth to violence. And violence spawns barbarism and bloodshed.'

13

The doors of the court reverberated with the sound of knocks that left them spattered with blood.

Those interminable summons maddened it. While the rat-tat-tat of a Chinese AK-47 could be heard in the west, the cries of families in flight from the north-west tapped yet another tattoo.

The court asked them, 'Who are you?'

They replied, 'We are Hindus from Kashmir, but in Hindustan we are known as Kashmiris.'

A bullet came whizzing in from the North-East. That was a summons from the ULFA extremists operating in the area's tea gardens. It was followed by those widowed during the riots of 1984 drumming on the doors. Naxalites from the south joined in. Twenty dead men, killed in the Meham elections, added to the bedlam. Corpses from the Batala bus massacre started shrieking and the Lok Sabha gave another rap. The 10,000 people killed in communal riots during the past year stood up and added to the din. Supporters of democracy stood beating the gateway and walls of the Nepalese martyrs' monument. The LTTE from Sri Lanka added to the cacophony. The victims of Karachi's riots had just risen, when new corpses joined their ranks. Before the court could give any of them a hearing, Simranjit Singh Mann appeared and rapped on the door with his sword. Abdullah Bukhari, the Shahi Imam of Jama Masjid, announced, 'If the Babri Masjid is demolished, rivers of blood will flow. This is the Shahi Imam's decree.'

A rickshaw puller tugged at the corner of the court's kurta and asked, 'Shahs have vanished; shahenshahs have died. Yet, how is it that shahi imams survive, even today?'

Those knocking at the door burst out laughing.

'Silence!' cried the court and the laughter died down. But the knocking did not cease.

From the corner of the court, Shahabuddin's cough was another echo—Shahabuddin, who had brought out, not the *Indian Muslim*, but *Muslim India*, and who now clutched to his heart the corpse of his Insaaf Party.

The court asked him the reason for his presence.

'These days, my plight is worse than that of the dead. I have something to say,' answered Shahabuddin, before he was overcome by a fit of coughing.

Courts never take cognizance of coughs, but this one was transformed into a summons as its germs spread far and wide.

In their strident tones, the leaders of the Vishwa Hindu Parishad and the Bajrang Dal joined in the knocking. 'The Ramjanmabhoomi Mandir will be built,' was their message. 'In fact, we shall not rest till we liberate Krishna Janmabhoomi and the Kashi Vishwanath Mandir.'

The adeeb's court then issued the order that all the windows and ventilators there be left open so as to allow easy access to every summons that arrived at its doorstep.

The moment this announcement was made, the corpse of Shiv Khera, who had been the chief manager of the Srinagar branch of Hindustan Machine Tools, made an appearance. Bearing six bullet wounds, the body was soaked in blood. The corpse announced, 'I was shot at one-thirty p.m. I was taken to Batmaloo and murdered in cold blood. Rubaiyya Sayeed's father Mufti Mohammed Sayeed was home minister at the time. Don't I have a father in this country?'

The court interrupted, 'Khera has become deranged. He should have known that those who love this country cannot possibly expect their fathers to survive here.'

'Adaab,' said another echo.

'Adaab,' the court replied. 'Who are you?'

'They call me Professor Mushirul Haq. I was the vice-chancellor of Kashmir University. Earlier, I was at Jamia Millia in Delhi. I am a professor of Islamic Studies. I was killed at Padshiya Bagh this evening.'

The court wanted to know what he was carrying on his shoulder.

'Sir, this is the corpse of my secretary, Abdul Ghani. He was killed at the same time.'

There was loud knocking from the rear. The peon came to report that it was a summons from those who had been killed in the Baroda riots in Gujarat. Among them was a fatally injured man who was likely to die at any moment.

'Well, let him die first,' the court admonished the peon. 'I have no time for the half-dead or the living. I only deal with corpses.'

The peon was incensed. 'If you don't pay heed to the voices of the living and the half-dead,' he retorted, 'the number of casualties will keep spiralling. Shedding more blood will get us nowhere. Turn off this tap of blood which flows without a pause.'

'Shut up!' the court yelled.

'I will not be quiet! Only political authority or the police can silence peons. But how can you, an adeeb, seek to have me silenced? Shame on you!'

The court instantly acknowledged its error: 'I apologize, Mahmood. But what is this sobbing I hear? I find it immensely disturbing.'

'That is Begum Mushir weeping.'

'But Mushir Sahib is standing right here, bearing the corpse of Abdul Ghani on his shoulder. Can't you see him?' the court asked.

'Sir, the point is, his spirit is here, but his body took its time reaching Delhi. It had been placed behind a curtain in the plane in which Begum Mushir was travelling. So, she hadn't even known her husband's body was there. It was her son-in-law Abdul Salaam who explained it all to her. Eventually, Mushir Sahib's body reached Jamia Nagar, but the Begum could not reconcile herself to his death. She kept pleading, "Call the doctor. He's still alive." From that moment onwards, all she does is weep.'

'Then tell her to accept his death,' declared the court. 'Whoever dies, goes away forever. One should come to terms with the fact as soon as possible, for only then can the world carry on living.'

At this moment, two bombs, filled with blood, exploded in the court, spattering everyone present. Wiping away the blood dripping from its face, the court asked, 'Since when are these bombs packed with blood being manufactured?'

'Since Independence.'

'And when was that?' inquired the court.

The peon let out a loud guffaw and exclaimed, 'Shame on you, O Man of Letters! You preside over a court without even a basic knowledge of events to your credit! Either you are trying to fool us or you continue to live in 1947, when wise men like you scoffed at Independence.'

It was now the court's turn to laugh. It replied, 'But even today, the Shahi Imam of the Jama Masjid scorns Independence. He hasn't changed a bit. Nor does he allow the times to change.'

'He never will,' remarked the peon, 'because, in Hindustan, he heads the band of the abysmally ignorant. Among leaders like him are Ashok Singhal who is not a Hindu, but a Jain, and Mahant Avaidyanath, a Gorakhpanthi. There are many others of their ilk, sir. This country has no dearth of such people.'

'When was the crop of these ignorant souls sown?' asked the court.

A moaning corpse stood up and replied, 'Sir, the seed was sown in 1947 and it was irrigated with blood.'

Corpses from Bhagalpur, Meerut, Ahmedabad, Baroda, Kanpur and a number of other places seconded him.

'Of which harvest are you a seed?' the court asked.

'We have been reaped from the same harvest.'

'No!' screamed the corpse of a young man. 'You might belong to it. I don't. I belong to a lineage that is purely Hindustani. I was born after 1947 and killed in Bhagalpur.'

'And you?' the court asked another man.

'Show me due respect, please! I'm not just any old corpse. I happen to be a martyr. I was killed by the police in the Mand region.'

'What were you doing there?'

'I was creating Khalistan.'

A mohajir's corpse from Karachi stood up to say that he had also been killed.

'Why?'

'Because I was creating a Pakistan within Pakistan.'

'Wasn't Pakistan created in 1947?'

'It was, but that's a matter of geography. The contours of Pakistan we carry in our hearts and heads have yet to take concrete shape.'

'They never will!' growled a trident-wielding voice. 'There will be a united Bharat now.' Then he raised the slogan, 'Ram, Krishna and Vishwanath, together shall we take all three.'

Three more blood-filled bombs went off, bathing everyone in blood. The bombs contained such corrosive matter that many of the corpses broke out in boils.

Licking its boils, a Sikh corpse screamed, 'I was killed in Shopian!'

'What do you mean by that?'

'I'm not a Khalistani. I'm a Kashmiri. I was killed in spite of it. I was ordered to change the time by my watch and synchronize it with Pakistani standard time.'

'Can Pakistan be created just by setting back watches?' the court inquired.

'I wouldn't know. All I know is that I had to wear a green pugri and shut down meat shops that did not adhere to the Islamic way of slaughtering animals. Kashmiri Pandits were told to flee, leaving their spouses behind. Many of those who fled are now approaching this court.'

'Some are already here,' the peon reported.

'So Mushir Sahib, are you a Kashmiri Pandit?' the court wanted to know.

'No,' came the reply, 'I am a Muslim...I say my prayers five times a day. In fact, I was going to say my prayers when I was kidnapped. I was shot the following day. You were right, sir, when you stated that Pakistan could be created by pushing back time.'

'How far can one push back time?'

'To the time of Babar!' screamed the wielder of the trident, 'because that is when the enslavement of our history began.'

'No!' shouted the voice of an old man from Bhagalpur. 'The history of enslavement began with the arrival of the British. They snatched away Bahadur Shah Zafar's kingdom. When they left, they should have handed it back to us. Babar was only a ghazi, a victorious invader.'

'Babar was a barbarian, a beast!' came the furious rejoinder. 'As soon as he arrived here, he demolished our Ramjanmabhoomi Mandir and built the Babri Masjid on its foundations!'

A strange chaos descended on the court. The corpses' eyes filled with terror. They tore away the scabs of the wounds on their bodies, causing the blood to well up again.

'Where has this fresh blood come from, now? You were all killed long ago.'

'Babar is the culprit!' declared the impassioned voice of the trident-wielder. His enthusiasm cast a shadow on the other faces.

'Sir, as long as Babar's name keeps cropping up, the blood of centuries will continue to ooze out,' the peon explained politely.

The adeeb was lost in contemplation. He could not decide what he should do. It was true that he occupied the judge's chair, not a puppet throne. He had to find a solution, in his way and in his own time. After pondering over it at length, he spoke. 'Let Babar be presented before the court,' he commanded.

The peon left to execute the order.

The faces of the corpses blanched.

14

Babar was exhausted when he appeared in the court. Being roused from his grave had been a very painful experience. He resented his eternal repose being disturbed. Yet, he had had to undertake the long journey from Kabul.

As soon as he appeared, the court asked the corpses, 'Do you recognize this man?'

'No,' replied the corpses in chorus.

'This is Babar,' the court announced.

A chilling silence fell over the gathering.

The court ordered that a chair be given to Babar so that he could be seated.

'No, I need a throne to sit on!' Babar thundered. 'After all, I'm an emperor! Leaders these days tend to rest their crushing weight either on the shoulders or the necks of their people!'

'Would you like to sit on the necks of these people?' the court asked him.

'I was lying peacefully where I was, but now that you have summoned me here, I'll sit wherever you ask me to.'

'All right, sit down wherever you wish to and answer my questions,' said the court.

Babar aquiesced.

'Why did you attack Hindustan?'

'What else could an emperor have done?' came the reply. 'When Farghana and Bokhara were snatched away from me, I had to establish another kingdom somewhere. I attacked Hindustan several times, but victory eluded me. The truth is...I eventually defeated Hindustan, because I was invited to attack it by Rana Sanga, the Hindu Rajput, and Daulat Khan, the subedar of Punjab who was Sultan Ibrahim Lodi's uncle.'

'This man is a liar!' protested the trident-wielder. 'Rana Sanga could never have been a traitor!'

'Silence!' the court roared.

The peon snatched away the trident from the corpse's hand with the warning: 'Calm down and be seated like the other corpses. Is that clear? Or you'll be sent down to be killed again.'

At this, the trident-wielder looked terror-stricken and, clasping his hands in supplication, pleaded, 'No! I don't want to die the same death all over again.'

'Why not?' the peon taunted. 'Hadn't you promised, when you were still living, to die not ten, but a thousand times, if necessary, for the Ramjanmabhoomi? What makes you so fearful now?'

'I'm human now and the fear of death overwhelms me.'

'Then what were you when you died?'

'I was a Hindu then.'

'Aren't Hindus human beings?'

'They are to begin with, but when the poison of hatred courses through my veins, I cast off the robes of humanity and become a Hindu.'

'Where has this bitter poison come from?' asked the court.

'It took birth in the harvest of 1947, sir. It urges both Hindus and Muslims to be zealots,' said the peon.

'Don't waste my time,' Babar said exasperatedly. 'Resolve your disputes by yourselves.'

'But you yourself are the root cause of all our disputes! Had you not destroyed the Ram Mandir, this dispute would not have arisen at all,' the trident-wielder replied apologetically.

'Let my Allah and history stand witness—in Hindustan, I neither destroyed a mandir nor had a masjid built in my name. Islam had come to Hindustan much before my arrival. Wasn't Ibrahim Lodi a Muslim when he sat on the throne in Agra? I defeated Lodi, a Muslim, at Panipat on 20 April 1526 and took over his kingdom. His head was severed and brought to me. I'd sent Humayun to Delhi and had proceeded to Agra, Ibrahim Lodi's capital, for some rest.'

'Babar, answer the questions honestly. Don't try to mislead the court by digressing from the issue at hand.'

'I had come to conquer Hindustan for myself, not in the name of Islam. I sought a kingdom and acquired it. When I was alive I

never heard of Tulsidas, the creator of Ram, the Hindu god. During
my reign, no such god existed. So, how could I have demolished his
temple? It was when I lay in my grave that I heard of Tulsidas. When
I sat on the throne of Delhi and a *khutba* of praise was offered in my
name for seven days, no one knew who Tulsidas was. At the time,
he must've been a little boy roaming half-naked in some street or
other.'

'What is the date you refer to?'

'I defeated Ibrahim Lodi at the battle of Panipat on 20 April
1526...that is, Friday, Rajab 15. The khutba in my name was read
on 27 April 1526, as my troops camped beside the Jamuna. O Legal
Scholar, I loved the water of Hindustan! At the time, I was homeless
and had come here looking for a land to call my own. In those days,
even that had to be obtained by the edge of the sword.'

'You are digressing once again.'

'No, sir, I am not!'

'Then relate without further ado the story of your Babri Masjid.'

'I told you, didn't I, that Agra was my capital city? At the time,
Krishna had been accepted as an incarnation of the gods. His
birthplace was Mathura, just fifty miles from Agra. If I were bent on
destruction, wouldn't I have ground to dust Krishna's birthplace?
Why would I have gone to Ayodhya to demolish Ram's birthplace?
Ram became a god only after Tulsidas, who was a child during my
lifetime, wrote the Ramayana. And that was after my death.'

'When did you die?'

'December 1530. I don't remember the exact date. Who wants
to remember the date of his death?'

'But the world claims that you had the Ram Mandir demolished
in 1528 and ordered your subedar Mir Baqi to build a mosque
there.'

'That is an outright lie. I had nothing to do with that mosque.
Do you really want to know the truth?'

'Absolutely!' the court cried, leaping to its feet. 'Absolutely!'

'Then the honourable Fuhrer should be summoned.'

'Fuhrer?' the court asked apprehensively. 'The Nazi Fuhrer,
Hitler?'

'No, not him, but A. Fuhrer.'

'Who is he?'

'This man reached Hindustan after my kingdom had been destroyed. He was the director-general of the British Archaeological Survey of India. You must summon him to confirm this.'

The court found itself in a dilemma. Babar was talking about events that had occurred 300 years after his death. Scratching its head, the court asked Babar, 'How will calling him help us? There is a gap of almost three hundred and fifty years between your reign and the era to which he belonged.'

'Just call him, will you?'

'But how will his presence help you?'

'In 1889, this man had read an inscription in the very same mosque which carries my name. You can't read that inscription today because vandals have defaced it. However, it was very much there in Fuhrer's time. Call him here to confirm it.'

The corpses present in the court were bewildered. What did Babar eventually seek to prove? He seemed to be talking sense. By now, the boils that had erupted on the corpses were subsiding and the pain from their wounds had eased somewhat. The chaos prevailing in the court had also died down after Babar's arrival.

The court issued an order for A. Fuhrer to be brought before it. The peon ran and fetched him. An arrogant man, Fuhrer thought it highly insulting that he should be summoned in this manner by the liberated citizens of a slave nation. Babar's presence, however, made him recognize the importance of his position. Unable to bring himself to show disrespect to the court, he stood up deferentially.

'When did you meet Babar?' he was asked.

'I met him sometime around 1910. In Kabul...at his grave.'

'Did you read the now-illegible inscription in the Babri Masjid?'

'Yes, sir, I did.'

'What did it say?'

'It said,' replied Fuhrer, 'that in the Hijri year 930, that is, near about 17 September 1523, Ibrahim Lodi had laid the foundations of this mosque. The building was completed on 10 September 1524 and was named the Babri Masjid. I had gone to Babar to inform him about it. This monument has not been destroyed by time, but rather, by people eager to perpetuate and keep alive the Babri Masjid–Ramjanmabhoomi conflict.'

The court wanted to know why no one had ever held Ibrahim Lodi accountable for laying the foundations of this mosque.

'No one blamed Ibrahim Lodi because firstly, no mandir had existed there. Secondly, Lodi's paternal grandmother was a Hindu. In her veins flowed Hindu blood. So, obviously, he could not be blamed...'

Babar interrupted loudly: 'So, I was the foreigner without Hindu blood! Lodi was the true-blue native with a Hindu grandmother!'

'But while pursuing Afghanis, you had reached the Ghaghra river—also known as the Saryu. Ayodhya is on the banks of the Saryu and your subedar Mir Baqi was there.'

'That is why he dedicated the masjid to me. You know how sycophantic people like subedars and mansabdars can be,' Babar explained. 'Do you know how many Gandhi Nagars, Nehru Nagars, Kidwai Nagars and Sanjay Gandhi Nagars exist in your country today? Have all these places also been constructed by my people?'

'Then why is it that your diary, the *Babarnama*, has no record of the five-and-a-half months between 3 April 1528 and 17 September 1528?'

'Now what can I possibly say to that?'

'We demand an explanation, because on 2 April, you went to the jungles north of Ayodhya for shikar. It is from this point that your diary maintains no record of subsequent events. The next entry mentions your presence in the durbar held at Agra on 18 September 1528. Where were you in the interim period? The English gazetteer H.R. Neville writes that in the summer of 1528, you were in Ayodhya. This means that you had ample time between April and August to go to Ayodhya, order the demolition of the ancient mandir and arrange for the construction of a mosque which you later named the Babri Masjid.'

'This is a gross untruth!' Babar protested. 'Lying in my grave, I have witnessed the passage of centuries. Till around 1850, everything went well. After 1857, the British government's policy underwent a change.'

'Babar is right,' interposed Fuhrer. 'As part of our changing policies, we had decided that in order to keep the British government from collapsing, it was necessary to create rifts between Hindus and Muslims who had been united in 1857. It was what motivated me to deface Ibrahim Lodi's inscription on the Babri Masjid. The translation of this inscription still lies in the files of the Archaeological Survey of India. No one has thought of destroying it. However, the two crucial pages of the *Babarnama* which prove that the king had gone to Avadh, not Ayodhya, mysteriously disappeared. Having played this dirty trick, the British and, particularly, H.R. Neville, the Faizabad gazetteer, went a step further. The latter placed on record the falsehood that Babar had stayed in Ayodhya for a week and ordered the demolition of the Ram Mandir.'

Tired and thirsty, Fuhrer was out of breath after this long narration. Since no water was available, he was handed a glass of blood.

The court put the next question to Babar. 'If pages have, indeed, been torn out of your *Babarnama*, at least you can tell us what you were doing between 3 April and 17 September 1528, when you were not in Ayodhya. While on shikar in the jungles of Avadh–Ayodhya, where had you disappeared? This is the most pertinent question of all and the root of all trouble.'

'Sir, it is true that I was in the jungles of Avadh for shikar till 2 April. At the time, Ayodhya was not so famous a place that I would want to visit it. Besides, I had no enemies to conquer there,' Babar replied.

'Why do you wish to hide the truth? At least, you can tell this court the facts as they stand.'

'The truth, Honourable Adeeb, is that after the uprising of 1857, the British modified their policy. They started dividing my homeland along the lines of religion. I was interred in the soil of Agra, but fanatics exhumed my grave and carried me off to Kabul. Anyhow, Honourable Adeeb, the fact is that after 1857, H.R. Neville deliberately resorted to deceit. In my handwritten *Babarnama*,

I had mentioned Oudh. Neville changed it to Ayodhya, knowing only too well that Oudh meant Avadh, the name that is used even today. Fuhrer also passed me the information that Cunningham, a British officer well liked by his compatriots, had been assigned the job of protecting the authentic facts about Hindustan's history and historical monuments. Exercising a great deal of cunning, this man had recorded in the *Lucknow Gazetteer* that during the construction of the Babri Masjid, Hindus attacked the building. In the ensuing battle, say his records, one lakh seventy-four thousand Hindus were killed and their blood mixed with the mortar used in the construction of the building.'

'This is horrifying indeed!'

'But it is not the truth,' retorted Babar.

'How can you say so? Where's the evidence?'

'Firstly, what Cunningham wrote has vanished like the lost pages of my *Babarnama*.'

'Oh really?'

'It's true...I also wish to place before this court another fact. In the *Faizabad Gazetteer*, the British officer Neville has recorded that the population of Faizabad–Ayodhya rose from nine thousand nine hundred and forty-nine in 1869 to eleven thousand six hundred and forty-three in 1881. This implies an increase in the population by two thousand in a mere twelve years. Honourable Adeeb, it's up to you to guess what the approximate figure must've been in my time, that is, in the year 1528. How, then, could one lakh seventy-four thousand Hindus have been killed at the time? It should now be quite clear to you that the British have played a dirty trick on us.'

The adeeb looked intently at Babar.

'That is all I can tell you,' continued Babar, 'but my daughter Gulbadan Begum has written as much in the *Humayunama. Tuzuk-e-Babri* is written in Tajik. Read it and you will come to know the facts.'

'I am a writer, but during this era, I've had no time to pursue my literary interests. Those days are over when one not only fought battles, but also enjoyed the leisure of dictating one's memoirs,' the court retorted with sarcasm.

'Your words remind me of...' began Babar. 'Look here, the point is...'

'Don't prevaricate, Babar. Tell us what you did on 2 April 1528, after the shikar in the jungles of Oudh–Ayodhya. Did you visit Ayodhya subsequently? Did you stay there for a week or did you not?'

'I certainly did not! Reason it out for yourself. After years had gone by without my seeing them, my wife Meham Begum and daughter Gulbadan were coming to Agra for the first time. They were to arrive on 8 April 1528. I had returned from Oudh to receive them. You can verify this by reading the details in Gulbadan's *Humayunama*.'

'Again this talk of reading! You are insulting an adeeb!' the court angrily reprimanded Babar.

'I beg your pardon, but you must ask Gulbadan...'

The peon whispered something in the court's ear. There was a nod of assent as the court issued the order: 'Let Gulbadan Begum be presented!'

As soon as she entered, Gulbadan Begum greeted her father and began to sob hysterically. 'How was I to know that my Hindustan would be devastated like this,' she began, 'and that your name, my honourable father, would be sullied...'

The court interrupted Gulbadan by praising her ability to speak in Hindi and asked her to recount where her father had been between 3 April and 17 September 1528.

'Sir, let me tell you about it. My honourable father had called us to Hindustan. My younger brother Humayun had accompanied him there two years earlier. With my ammi, Meham Begum, I reached Hindustan before any of my other female relatives did. Much before 7 April 1528, my father had left the jungles of Avadh to receive us at Agra. We had travelled via Aligarh. In those days, it was known as Kul-Jalali. On 9 April, we reached Aligarh. My father had set out from Agra on foot to receive us and we met near Mehamnanacha's house, four miles from Agra. Our entourage entered Agra on foot. The date was 10 April 1528 and my father wanted to spend some time with Ammi.'

'What has all this got to do with history?' the court inquired.
'It's surprising that you should ask. You are a man of letters, an
adeeb presiding over a court. Yet, you seem to be fighting shy of
human emotions. Isn't every individual, even a shahenshah, a human
being? Don't love and affection spring from his heart? Are you
incapable of grasping even this much? Three months...yes, three
whole months, from 10 April to 10 July, my honourable father spent
with us. Then he took us to Dholpur and, from there, to Sikri. Here,
he had a throne built out of stone. It was surrounded by water and,
seated on it, he either wrote or dictated his memoirs.'

'So Babar, your honourable father, never reached Bihar when he
passed through Jaunpur, Buxar, Chausa and Saaran in pursuit of
Sheikh Baazid?'

'How could he have done so? He had returned to Agra to
receive us. It was his army, under the command of Mohammed Ali
Jung-jung, which pursued Sheikh Baazid through these places. My
honourable father returned from the confluence of the Ghaghra and
Sarda rivers; he never went on to Ayodhya. After spending three
months with us, he left for Dholpur and Gwalior on 10 July. He
returned to Sikri in the first week of August, arriving in Agra around
15 September. Relevant pages from my *Humayunama* can take the
place of the missing pages from the *Babarnama* and explain where
my father was. I wish to categorically state on his behalf that for him
Ayodhya had no special attraction and that he never visited it.

'During the three months we were together, we went to
Sirhind, because the imam of Lahore had rebelled against him. In
Sirhind, Kambar-e-Ali Argun was ordered to arrest the imam and his
supporters and produce them before the Agra durbar. All this while,
Muslim had been fighting Muslim, and no one—be it emperor,
sipahsalar, or subedar—could establish their rule over this country
without the collaboration of the Hindus. Involved as he was in
defeating the Afghani Muslims, where could he have found the time
to go to Ayodhya, demolish a mandir and build a masjid in its place?
The question of religion did not arise when my honourable father
attacked Hindustan for the last time. That battle was fought over a
kingdom. As Muslims were fighting each other at the time, the
Hindu–Muslim question was simply not relevant.'

'Lend me your ears!' a voice called. 'During Babar's reign, we received the decree for the Dantdhavan Kund Mandir in Ayodhya.'

The court asked for the voice to be identified.

'I am Chhatradas,' came the reply, 'the first mahant of the Dantdhavan Kund. I came to know that Babar was present in this court. So I emerged from my samadhi to pay obeisance to my emperor.'

'What the hell is Dantdhavan Kund and where is it?'

'It is the place in Ayodhya where Ramchandraji used to clean his teeth with a herbal twig called datun,' Mahant Chhatradas replied. 'It was here that Gautama Buddha spent sixteen *chaturmas*,' he continued in a monotone. 'The Chinese traveller Hiuen Tsang had also come here and has described the place in his travelogue. This place exists in Ayodhya to this day. My disciples are present there. On a bronze plate, Babar had given me a decree waiving taxation. Later, the British certified the same on a piece of fabric which exists even today.'

'Does this mean that Babar had come to Ayodhya?'

'Zahiruddin Mohammed Babar was an emperor. In those days, emperors did not deign to grace a place with their physical presence. Rather, their benevolence did. They were not like the politicians of today who come to disburse paltry sums of money. Till today, we merely collect *lagaan* from the area; do not pay any. We retain in our possession both Babar's decree and its certification by the British.'

'I'm not interested in the benevolence showered on you by Babar. Since you are a contemporary of his, I'm only interested in knowing whether he built the Babri Masjid or not.'

'There is no doubt that I'm one of Babar's contemporaries. The masjid was built on a vacant plot of land by Ibrahim Lodi. It's quite possible that Mir Baqi Tashkandi had got some alterations done to it. Mir Baqi's descendants can be found in his village of Sanewa even today. Why don't you ask them?' the mahant suggested.

'All right, in that case, the court is adjourned for some time.'

A commotion arose among the dead. The knocking started again. The uproar resumed. Some new corpses had arrived. It was revealed that they came from the North-East, where ULFA insurgents had killed them. The court could not understand what the Bodoland issue was about. So, the peon had to explain.

'Sir,' he began, 'this is a movement embraced by the ethnic Assamese. The first movement of its kind was born in Andhra. It was, subsequently, taken up by the Shiv Sena in Maharashtra.'

The adeeb thanked the peon and, tucking him into his pocket, set off for Faizabad–Ayodhya. His purpose was to locate Mir Baqi's village—Sanewa.

The corpses surrounded him, screaming, 'You can't postpone the court hearing like this! After all, only one court remains! All the other courts in the nation are useless. Their uselessness stems from half-baked laws.'

With great difficulty, the adeeb was able to convince the corpses that the court had only been adjourned, not dismissed, and persuaded them to disperse.

15

The adeeb had just stepped down on the platform at the Faizabad railway station when he received a stinging slap from a slogan painted on the wall. Then the slogan spoke up: 'Now that you've come to Faizabad–Ayodhya, you must read this.'

Hindustan, said the writing on the wall, would not tolerate any desecration of its religious sites:

'Never will tolerate Hindustan

Any insult to its *dharam sthans.*'

'Where have you come from?' the adeeb asked the slogan.

'From Delhi,' it replied.

'To which place do you belong?'

'Delhi...but I was born in the Gorakh ashram of Gorakhpur.'

'Where do you live in Faizabad?' the adeeb inquired.

'Here, in this station.'

'Don't you go into the city?'

'Occasionally,' the slogan replied, 'when our bands, the jathas, come here.'

'Otherwise?'

'I stay here...because the townspeople don't make me feel welcome.'

'Is that why you live in the station?'

'Yes...mostly.'

'I am going to the house of Mir Baqi Tashkandi, so I'll take your leave for the time being. On my way back, I shall speak to you again.'

The slogan continued shouting:

'Never will tolerate Hindustan,

Any insult to its dharam sthans.

Never will tolerate Hindustan...'

When he came out of the station, the adeeb was besieged by a crowd of rickshaw pullers and auto drivers. Then he witnessed a miracle. The slogan flew away and got tossed around amidst the clouds in the sky. Moments later, a storm brewed and it began raining money—currency notes and coins. As the storm grew fierce, the money showering down was blown away towards Ayodhya. Some fell into the hands of the poor, but most of it was carried away in the direction of the Saryu.

On his way to Mir Baqi's village of Sanewa, the adeeb passed through the streets of Faizabad where everything—the bazaar and the hustle and bustle of life—seemed quite normal. Bundled into a rickshaw, children were on their way to school. Burqa-clad Muslim women were busy making purchases in the bazaar or trying on glass bangles. Hindu bangle vendors slipped the bangles over the women's wrists while the latter sat at ease in their presence, their veils swept back from their faces. They looked upon these vendors as they would members of their own community and addressed them as 'bhaiyya' or 'chacha'.

The bazaar overflowed with foodstuff and ready-made clothes. The shops were neither Hindu nor Muslim—they were just shops. The dust and filth around the place were no different from anywhere else in Hindustan. The clothes people wore were very similar to those seen in other parts of the country.

And none of the walls here were given to shouting slogans. No bloodstained wall, pockmarked with bullets, came forward to narrate its tale of woe. The adeeb was relieved to see that these walls in Faizabad cared for their people. They advertised gripe water, red herbal massage oil and feeding bottles for babies. The walls exhorted young men to purchase motorcycles and encouraged young women to buy lipsticks and brassieres. They urged men suffering from impotence to visit hakims and vaids, whose herbal cures promised to transform them into the epitome of virility and manhood.

The children played with the same kind of wooden or plastic toys. They all wore similar rubber chappals, though in different colours—green, blue or cream. They used the same kind of feeding bottles and nipples, while the same type of brush was used to clean them. Even their tantrums were similar in nature; each child kept tugging at his mother's arm, adorned with bangles, in a bid to drag her to his favourite shop. Everyone seemed to be eating chaat from the same kind of plates woven out of leaves. The lips of all the young girls chewing paan seemed to have taken on the rosy hues of the gurhal flower.

The adeeb could not believe his eyes, because he had expected something quite different. He could only gaze around him in wonder. He ran into the office of the *Janmorcha*, a newspaper, to confirm that all he had seen was true and not a web of deceit woven by some malign power. Was he really in Faizabad or some other town? It certainly didn't look like Faizabad. It seemed more like a magical place, a Tilismabad. Sitla Singh, the editor, gaped at him in disbelief and he left the newspaper office.

He was passing by a beautiful mausoleum, when he felt a pale, emaciated hand on his shoulder. Turning round, he started. The hand belonged to an old woman who resembled his graceful great-grandmother. Her wrinkles and silvery mane reminded him of the Saryu's waves.

'Don't you recognize me?' she asked. 'I'm Bahu Begum, Faizabad's daughter-in-law. I didn't leave my Faizabad...he went away, taking even his capital city along to Lucknow. All I said was: "Go...just go away! You are not the only son I have. I am blessed with several and I'm not going to leave Faizabad."'

'Dadi, where do you live?' the adeeb asked.

'Arrey...don't you know? I live right here, within the mausoleum. I am buried here. I saw you passing by; so, I thought I'd come out and meet you. After centuries I felt like seeing you. You belong to Amir Khusrau's family, don't you? You're a writer, aren't you?'

'Yes, Dadi, I am, indeed, a writer. Amir Khusrau belonged to Etah. I come from Mainpuri, just thirty miles away.'

'How do a mere thirty miles matter? Writers traverse centuries. My children—Valmiki, Vyas, Kalidas, Kabir and Meera—are the elders of the same family of which you are now the heir.'

Before the adeeb could reply, she continued, 'I recognized you the moment I saw you. Tulsidas too belonged to the same family. Khusrau lived in Etah, but Tulsidas lived right here in Ayodhya. You must live here as well. Why wander from place to place? Just settle down here and write. Your words will transcend centuries...they will reach across to people. You are not old. Yet, your eyes are misty and your brow furrowed and you are short of breath. Why? What are you fleeing from? Tell me, my son, please tell me!'

'Dadi, the times are such that I have no peace of mind. I cannot write. These days, I bathe in blood and live on bullets.'

'Arrey Beta, even I have received a bullet wound. Ask these Kashmiri mujahideen—what harm I did them. But, son, do look after yourself. No king, emperor, politician or prime minister is ever going to answer for his deeds. Having done good or evil, they will die. It is either you or the nation who will be held accountable. That is why, my son, you have to take care of yourself.' With these words, Bahu Begum wiped away her tears and vanished.

From where he sat in the adeeb's pocket, the peon tapped him and urged, 'Please finish your work.'

'What?' asked the adeeb, dazed.

'Well said!' came the reply. 'You've even forgotten why the adjourned court came here in the first place! Do remember your mission and ask the way to Mir Baqi's village.'

'Oh!' the adeeb exclaimed and asked a passer-by for directions.

'Who...which Mir Baqi?' was the response, each time he inquired.

When no one seemed able to give him the address, the adeeb entered a printing press. Only two things were being printed there—*Ayodhya's Bloody History* and receipt books for recording donations. Piles of these receipt books were being sent to Ayodhya's mandirs.

The post office was jammed with the agents of Ram Mandir committees, bhajan singers and various other groups like dals and parishads. Armed with rubber stamps, they were busy receiving the donations that came by money order.

Eventually, the peon emerged from the adeeb's pocket, got hold of a copy of *Ayodhya's Bloody History*, discovered Mir Baqi's address inside, and passed it on to the adeeb. Mir Baqi's village Sanewa, it turned out, was described in the book and lay just four miles away.

Sweltering heat. A dirt track. Blazing sunlight. Billowing clouds of warm dust. Somehow, he reached the heart of the village. The wheat had already been harvested and the fields lay empty. Only the wheat stacks stood piled on one side. The village consisted of an assortment of mud and brick houses. A dozen children could be seen playing. No adult was in sight.

Then a little girl came forward and asked, 'Do you want to meet Abba?'

'Where is your abba?'

'There he is...sleeping on a cot.'

The peon went to wake him up and the man came over.

'Can someone help me?' asked the adeeb.

'What do you want?'

'Does anyone know where the descendants of Mir Baqi Tashkandi live?'

'Which Mir Baqi Tashkandi?' asked the elderly villager. 'This is Sanewa. If you need that information, go and seek it at Tashkand village...why bother us?' With these words, he retreated into his thatched hut and did not emerge again.

The adeeb found himself in a quandary. Gazing at the village scorched by the searing heat, he noticed a small masjid and a mausoleum in the distance. A lamp had been placed at the head of the grave there. He called out to his crew. The cameraman and the sound technician were prompt to respond and the production unit became alert.

'Since this village seems to have no other masjid or mausoleum, this must be the one Mir Baqi built...and that must be his grave,' the adeeb observed. At this, the crew doffed their footwear and climbed up the steps leading to the mausoleum's courtyard. They had just begun filming the place, when a crowd of people suddenly came running out of a back street and created a furore.

'You are the culprits who set our Bharat aflame!' yelled a middle-aged man resembling a maulvi.

'How dare you climb up here without permission?'

'Who allowed you in?'

'Who are you?'

'Get down!'

'What is your motive in coming here?'

'Do you take this for your own village that you can come here whenever it suits you?'

The screaming mob threatened to get out of hand any moment. If anyone had merely picked up a stone and flung it, the act would have provoked a shower of brickbats. The adeeb gently tried his best to contain the mob. In vain, it seemed. A group of young villagers, still busy shrugging into their kurtas as they wrapped *tehmads* around their waists, joined the mob. The tension escalated.

Suddenly, two angels appeared before them. 'Arrey bhai,' declared one, 'this is our Sitla Singh Babu of the *Janmorcha*. He can do no wrong. Quiet, now! Quiet!'

In the blistering sun, everyone miraculously forgot their anger and wanted to know why the strangers had come.

When Sitla Singh told them, the man who looked like a maulvi, came forward. 'Now, the fact is,' he explained, 'we all live here in harmony. This is a Muslim village. Both Shias and Sunnis live here. And I...'

'What do you do?'

'I have a small provisions store and I also happen to be the pesh-imam who leads the prayers here. No Mir Baqi has ever lived here...nor is anyone here related to him.'

'Whose mausoleum is this, then?' asked the leader of the expedition.

'The man was a *buzurg*, a much-respected elder from the family that lived opposite our house. We all had great faith in him. This is his grave. Just think for a moment—could Mir Baqi's mausoleum and masjid be quite so nondescript? Actually, misguided historians and Delhi's newspapers have inflamed passions. They came here, took photographs of the place, then went back and wrote that this was Mir Baqi's grave and that, the masjid built by him.'

'Those bastards should be hanged.'

'Such people just go around rousing feelings to fever pitch and inciting others to violence...it never occurs to them to wonder what will happen to Bharat. First, they tried to create a Hindu–Muslim divide here. That didn't work. Now, they're trying to foment trouble between the Shias and the Sunnis.'

The signs of village hospitality were beginning to manifest themselves. Water, sherbet, biscuits and *dal mot* were being offered to the guests.

'We know that you are trying to douse inflamed passions. Do take photographs of whatever you wish to.'

At this, a member of the production crew climbed up the steps, once again, to the mausoleum's courtyard. Conversation resumed. Under a tree nearby, an altar had been built for earthen lamps.

The owner of the provisions store explained, 'That altar was built by our Hindu ancestors. We light scores of lamps here when the tazia processions are taken out...'

'Who leads the prayers in the masjid?'

'I do,' the same man replied.

'Does this village have only one masjid?'

'Yes...both the Shias and the Sunnis pray here. We Shias say our prayers first; then the Sunnis say theirs. There is no dissension here, but certain people are keen on creating it. As a result...'

'By the way, what is the difference between Shias and Sunnis?' the adeeb asked.

'Not much, sir,' explained an elder. 'The Shias are those who have a deep regard for Ali. The ones who have less of a regard for him are the Sunnis.'

Just then, a wailing woman arrived on the scene. Beating her breast, she hurled an accusation at the imam. 'Let the Sunnis and Shias go to hell!' she cried. 'Imam Sahib, you have killed my Bilqees. Bilal of the Emirates is responsible for this.'

Her words caught the adeeb's attention and he asked what the incident being referred to was all about. In the meantime, the peon who had been surveying the village had come back and was standing by him.

The court now required Bilal's presence. The peon was sent to look for him, but returned alone. 'Sir,' he said, 'Bilal is nowhere to be found. He is neither in this world nor in the other.'

'How is that possible?' the adeeb retorted. 'All faiths and cultures have evolved the principle of only two spheres of existence. How can there be a third one in which a man like Bilal can go missing.'

'I really don't know, sir, but I have failed to find him. The last I heard of him was that he had fled towards Egypt.'

'Towards Egypt? Then we'll surely get him. How can the Egyptians ever forget me? I speak of an age when human beings were united by blood, shared a common culture and coexisted on the banks of the Nile. It is we who nurtured Egyptian civilization. Go and tell the Egyptians that Bilal's presence is required by the individual who has given them their culture. Have the people of the Nile Valley forgotten that it was I who irrigated the entire expanse of fertile land from the Mediterranean to the source of the river? Six thousand years before Christ, my companions and I had constructed the pyramid for the Pharaoh Cheops. Even Herodotus, that Greek historian, you know, had gone to see it. There is little point in going into the nitty-gritty of what King Menes did, but the fact remains that it was I who devised the concept of paving the way for the spirits of ancient Egypt to enter this world and to return where they came from.'

'Sir—'

'Quiet! Six thousand years ago, I was the one to obtain an

insight into the two spiritual aspects that coexist within man: the worldly and the divine. Even after death, the spirit seeks its old abode; that was why I felt the pyramids were essential. It was within these structures that the body could be preserved, so that the spirit could come and go as it wished. And do you know—'

'Sir—'

'Do you know that in me reside not only centuries, but also civilizations? Within those pyramids, I had created paths to direct the spirit on its way back, so that there would be no chance of it going astray the way we do today.'

'Honourable Adeeb...' a worried Babar intervened.

'Hear me out, Babar. If you don't care to appreciate the humanitarian roots of mankind, you will never be able to understand the cause of all the sorrow and suffering in this world.'

'Honourable Court, what have I to do with the world today?' asked Babar.

'You have much to do with it. Future generations are affected by the world we create. If you had nothing to do with it, you would not be present in this court today. No one can claim an independent existence...the past is inextricably bound with the present.'

'That's true.'

'Now, listen. All of us have a definite link with Egyptian civilization. It was I who envisaged my rebirth in it, because I refused to accept the finality of death. Life after death was the biggest truth of all.'

'Perhaps, it was you who abolished the tradition of worshipping spirits and established the principle of the unity that bound together the soul and its creator,' Fuhrer interposed gently.

'Why do you use the word "perhaps"? I say "definitely"! We regarded the sun as the supreme deity and reverentially called him Ra. He gave us strength and energy and presided over all creation, the seasons and our happiness. To strengthen monotheism, the Pharaoh Amenhotep worshipped Amon-Ra and brought about the cultural confluence of Thebes with Karnak in the south and with Memphis in the north. He conceptualized the orbit of the sun and bestowed legitimacy on the belief of ancient Egyptians that the sun travelled to the land of the dead when it set and returned to the land of the living at dawn.'

Hardly anyone was paying attention to the adeeb's lengthy monologue. Babar looked at the peon who whispered in his ear, 'My master often tends to digress and ends up giving these long, irrelevant speeches like politicians...but what can be done? After all, it is he who has to judge mankind's bloodthirsty impulses. Who can stop this court from performing its duty?'

Once again, the knocking resumed. The babel of voices reached a crescendo. The adeeb tried to shut out the noise by clamping his hands over his ears, but even that failed to work. Finally, he roared in a thunderous voice, 'Silence! The earth has banished you! If I do the same, where will you go? Tell me, where?'

When the chaos had subsided a little, he continued, 'Listen. Every civilization, every faith has to pass through a phase of domination by its priests and its upper class. Though that phase was late in coming to Bharat, it was there in Egypt as well. It is a symbol of stasis. In my Egypt, the offerings made to the presiding deities eventually served to satisfy the gluttony of the priests. The latter lived a life of luxury, enjoying the benefits of exemption from hard labour, military service and taxation. Ultimately, this breed was the real cause of the downfall of its civilization. Such was also the fate of the Sumerian civilization which worshipped the moon, not the sun, and placed a great premium on individual freedom.'

Now, Babar raised his voice: 'Sir...Honourable Adeeb—'

Fuhrer interrupted him, 'Allow me to hear what he has to say!'

'Then, listen,' the adeeb continued. 'The Sumerians did not build pyramids for the spirits of their dead. Rather, they constructed temples honouring their deities. When the Sumerian priesthood became corrupt, their civilization met its demise. From its ruins rose the Babylonian one. The first civilization to acknowledge composite culture, it brought prosperity to the valleys of Dajla and Furat. But even in Babylonia, the feeling of class superiority reared its ugly head and society split into numerous categories. It was a fate shared by the Assyrian, Hittite, Armenian, Hebrew and Greek civilizations as well. The latter could not prosper for long, because there arose a class of people who appointed themselves as priests by claiming their superiority to others, and established sovereign rights over temples, scriptures and rituals. These priests symbolized and perpetuated arrogance, selfishness and corruption—the inevitable fallout of class consciousness—and lent their active support to social stratification. They were obdurate in resisting change and impeded the path of progress...' By now, the adeeb had worked himself into a frenzy that made him fling his arms about, jump around and, occasionally, tear at his hair.

The knocking, the murmurs and the lamentations peaked again. With a start, the adeeb asked the peon, 'What is this hideous noise?'

'Sir, while you wax eloquent, somewhere in the world, there is bloodshed and some violent man or the other emerges to stir up passions in the name of race or religion. Then, those incited by him set out to wreak revenge.'

'Who are these people seeking to put a stop to the narration of the saga of civilization so that they may recount their tales of barbarism?'

'Sir,' replied the peon, 'here are the thirty-nine people who have just arrived from the Boipotong region of South Africa. They are black Africans, killed at the behest of South Africa's white rulers.'

'But an agreement has been reached there between Nelson Mandela's African National Congress and the white regime under de Klerk. Together, they will draw up a new constitution that is supposed to grant the blacks their fundamental rights. So, why did this massacre take place at all?'

'Sir, the whites who have managed to split the Inkatha Freedom Party of the blacks are responsible for these killings.'

'Hmm, what do these thirty-nine corpses want?'

'They want justice.'

'But who are the others knocking at the door? Until this racket dies down, how can justice be dispensed?'

'There's nothing we can do about it, sir,' replied the peon. 'I suggest that you carry on dispensing justice while the knocking continues at its own rhythm.'

But the knocking became increasingly frenzied. 'Well, sir, you'll just have to speed up the pace of dispensing your brand of justice. If the judicial process is swift, some solution is bound to emerge.'

Yawning, Babar and Fuhrer spoke in unison. 'Honourable Adeeb!' they said. 'Please allow us to take your leave. There are people coming to offer prayers at our graves. If we are found missing, a needless controversy will arise and thousands of innocents will be slaughtered.'

'All right,' the adeeb conceded, 'you may leave. But please ensure that you go right back to your graves so that you can be summoned when required.'

When the two left, the volume of noise increased dramatically. Voices screamed, 'We have come from Karachi! We are Sindhis. We were killed by the Pakistani army at the instigation of the mohajirs.'

'We're Lebanese...the Christians killed us.'

'We died in Moldova. The Russians butchered us.'

'Sir, we've arrived from Bosnia where we died at the hands of the Serbs.'

'All right, all right...now that you're dead, do please sit down quietly! Life brings stress, but death brings serenity. This is what Egyptian civilization always maintained. It is why both the Egyptians and the Aryans believed in reincarnation. The only difference is that for the latter, rebirth could manifest itself in different life forms. For the Egyptians, though, man was always reborn in his human avatar. I support the Egyptian interpretation, because from the point of view of civilization, it is man alone who has evolved.'

'Sir, what makes you say that? If mankind has truly evolved, why is there such a clamour in your court?'

'Hmm...that's a pertinent question,' replied the adeeb and sank into deep thought. Then, with worry writ large on his face, he commanded, 'Summon Life...Life should be brought here this very instant.'

'Life?' exclaimed the peon, his eyebrows shooting up.

'Yes, Life.'

'You mean Storytelling, don't you?'

'Whichever way you choose to interpret it. Today, there is hardly any difference between life and storytelling,' replied the scholarly court.

On his way out, the peon suddenly paused to say, 'Sir, you'd ordered me to get Bilal from Egypt. Should I do that or not, because the Indian girl Bilqees is crying her heart out and demanding justice.'

'Oh, I'd quite forgotten. Get Bilal from wherever he is and produce him before me.'

In the blink of an eye, the peon reappeared. He had brought with him Mohammed Bilal, an officer in the social welfare department of the Emirates. He held Bilal by the ear and announced, 'Sir, here's Bilal...I've finally brought him before the court.'

Bilal could not quite figure out what kind of court he had been summoned to or the reason for his presence here. When he was told about his offence and asked to give an account of the circumstances surrounding Bilqees's death, his response to the court was a withering look and an enraged reply: 'Oh, Bilqees...no Hindustani woman's life is so precious that I should have to answer for it! In your own country, many Bilqeeses lose their lives in riots. Many of them are molested, but you choose to remain silent. You don't hold your own people responsible for the crimes they commit.'

Bilqees's sobbing grew louder and the situation became more difficult, because now, another woman wept along with her. This was Kim Huk Sun, a seventy-year-old from Korea.

Shocked and dismayed, the court ordered that the living be kept away from the dead. Or else, it would complicate matters. A Japanese, it seems, had whispered in the court's ear, raising the issue of legal propriety in having a living person appear in the court of the dead.

The court struck its own forehead in frustration and said, 'This is a constitutional matter...I am only empowered to listen to petitions from the dead, but...'

'Sir, please don't delve into the legal ramifications. Injustice is injustice, after all. A woman suffering the consequences of injustice is worse than dead.'

'You're right,' the court told Mahmood Ali, the peon. But

Creation itself was shaken, when the court shouted, 'No! Apart from the petitions of the dead, I also reserve the right to give a hearing to those who are taken to be dead while still alive.' The court looked in Kim's direction and asked her to narrate the story of her life.

Kim Huk Sun then spoke up. 'I am Korean, sir,' she began. 'I was born in Jilin in 1924. In 1941, when I was just seventeen, I was abducted by Japanese soldiers from Beijing. They raped me fifteen times a day without respite. I was conscripted into the Teesintai or "sex core", and became a "comfort woman". Forty thousand women were forcibly conscripted here and every single day, each one of us was forced to sexually satisfy more than a dozen Japanese soldiers.'

Bilqees's sobbing grew more intense. Then she spoke. 'Kim Huk Sun,' she said, 'this happened to you in wartime; what I endured, happened at a moment when no war was in progress. I was forced into this despicable profession through photographs and letters that promised me marriage. Honourable Court...' Here, Bilqees began to cry piteously. 'I knew nothing of the Arabic language or culture; yet, it was an Arab who took me away after pretending to marry me. My husband was twenty-eight years older than I was. Like Kim, I had to satisfy his lust. Countless times was I forced to submit to his unnatural acts. Children born of a union like ours were called "teli" and segregated from society.'

Frowning, the court shouted, 'You, Officer Bilal of the Emirates! The Japanese will have to answer for Kim's lost virtue, but you will divulge to this court the details of Bilqees's "teli" child...how he was born...'

Noticing the peon who hadn't budged from his place, the court reprimanded him. 'Why are you still here? I'd ordered you to fetch Life. I shall record Bilal's statement and those of the savage Japanese in the meantime. Be off with you now! Make your way, post-haste, to Karachi airport and fetch Life which, despite being alive, has never really lived.'

As soon as the peon left to execute the order, the court was attacked. Numerous slogans were raised and bullets fired. Chaos prevailed and, strangely enough, the dead started perishing all over again. In the throes of death, the corpses screamed and shouted and moaned. It was unclear as to who was killing whom, because bloodthirsty citizens of the world's many 'Pakistans' were shooting their own people.

Greatly perturbed, the adeeb yelled, 'What nonsense is this? We are here not only to determine man's destiny, but also to decide the issues of the living. We address questions related to the rights of both the living and the dead.'

One of the attackers intervened: 'Spare us your equivocation! If this court was established to address the issues of the living, why should a gathering of the dead be present?'

'Because the dead here were killed long before their life could come to a natural end. I am only giving an audience to those who have met an unnatural end much before their natural death was ordained. Who is accountable for them, suspended as they are between life and undeserving death? Where will they wait till the Day of Judgement? Who has kept account of their deeds to determine the form in which they will be reincarnated? These restless spirits are the victims of untimely death. Who is to be held responsible for their plight?'

The adeeb's voice was lost in the pandemonium of gunshots, explosions and screams. Fire, smoke and discord swept through the place. Observing it all, the peon swiftly returned and somehow managed to escort the adeeb to safety.

16

Exhausted during their flight, the two found themselves in a vast desert. Running across sand was not easy and a storm served as an added impediment. There was sand everywhere—in their eyes, ears, nostrils, hair and clothes. All around them lay the bleakness of the desert with its billowing clouds of warm sand and its dunes sculpted by the wind.

Panting with exertion, the adeeb collapsed and the gasping peon sat down near him. When their breathing eased a bit, the adeeb asked, 'Where are we?'

'Sir, we're in a barren desert.'

'Friend,' said the adeeb, 'I am terribly tired. I wish to call out to my friends and contemporaries. Besides Rakesh, Renu, Dushyant, Rahi, Parsai, Raghuvir and Shrikant, I am eager to communicate with all my living friends who have not used their imagination for personal gain, but have dedicated it to the world. All the while, their creative powers and pens have persisted in their efforts to make the world a better place. Tell them I need their support, since I stand alone. Beg them to come forward as the world needs them. But tell me, first of all, which desert this is. What is it called?'

'I have no idea,' replied the peon, brushing the sand off his clothes. 'There's nothing here but sand, sir.'

The adeeb too brushed away the sand and sat down comfortably. He was amazed when he looked up at the sky. 'Look!' he cried. 'Just look at the white swans...observe how they fly...'

'They aren't swans, sir. They happen to be birds of the desert and will ultimately merge with its white sands.'

The adeeb kept looking at the birds for some time. Then he stood up and started walking again.

'Where are we going, sir?' asked the peon.

'Direction is irrelevant now. I'll go where my feet take me. These birds of the desert are helping me out a little by giving me some direction.'

The desert was a vast stretch of nothing but sand. No shelter was to be found anywhere. Just sand. The two men had no idea of the distance they had covered or for how long they had walked. Days had dawned and nights had descended and passed, but they were simply not aware of the lapse of time. Wherever they walked, it seemed to them as though they were where they had started from. Their footprints vanished without a trace and it was impossible for them to decide whether they had actually walked at all.

Then one day, the peon said in desperation, 'We walk so much every day, but never arrive anywhere.'

'Walking is one thing, but arriving at some destination is quite another. Why do you confuse the two? Evidence of this lies in the pause of centuries. Millions of years ago, they started out, but have only succeeded in reaching the point they started from. Sometimes, these centuries came across shelters of religion, but were pushed back into the desolate wastes of the desert.'

Since the peon failed to grasp the import of what he was saying, the adeeb explained: 'Look, everything does its assigned work. Darkness comes, but never does it seek to know how much it has travelled. Light shines forth, but it keeps no record of the distance it has covered. Even this sand which flies about cannot tell us the range it has spanned.'

The peon thought it wiser to remain silent. He realized his master was digressing again. Then, in the distance, he noticed a shadow. It seemed to melt away before reappearing. With narrowed eyes, the adeeb observed the phenomenon. The shadow also seemed to have seen him and was approaching at a run. It embraced the scholar and said, 'You're here! O Adeeb, when did you get here from Hindustan?'

'You! Comrade Imam Nazish!' exclaimed the adeeb. 'When did you get here from Pakistan? Arrey, where is Banne Bhai, our Sajjad Zaheer? And how are you?'

'I'm not too well, as I'm both dead and alive. I had gone to Pakistan for the sake of democracy...to wage war against poverty...I'd gone there, leaving my wife and my home in Amroha.'

'Yes, Nazish, I remember. You too, had raised slogans in favour of Pakistan. In the Sindh Assembly, G.M. Syed had also welcomed its formation. Banne Bhai had forgotten then that Pakistan was not a country consisting of individuals who persevered. Rather, it was a nation of those who wallowed in wealth. Its foundations had been built on religious hatred. You Marxists had considered this hatred a necessary evil born out of religious and communal compulsions and had supported the partition of the country. With your faith in religion being the opium of the masses, you had all given precedence to racial, religious and linguistic superiority.'

The adeeb's acerbic references enraged Imam Nazish who retorted, 'At the time, you too were part of our group...along with Amrita Pritam, Kartar Singh Duggal, Mohan Rakesh, Bhishm Sahni and Devendra Satyarthi...to the extent that even people like Yashpal, Ashq, Agyeya chose to remain silent. After Partition, you did lay bare the traumatic scenes it had given birth to...but that was only in the role of honest onlookers. It was Manto alone who dared to throw Toba Tek Singh's corpse right on the unnatural border that divided the two countries. We committed an error all right, but you were party to it. When Sajjad Zaheer became the General-Secretary of Pakistan's Communist Party, I moved from East to West Pakistan. It was there that I obtained an insight into the realities of a country built on the foundations of religion. It was my visit to Bengali East Pakistan that made me realize how wrong it was to determine national identity on the basis of religion.'

'But now, efforts are on to create Pakistans of hatred in every nation in the world. That's what happened in Bosnia, Cyprus, the fragmented Soviet Union and the new Russian Federation. And it is happening in Afghanistan today. Using hatred as a prop, everyone is involved in creating new Pakistans against the interests of their own people.'

A voice called out in the lonely expanse of the desert: 'Hatred determines man's identity and caste today. The past comes in handy to unite hatreds, especially those painfully bitter memories that ooze and fester. History, which can provide remedial insights into the past, is often cast aside. The analysis of history, its perspectives on society, often appease and serve to eliminate hatred. But the past spurns this logic of countering hatred. It merely weaves half-truths into tales of actual recollection and perpetuates these tales for centuries. Hatred is a "school" where one begins by inflicting pain, humiliation and suffering on oneself. Hatred then enriches the soil of ill will and strengthens the resolve of revenge. Similarity and uniqueness serve as the hallmarks of revenge whose practitioners speak in one voice, raise identical questions and offer the same arguments. This unity forges their identity.'

Listening to these words, the adeeb asked his peon to find out who had spoken them.

'Sir,' replied the peon, 'that is the Jewish writer Amos Oz.'

'What is a writer doing in this desert?'

'I've discovered the reason. He lives in the city of Arad in the Negev desert.'

'Is there a town here?' asked the adeeb.

'No, sir, it's just a small settlement.'

'A settlement!'

'That's right, sir. All the world's exiled writers have come to live here in this settlement.'

'Come on,' urged Oz's shadow, 'I'll be your guide.'

They did not know how long they walked in the desert. Along the way, Imam Nazish related his tale of woe. 'Look, Adeeb,' he said, 'I have nothing left in my life but regrets. The flood of hatred we had once allowed ourselves to be carried away by, has taken us nowhere; it has left us high and dry. I had been married for just three months when this deluge of mindless fanaticism carried me away from my wife and Amroha, and swept me far from my homeland to Pakistan. There, I had to constantly remain in hiding. I felt that I would never be able to return to Amroha. My wife eventually became a teacher back home and dedicated her entire life to educating children. While she was crafting a new generation in Hindustan, all I could do was destroy one. In the bargain, I destroyed myself. After many years, I chanced to reach Amroha. I found that all the children I'd left behind—my nieces and nephews—had children of their own now. When I finally met my wife, she was on the verge of retirement. Only a Hindustani woman could have led a life inspired by so noble a purpose, when all around her lay a desert of loneliness! I was part of a destructive wave; my wife, part of a constructive one.'

'Very often, regret illuminates the paths of life,' observed the adeeb.

Oz replied, 'But the problem is that the floods of darkness don't all sweep in at the same time. Neither does the awareness of regret. Between them lies the interregnum of time. Consequently, generations and centuries continue to be steeped in blood.'

'True. By the time one collective regret emerges, the flood of ignorance surges elsewhere in the world. When the era of regret for that particular deluge is about to dawn, subsequent waves of darkness submerge other corners of the world...'

As the adeeb was uttering these words, Oz pointed ahead.

'There,' he said, 'that's the refugee camp for the world's exiled writers.'

Ahead lay a settlement of white tents. Circling overhead were the white birds of the desert. The adeeb ran ahead. When he reached the tents, he was stunned to see that they were all there—Kabir, Tolstoy, Tagore, Agnon, Kazantzakis, Rahul Sankrityayan, Dinkar, Chekhov, Camus, Premchand, Lu-Xun, Milan Kundera, Brecht, Nirala, Sartre, Hazariprasad Dwivedi, Mir, Sauda, Ghalib, Faiz, Faizi Nizami, Manto, Krishan Chander, Rajinder Singh Bedi, Dushyant Kumar, Renu, Rakesh, Raghuvir Sahai, Parsai, Shrikant and Muktibodh. He knew them all, these writers who now lived as refugees in their tents that stood by a river where time flowed like the ripples of the desert sand.

It was a strange experience for him to see time flowing by. Sometimes, many centuries would float by together. He felt greatly soothed as the water from the river splashed him.

The peon offered a suggestion: 'Sir, if you want me to, I can capture time for you.'

'Where is the need?' replied the adeeb, as he moved on with Oz. 'These writers have captured it in their works. Each word they've written has proved to be more forceful than all the strength of time put together.'

A tranquil calm pervaded the camp. Fireflies of sand swarmed around it. Desert hares ran here and there, pausing occasionally in their paths. Sheets of sand seemed to swirl around the place. Sometimes, they would be rent asunder and each fragment became a butterfly fluttering away from the camp.

The writers all sat in a group discussing the saga of mankind. Hazariprasad Dwivedi was telling the others that the *mithak* was a supernatural tale depicting man's first encounter with nature. 'Man,' he explained, 'then resolved to transform it. So, he made it divine and immortal. These ancient tales, songs and ballads which began as an oral tradition, gradually evolved into ancient history. From the latter emerged the narrative of faiths and philosophies which, in turn, gave birth to the narrow confines of different religions.'

'True. Otherwise, godhead did not exist. These insular religions created their own gods. In Nineveh, history, written on clay tablets in the archives of the Assyrian king Ashurbanipal, establishes that there was no omniscient, omnipotent or omnipresent god. It was the Babylonian civilization that created this belief. The eminent Marduk who came from that civilization, and rose to be a god, always remained a mortal, though the gods had graced his coronation. They had designed his throne and had even declared him the Supreme Being, the Creator, the Destroyer and the Preserver. They had bestowed on him powers and weaponry similar to that gifted to Brahma, Vishnu and Mahesh. Marduk had then created the universe. He had made his paternal grandfather Anu the monarch of the skies, and his father Iaea the ruler of the earth. He had built a grand temple, so that his divine subjects, the other gods, could reside in comfort when they descended to earth. He named this temple Babylon. The same Marduk then ripped the flesh of woman who had been created before him and crafted from it the myriad other forms of earthly existence. Her torn flesh brought on a flood of tears which were transformed into the Dajla and Furat rivers. The story of creation began from here. It was from the bones and blood of woman that primitive man was born.'

A harsh voice shattered the silence of the desert: 'Absolutely! That was precisely how the true Aryan civilization arose from the Caucasus. I am its legitimate heir.'

When the adeeb inquired about the identity of this ruffian, the peon replied that it was the Nazi—Hitler of Germany.

'He's the brute who was determined to destroy the world! My head spins and my blood boils at the sight of him here. Arrest him! He must appear in my court when I set the date. Now I'm dog-tired. I need some rest.'

'Well, why don't you...' the peon began but was interrupted by the uproar of the thirty-nine corpses killed in the Boipotong firing. 'My sahib is resting,' the peon continued after subduing them. 'Besides, there is such a thing as manners...you can't just disturb him whenever your whim so dictates.'

The knocking, accompanied by groans and shouts, reached an unbearable pitch. The adeeb, rudely awakened, shouted to the peon,

'Let them in! These are victims of inhuman treatment, of brutality, suffering and torture, and mine is a court of humanity, not a cowardly, paralysed legal system. My court is open to all victims of human tyranny...so, let them all in.'

At this, the corpses cried in one voice that they had met their untimely end at the hands of Zulu extremists.

'Where have you come from?'

'From South Africa. We were killed in the township of Boipotong at the behest of Prime Minister de Klerk. Tell us, please, what was the nature of our crime?'

'Crime? Your only crime was that you belonged to the poor, exploited class.'

'But even the Zulus are as poor and exploited as we are. We belong to the same race, but the whites use our own people to kill us.'

'Poverty and hunger have no racial identity.'

'But we will exact revenge on these whites...revenge...'

'Stop this talk of revenge! After all, how many centuries will wreak revenge on other centuries? You've all gone mad.'

'Sir, you are tired. You should rest. Till then, we will wash our wounds,' said the corpses before leaving.

The adeeb heaved a sigh of relief and drew a pillow towards him. In the process, sheaves of paper that had been lying trapped under the pillow were released, one by one, and flew off in different directions like the feathers of a pigeon.

Startled, the adeeb murmured, 'Arrey...Life? Was it you pinned down under the pillow?'

Life gave no answer. Silence prevailed.

'Life, where are you?' the adeeb shouted, but the only reply to his query was silence.

'Sir,' interposed the peon, 'you look worried. Can I be of some assistance?'

'Yes, my friend, go and fetch Life from wherever it is. I want to live a little longer. No matter what it takes, retrieve my half-written existence and bring it back. Please, please get it back for me.'

'I shall do so right away,' the peon promised before he left.

17

When the peon returned, the court was sitting there, eyes shut, ears stuffed with cotton wool. Not daring to disturb the court, the peon paced about agitatedly and even fished out a cigarette from his pocket and lit up.

Eventually, he fetched Memory and made it sit in a chair facing the court.

When, at last, the adeeb yawned and opened his eyes, he was surprised to see an unknown face before him. 'You?' he asked, 'and who may you be?'

'Yes, it's me. You may have sent for me...your peon brought me here.'

'Where from? Pakistan?'

'No sir, you've got it wrong. You made a similar mistake at Lahore airport. There, too, you'd taken me for a Pakistani and I'd had to remind you that I wasn't; that I was, in fact, a Hindustani.'

'I can't understand how we get embroiled in Hindustan and Pakistan, Lebanon and Syria, whenever we talk about man and his natural identity.'

'How should I know? This has been happening since the time of Socrates,' Memory retorted.

'Well, I'll speak to Socrates later. But tell me, why are you here?'

'Living among the dead, you seem to have forgotten how to recognize Life. It was your peon who summoned me. Try and recall the time you were travelling from Lahore to Karachi. You had to go to China and your connecting flight was from Karachi. I was also travelling to Karachi and we got talking while waiting to board the aircraft.'

'Oh, Salma!' the adeeb suddenly yelled, startling the peon. With an intense look on his face, the adeeb travelled down memory lane. 'Ah,' he murmured, 'everything is coming back to me...' as he embarked on his narrative of the past...

*

The adeeb had asked her, 'You must have relatives in Karachi?'

'No, most of them are in Patna,' she'd replied. 'Patna, as you know, is a town in my country. I have only a few relatives in Karachi and I have to travel on to Quetta. I shall be staying in a hotel in Karachi for a few days.'

'Which hotel?'

'The Holiday Inn, possibly.'

'Then, perhaps, we might meet for breakfast tomorrow, since I shall also be staying at the same hotel. I think the airline is putting us up there.'

'Inshallah,' Salma had said.

The announcement of the Karachi flight was expected any minute.

'May I demonstrate something to you?' Salma had asked.

'What is it?'

'I'm wearing a sari and I want you to see how Hindustani women are treated by men at Lahore airport. Normally, they make things difficult for women...more so, when the women happen to be Hindustani.'

With this, Salma had gone and stood before a counter. The Pakistan Airlines officer had glared at her and, without looking at her ticket, had asked, 'How many saris, blouses and brassieres have you brought?'

'Why, have you taken over the duties of a customs officer?' Salma had retorted. 'Why not let them ask me the questions.'

'How many petticoats and panties do you carry in your luggage and how long do you propose to stay in Pakistan?'

'This, again, is a question for the customs officer to ask and to verify my answer by looking at my passport,' Salma had reprimanded him. 'Your duty is to allot me a seat after examining my passport.' The officer had observed her glancing at the adeeb, and he'd asked, 'Is that gentleman with you?'

'Is that any concern of yours?'

'Yes, it is,' he'd retorted and walked away after putting her ticket in a drawer.

His action had taken Salma by surprise. She had begun to

wonder if the joke had gone too far and she would needlessly find herself in a spot.

The man at the counter had then returned with a police inspector, summoned, perhaps, with the specific intention of interrogating Salma. As she drew back, the inspector seemed to recognize her. 'Excuse me,' he said, 'are you...'

'Yes, indeed, I am,' she had exclaimed, her confidence surging back. 'I am the granddaughter of Janab Aftab Ahmad of the CSP. And I have arrived from Hindustan.'

The inspector had been upset with the man at the counter and had reprimanded him, telling him that he should closely observe passengers before reporting them.

The man at the counter had remained unconvinced, but had decided that if the police did not want to do their job, he would not take it on for them. He had handed Salma her boarding pass.

Before the adeeb embarked on his journey to Quetta and Beijing, Salma had met him in the restaurant of the Holiday Inn for breakfast.

Some unexpected things had occurred while they were eating. She had been there at the restaurant before him, awaiting his arrival. He hadn't been able to take his eyes off her. She seemed to be the woman he had been yearning for all these years. He had realized that when a desire is suddenly fulfilled or a dream comes true, one is overcome by feelings of self-consciousness. The night before, he had been rapt in dreams about her. In those dreams, he had seen Salma in the same clothes she was wearing for breakfast—a Punjabi suit. She had made him feel totally at ease.

'Please sit down,' she had invited. 'I knew I would meet you before you left for China.'

He had been overcome by diffidence. This was the way he had wanted it. His reverie had been broken by the arrival of the bearer. He had ordered cornflakes, eggs on toast and chilly sauce.

'Excuse me,' he'd said to Salma, 'I'm really fond of chilly sauce...what would you like to have?'

It turned out that she had already placed her order.

Their breakfast had arrived at the same time and he had

observed something else that was unexpected. They had both ordered the same items—the same combination of cornflakes, fried eggs and chilly sauce.

'It seems they serve the same breakfast to everyone,' he had remarked. 'You've got the same things that I ordered.'

'No,' she'd replied. 'It's a coincidence that we both ordered the same dishes.'

'Even the chilly sauce which I'd asked for specifically?'

'Yes. I do like to have a dash of sauce with my fried eggs. It seems you like to have them the same way. It's quite amazing really.'

A strange silence had descended in their midst, a silence that came from reflecting privately on the sheer coincidence of it all. It was Salma who spoke first: 'I seldom have dreams. Usually, I forget them, but the one I saw last night was really strange.'

'What was it about?' he'd asked in awe. Would the dream, he had mused, turn out to be like the identical dishes they had ordered for breakfast, similar to... He'd dreamt that their plane had met with an accident. It had made a forced landing in the desert and had ploughed through the sand before coming to a stop. All the passengers had been safe.

'I dreamt,' said Salma, 'that our plane had been forced to land in the desert and had ploughed through the sand before coming to a stop, and that all the passengers were safe.' She then sipped her coffee.

He had felt breathless at the eerie coincidence. Taking a sip of his coffee, he had managed to speak with some difficulty. 'Salmaji,' he had said, 'I don't know how to say this, but...I had the same dream...exactly the same one that you've just narrated to me.'

They had silently sipped their coffee, wondering whether it was actually possible for two strangers to have the same dream at the same time. It seemed quite incredible.

Salma had gazed at him for a while, wondering if he might have had a motive in claiming to share the same dream as hers. What could possibly be gained or lost, she wondered, if two perfect strangers chose to lie to each other, knowing fully well that they were going to travel in different directions and would, in all likelihood, never cross each other's paths again. There was no place, no need for such lies.

For a long while, they had sat there in silence. The dream they had shared acted as a hurdle, putting a stop to further conversation.

For the sake of mere civility, he'd asked her, 'Have you always been a Hindustani?'

'How do you mean?'

'Oh, simply this…were you born in Hindustan?'

'I was. However, although I was born in Hindustan—in 1947—I was actually conceived in Pakistan. The fact is, we come from Bihar's landed gentry. My nani, who's still alive, continues to live there. It was my nana who came away to Sindh a very long time ago—when India was still undivided. My parents had also come away when Pakistan was created. In a sense, my nana was a mohajir. He still remembers Bihar and declares that his country may be Pakistan, but Hindustan is his homeland. Even his memories are Hindustani. Nana is in Quetta. I'm going to meet him. We all remember Bihar and speak of it.'

'It's a bit puzzling, the fact that you were conceived in Pakistan, yet born in Hindustan.'

'Why is it puzzling? When the moment for Partition came, I was in my mother's womb. Terrible riots were taking place in Bihar. Muslims were being massacred there. Nana tried his best to stop Ammi and Abbu from leaving, but they were adamant, declaring that Nani was all alone in Bihar and, in any case, they could not forsake their homeland.'

The adeeb had looked surprised. Then he had hesitantly said, 'It's amazing that when lakhs of Muslims were leaving Hindustan to go to Pakistan, your ammi and abbu had, in spite of being Muslims, decided to return to Hindustan. Two Muslims…'

'No, three…I was the third. I was there in my mother's womb. Adeeb, you can never comprehend the spiritual suffering that Muslims go through. If you Hindus have been Hindustan's citizens since ancient times, we Muslims too had sprung from the same roots at the same time. So what if we embraced Islam? One's origins do not change with one's religion.'

The adeeb had given Salma an intense look and she'd asked, 'Why do you stare at me so? I have witnessed many deaths in my family. When we confront death, our thoughts don't turn to the Kaaba or Karbala; we only think of our homes. If you don't believe what I say, go and ask a Muslim from any part of the world...even those living in Riyadh and Dhahran. The house of God is for everyone, but, when death is imminent, what matter are one's hearth and home. This is an eternal truth and every Muslim, whether he belongs to Spain, Turkey, Egypt, Indonesia or anywhere else, wishes to die on the soil of his homeland, not in Mecca or Medina.'

'But—'

'But what? You Aryans have destroyed your religion by segregating it within mutually exclusive compartments.'

'How can you claim that, Salma?'

'I claim it on the basis of your Brahminical texts. Your caste system has become your true religion. Every child is born from a mother's womb. Yet, your Brahmins and their scriptures insult all wombs. By asserting that individuals are born from different parts of Brahma's body, they have established a faith built on the difference between one human being and another. In today's terminology, one could well say that your Brahmins have created a Pakistan for themselves.'

The adeeb had been dumbstruck at these words.

Salma had continued, 'Your Upanishads had tried to protect human values and wealth...' While the adeeb fumbled for words, Salma had carried on, 'The Upanishads, however, were nothing but writings that on the ploy of re-establishing faith in divinity condoned misconduct within the parameters of the caste system and encouraged the kind of tyranny that was practised on society by the Brahmins. Though they were read as scriptures advocating penitence, the Upanishads merely ended up protecting Aryans of noble descent. They were unable to adapt their interpretation to the world's evolving mental map. The realities had changed, but you Aryans could not bring yourselves to come to terms with them. This was the cause of your downfall. The roots of culture lie in religion, but with the passage of time, culture liberates itself from the shackles of faith and takes on a humanitarian aspect. Yet, you and your kind constantly try to drag culture back towards religion.'

'But this hardly justifies what Iqbal and Sir Syed Ahmed Khan did later, does it?'

'Who's trying to justify it? But the change that came over these men was triggered by Lokmanya Tilak, when he sought to identify the quest for Independence with the Ganapathi Utsav celebrations and turned the former into a purely Hindu movement.'

'But Gandhiji came forward to undo the wrong, didn't he?'

'By then it was too late. Hearts had been divided.'

They had looked at each other in silence and again it was Salma who broke it: 'Consider the subsequent pattern of events, Adeeb. What happened? It is true that Gandhiji did all he could, but by then, the English had taken advantage of the situation. And what happened later? Eventually, it was Lokmanya Tilak who would be instrumental in rallying together the Hindu rightists. Even a progressive like Savarkar became one, and his generation produced Gandhi's assassin Nathuram Godse. What hope was left for the Muslims despite the presence of Gandhi, Nehru, Patel and Maulana Azad? Suspicion had crept into people's minds that as soon as power was transferred to Nehru, secularism would gradually lapse into a dormant state, while Hindutva, which had been passive all this while, roused itself.'

'Was it for this reason that Muslims became suspicious and felt compelled to establish kinship with the likes of Babar, Taimur and Changez Khan?'

'How else could Muslims, beset by doubts, have reacted? The double-edged sword was already in the hands of the British. Why should they have hesitated? And don't forget, Adeeb, that all the rulers of the Middle Ages wanted to build empires. They were neither proselytizers nor preachers of any particular religion. Changez Khan, a Mongol, was not even a Muslim, since Islam hadn't even been born during his time. He was a worshipper of idols who lived much before the advent of Buddhism.'

'Your knowledge of history is formidable,' the adeeb had remarked while finishing his breakfast.

'I was, after all, a student of History at Allahabad University, the same institution which made you an adeeb. And shall I disclose another significant fact?'

'Please go ahead.'

'Jinnah Sahib did not create history; history created him. Learn from history. Don't set the cauldron of religion over the flames of history. If you do, be prepared to witness a repeat of what happened during the partition of India and is taking place, even today, in Pakistan.'

He had been amazed to note that Salma could speak so openly in Karachi, Pakistan. It was a relief that no one was loitering near their breakfast table at the time.

Then...

*

A battery of knocks rent the air. It sent a chill down his entire being. Salma had vanished and the adeeb asked his peon about his own bearings.

'Sir, you are present in your court,' the peon replied.

'In court? Are you sure? I was sitting and talking to Salma in the restaurant at the Holiday Inn in Karachi.'

'Sir, I don't know how you describe the shadow of memory, but I carried out your orders and presented it before you,' said the peon politely.

As the knocking and shrieking intensified, the court ordered, 'Let the petitioner be produced.'

Beating her breast, Shahin came forward.

'Who are you?'

'Shahin.'

'Where have you come from?'

'From Bombay, the graveyard of Hindustan.'

'What happened to you?'

'The whole of Hindustan was on fire when the Babri Masjid was demolished. Bombay was devastated by an orgy of bestial violence. Sleeping though I was in my grave, even I was not spared. I was wrenched out and forced to abandon my grave. As I await the Day of Judgement, I have no resting place. That's why I am here before you.'

'But this is a court, not a graveyard.'

'All the courts in Hindustan have been transformed into graveyards. They provide no shelter. I've come here seeking refuge.'

With a look of inquiry, the court said, 'You look quite young. What right had Death to drag you to your grave?'

'It wasn't Death that maltreated me. It was I who longed for it,' replied Shahin.

'But why?'

'Because Pakistan had been created and I had no desire to go there.'

'So, the savage Hindus killed you during the riots?'

'No, honourable sir, the tale of my death has no parallel. When the country was partitioned...'

At this moment, the countless years that had gone by, came trooping in. Bloodied and battered, 1947 stood before the court.

Hordes of vultures began swooping down on them. The sheer number of these birds of prey cast a giant shadow over the place. The rivers from Punjab to Assam turned crimson with blood. In celebration, millions of corpses performed a macabre primitive dance. The wounded and the dying screamed in anguish, as terror, barbarism and bestiality took them hostage. Trampling over the dead and the injured, Jinnah hoisted the flag of free Pakistan. On his side of the border, Nehru did the same, unfurling the tricolour.

All around, voices were audible, but the words they uttered were indistinct. All that came through clearly in their tones was fear and despair. The voices then echoed with the resonance of thunder, lashing the adeeb's ears like whips being cracked.

'Hindustan has one destiny. Give me your blood and I will give you freedom. The Red Fort of freedom shall be built on the foundation of love, not loathing.'

'Pakistan is another name for hatred.'

'Pakistan has been built on the abhorrent principles of animosity.'

'Jinnah did not make history...he was created by the powers of imperialism.'

'I don't accept this.'

'I still maintain...religion does not make a nation...only blood and history can do so.'

'If you believe that religion determines national identity, you are dooming the world to destruction.'

'Arrey, did you hear that Quaid-e-Azam Mohammed Ali Jinnah? Even you will fail to integrate the Pushtuns, the Punjabis, the Baluchis, the Sindhis, the Bengalis and the mohajirs. They will continue to feud among themselves.'

'Religion will serve no purpose in such a situation. Only culture, history and the blood flowing in these veins will come in handy. These are the elements that determine the realities of nationhood.'

The voices grew louder and more embittered. The adeeb summoned the peon and asked him to find out whom they belonged to and why they were bent on disrupting his work.

The man went running to do his bidding and returned almost right away. 'Sir,' he said, 'they are the voices of four insane men.'

'Who are these deranged people?'

'Sir, how shall I put it...?'

'I have to save the world from lunatics like these.'

'Sir, it is in trying to save the world from madness that these men have lost their own minds.'

'They are strange people indeed!'

'You're right, sir, they are,' the peon replied angrily. 'Such people are rare in the world today. If they had been around, the Soviet Union would not have collapsed, Yugoslavia would never have witnessed the massacre of its Bosnian Muslims, thousands of Somalis would not have perished in a famine, and four hundred hungry and freezing Palestinians would not be awaiting death on the borders of Israel where they have been stranded. The Israelis would never have been allowed to push them into the jaws of death the way they have done.'

The adeeb smiled and remarked, 'You've become quite an intelligent man, haven't you, while carrying out your duties! But, tell me, who are these people?'

'Honourable sir, I've managed to find out that these are demented men.' With these words, the peon knocked on the panel of Memory. 'Yes, here they are...the craziest of them all, Mahatma Gandhi...the second, Subhas Chandra Bose...the third insane fellow, Khan Abdul Ghaffar Khan...and the fourth, a writer.'

'Shut them up.'

'Sir, they are extremely placid people. It's only when history is unravelled that their spirits start raging. That is when they emerge from their graves and samadhis and declaim in this manner.'

'Just restrain them for the present.'

'I've done so, Your Honour. I have confined them, once again, in the asylums of their graves and samadhis. They shall not disturb you now.'

Driven by boredom, perhaps, Memory sat down before the adeeb once more. Mirrored on Memory's body were undulating waves that shimmered like the waters of a lake. Impulsively, the adeeb remarked, 'Salma, you are beautiful!'

Unsurprised, she merely replied, 'Had Partition not taken place, Creation itself would have been just as beautiful.'

Then she glanced at her watch and observed, 'We should be going...when is your flight?'

'Eleven o'clock. All right, then. I don't know if I shall ever see you again.'

'I had imagined you bidding me farewell with a profoundly meaningful sentence.'

'What...what sentence? I'm sorry, I didn't quite get what you meant.'

'Something like the following couplet: "Whether you be evil spirit or scourge, how I wish you could be mine!"' Salma laughed, then bade him khuda hafiz.

'Khuda hafiz,' the adeeb replied. 'When you reach India,' he continued, handing her a napkin on which he had jotted down his address and telephone number, 'you won't need this, but still...'

She thanked him and left. He was immediately swamped by the desolation of centuries. It dawned upon him that he was, indeed, in a foreign land. It had escaped his mind while he was travelling from Lahore to Karachi. Salma had departed for Quetta, but her very special scent stayed with him.

He ordered another cup of coffee, as he wanted to bask some

more in that lingering fragrance. While drinking the coffee, he wondered what Salma's nana was like. Here, he thought, was a Pakistani on the one hand, and a mohajir with memories, on the other. What must her parents have been like, he wondered, to insist on crossing the ocean of blood that swelled with each spilt drop, as Muslims from Hindustan fled to Pakistan. The Muslim couple that preferred to go back to its roots for the sake of the future.

18

The adeeb was back from China. Salma, too, had returned from Quetta after meeting her nana. He had not expected her to save the paper napkin on which he had jotted down his name and address. Yet, she'd kept it and that's how she had managed to call him. How fortunate it was for him that her call had come through before he moved into his new house. Otherwise, his address and phone number on the napkin would have served no purpose.

That breakfast at Karachi's Holiday Inn, the dream they had both shared and now...now, this call that had come through on his very last day in the house he would be leaving.

'Where are you calling from?' he asked.

'Patna...why? I'm sure you didn't expect a call from me.'

'Well, every day, there was a glimmer of hope that you might. But then, where does the hope lie, if it is fulfilled?'

'What do you mean?'

'Just this—that hope spreads its tentacles like roots. If you hadn't rung me up, I would've waited in eternal hope for your call. Now that you have, you've breathed life into other hopes.'

'I'm coming to Delhi. Actually, I might as well tell you...I am in Delhi. Could you meet me somewhere?'

'Wherever you like.'

'At India Gate, at the intersection of Man Singh Road, near the pool of water behind a masjid.'

'Why specifically behind a masjid?'

'Because Allah's abode always stands behind a masjid. This evening...'

'It would be better if you didn't tell me the time.'

'Why not?'

'Because you've indicated the place. If I have enough life and time, I shall wait for you there forever.'

'We'll know soon enough who waits for whom, won't we?'

When the adeeb reached the spot they had agreed on, he saw Salma seated on a green rug, idly pulling at tufts of grass. As he parked the car, she recognized him and rose to her feet. Her downcast eyes resembled a wave that had been frozen midway. They stood before each other. No pair of hands reached out to clasp the other's. Only the eyelashes rose and fell like gentle waves.

'I knew, or should I say, felt that...' she began.

'Yes?' he asked.

'...that you would come in a kurta and pyjama ensemble. And as it turned out, I was right.'

'Something similar had happened at the Holiday Inn in Karachi. Remember that dream we had about the plane crash? The clothes you had worn in my dream turned out to be the very same ones that you wore at breakfast. How could such things possibly happen? How is it that what hovers in the mind suddenly appears before the eyes?'

'Who knows? Only Allah can tell. Won't you buy me chocolate ice cream?' she asked.

Salma did not accompany him to fetch the ice cream. After he had returned, both of them sat down on the grass. Dusk had fallen. There was quite a crowd around the ice-cream vendor.

Then he asked Salma a personal question: 'Isn't it strange that when the country was partitioned and Pakistan created, your people fled to Hindustan? I'm sorry if I'm being inquisitive.'

'It's perfectly all right,' she reassured him.

'Yours is an unusual family...your nana living in Pakistan with his memories of Hindustan...your parents fleeing from Pakistan to Hindustan at a time when Muslims were desperate to reach Pakistan. Don't you think it's strange?'

'What's so strange about it?' she asked. 'My abbu has explained to me that the very creation of Pakistan is a sin from the point of view of Islam. "There is no place for hatred in Islam," he had declared, "yet, the very foundation of Pakistan is built on hatred. A religion like Islam cannot be confined to a nation." For that matter, no religion can be shackled...'

Salma suddenly found herself being interrupted by a man who stood before them.

'Young lady, what nonsense are you spouting?' the man asked loudly. 'Pakistan came into being because hatred and suspicion between Hindus and Muslims predated Independence by many years. Muslims had no rights in undivided India. That is why Pakistan was created. Is that clear?'

'Who are you?' the adeeb asked him.

'I'm Ghulam Mehmood Banatwala, the president of the Indian Union Muslim League.'

'Banatwala, why don't you go to Pakistan?' interrupted another man.

'And who are you?' Banatwala inquired.

'Me? I'm Chandrakant Bhardwaj, chief of the RSS in Aligarh. You communal-minded Muslims have a long tradition of being traitors. You are incapable of patriotic feelings.'

'You're absolutely right there!' claimed another voice. 'Islam does not accept boundaries. It negates nationalism. We subscribe to Darul Islam, the land of faith and peace; not to Darul Harab, the land of faithlessness and turmoil.'

'And who may you be?'

'I'm Maududi, Maulana S.A. Maududi.'

'I know exactly how your mind works, Maududi!' yelled yet another voice. 'You want to make Hindustan Darul Islam, but you must understand that on the map of the world, only an undivided Hindustan will be allowed to exist. We shall oppose traitors like you who endeavour to establish Pakistani influence within Hindustan. We are not about to allow this to happen. Understand?'

As Salma became increasingly apprehensive at this exchange, the adeeb asked, 'Who are you?'

'I am Vinayak Damodar Savarkar.'

'But you were a nationalist, not a rightist Hindu.'

'That Pakistani fellow, Iqbal, the one who composed *Saare jahan se achcha Hindostan hamara*, was also a nationalist. Right before our eyes, the man underwent a metamorphosis and became a devil. Then he changed his tune along with the lyrics of his composition: "From China to Hindustan to Arabia extends our realm, and the entire world is our homeland." Why shouldn't I be allowed to change? In this sacred land of the Hindus only that legislation shall prevail which has our religious sanction,' Savarkar declared. At that moment, he was interrupted by Nawab Dewan of Murshidabad.

'India is a Muslim nation. Here, the laws of the Shariat shall prevail, not the laws of the Shastras.'

'Oh, be quiet, Nawab Dewan of Murshidabad!' Savarkar exclaimed. 'Your ancestors were all Hindus, as were those of Allama Iqbal, Jinnah and Sheikh Mohammed Abdullah. Who can deny their Hindu blood? But you people have never acknowledged these blood ties. You have even denied your lineage. Religious conversion does not change one's blood or lineage. Even after the drubbing you got at the hands of the British, you retain the arrogance of rulers, imagining that yours was the final victory. You are half-breed Hindustanis. Yours was the religion of rulers way back in the Middle Ages. The rituals of your worship have changed, but neither has your culture nor your history. Is that clear?'

Savarkar's little speech had created quite a stir. Some constables on duty rushed forward to see what was happening.

Noticing the policemen, Banatwala, Maulana Maududi and Nawab Dewan Sahib rushed to hide in the masjid on Man Singh Road. Savarkar scurried to Bombay and quickly merged with his statue in Dadar.

The adeeb and Salma were amazed. They just could not figure out what had happened. How and why had these people come in their midst?

'Listen,' she suggested, 'isn't there a place where we can sit without being bothered by such an inhuman, uncaring lot?'

'Let's go and sit in the car.'

But how long can one sit in a car? The adeeb started the engine and they drove around aimlessly. In the end, it was decided that he would drop Salma near Baroda House, so that she could walk down to her apartment close by, on Curzon Road. He had just taken a turn in that direction, when an agitated Salma gently placed her hand on his thigh and beseeched him, 'Please, stop the car here, on your left, or just drive on fast.'

'Why, what's wrong?'

'Shahid, my brother, is driving the car ahead of us. My son is with him. They must've gone for a spin in the car and had ice cream. Please, stop the car,' she implored.

He did as she asked.

'I'll walk the rest of the way,' she told him.

As she got out of the car, the adeeb went around to her side.

'I didn't know,' he said, 'that you had such a great responsibility on your shoulders.'

'But I happen to know that you shoulder far greater responsibilities.'

The adeeb was flabbergasted at her words.

'What do you know about me?'

'I know that you are married. Your wife is a simple, virtuous woman. You are the father of a beautiful, intelligent girl who is more a friend to you than a daughter.' As she spoke, the withered leaves of the neem tree nearby kept drifting to the ground. They gleamed in the dark, like blinking eyes, before disappearing in the gloom. At that moment, it occurred to him that turmoil in the human mind could even stir nature.

'Well, you seem a bit confused,' she observed.

'No...not at all. It's just that these drifting neem leaves...'

'Well, this is the season during which trees shed leaves.'

'No, it's the season of darkness,' he replied. 'It descends like falling leaves.'

'Then why don't we do it?'

'Do what?'

'Ask no questions. Nor seek answers. Let's not interrogate each other about the mundane matters in our lives. Let's put aside our mental blocks and live life the way we want to...like the pearl diver who brooks no questions while descending to the depths of the ocean.'

As Salma said this, the neem leaves seemed to drift down faster.

Then voices called out. From the South Pole, Bernard Pierre beckoned: 'Come here, Adeeb. True love is that which is forbidden. Love without barriers is prostitution. Yet, society accepts it. Just forget society. All I am certain about is the fact that your love yearns to be possessed. If you allow your head to rule your heart, you'll never really be able to live life to the fullest. This world won't allow you to do so. Rise above your conscience and acknowledge the primacy of love. It is only in love that pleasure is to be found. Love is the ultimate goal, whether achieved fairly or by deception.'

'Then, was it from deception that the eternal love of Paul and Virginie had sprung?' asked the adeeb.

'What else?' came Pierre's reply. 'If Mrs Poivre had not existed, I would never have paid attention to her husband. In fact, here lies the core of the real story. It was for Mrs Poivre that I had halted in Mauritius. It was there that this woman with the divine voice became the heroine Virginie in my novel and I became Paul. I'd made her husband an old fool. Dear adeeb, what holds you back? Just go to Mauritius with your beloved. Choose to celebrate forbidden love; experience it. Man's most tender and committed moments arise out of love sanctified by nature.'

Salma had been listening to it all. The adeeb pondered over what he had heard. Then he said softly, 'Salma, the sacred beauty of nature lies scattered all over Mauritius. People perceive only the beauty. The entire world does not have a spot more sacredly beautiful than the Grand Bay there. Beauty lies around us, but we never seem to recognize its sacredness. It's there in Trobish...it's everywhere.'

'Adeeb, dreaming is easy. The difficulty lies in living your dream. Will our circumstances ever give us a chance to live the way we want to?'

With the neem leaves drifting down in the dark, the conversation veered towards the silver beach of Trobish.

*

It was a moonlit night. The waves of the ocean undulated gently like a veil of white flowers. The moist grains of sand seemed to softly hum a melody. The corals lay scattered about like silver. Tiny moss-coloured sevanti flowers bloomed. As the wind flipped their leaves over, they looked like silver salvers.

'Seems like a full-moon night,' the adeeb observed, looking around him.

'No, the moon isn't full tonight,' she countered, looking up at the moon. 'It will be—tomorrow.' The moon came down to pat her silky hair before rising to its place in the sky.

As they sat down on the sand, Salma asked, 'Wouldn't it be better if both of us remained like this, so near and yet so far, thinking of and living for each other.'

'Well, what stops us from doing so?'

'No, nothing, really.'

'Any memories...'

'Memories? There could be so many, but none that can bind me.'

'I hope we're not sacrificing some beautiful memories by being selfish.'

'Perhaps, you're right there,' Salma replied. 'Memories, like lingering pain, are a constant in our lives. We are forever trying to make our splintered memories whole.' Her tear-filled eyes told a different story, however.

'Memories are sacred, Salma,' the adeeb said. 'That's why they linger on. No memory is great or insignificant, but each has its distinctive impact. Is it possible that we set out on a journey to make our fragmented memories whole?' Having uttered these words, he planted his lips on her throat. Salma's own lips quivered like the wings of a butterfly; her eyes closed shut like the oysters at Trobish.

Her teardrops fell like pearls on his palms. He could only gaze at them as they slowly evaporated. The imprint of these tears would forever remain on his palms. It was the first time that he had experienced anything quite like this.

They had no idea when night descended and day dawned. Moist ocean breezes announced the departure of the night. Moonlight had merged into the hues of daybreak. They had risen from the sands and walked into the cottage.

A bed awaited them there, pristine as the sands of Trobish.

'I hope my touch, my caress, won't awaken your inhibitions?' he asked.

'No, nothing of the sort,' Salma replied, gazing deeply into his eyes, 'but...'

'What is it?'

'It's just...' she hesitated.

'Just what?'

'Just that nature has devised certain laws. The law governing the man–woman relationship dictates that woman gives before receiving and man receives before giving.'

'But this law negates equality.'

'No, equality isn't a commodity that can be weighed in the balance. Equality is only manifested in our dreams...our yearnings.'

'What was the dream you had tonight?' he asked her.

'Night never did descend on us this time, did it? Rather, we enjoyed our dream today, fully awake, with our eyes wide open. The coincidence lies in both of us having seen the same thing in our dream. Just like the one we had at the Holiday Inn. Perhaps, the greatest truth of our lives lies in...'

'...that which has never happened anywhere in the world, is far removed from reality, yet, continues to be an eternal truth for us.'

'This is our reality,' she affirmed.

Her words escaped from the cottage and echoed around the world: This is our reality...our reality...

Then restraint gave way and they were swept into the world of passion.

The material world is made of bricks and stones and bodies. But theirs evolved from their very breath, frothing and foaming like the waves that struck the distant coral reefs in the Indian Ocean. A shower of sparks flew from their deep embrace and cleaving forms.

'It seems as though we're lying in a forest of palash trees,' Salma said hesitantly.

'Yes,' came the husky reply, 'millions of years ago, a volcanic eruption in the ocean had given birth to Mauritius. Today, another volcanic eruption has given birth to what we share. How beautiful this palash forest looks, bathed in the fountain of fire!'

They looked deeply into each other's eyes, as if trying to commit to memory some special feature belonging to the other.

'What are you looking for now?' she asked.

'Perhaps, it's also what you seek—a touch, a caress that is more intense, more powerful than the merely physical.'

'Adeeb, try and imagine how the earth must have felt when the first breeze caressed it.'

These words made the adeeb look at her in amazement.

'Salma!' he cried.

'Yes, what is it?'

'When did you bathe and put on your make-up?'

'Make-up! We never even saw the dawn and half the day has gone by...so, make-up is hardly...'

'But why have your lashes turned purple? When did you adorn your forehead with silver kumkum?'

'What...what else do you notice that's different?'

'How is it that every joint, every fold and orifice of your body gives out the fragrance of musk?'

'Mm...why am I faint with the scent of your body? It is like the fragrance of parched earth after a shower...'

'I don't know what this is, Salma. Perhaps, we are in ourselves the indestructible universe, a link in the chain of creation.' Having uttered these words, the adeeb drew her close.

'Hush, don't speak, Adeeb. Don't even allow yourself to ponder. Not another word...or this castle of dreams, of our shared passion, will come crashing down. Just let your heart's desire have its way. Let things take their course...as they always have...and always will.' With these words, Salma too drew closer, her body merging with his, as though they were one, she, a part of him, as intimate as his very breath. On their prone forms bloomed a thousand blue flowers.

Suddenly, there was a knock on the door. Languid with passion, they turned to it and called out, 'Come in.'

As the room boy entered, they tried to get a hold on themselves.

'Sir,' he said, 'you neither asked for tea nor appeared for lunch. If you want me to clean the room...'

'Thank you,' Salma replied, 'but there's nothing here that needs cleaning. If you have to dust the furniture, do it tomorrow.'

'No problem, madam.' The room boy departed.

Gazing at the adeeb, Salma murmured, 'Never shall we share this bed again.'

'Why not?'

'Because love has lain here once. Our love might be sullied if we use the bed again.'

'Go brush your teeth now and have a bath. Let's go out and have a meal. As it is, here in Mauritius, you get nothing to eat after eight p.m.'

'Even if we have a bath, these blue flowers will remain with us. They won't wither away. What shall we do with them?' she asked.

'Who's going to ask us about them, anyway?' the adeeb replied, gathering Salma into his arms once again.

19

A profusion of blue flowers bloomed on their bodies when they emerged from the cottage. Some of those blossoms were hidden within the folds of Salma's sari. The blouse she had on concealed the others. As for those that bloomed along her arm, she knew not what to do with them. Again and again, she tried to shield them with the pallu of her sari, hoping to seal in their fragrance.

The sun was sinking in the west. A veil of clouds persevered in vain to block out its rays, but the sun could not be kept from glancing back often at Trobish. The placid waves of the Indian Ocean gently caressed the beach. Boats bobbed around aimlessly on the sea. Some were carried in the direction of the coral reef, others towards the Grand Bay. Their sails glimmered like veils of light.

'What a joy it is to watch the silent waves,' she remarked. 'They look like blue chunnis spread out to dry in the sun. At night, they take the form of embracing arms.'

With his arm around her shoulders, he guided her towards a beach umbrella fashioned from sugar-cane strips. A table had been set up below it. They had no desire to go to the hotel's dining room. The sun had set by now. The silvery sevanti leaves swayed in the breeze. A carpet of shimmering shells shone along the beach.

'How pristine the sand looks...' she started to say, as the waiter arrived.

'India. Bharat...'

'Yes. India...Bharat!'

'Sir, I've heard that a huge sun rises there,' the waiter said with an all-encompassing gesture that suggested the idea of immensity.

'No, really, it's no different from the sun here,' Salma told him.

'But how is that possible?' The waiter sounded dubious, but refrained from further argument.

'Could you take the order after ten minutes, please?' she requested, and the man went away.

'See? A mighty culture has to have a larger sun,' remarked the adeeb, placing his hand on Salma's. Gently, he played with her fingers.

'A strange thought comes to mind,' she reflected.

'What is it?'

'It seems as if we set out in a boat two centuries ago, like indentured labourers. The contractor had counted each one...even the cadaver that had made a transition from life to death. The English had disinfected us and made us put on a numbered collar. We had set off to work on the sugar-cane plantations...' Salma seemed to have travelled back in time, rapidly receding into the centuries gone by.

A gentleman had approached them in the meantime. 'Excuse me,' he said, 'could I intrude for a moment?'

'Go ahead.'

'Actually, it's not you I want to talk to, but her.'

'To Salma? Well, go ahead.'

'Can we go and sit under that beach umbrella?' the man suggested to Salma.

'Why, what for?' she quipped.

'I'll not intrude on your privacy,' the adeeb said.

Salma asked him in a worried voice, 'Where will you be?'

'Oh, nowhere in particular...I'll be around. People who are secretive should know that nothing remains hidden for long. Whenever you look for me, I'll be there.' With that, the adeeb vanished.

'Well, now, what do you have to say to me?' Salma asked the man.

'Let me tell you a little about myself. I'm Naim. I work for the Pakistani civil services. And you, I think, are the granddaughter of Aftab Ahmad Khan who retired from the CSP.'

'That's right. I also happen to be the widow of Salman Hussain of the Indian Civil Service—the IAS,' Salma retorted with some irritation.

'Yes, I'm aware of that. I happen to be Salman's cousin. I also know that he died in Shimla.'

'And, by producing a counterfeit will, Salman's family cheated me of my share of his property that would have amounted to a good two-thirds of the whole,' Salma retorted angrily.

'Yes, I'm aware of that, even though it isn't from India that one gets most of the news.'

'Then you must also be aware that your relatives had dragged me to court,' she said bitterly. 'Their allegation against me was that I'd been involved in a relationship with another man before my marriage.'

'That's right. And after placing you in the witness box, the court had even claimed that it was impossible for such a beautiful woman to be faithful to one man.'

'Yes, and the media loved those titillating stories! Relatives on both sides of the border heard, read and knew about them. And, of course, your bureaucratic brotherhood always stands united, whether it's the Hindustani IAS or its Pakistani counterpart, the CSP.' Salma's rancour made him uneasy.

'No, actually, that isn't really the way things are...' he muttered.

'It most certainly is!' she lashed out. 'Naim Sahib, any man is allowed to break away from your brotherhood and still remain the master of his destiny. But you and your brethren look upon women as chattel. If, having gone through a traumatic experience, a woman turns to a man outside your community, people like you refuse to put up with it.'

'That's a misconception on your part.'

'It most certainly is not! To begin with, you strive to keep your women confined within the strict boundaries of your community. If they resist, you try and break them by citing their obligations to family and society. If that doesn't work, you use religion as a ploy.'

'Perhaps, you're right! You are a Muslim all right, but the path you've chosen to follow with a Hindu man is outright heresy!' came Naim's stinging reply.

'So you've dragged your crude notions here as well! Does anyone ever inquire about a beloved's religion before falling in love? Naim Sahib, can't you tell the difference between the two kinds of love—the sacred and the profane? Instinct has always taken precedence over religion.'

Groping for a reply, Naim could only manage, 'I merely wanted to say that—'

'—that I should not seek my emotional, physical and spiritual fulfilment with a Hindu?'

'You have a son, too. What about him?'

'He's my son all right, but then, a male encounters few problems in life.'

'As a friend and relative, I advise you to take your son and join your nana in Pakistan.'

'You're behaving just like Yezid,' she observed.

'Like Yezid? I don't understand what you mean.'

'Why would you ever admit that you understand?' she shouted. 'Yezid too had invited Hazrat Hussain to Iraq from Medina. On the plains of Karbala, he killed Hussain after putting him through the ordeals of hunger and thirst. Your advice echoes Yezid's invitation and your Pakistan will be my Karbala. By depriving me of all that matters to me most and by sexually abusing me, you will hand me a life that is worse than death. While Hazrat Hussain was merely martyred at Karbala, every Muslim woman's life is a Karbala. And what, pray, is so special that only a Muslim man can offer a woman and a Hindu cannot?'

'No other religion can claim to offer a woman all that Islam has ordained for her,' was Naim's reply. 'As far as sexual matters are concerned, all men, irrespective of faith, can give a woman the same thing. But from the social and spiritual point of view, only a Muslim can offer a woman much more. He alone has access to the sacred Koran and the hadith.'

'But it's the Arabs who have that in their possession. They have the original copies that they have chosen not to share with anyone else. It is only the *fiqh*, the series of Islamic injunctions that lends Islamic law its distinctive identity. And I'm sure you're well aware that this accounts for the variations in the sharia laws. The Sunnis were split into four schools. Then the Shias chose to establish their own school, the fiqa-e-asnashari. It is true that the adherents of these schools are all Muslims, their khuda and Prophet are one, and they share the same religious scriptures. Yet, the rituals and customs involving their daily lives are so very different from one another's.'

'Right. Anything else?' Naim asked in a challenging tone.

'Only this—you might be with the CSP in Pakistan, but your loyalties lie elsewhere. You wish to conceal your shortcomings by quoting Islam. It was the British who gave you a country as a jagir, a grant. You never apply yourself to improving the lot of the common people. On the contrary, with your perverse religious goals driving you, and your warped interpretations of Islam, you are capable of ruining several generations of men. Islam has never preached hatred. It's people like you who perpetuate hatred. You wish to do to others what Israel's Judaism has done to Islam.'

'How can you make such an allegation?' Naim retorted. 'The foundation of Pakistan was built on a sound principle.'

'And which sound principle is that? Religion does not establish the parameters of national identity. Much before organized religion came into being, every society functioned on the basis of some kind of faith or principle. If the whole of America embraces Islam today, does that mean it loses its identity as a nation? Will its culture turn Arabic or Iranian?'

'You are bent on arguing and are needlessly dragging Islam into the issue at hand.'

'That's because, as a Pakistani, you consider yourself the flag bearer of Islam and are given to constantly quoting Islam. Pakistan was created in the name of Islam. This was a phenomenon without precedent. Religious identities had always emerged from within a nation. Despite the arrival of the Prophet of Islam Hazrat Mohammed and the descent of the sacred Koran from the heavens, Arabs remained Arabs, Iraq was distinctively Iraq, Egypt retained its unique identity, but Pakistan did not remain Bharat or Hindustan!'

'What are you trying to imply?' Naim asked.

'I only repeat what your President Zia-ul-Haque had said—that Pakistan is the outcome of religious strategy, just as Israel is the gift of Judaism. If Judaism were obliterated from the country, Israel would cease to exist. Similarly, Pakistan would be no more, if Islam ceased to be the pillar of its existence. Nations might die out, Naim Sahib, but race and ethnicity never do. Did Christianity succeed in wiping out the different races? No, the conceptual framework of race is at variance with religion. Could the advent of Buddhism alter the racial and ethnic realities of China, Japan, Cambodia, Burma, Sri Lanka and Indonesia? Many people in these countries embraced Christianity or Islam. But could the hold of religion weaken their racial bonds and customs?'

'You're wrangling in the most unreasonable manner.'

'You've come to Mauritius alone. You are also my late spouse Salman Hussain's cousin. If, in the name of Islam, I were to spurn the adeeb tonight and agree to sleep with you, your shariat, your hadith and your revered Koran would rush to accommodate me! And that would be because you seek to restrict the vast scope of sacred human concepts using Islam as your pretext. So, Naim Sahib, don't bring up the issue of religion! There are many depraved bastards like you who use religion as an instrument to satisfy their own carnal desires! Another weapon, imprisoned below your belt, is always raring to go and, depending on its need, people like you are always willing to justify your actions in the name of religion.'

'You are nothing but a filthy bitch!' shouted Naim, smashing his fist down on the table.

'And you are nothing but a man with a filthy mind who wants to imprison a noble religion within the narrow confines of Pakistan's borders!' Salma shouted back. 'My Islam hasn't sunk quite so low yet! In the name of Pakistan, you once divided a mature nation. Now, once again, you're trying to use religion to keep me apart from someone I love and in the process destroy my very being!'

Her words had created a commotion. Considerably flustered, Naim composed himself with some effort and scurried away.

The moon had risen. The sands shimmered in its beams. The breeze wafted in from the ocean, flipping over the sevanti leaves. Waving in the gusts of breeze, they looked like hands caught in applause. The pines hummed a melody and in the distance, the silvery leaves of the sugar-cane plants twined around each other in the wind.

It was the night of the full moon. Salma's anger had lent her face the glow of beaten silver. Naim Sahib had made himself scarce. A hush had descended on Trobish. God knew where the others were. In the distance, anchored boats danced on the surface of the gleaming waters and the jetty seemed covered in squares of icing. Cliffs of lava resembled deer at rest. Like a million scattered pearls, shoals of fish flicked back and forth in the water.

Lost in eternity, the adeeb suddenly recalled that Salma was alone. As soon as he approached her, she dissolved at his touch like a crumbling pillar of sand and gave herself to him.

The adeeb gathered up each individual grain of this sand and painstakingly put them all together. And behold! There, once again, was Salma, standing before him. But there was a difference—instead of tears, sandstorms raged in her eyes and her breath smelt of acid.

'What's wrong with you?' he asked, shaking her.

'Nothing's wrong with me, Adeeb!' cried an enraged Salma. 'Why do Pakistanis like Naim fail to understand that they cannot take it upon themselves to speak on behalf of Muslims and Islam? People like him ought to know that there are more Muslims in Hindustan today than there are in Pakistan, that Hindustanis have a better grasp of Islam than their Pakistani counterparts and that Hindustan has far more genuine practitioners of Islam than Pakistan could ever dream of having. What right have these Pakistanis to voice their criticism?'

'Just get it out of your mind. Let's go and eat,' the adeeb suggested.

'Yes, let's do so. I'm famished.'

As the adeeb turned towards the hotel, he noticed that its lights had been dimmed. When they reached the place, they were informed that it had closed for the festival of Holi. Meals were not being served.

'But the waiter took our order,' the adeeb protested.

'Yes, sir, he did. And he waited a long time for you. After all, today is a holiday. He grew tired of waiting. When the kitchen closed for the day, he left.'

'So, there's nothing available now?'

'We're sorry, sir.'

'But you serve the South African guests throughout the night, don't you?'

'Yes, we do—on working days. They usually prefer to have their dinner by eight-thirty p.m. We close our kitchen by nine p.m. It's almost eleven-thirty p.m. now.'

When the adeeb returned to the cottage, Salma was stretched out on the bed, weeping bitterly. Naim's words and her own hunger pangs had driven her to tears.

'Salma!'

'Don't mind me...it's just that I was ravenously hungry and there you were, arguing at the hotel reception. You didn't seem bothered that I was hungry, so I came away. They have closed the hotel kitchen on account of Holi, but everyone is not a Hindu. Even non-Hindus can feel hungry!' She started crying again.

'Look, I'll try and do something about it,' he reassured her. Getting into his car, he began driving towards Port Louis.

Sugar-cane fields, the narrow, winding road running past the village of Triole. In a house to his left, he noticed that the lights were on. He instantly felt that this house belonged to a descendant of Bernard Pierre. When he stopped to inquire, it turned out to be the residence of Abhimanyu Anat, a writer of Indian descent. While Mauritius switched off its lights and slumbered, this reclusive writer used his pen to illuminate a dark world.

The light emanating from the writer's pen accompanied him all the way to Port Louis. When he reached the port town, he found it reeking of onion and garlic. He discovered that these were imported from India. Cream and cheese came from Australia, mutton from New Zealand, cereals from Europe, petrol from the Gulf and tourists from everywhere. There was no shortage of anything; it was just that the shops were shut.

As in Triole, he noticed a glimmer of light. When he approached it, he was told that it was the residence of the prime minister, Sir Seewosagar Ramgulam. Just below it stood a stall, its shutters open. Samosas, pakoras and bananas were being sold there. While he was buying them, he learnt that the place belonged to a man from Madagascar and served Indian breakfast in the mornings. He came to know that the prime minister himself had given the man permission to set up the shop near his residence. The adeeb pondered over the land that was Mauritius, more unspoilt than any in the world.

He laid his hands on whatever food he could manage, paid for it and raced back to Trobish. Half the night was over, but the lights in Abhimanyu Anat's house were still on.

Salma was waiting for him at the cottage. He arranged the food on a plate.

'Come, eat,' he urged her.

'Appetite is a wise instinct, you know,' she told him. 'The moment you left to fetch food, my stomach felt quite full.' She kissed him and murmured, 'I'm thirsty...'

As he rose to fetch water, she stopped him and put her arms around him. 'To quench this thirst, one needs a different kind of water, Adeeb...'

The room's natural odours receded to give way to the aroma of their union. Like the currents of a river, it swept through the room, transforming it into a forest of perfumed spices.

'Ah...never let me go...in each other's arms we shall one day be transformed into stones, my beloved adeeb.'

The waters rose ever higher in their river of passion.

'May I say something? Like your sweat, your passion is raw and instinctive. Oh God, my sustainer,' she prayed, 'I beseech you never to rob me of my hard-won, ethereal happiness. If need be, snatch away my physical pleasures, confine them in fetters. But please leave him for me. Such wealth is not bestowed in charity. But then, this

is hardly charity. It is my bounty, my reward. Allow me to revel
in it.'

'Amen!'

'Was it you who said "Amen"?' she asked with a start.

'I didn't, actually.'

'There is a third presence constantly hovering over us.'

'Who offers us identical breakfasts and dreams?' asked the
adeeb.

'Adeeb...'

'What is it?'

'In so short a span of time, you've given me the sense of
fulfilment my husband couldn't offer me in eight years.'

'You don't mean that!'

'I speak the truth. You have drawn me out from a world of fear,
Adeeb, and placed me in a world of faith. I wish...'

'Yes?'

'I wish you had been my *shareek-e-hayat*, my wedded partner,
during the journey of my life,' Salma murmured, beginning to cry.
The adeeb kissed away her tears so as to prevent a single drop from
spilling out.

'Your tears are so different, not like my briny sweat. They're
sweet like the waters of the Dajla-Furat, the Nile and the Ganga,'
the adeeb whispered, as he gathered her up in his arms once again.

'Where were you that year?'

'Which year is that?'

'The year I was married to Salman.'

'I was like a tree growing in the corner of your yard. Streamers
of decorations and lights adorned my branches to welcome the
baraat,' mused the adeeb, smiling. 'In my helplessness, I had no
choice but to release you to seek your happiness.'

'It's not that Salman never gave me a single moment of happiness.
It's only that certain things he did make me pause to reflect. I cannot
stop pondering over those eight years. Even after his death, Adeeb,
I continued to search for that one steadfast face I might identify as
my husband's, but it always eluded me. Where every woman errs is
in her quest for a man with a single persona.'

'Salma, I might not have many personas, but I do have at least two—one that my wife knows of; the other that lies bare before you.'

'I'm aware of it, Adeeb.'

'How much do you know?'

'Just this, Adeeb—that you can neither give me up nor leave your wife.'

'And how do you know about it?'

'Because I know you,' Salma replied, gazing into his eyes. 'You cannot bring yourself to let someone else pay for the consequences of your own desires. I know only too well that you can live for your yearnings, breathe life into them, carry them with you to distant deserts and suffer for their sake. But you'll never inflict pain on someone else.'

'What exactly do you mean?'

'That you can leave your wife Shanta for my sake, but that you cannot leave her to languish alone. You are willing to endure the suffering that comes from your yearnings, but you can never inflict it on Shanta. That is why I am confident about you never abandoning me. If you could have deserted Shanta, you could've left me too, any time.' Salma's hands touched the adeeb's feet.

'Salma, I cannot decide whether you are a woman or an angel!'

'Adeeb, I agonize over the possibility of men like Naim who share my religion never ever allowing me to live with you. Why don't we do something about it?'

'What could we do?'

'Why don't I become a Hindu and you a Muslim—just so that we may live in peace? The Muslim mindset is quite willing to accept a Muslim man marrying a Hindu woman, but it will never allow a Hindu man to share a Muslim woman's bed. So, why don't we interchange our religious identities just to appease people like Naim, so that they'll leave us alone? Otherwise, such people will never let us be.'

20

Though Salma and the adeeb did not actually convert to each other's religion, they enjoyed indulging in the charade. It became a game for them. The first thing they did was travel eastwards. Crossing the dense jungles of the Black river, they came upon a flower-strewn path. Walking down it, they met the old man of history who asked them, 'How are you? And why are you running away?'

'We're fleeing from our present,' the adeeb replied, out of breath. Perspiring profusely and panting even more laboriously than the adeeb, Salma rested her head on his shoulder and explained, 'We're running away from the centuries. O, Father Adam, when shall we enjoy the liberty of living in peace?'

The old man laughed. His laughter rang out over the ancient trees of the Black Forest, over waterfalls and the colourful soil of Shamarel. It briefly took shelter in Qupip, echoed in the silent mouth of a volcano and after touching the eternal peak that stood sentinel over Kalidas, returned, softened in timbre.

Salma and the adeeb gazed at the old man incredulously.

'How long will you two keep running away? Mankind has always been in flight, but this is not the response of a committed individual. I've seen Indian labourers escaping the tyranny of British imperialism. Some of them committed suicide. Others jumped into the Indian Ocean, hoping to reach home, but were claimed by the sea. A few were torn apart by the hounds of the imperialists. Others were axed as they cut down the *abnus* forests. But tell me, where can Tibet hide? Where can Nigeria or Bolivia escape? Mexico cannot run away and merge with India, just as Cyprus cannot flee to Spain. How far can you run? You cannot change the world by running away...you have to face it.'

'That's exactly what we'll do, Father Adam. Hope to see you again.' With these words, Salma and the adeeb entered the Dushrock Hotel.

Mauritius encloses within it the many secrets of the sea. All the pearls in the world have contributed to the creation of its beaches. Its seas have absorbed the luminous tears of mankind. They lend this island its air of pristine innocence and a touch of the divine. Here, every tree has a song, every leaf a message. Each bird is a courier, bearing the songs of the trees to faraway places. Every moment, the Kalidas of the mountains, wreathed in mist, calls out to the clouds as they hang suspended over the island. Here, the breeze wraps itself around the clouds, driving them, at times, towards the land and blowing them away, at others.

They were just about to have tea, when the old man of history reappeared out of nowhere before them. They could only gape at him.

'Would you like to have some tea?' the adeeb asked.

'Can tea served in a hotel ever exude an aroma?' he replied. 'I only drink the beverage yielded by the tea gardens of my homeland. Go ahead and have your tea. I dared to invade your privacy because I found you both in a state of utter indecision. Complex situations like this often impede the pace of one's normal life. Love should fill life with music, not with bestial physicality.'

'True...that is, indeed, how the situation stands. We are fearful. Yet, we seek a path that will liberate us from fear.'

'The only way to break free from fear,' explained the old man, 'is to have unshakeable faith in each other and to accept and rely on the promise the future holds. Those who refuse to acknowledge this reality are resisting the possibilities of that promise whose flame burns so steadfastly within mankind. It is man himself who has created the promise which lends life a sense of continuity.'

'But no one acknowledges the invention of promise and its burning flame within man,' said Salma.

'You are both the future users of this invention and its steadfast flame. Because of this flame that burns within you, you are Day. As surely as Day can never be Night, this glow is eternal. Even when thick clouds encircle Qupip and its environs, casting a pall of gloom on everything, the awareness remains that night has not descended. It is still daytime.' With these words, the old man of history disappeared.

Till late in the night, the adeeb and Salma strolled around, exploring the area around the Dushrock Hotel. Water, limpid as tears, flowed like the currents of the sacred Zamzam. For a long while, they watched the fish swimming in the water, bubbles rising from their mouths, and observed the waving fronds of the coral. Then, taking a boat, they visited a neighbouring island. They returned intoxicated on martini. Salma quipped, 'You should now become a Muslim.'

'I am one already.'

'And I'll be a Hindu.'

'Then become one in earnest.'

Thus they embraced each other's faith.

'May I hold your hand?' the adeeb asked.

'Of course you may.'

'How does it feel to hold hands with a Muslim?'

'Converting to each other's religion has not made an iota of difference. Holding your hand in mine affords me the same sensuous pleasure that I enjoyed when you were a Hindu. Like the lashes of a painfully shy woman, mine sweep down over my eyes at your touch,' Salma replied.

'What else?'

'My lips still thirst for yours. My desires diminish not a whit with our religious conversion,' she replied huskily.

'I think we've adopted the wrong course. Come, let's both become Muslims. Or convert to Hinduism.' The adeeb's embrace tightened.

'Even now, your arms hold the same overpowering fascination for me.'

'And now?'

'Even now your hands seek what they had always sought before—their favourite spots, like weary travellers in quest of a refuge in the desert. Let yourself go, Adeeb, and take me, offer me release.' Their arousal soared to its peak. Their breaths and bodies merged, locking them into a world of passion.

When they came to their senses, Salma lay stretched out before him as though she were the desert and he the ripe dates that dropped from the trees on to its soft, silky sands. Both had burrowed into the sand like the roots of a desert shrub that seeks sustenance below the topsoil. They wanted to remain that way forever.

'Inscribe your name on these peaks, Adeeb.'

'But my name will fade away.'

'No, it will be preserved forever. Now, do write your name, Adeeb.'

Picking up a pen from the bedside table, the adeeb wrote his name on the taut peaks of her body. Not once, but hundreds of times.

'Don't stop, Adeeb, just keep writing.'

'I'm not hurting you, am I? The nib of this Dushrock pen is sharp. It must be painful.'

'Adeeb, the sand can absorb all pain. Just write your name on every inch of my body.'

When the adeeb had done so, she pulled him into her arms once again.

'Now I feel complete,' he said.

'Then just surrender to my embrace.'

'Salma, the feeling of satiation that love brings us is so soothing. No religion can offer this kind of release.'

'Come, let's interchange our religions once again and see how it feels.'

'No religion can ever bring us this overwhelming sense of peace, this indestructible serenity, all the way to the Day of Judgement. And we have to go on living till then.'

'For the time being, you're a Muslim. So, how can you talk of life after death? You should only be talking of life,' said Salma.

'Well, you're a Hindu now. But do you believe in reincarnation?'

'Whether I believe in it or not, I enjoy visualizing it.'

'Oh, Salma, then you're special. You transcend religion. You are the symbol of faith in the immortality of mortal man.'

'What's new about it, Adeeb? The Iranian mystics and the Hindustani scholars of the Vedas have said as much.'

Then, a grating voice from the unknown spoke up: 'Woman, you grow rebellious. May you be damned! The life you have chosen and the philosophy you've adopted—Dara Shikoh's—is sacrilegious. Ultimately, you will have to step out of your hotel room. When you walk the streets of this earth, you will be walled up alive. On Judgement Day, half the body of a sinful man will disintegrate into fragments. But yours, you depraved woman, will dissolve into oozing blood and pus.'

The voice cracked like lightning and leapt into the room. 'Adeeb, who's that?' asked a frightened Salma, hiding behind him.

'I? I am a *jallad*, an executioner. I am not only Alamgir Aurangzeb's instrument of punishment, but also a kotwal. I am the man who beheaded the Sufi Sarmad on the steps of the Jama Masjid. I was the one to sever the tongue and gouge out the eyes of Shivaji's son Sambhaji who had looted and torched the storehouse of books at Kot Pithora.'

'Silence!' ordered another voice. 'This happens to be the representative of the evil powers of darkness who wishes to crush all promise the future holds and destroy its luminous past. It is monsters like him who have prevented the world from evolving. No executioner can claim to be the spokesman of his time. Do you know that a book never dies? It only reappears in a different manifestation. The books you had destroyed were resurrected as white pigeons that took flight. You never managed to see them.'

The old man of history stood, once again, before them. 'Why do you vilify Aurangzeb, the emperor of Hindustan? Though he oppressed his subjects, he was, after all, an emperor. Despite the many wrongs he inflicted on his people, he must have done some good. If Aurangzeb followed the path Akbar had forged, the map of the world would have been radically different today. Islam would have been the beacon of the world's religions. But Aurangzeb failed in this endeavour. Whatever might have been his compulsions, Aurangzeb does not need worthless supporters like you. In fact, thanks to monsters like you, he has earned a bad name. Look...if you have the eyes to do so, observe...you have disturbed Aurangzeb's heavenly repose. In his grave at Aurangabad, he turns restlessly from side to side. You remembered Sambhaji, but how could you forget that Aurangzeb had given shelter to his seven-year-old son Sahuji? Did you know that he bestowed on the boy the titles of Haft Hazari and Raja, placed him under the tutelage of pandits, and appointed a dewan and a bakshi to supervise his upbringing? He even conferred on Sahuji's two younger brothers the status of princes. Though Aurangzeb strove hard to change the history of south Asia, it would have been infinitely better had he not exploited religion to fulfil his goal.'

'No!' yelled the jallad, 'religion is the ultimate weapon of victory for Muslims. Aurangzeb taught us to live the way Muslims ought to. He taught us never to acknowledge "namaskar" or "Ram-Ram", instead of "Assalam-alaikum". He put a stop to the tradition of darshan reserved for emperors, because it perpetuated idolatry and its discontinuation would help to segregate the kafirs. So what if the practitioners of darshan were kings? We put an end to this Hindu tradition.'

'And?'

'And, as Islam would have it,' the bigoted jallad replied, 'we opposed both Akbar, Aurangzeb's great-grandfather, and Dara Shikoh, his brother. This was necessary, because both were close to being kafirs.'

'It was necessary,' explained the old man, 'because Akbar and Dara Shikoh aspired to infuse Islamic tradition and thought into the faith and spiritual traditions that prevailed in Hindustan. Aurangzeb let this momentous occasion in history go by, because he was more committed to consolidating his position on the throne. So, he killed off relatives he regarded as threats to his authority and kept dreaming of creating an Islamic state. Ironically, the foundations of this state were not based on solidarity between fellow human beings, but on hatred. In his quest to fulfil his dream, Aurangzeb rejected the multi-religious and multi-cultural strengths of a kingdom stretching from Tibet to Golconda–Bijapur, on the one hand, and from Bengal to Kabul and Kandahar, on the other. That is why he ended up as the last Mughal emperor. He died an obdurate Muslim monarch, defeated by the Marathas and forced to hand over the reins of his kingdom to the British.'

'No, this is factually incorrect. The reins were handed over by his worthless offspring.'

'Every year, he would send the Sharif of Mecca a sizeable amount of the country's wealth. From the sacred city would come people to carry it all away. This was the wealth that accrued from the jaziya tax imposed on the kafirs. He never acknowledged Hindustan as his own country. That is why he allowed the British to establish trading posts at the ports of Bombay and Surat. For this reason alone, the English historian Lenpool has described him as a wise and just monarch. He has written that if the kafirs were tyrannized at all, it was because Aurangzeb was a radical Muslim.'

'If he didn't acknowledge Hindustan as his country, why does he still lie buried in Aurangabad? Whatever be the reason,' yelled the jallad, 'all historical accounts confirm that the world never produced a Muslim ruler greater than Aurangzeb! Books tell us that he dedicated his life to religion and was the one to bring everlasting glory to Taimur's lineage.'

'Glory be to the same Taimur who had mocked Islam with the words, "Your khuda in heaven is invisible, but the khuda on earth, an emperor, can be both seen and heard. Just as the heavens have one khuda, the earth too needs just one emperor." Casting Islam aside, he had bestowed on himself the status of God,' the old man of history declared. 'The wisdom of Dara Shikoh is not yours to possess. You are as illiterate and ignorant as Taimur, Abdali and Aurangzeb. Only jallads like you can be flag bearers of illiteracy and ignorance. Anyway, let's be done with this sparring. Just tell us if you will grant Salma and the adeeb some moments of togetherness, a little more time to live in the manner they seek to?'

'Our hadith, our shariat...'

'Don't refer to books, jallad. The Islamic scriptures are far beyond your grasp. You have trivialized their contents. In the name of books and scriptures, you propagate yourself. Tell me, which book do you wish to quote now? All sects have presented their fiqh—the Hanfis, the Malikis, the Hambalis and the Shafais. These four sects, however, remain unacknowledged by those who repose faith in the hadith, a clear indication of the internal conflicts existing between the Sunnis. The Shias have their own interpretations. Whose parameters do you propose to adopt when you take up the case pertaining to both? For God's sake, don't quote scriptures to justify your private agenda! Allow these two people to live with God's grace. Each one has been given the divine right to live in peace. Just let these two be, jallad. Let them live their life. Don't bind them by what is written in books,' the old man pleaded.

'I have no faith in words.'

'That's because you are devoid of a soul. By quoting caliphs and kings, you torment the world. You forget that when the Prophet Mohammed evolved laws for the desert tribes, the rest of the world was not living in deserts and jungles. The advanced civilizations of Iraq, Syria, Egypt and Iran existed at the time, and the laws intended for the desert tribes were obviously irrelevant for them. These cultures accepted the monotheistic god of the Prophet, but the Arab way of life had not found favour with them.'

'I'm not interested in quibbling with you. The issue at hand is this woman. She has sunk to the depths of depravity. She has crossed all the limits set by Allah and so…'

Caught in the midst of these arguments, Salma felt faint. She was unable to comprehend what had happened. Had leading the life of a good Muslim been made so difficult? Were the terms by which a Muslim lived to be forever dictated by books? Was there no place at all for principles that originated from concerns about life and nature?

'There certainly is place. Islam has taken into account all issues involving nature. But when religion is manipulated for political ends to engender hatred, not one, but many Pakistans are born. My child, your life has been destroyed by the unnatural partition that has split apart one nation, one identity, one culture.'

When Khan Abdul Ghaffar Khan spoke these words, Nasira Sharma suddenly appeared before them and asked, 'Can culture ever be divided? Afghanistan has its own currency and my airline ticket carries the pictures of the Bamiyan Buddhas. For years, Afghanistan has been exposed to the influence of Hinduism and Buddhism. This cultural and historical link has survived till today, despite the redefining of boundaries. It is my impression that the walls built by the Buddhist king Kanishk to protect Kabul still stand today. Before the advent of Buddhism, the Vedas were composed on Afghan soil.

The names of Afghan mountain ranges, valleys, towns and kings are to be found in these texts. Paeans were sung here in praise of the gods of fire and later, it was here that the tradition of monotheism was established. By then, the Aryans had completed their quest for morality and truth. No one had heard of Greece or Rome at the time. When Europe was trapped in the Dark Ages, the Aryans in Afghanistan had already introduced the age of fire. Their fire god was Ahura Mazda.'

'My child, you're so right. Culture can never be segregated,' Khan Abdul Ghaffar Khan replied, patting Nasira's shoulder. 'Let's leave these two people now to consecrate themselves to the sacred fire so that in times to come, they may offer the world a new perspective.'

'May Salma and the adeeb be given more years to their lives. Let them not be fettered by the outdated tenets laid down by the written word,' the old man pleaded before Ghaffar Khan. His request was immediately granted.

'Let's go elsewhere to resolve our differences over religious and scriptural issues. Come, come with me.' Leaving Salma and the adeeb alone, the old man of history from Mauritius led them all away.

The night spent at Dushrock Hotel was transformed into a night out in the forest.

'In this dense forest, even the wind can lose its way,' Salma observed.

'That is why man has drawn in the wind to make it a part of his very breath,' the adeeb replied. 'By confining it within his breast, he hopes never to go astray.'

Salma seemed shaken by all that had transpired. It took her quite a while to speak again. 'Something has died within me, Adeeb,' she confessed. 'It's the jungle created by mankind that terrifies me so. All around me, nothing but graveyards seem to stretch in the distance. Caught in their midst, I lie dying, inch by inch.'

'Salma, this corporeal frame preserves within itself a soul that is both temple and crematorium. Don't let the lamps that burn within either be extinguished.'

'How can I keep them burning? Even as they burn, they release the stench of a graveyard. It is not light that burns within these lamps, I feel, but the fragments of my broken spirit and body.'

'Keep your dreams alive, Salma,' the adeeb urged. 'They alone light up my spirit with a steady flame. What purpose would my body serve otherwise? Without your dreams to keep it alive, it would be little more than an empty shell in which the light has been snuffed out. Those within whom the light continues to burn, sail across the river of life; others, whose light has been put out, drown in its waters.' He kissed her dew-moist neck.

'Whatever be your explanations, Adeeb, I still feel as though I'm lost in a dark jungle,' she said, looking around her fearfully.

'Have courage, Salma. We have not come together at this point in our lives to forge the paths of suffering. If we keep discovering narrow tracks of happiness in this vast jungle, we will have reached our journey's end.'

'I'm afraid that my legs may not be able to support me any longer. It feels as though a great blow has shattered them irreparably.'

'Having advanced so deep into the recesses of the jungle, life cannot come to a standstill now. It has to take some direction or other. Well-trodden trails can take one back to where one started from, but travellers carving out their own paths never go back. They just keep moving forward.' As he uttered these words, the adeeb shot her an intense look.

'Hmm...Perhaps, you're right. You, at least, have a path to take you back home if you should so choose. I have none. Except for my son Sohrab who lives independently in a hostel, but still walks holding my hand...' Salma broke down again. 'There's nowhere for me to go back to in this jungle...'

The adeeb gathered each of the harsingar blossoms that fell from her eyes.

'Salma, we can reach our destination only by forging our own paths. In this dense jungle, we shall keep in touch by constantly calling out to each other. This will ensure that we don't lose our bearings. Even if we do so for a moment, we will not be overcome by frustration or despair.'

'As we have no option but to cross this jungle, Adeeb, let's set out together,' Salma declared.

'Amen!'

'Amen!'

The echo carried back these words from all directions.

'Adeeb, this jungle is now mine and so are you.' Drawing close together, they entered the jungle, heavy with dew. Moisture-laden wild breezes swept over them and the tendrils of vegetation caressed them, seeming to drown in the turbulent waves of the Indian Ocean at Gris-Gris.

When the tide of passion had receded, they found themselves stretched out in a vast expanse of darkness. Naked, they lay on a cliff beside a beach. The restless waves of the ocean murmured, 'Mamma... mamma...'

Startled, Salma exclaimed, 'That's Sohrab's voice!'

Here on vacation, Sohrab was looking for his mother. Hastily putting on her clothes, an extremely agitated Salma stumbled off. In her hurry, she had worn her blouse inside out.

All that the adeeb could remember was the sight of Sohrab and his mother hugging each other and crying. They cried for weeks on end and their weeping abated only when the boy returned to his hostel.

Then Salma and the adeeb met again. For a long time, they sat silently on the silvery sands. At last, gazing at the sun setting over the blue waters of the ocean, the adeeb asked, 'So what shall we talk about?'

'About the first day...when we met at Lahore airport.'

'And then?'

'Each time our conversation will begin from there and end with the cliffs of Gris-Gris, where Sohrab had called out to me.' Her eyes twinkled like fireflies. 'You are my happiness and my fulfilment. If I can't say this to you, to whom shall I say it? I think I have a right to live honestly for my god, my son and myself. Where there is deceit and fraud, there is sin. I confess before my god that I wish to live with you; and I wish to live for my son. My god bears witness and knows of my desire to live an open, honest life.' With these words, Salma walked into the room. The adeeb followed her.

Sitting on the bed, he observed, 'You speak of profound matters, Salma.'

'Not profound, but urgent. The British and Jinnah Sahib had never foreseen that the partition of Hindustan would create Salmas like me. How would we be partitioned and where would we look for our honour and our hereafter?'

'Salma,' he murmured.

'Yes, Adeeb,' she replied, 'I shall live with you as Salma; with Sohrab, I shall exist as his mamma. When I pause on the steps of my house after having been with you, I will quickly open the door and hasten to change out of my clothes, so that your odour does not linger on them. I'll become Sohrab's mother then and tell myself that this is my reality. My reality, too, has been divided like Hindustan and Pakistan. Perhaps, this is the reality of all Indian Muslim women. Whether a woman belonged to this side of the border or the other, she was never whole. The Partition has diminished her even further.' Salma uttered these words sorrowfully, as she gathered the withered petals lying around the base of the flower vase.

There was a silence.

The adeeb picked up a book from the cabinet and flipped its pages.

'What book is that?' she asked.

'It's the Bible.'

'For God's sake, close it!'

A ghazal drifted into the room at the Dushrock Hotel. It brought in its wake Dushyant Kumar, Shahryar, Nida Fazli and Jagjit Singh.

'Who are you? I'm sorry, I don't know you,' Salma said.

'I'm a ghazal fresh from Hindustan. I was born from Dushyant Kumar, Shahryar and Nida Sahib. I grew up with Jagjitji.'

'Have you something to say?'

'Yes, I have. Don't worry about the political events that have divided you. You cannot imagine how terrible it has been for me. Faiz was confined on the other side. Firaq found himself alone on this one. Though I was severely castigated, I continued to survive.

I did not care to accept borders that had been forcibly imposed. The common ground of the language spoken on either side of the border saved me. On the other side, it was poets like Ahmed Faraz who protected me; my saviours here were ghazal composers like Dushyant and Shahryar. Simply cast out the sword of Partition embedded in your heart.'

'That is what I have failed to do. This sword dogs every moment of my existence—as I breathe, sleep, walk...'

'Rely on these lyrics to help you through.'

'Which lyrics are those?'

'The following: *Dhoop mein niklo, ghatao mein nahakar dekho, zindagi kya hai kitabon ko hatakar dekho*—Exult in the sunlight, bathe in the rains...and discover life beyond the confines of books.'

The words echoed around them. Salma rose and lifted a corner of the curtains at the window facing the sea. She stared at the Indian Ocean. The adeeb came and stood beside her. As they watched the waves, a ship appeared on the horizon. Then, another...and another...and another...

'What's that, Adeeb?' she asked.

'Perhaps, they are pirates...'

'Where are they headed?'

'Towards the East.'

21

Churning the waters of the Indian Ocean, these Portuguese ships moved eastwards. Mauritius was then a virgin isle and had no port facilities. In southern Africa, Vasco da Gama had run into an Indian fisherman who was now guiding him towards Hindustan.

The old man of history had launched into his narration...

The Dutch had been the first to cast anchor in Mauritius. The French and the British sailed south of the island in their hurry to reach the shores of Hindustan. Their mission was to acquire the wealth of the East. These ships did not carry astronomers out to discover the New World. On board, rather, were men who were traders, discoverers and pirates, all at the same time. Their interests were at variance with each other's. Yet, they sought destiny and wealth together. Like them, Columbus had started out in search of Bharat but had, instead, reached the shores of America. If these vessels had carried astronomers, they would have shared a common goal—the discovery of the New World. But that was not the case. They were rivals and often fought each other on sea and land.

The seventeenth century was about to dawn. It was a time when three-fourths of the industrial produce came from Bharat and China. Agriculture did not dominate Bharat's economy. The country was famous for its spices, fabrics, and wood and leather products.

Traders from the West were seeking land and sea routes to Bharat and China. It was during this era that Thomas Roe, the English trader, presented his credentials to the Emperor Jahangir one morning. Jahangir and Nurjahan, along with their palace guards and retainers, were all present. Seven envoys representing the Caliph of Turan had been put up a short distance from the fort. For days, they had been waiting for an audience with the emperor. Also waiting for an audience with Jahangir was a delegation of select traders who wanted to present the emperor with their balance sheets of trade with other countries. Waiting along with them were some senior officials of the land. The latter were men entrusted with the task of protecting and maintaining the trade routes within the realm. They also saw to the job of repairing and constructing serais that served as inns for travellers. They were accompanied by a group of munshis who kept an account of the passing caravans and collected small tithes from them. The amount of these tithes was determined after taking into consideration the number of camels or mules and cars in each caravan. Shelters had been constructed for the traders' animals and there was no shortage of water troughs along the way.

A special battalion of soldiers was maintained to provide protection to foreign traders who passed through the country along the Silk Route. Once they had entered the kingdom, these traders had no reason, therefore, to fear for their own safety or that of their merchandise. The guards who had set out from the traders' own countries to accompany them were stopped outside Bharat's borders. From this point, the emperor's soldiers took over, escorting the groups of traders through the realm to the frontiers. From there onwards, their own security guards would take charge. Thus, every year, the emperor was presented with a detailed account of the complex arrangements and smooth administration of trading facilities within the land.

Even the man in charge of the Silk Route was awaiting an audience with the emperor. The old man of history reported, 'Due to the princess's illness, the emperor was unable to spare time for visitors. But today, there is a possibility, as the princess has recovered.'

Standing in the fort's tower, Jahangir bowed his head in obeisance as the sun came up. His subjects, gathered below, chanted in unison, 'Long live the king!' Wafting in from a mandir in the background were other chants—hymns in praise of the sun.

Jahangir addressed his wife Nurjahan: 'What an exquisitely lovely sight! My father, Emperor Akbar, always worshipped the sun from this latticed window. It was my mother, Jodhabai, who had initiated him into this ritual.'

'Greeting the rising sun and bidding it farewell with evening prayers is an intrinsic part of our Hindustani traditions,' Nurjahan replied.

'Yes, Begum, it is symbolic of the new trends emerging in Hindustan. The rituals and traditions of this land are as old as nature itself. Religions here have emerged from the womb of Mother Nature who has also blessed us with the seasons and with food grains. It is these religions that bind us to her.'

An account of this exchange reached the ears of the seven envoys. It made them raise their brows and frown. One of them murmured, 'Did you hear that? Despite being followers of Islam, the perspective of these Hindustani emperors is undergoing a change.'

Pointing to the crowd gathered below, Nurjahan observed, 'Look, Your Highness. Your subjects are overwhelmed at your appearance after a long absence.'

Slogans rent the air.

'Long live the king!'

'Blessings for the recovery of the princess!'

'Long live the just Jahangir!'

'May the emperor always shower his benevolence on us.'

Then a courtier announced: 'Your Royal Highness, besides the envoys, the traders and the officials in charge of protecting the Silk Route, a few others await an audience with you. Prominent among them are two Englishmen—Thomas Roe and William Finch.'

'Thomas Roe! The man who helped my daughter recover, who reclaimed her from the jaws of death?' Jahangir inquired. 'We will shower these Englishmen with priceless gifts and rewards! Let them be brought before me.'

Moments later, these men appeared and bowed before the king. Thomas Roe stepped forward, paid his respects and said, 'Emperor, Thomas Roe stands indebted to you.'

'It is we who are indebted, Thomas Roe! You have given our daughter a fresh lease of life. What delights us still further is the discovery that you are an artiste par excellence in the sphere of music and have also brought along some exquisite paintings.'

'We treasure the happiness of the Emperor of Hindustan, Jahanpanah, Ruler of the World!'

'But, Thomas Roe, we are still at a loss as to who you really are—a hakim or an artiste?' Roe looked reverentially at the king who continued, 'And it is also imperative for us to know why Thomas Roe has come all this way from his far-off land.'

'This humble man you see before you happens to be a trader, Your Royal Highness. He has come here for the sake of furthering trade between his country and yours. Alampanah, the inhabitants of England wish to establish trading ties with your subjects.'

'We grant you this wish. Hindustan's traders and its men of means are capable of conducting all kinds of trade.'

'Your Royal Highness, this humble man seeks a detailed exchange with you on the subject.'

'Yes, I understand. The empress will give it some thought. Now, there are other issues at hand I need to address.' With these words, Jahangir turned in the direction of the court and left with his courtiers. The Empress Nurjahan said, 'His Royal Highness and I are deeply indebted to you. What is it you desire?'

'O Great Empress, around 1600, a few traders like us had established a trading company. For its sake...' Thomas Roe paused.

'Why do you falter? Speak boldly, without fear.'

'Empress, we wish to establish a factory at the trading port of Surat for our East India Company.'

'Factory? I don't understand...'

'It means setting up a warehouse where we can store our merchandise.'

'Is that all you desire? Your wish is granted.'

The minister of trade, however, cautioned her: 'Royal Empress, the trading vessels from Portugal also anchor at Surat with our permission. Please think this over carefully.'

Thomas Roe interjected, 'O Royal Empress, we have nothing to do with the Portuguese. Holding you in the highest esteem, we merely wish to avail of the facilities at port towns like Surat and Machhlipattam to earn our bread.'

'It is our pleasure to grant you these trading facilities.'

*

In the meantime, the seven envoys had had an audience with Emperor Jahangir. Then they held secret parleys with the realm's wealthy and powerful personages. One of the envoys had declared, 'It is highly inappropriate that nationalism supersede religion, that attachment to Hindustan override devotion to Islam. You, gentlemen, should keep a vigilant eye on these developments. More important than national interests is devotion to one's faith.'

Grieved by these words, Time took a deep breath. Suddenly, leaves began to wither away. Without so much as a fire in sight, they crackled and crumbled into cinders. The birds became agitated. They could not comprehend why nature had reduced their nests to ashes. Those fledglings that had learnt to fly were led away from their nests by their mothers and flew about aimlessly. The others all perished in their eggs or in their nests. Their frantic cries, as they tried to escape death, rang out over creation. Their scorched and broken wings lay strewn over the whole world.

Then the seasons changed. The sun made its appearance. The moon shone in the sky. Grain sprouted in the fields. Festivals were celebrated. The earth sang. Everyone bathed in the rains of Asadh.

But a century later, Time took a deep breath again and the leaves started wilting on the trees once more.

Then, from somewhere, came the voice of the old man of history. 'Birds!' he exclaimed, 'have patience. We are aware of what has taken place and where. Do not fret. Any thought that negates humanitarian principles and operates in the name of religion is capable of having an incendiary effect on other lines of thought. But, it can never reduce these thoughts to ashes. Otherwise, people like Kabir and Nanak and other sants and Sufis would never have been born.'

His words gave the birds hope. The voice continued, 'Even in Hindustan, Islam became the victim of a kind of outdated Islamic Brahminvad, controlled by the vested interests of priests. Born out of Islam's spiritual leanings, Sufi liberalism was rejected outright by these radical Islamic "Brahmins". In Hindustan, the priests moulded Islam into the Hindu system of caste. How else can one explain why none of the Hindustanis who embraced Islam after reciting the kalmah rose above the lowly ranks of *khadim* and *chobdar* during the reign of the Mughals? This was the insidious caste system their dynasty perpetuated and with disastrous results. The Mughals ended up being deprived of cooperation from the country's native Muslims. Earlier, a similar caste system had destroyed the Hindus. Just as the Dalits of the Hindu community had never supported its Kshatriyas, native Muslim Dalits withheld their support to the Mughal Kshatriyas. This Islamic Brahminvad resulted in Akbar's endeavours coming to naught and dealt a severe blow to Jahangir's reign. Shahjahan became its victim, but Aurangzeb who followed, perpetuated it in the name of Islam. He became a Muslim "Brahmin" who gave precedence to religion over humanitarian concerns.'

'This is an utter lie!' interrupted another voice.

The argument over what was true and what was not had just begun, when a boat that had obviously gone astray, cast anchor at the jetty of the Dushrock Hotel. Salma and the adeeb thought they recognized the boatman. His face seemed familiar, but his condition made recognition somewhat difficult. Salma said, 'I think it's your peon.'

'Yes, you're right. How did he get here?'

'I had to come here, sir. Once you took on the responsibility of trying to make sense of the wounds inflicted on civilization, you forfeited the freedom of enjoying your private life.'

'What has transpired in these last few moments that makes you come looking for me?'

'A few moments? Each passing moment weighs so heavily on the world as to defy description. Afghanistan has turned into a graveyard. Based in Lebanon, Pakistan's Murtaza Bhutto plots to make rivers of blood flow in his homeland. He demands from his sister Benazir a share in his father's political legacy. Kurds in Iraq are involved in a struggle to create their own little Pakistan. Saddam Hussein has bombed their territory. Western powers have liberated Kuwait from Iraq. And you ask me, what has transpired? Corpses litter Afghanistan. While you relax here, the world is wrecked by destruction and the dead die a second time, waiting for the court to resume its session,' explained the peon.

His revelations made Salma feel as though she had sinned. When she looked at the adeeb, he tried to assuage her feelings of guilt by replying, 'We are not simply relaxing. From this place, we have identified the vessels of the Portuguese, the Spaniards, the French and the British. They sailed by, in hot pursuit of each other.'

'Well, that's all right, then. Following their individual charted routes, they are all headed towards the East. I wanted to give you this bit of news centuries ago. Only the East is aware of the saga in which these ships played a vital part. History waits to peruse this record. If you can just meet the dying corpses for now...' The peon lapsed into silence.

Salma understood the reason for the peon's silence. She looked up at the adeeb and said, 'Khuda hafiz.'

'What do you mean?' he asked with a start.

'It's time for me to go. Whenever you call out to me, I shall return.'

'But why...why are you going away?'

'I have to. Otherwise, Time will never forgive you. Before leaving, I have just one request. You must see Sara Shagufta of

Pakistan before resuming the court hearings. After committing suicide, her restless spirit roams the earth.'

'Sara Shagufta?'

'Yes...and now I must take leave. Khuda hafiz.'

'Khuda hafiz,' the adeeb responded sadly.

Greatly relieved, the peon took a deep breath.

The adeeb was lost in thought. He had never met Sara. Yet, her face was among the many that shimmered before him. He knew that she was an exceedingly beautiful woman and a fearless poet, that tears rolled out from one of her eyes and sparks flew from the other. She had paid the price of her desires and her dreams with her life.

'Where is Sara Shagufta right now?' he asked the peon.

'At this moment, she's in Hauz Khas, Delhi, at the residence of Amrita Pritam.'

'At Amritaji's place?'

'Yes. Where else could she be? Asia has only one institution for tears and words—that's Amrita Pritam's house.'

It did not take him long to reach Hauz Khas from the Dushrock Hotel. Having arrived at his destination, he greeted Sara with the words, 'O Asia's Foremost Poet and Lady, when did you arrive from Pakistan?'

'I'm not Sara Shagufta. I'm Amrita Pritam,' explained the woman standing in front of him. 'Sara is in the next room, counting her tears. I'll fetch her.'

Another woman appeared before him. The adeeb was startled and blurted out, 'Arrey, Salma. You were with me in Mauritius a while ago. How come you're here?'

'Adeeb, I'm not Salma. I'm Sara Shagufta.'

It was Amrita Pritam who dispelled the adeeb's confusion, 'All women look alike once they've been through the experience of motherhood. It's hard to spot any difference between them. Please make yourself comfortable. I'll send in some lemon tea for you.'

As he sat down, the adeeb told Sara, 'The entire brotherhood of scholars salutes you. I've read *Aankh*, your collection of poems. Your conclusion there is the very last word in poetry—the *harf-e-akhirat*.'

'No,' said Sara, 'there will be no tears left to shed on the day the last word of poetry is written. Desolation will overwhelm the human race. My last lines are a dirge for a mother's tears.' Even after exhaling her last breath following her suicide, Sara continued to breathe.

The lemon tea arrived.

'I speak of the time when someone was trying to breathe in my womb. A life was asking to be born. I moaned in pain to give birth to it. My landlady heard me. She got me admitted to hospital, put a five-rupee note in my hand, and returned home. I gave birth to a son. It was a bitterly cold night. There wasn't even a towel available in the hospital to wrap my son in. The nurse had laid him in the crook of my arm for five minutes. He had stared at me with his bright eyes, and then...I don't know what happened...what thoughts went through his mind. He simply closed his eyes and went to sleep forever.'

The adeeb looked at Sara with sorrow and alarm.

She continued, 'Since then not just a pair, but thousands of his eyes have taken root in my body. They blink. They stare at me. They plead for a shroud...and then, they vanish. It had taken him just a few moments to realize that this world was not worth living in. All I had was five rupees. I sought permission for my discharge from the hospital. I was refused—firstly, because I was in no condition to go home; secondly, because my son's body lay there.'

'Go on, Sara Shagufta...'

'I had to make arrangements to clear my hospital expenses and organize my son's burial.'

'And then?'

'I was running a high fever—a hundred and three degrees. The hospital was demanding money. I told them, "Keep my son as security. I'll take him away only after paying you." The man at the hospital had looked unconvinced. I insisted, "I won't run away. I will come back." What was truly remarkable was that everyone believed me. They believed that a mother would always return to claim her child—whether he was dead or alive. When I left, I felt my breasts bursting with milk. Once I arrived home, I squeezed the milk out into a glass and was putting it away, when a number of poets and scholars arrived to offer their condolences. For a long time, they stared at the glass in silence. Then they plunged into their usual conversation—about Freud, Rimbaud, Saadi, Camus, Kafka and Allama Iqbal. They'd forgotten about my dead son.'

'And?'

'And then...I reclaimed his body.'

'Go on...'

'Look, sir, the corpse of Sara Shagufta's son still lies in her lap,' the peon cried.

It was from this moment that the bazaars of corpses were thrown open. A huge heap of Pakistani soldiers lay dead, killed during their peace mission in Somalia. The bodies of Muslims slaughtered in Bosnia were being wrapped in shrouds, in preparation for burial. A market of corpses was opened in Azerbaijan, where jackals, dogs and birds of prey tore at them. Bodies were being identified in Nigeria, while others in Bolivia waited to have accounts of their martyrdom read out. Corpses of both Kashmiri Muslims and Pandits waited to register their statements. There was a dearth of burial space for the corpses in Afghanistan. Incredile though it seemed, despite their defeat at the hands of the Taliban, Ghulam Rabbani, Ahmad Shah Masood and Gulbuddin Hekmatyar stood proudly on the piles of corpses that had once been their own supporters. Mohammed Umar, the Taliban tyrant, stood on a similar mound of his own supporters. All these men wore the crown of Islam on their heads.

At this point, a corpse came running forward and shrieked, 'O Adeeb! Afghanistan has been turned into a graveyard in the name of Islam. This shameless lot stands proud, flaunting the crown of Islam on its head, but has anyone taken the trouble to find out what has befallen ordinary Muslims like us? Thousands of us have been butchered! The robes of these four men are drenched in our blood! The entire country has been devastated!'

The corpse was interrupted by the arrival of a moaning Babar.

'O Adeeb,' he began, 'I'd returned to my grave with your permission, but the incessant noise of bombardment made it difficult for me to lie in peace. Now, even ancient corpses like us have to flee Afghanistan, as our graves have been desecrated. Corpses lie rotting in the open like overripe mulberries. The sour stench of putrefying flesh has even driven away carnivorous beasts. Afghanistan is dead; my Kabul is gone. In the name of Islam's wrath, my city stands in ruins.'

'Babar, how dare you even raise the issue? You yourself had wrought similar devastation in Hindustan in the name of Islam,' challenged Rana Sanga, emerging from the pages of a history book.

'No, you're mistaken. For me, Hindustan was not the land of Hindus, but the land of gold. In your Hindustan, grains of gold flowed in the Sindhu river. You are illiterate. Have you any idea what the Greek Herodotus has written? The Raja of Sindh had had tons of this gold mined. He had traded it with Cyrus, the King of Pharis. I desperately wanted to acquire this golden goose called Hindustan. I needed to have a powerful kingdom. My enemy happened to be Agra's Muslim ruler Ibrahim Lodi, not the Hindus of Hindustan. And have you forgotten that you, along with Lodi's uncle Daulat Khan, the subedar of Punjab, had sent me a message?'

'You bear false witness, Babar!' Rana Sanga shouted back. 'Like Mohammed bin Qasim and Mahmud Ghazni, you too had come to wage war on the kafirs! You came to spread Islam by the power of your sword!'

'It is arguments like these,' observed the adeeb, 'that change the parameters of social, religious and historical realities, and lead to disunity, ostracism and ill will in the future. The vanquished deliberately erase truth and memory. They record in word and deed a history warped to suit their own perspective.'

Expressions of concurrence and disagreement with the views being expressed flickered across the faces of his audience. The adeeb continued, 'On the other hand, when the victors are confronted by these collective realities, they take up the weapon of religion. By incorporating religion into statecraft, they go to the extremes of selfish opportunism. This is the reality underlying the initial offensives carried out during the early years of the Middle Ages.'

'This is an incomplete picture,' interrupted Rana Sanga. 'It is

not the whole truth. Ask this man Babar, why, if he had no
objections to religious conversion, did his mullahs honour him with
the title of Ghazi?'

'Before that, I wish to put a question to Rana Sanga,' Babar
interjected coldly. 'Did he want me to convert Hindus into Muslims
when he, along with Daulat Khan Lodi, invited me to attack
Hindustan?'

'I never sent Babar any such invitation!' came the wrathful
reply.

'My autobiography, the *Babarnama*, has your invitation on
record. This document goes back to the sixteenth century. Why did
you not raise your objections at the time? During the centuries that
followed, why did your descendants fail to take issue with it?'

'I don't accept your Islam!' came the enraged reply.

'Whether you accept it or not, time, evidence and history stand
witness. You offered me a longed-for opportunity. I wasn't foolish
enough to let it go and give up the golden goose. This was where
the seeds of our enmity were sown. To run the kingdom, I required
religiously inclined Muslims and loyal Hindus.'

'And so you bestowed on yourself the title of Ghazi?' the adeeb
taunted.

'The circumstances then were different,' replied Babar. 'My
warriors, who came from Kandahar, Khorasan, Badakshan, Tajikistan
and northern Iran and had fought many battles, were exhausted.
They were unable to adapt themselves to the climate of Hindustan.
Heat, scorching winds, blinding sandstorms and profuse perspiration
had made them break out in sores and boils. They were in a pitiable
state. The rains reopened their old wounds. Trapped in these
circumstances, all they wanted was to return home. They had even
pleaded with me to go back to Farghana after handing over the
kingdom to a representative subedar. But for me to take such a
course of action would have been both impossible and inappropriate.
I had to take recourse to means that would compel them to stay
back. The lure of wealth and position had failed to work its magic.
Religion was all I had to fall back on. I wanted to stay on in
Hindustan. That's why I was buried at Agra. It was only later that

my body was exhumed and taken to Kabul and radical Muslims declared me a Ghazi.'

Rana Sanga wanted to intervene, but the adeeb stopped him. Instead, he ordered that Mohammed bin Qasim be produced before him.

In a flash, the peon went to the capital city of Caliph Al-Walid and returned with Mohammed bin Qasim. Around twenty-four years old, this young man was made to stand before the court. On the way, the peon had already told Qasim why he had been summoned. The young man paid his respects to the court and gave his statement: 'Honourable Court, with all due respect, I wish to state that I am an Arab. Hajjaz was the master of my tribe and the honourable Al-Walid, our caliph. In those days, innumerable stories abounded of the wealth of Hind. Our own lives revolved around dates, deserts and sandstorms. Our tribe had recently embraced Islam. We only knew about adopting religion; we knew nothing about conversion. I was only seventeen years old at the time. I had absolutely no idea of how one could convert to another religion. The accusation that I converted the people of Hind to Islam at the point of a sword is absolutely baseless.'

'Then why had you come to Hindustan?' the court inquired.

'Sir, it was Hajjaz who sent me to plunder Hind. He had even given me a loan to help me carry out this venture. The understanding was that I would return the loan, along with an annual tax of five lakh dinars, after helping to establish his rule in the fertile region of the Hind river. He also made me privy to a special secret. Sir, when we go to war, even our children take up arms. Hajjaz told me that in Hind, this was not the case. In keeping with tradition, only Kshatriyas fought wars. If the Kshatriyas lost, everyone conceded defeat. This, in fact, proved to be true. When Raja Dahar lost, everyone surrendered, even the Hindu Brahmins and Buddhists. I pillaged the overflowing coffers of their mandirs and viharas. These Brahmins then informed me, sir, that Jibavan, the subedar of Kashmir's maharaja, had built a grand mandir on a lake east of Multan. The treasure of the Hindus was usually buried under mandirs. In the lake mandir, I discovered gold hidden in forty strongrooms under the building. Before breaking into these rooms, I had smashed the idols in the mandir. They yielded a hundred tons of gold. The rooms below the mandir yielded another thirteen thousand two hundred tons. Why, then, should I have refrained from demolishing mandirs?'

The court listened to him, mesmerized.

'At that time, Your Honour, people did not have faith in one Allah. Every Brahmin had a different god. When one god plundered, none of the others came to his rescue. Circumstances such as these helped me immensely in my quest. For me, the Hindu/non-Hindu issue never arose. From the mouth of the Hind river, I made my victorious way through Taxila right up to Kangra, killing and looting Buddhists and Brahmins as I went.'

As Mohammed bin Qasim was relating his story, a tremendous din rose in Kashmir. Tajikistan screamed. American bombings over Iraq resembled a fireworks display. Bosnian Serbs attacked Muslims again. The 3000 Sri Lankans Pirabhakaran had killed, groaned from beneath the ground where they lay buried. In the name of jihad, terrorists from Saudi Arabia, Sudan, Afghanistan and Pakistan had killed, torched, abducted, tortured and looted innocent citizens in Doda, Udhampur and Kulu–Manali.

At this moment, the voice of the wounded from Karachi called out. 'Listen to us, O Honourable Court,' it said. 'Based in London, the mohajir Altaf Hussain spews venom to create rifts in our land. The same powers that partitioned Hindustan are out to split Pakistan.'

The adeeb cried, 'Listen, you citizens of Karachi! Forget that which has already been broken. Don't allow whatever you have retrieved from the rubble to splinter again. The more nations you create, the more fragmented mankind becomes. This world has been unnecessarily divided into a myriad segments. For God's sake, control this urge to divide and destroy!'

'But it is imperative that we undo the wrong already done in the past,' boomed the voice of the Sindhi leader Dr Halepotha. 'Or else the massacres and bloodletting will never come to an end. In the name of religion, civilization is becoming insatiably bloodthirsty. Look at the fate that befell our Sindhi community. For centuries, we were independent. Our language, culture, philosophy and civilization stand apart from that of these Pakistanis. We, forty million Sindhis have been demanding the right to self-determination. We were deceived in 1947. Read the announcement made in Lahore in 1940. It promised the Sindhis local self-rule, but after the creation of Pakistan, the political agenda changed. Puppet administrators and military dictators reneged on the promise made. This led to the break-up of Pakistan when the Bangladeshis created their own Pakistan. Now, we want Azad Sindh, our own independent nation, because Sindhi Muslims and Sindhi Hindus share the same language, history, culture and civilization.'

*

Three people were sitting in a room of the Hotel Kanishka. They were G.M. Syed, founder of the Jiye Sindh movement, Baal Kavi Bairagi and Rameshwar Nikhra. Syed was saying, 'Dr Halepotha is right. Sindhi civilization is distinctly different, being a confluence of Islam and the Vedic religions. It is a fact that in 1943, I had, as a member of the Muslim League, presented the proposal for Bharat's partition in the Sindh Assembly. Two years later, perceiving the element of hatred that marked Pakistani ideology, I had grown suspicious. I was wary of Jinnah, as I had seen him run a campaign of hatred against Hindus. There was a possibility of him running a similar campaign against Sindhis in the future. It was with such misgivings that I had grudgingly welcomed the formation of Pakistan in 1947.'

A question crashed into their midst like a stone: 'If you believe that Sindhi Hindus and Muslims share a common language, culture and civilization, why is it that so many years after Partition, Bharat's Sindhi Hindus hate you so much?'

'This is quite untrue. It was certainly our fault that Partition was allowed to become a reality. But even in those terrible times, Sindh did not witness any killings. We had silently acknowledged our grievous mistake and with heavy hearts, bade our departing Hindu brethren farewell. Hindus leaving Sindh did so with a sense of security so powerful that they even took their parrot cages along with them. Sindhi Muslims revealed no resentment towards their Hindu brothers. If at all any resentment surfaced, it came from Punjabi Muslims who had settled in Sindh. These Muslims were as ignorant then, as they are today. We Sindhis were at odds with them in those days, just as we are today. It's a perpetual battle we're engaged in—not for our religion, but for our culture.'

'All you've said has been calculated to stir passions, but the real issue is quite different,' interrupted the question that had so violently intruded into their discussion.

'Yes, the issue is that at the time of Partition, non-Sindhis constituted only eleven per cent of the population in Sindh. Thirteen lakh Hindus had fled Pakistan. Today, non-Sindhis, constituting forty-eight per cent of the population, breathe down our necks. Inevitably, it's a lifelong battle we're engaged in now.'

'This implies that you are fighting the legacy of Mohammed Ali Jinnah and poet Allama Iqbal, one of Pakistan's founding fathers,' said the question, now turning over.

'Yes, we are and that is hardly a legacy. It is merely a region plundered in the name of religion and described as a nation. This nation has to break up; no power on earth can prevent it. All that bloodshed took place because of Jinnah's weakness, Mountbatten's conspiracy and Iqbal's despairing verses. Jinnah was obsessed with immortalizing himself in the pages of history. The price that was paid for his obsession is there for all to see. Iqbal was a talented poet, but his constant struggle to obliterate his Hindu heritage, turned him into a dangerously bigoted man.'

'Syed Sahib, this court cannot tolerate the derogatory words you have used in referring to a great poet like Iqbal.'

'I beg your pardon,' Ghulam Murtaza Syed said in respectful tones. 'I hold this court in high esteem. I wasn't aware of the fact that I stood before the tribunal of an adeeb. All I know is that I've come to Bharat after thirty-eight years and I'm sitting with Baal Kavi Bairagi and Rameshwar Nikhra in my room in Delhi's Kanishka Hotel.'

'The "personal" has no place for people in public life,' came the adeeb's rejoinder. 'They are considered to be ever-present in the court of the people. If their personal opinions run contrary to their public stance, they have no moral right to continue in public life.'

'But, sir, my perspective has not shifted. You will acknowledge that there's a difference between opinion and advice. There is no contradiction between my personal and public views, but the poet Iqbal has corrupted his poetry. Initially, he wrote *Saare jahan se achcha, Hindostan hamara*. Nothing in the world, he declared, could surpass Hindustan. By revising his lines, hasn't he made a mockery of the poet's ethics? By writing *Chin-o-Arab hamara, Hindostan hamara, Muslim hain hum, watan hai Hindostan hamara*, the same man went on to assert that the entire world was the legacy of Muslims. Sir, I'd like to know which ethical principles guide his poetry. Do you scholars and writers have scruples or do you consider yourselves to be above the law?'

For a minute, the court held consultations with the peon and Sara Shagufta. Then the peon went and silently stood in a corner. The adeeb said, 'Syed Sahib, every individual is a court. Whether or not one is an adeeb, one cannot evade one's responsibility as a court. But this particular court considers the cases of people whose souls died while they lived or lay dying. It also arranges to bring before it those individuals who have in the past posed a threat to the few who wished to live in peace, and continue to do so now and will not hesitate to do so in the future.'

His words invited a silent applause from the peon.

'Sir, I was referring to the same danger. Jinnah and Iqbal are responsible for instigating people to think along dangerous lines. I'm not concerned about the poet in Iqbal. A poet is one who understands the spiritual suffering of the world. What kind of a poet is he who pushes folk into the river of suffering? Even Bulle Shah and Kabir were poets, but Iqbal has manipulated his poetry to make torrents of blood flow. He was the one to declare that Muslims alone had a claim to God. Before Iqbal made his claim, God belonged to everyone—to Hindus and Muslims, to Meera, Kabir and Nanak; to Tagore, Subramanya Bharati and Nazrul Islam. He belonged to Sant Raidas and Gyaneshwar. Khuda was everyone's god. It was Iqbal who committed the sin of confining Him to masjids. Jinnah and Iqbal were the devils of the century...the most notorious devils!' lashed out Syed Sahib.

A stunned silence prevailed.

'Sir, I wish to visit Mahatma Gandhi's samadhi and light a candle there,' came G.M. Syed's request.

'You may go,' the peon said after consulting the scholar.

The voices of Karachi's terror-stricken people angrily responded, 'Does this mean that whatever Altaf Hussain is doing in Sindh is right?'

'No, it certainly isn't. While this court considers Pakistan's unity to be vital to its welfare and grants it top priority, it also believes that the passions sparked to bring Pakistan into existence were both misguided and dangerous. What the mohajir Altaf Hussain is doing is reprehensible. If his ideology is not nipped in the bud, the coming centuries will be witness to a bestial world. Our planet will become a graveyard, with each individual trying to establish a grave built out of his own ideology that he calls his Pakistan. What shape will the coming centuries assume?' the adeeb raved. 'Altaf Hussain and Dr Halepotha have no right to drown the citizens of Pakistan in a river of blood.'

'The Punjabi dictatorship of Pakistan cannot snatch away the aspirations of Pakistanis like me! These aspirations lie not in our hands, but in our hearts!'

'That is the greatest danger. O Altaf, strive to prevent the impulses of the heart from being transformed into weapons of destruction. Allow divine benevolence and human sensitivities a chance to thrive in the human heart. If you nourish it on the kind of aspirations that lead to bloodshed, Pakistan will become a wasteland whose desolation will engulf all countries, cultures and civilizations. So, Altaf Hussain, try to understand the basic conflicts of mankind and don't open the doors to military dictatorship in Pakistan. Today, courage is a slave to materialism. All soldiers and civilians today rely on courage inspired by materialistic instincts. Absorb this truth and try to break free of a world of personal suffering and hatred. Lend your hand in creating a just society in Pakistan.'

'We must avenge ourselves!' shouted the enraged Altaf Hussain.

'We created Pakistan, not these Punjabis, Baluchis, Sindhis and Pashtuns. We Muslims from Avadh and Bihar have paid the price for creating Pakistan. We are the real Pakistanis and we have to settle scores with these fraudulent ones.'

'Altaf Hussain, liberate people from the compulsions of revenge, hatred and bloodshed, so that in the centuries to come, future generations are not led astray by misconceptions.' There was a sudden disturbance in the court. The peon had stormed in, bringing with him Saddam Hussein whom he was trying to restrain.

'Sir, this is Saddam Hussein of Iraq. He was making such a racket, raving and ranting!'

'What is the matter, Saddam Hussein?' asked the court.

'Honourable Adeeb, today happens to mark the anniversary of the end of the war between Iraq and Iran.'

'That's good news.'

'No,' replied Saddam, 'it is not. Because on this day even as we celebrate peace, America, Saudi Arabia and Iran have pledged, for their own vested interests, to destroy us.'

'But why would they do so? After all, Saudi Arabia and Iran are Islamic nations. How can there be enmity between countries that share a religious faith?'

'Shiite Iran is bent on establishing a regime that is opposed to Sunni Arabs. It wants to appropriate Islam. Therefore, it opposes my regime and my leadership. In Iranian veins flow Aryan blood, which refuses to recognize Arabs and Sunnis.'

'But, Saddam Hussein, Saudi Arabia has more Arabs than your own country does and it is also Sunni. So, why does it withhold its support to you?'

'Because it suspects that we Arabs from the Dajla-Furat valley are, primarily, Aryans. It is for this reason that Saudi Arabia and its cohorts spurn us. Though we are all Sunnis, the Arabs consider our lineage to be different from the Arab–Islamic one.'

The peon interrupted. 'Sir,' he protested, 'you've got entangled in all kinds of digressions, while the centuries stand waiting for a hearing. Hitler is here. Mohammed bin Qasim has been waiting from the eighth century onwards, while Mahmud Ghazni has been ready with all his evidence from the tenth century. Babar of the fifteenth century was interrupted before he could finish what he had to say. In front of the closing gates of the seventeenth century, stands Aurangzeb, awaiting his turn. Salma, who departed after bidding you farewell, endeavours to halt this important court's functioning and wants you back in her life. Your friend Bhawani Sengupta has got back from the Iranian capital Tehran and wishes to speak to you urgently. I await your orders. Whom shall I summon first?'

'Look, my friend. Not only has Bhawani Sengupta returned from Tehran today, but Hindustan has lost Nurul Hasan, one of its greatest sons. My heart is overcome by grief and I need a break.'

'Oh...that's all right, then.'

'Just pacify everyone. Request Bhawani Sengupta to pay a visit some other time. Shahin will have to wait a little longer. Mohammed bin Qasim is free to go back if he so wishes. Mahmud Ghazni must be ready with his account of all that he plundered. Tell Babar not to bother about the bombardment by the Taliban. Once you have made these announcements, tell Aurangzeb to appear in this court in a short while.'

22

As Aurangzeb peacefully slept in his grave at Daulatabad, the peon rapped on it softly.

'Who is trying to rouse me?' Aurangzeb's voice asked from the grave.

'Honourable sir,' the peon replied, 'the future wishes to speak to you.'

'Well, go on.'

'A thousand pardons, King of Kings! Times and legal procedures have changed. Now you must appear in the court of an adeeb.'

'What? An adeeb...you mean a poet? Such people belong to the clan of singers, the *mirasis*. In my time, I had expelled them not only from the durbar, but from the kingdom itself.'

'Today, Time has rendered you irrelevant. That is why you have been summoned.'

'All right,' agreed Aurangzeb, rising from his grave. The earth shook. The waters in the rivers retreated to facilitate his movement. And Aurangzeb set out with the peon. After crossing Burhanpur, he halted at Dharmat. It seemed as though Time itself had paused here. 'On these plains of Dharmat I had faced the army of Raja Jaswant Singh, Dara Shikoh's sipahsalar,' Aurangzeb mused. 'It was Dara's way of preventing me from meeting Hazrat.'

'Hazrat...?' asked the peon.

'That was Abba-huzoor, my honourable father—Shahjahan, King of Kings,' Aurangzeb explained. 'He was fretting over his kidney problem at the time. From Bijapur, I had set off for Burhanpur. In the course of the battle with Jaswant Singh at Dharmat, thousands were killed. Corpses littered the field. The earth was slushy with blood. Today, fields of grain flourish on this blood-soaked plain. And what a pleasant sight it is!'

All of a sudden, four shadows materialized before Aurangzeb and bowed to him. 'So, it's you!' he exclaimed, recognizing them. 'Kazim Shirazi Sahib and Mohammed Saqi Mustad Khan Sahib...Ah there! Khafi Khan Sahib and Aqil Khan Sahib! It is, indeed, my good fortune to have come across historians like you at the precise moment that I was due to appear before the court of Time.'

'In fact, that is why we are here.'

'I have made a special effort to bring along Aqil Khan, the author of *Vaqaat-e-Alamgiri*,' Kazim Shirazi declared. 'He is not one of those historians accused of being a royal lackey.'

'Your Honour, let us proceed,' the peon urged.

When Aurangzeb appeared before the court, the adeeb could only gaze at him in amazement. Aurangzeb, a slim, attractive man of medium build who stooped, nevertheless, under the burden of age and accusations. He had an aquiline Aryan nose, a fine, sculpted face and a trim white beard that set off his olive complexion and enhanced his appeal. He wore a pristine white angarkha and a glittering jewel in his turban.

Aurangzeb cast the adeeb a hostile look. Several pigeons soared up into the sky as the adeeb stared back at him intently.

Aurangzeb stood with his retinue of historians. The peon brought him a chair. In a manner befitting royalty, the emperor seated himself.

'Alamgir!' the adeeb called out. 'Many charges have been levelled against you. The most serious of them describes you as a bigoted ruler and a radical Sunni. That is why you destroyed the Shia kingdoms of Golconda, Bijapur, Khandesh, Birar and Ahmednagar, it is alleged. You are also accused of persecuting your Hindu subjects, converting them to Islam under duress, banning their festivals and demolishing their mandirs. You fought with the Marathas who could have been your greatest allies. You had your father, Shahjahan, thrown into prison and your brothers, Dara Shikoh and Murad, murdered. You sent Shuja into exile and ascended the bloodied throne of Hindustan. You conceived Hindustan as the Dar-ul-Harab and wanted to convert it into Dar-ul-Islam. Like a radical Muslim, you blurred the distinction between statecraft and religion.'

Aurangzeb sat very still in his chair.

A procession of people passed by, abusing him loudly.

'He was the first ruler to impose curbs on a man's religion!' yelled one.

'To ascend the throne, this man became an abject slave of the mullahs,' accused another. 'He sought the sanction of radical ulemas to have his brother, Dara Shikoh, killed, so that none could accuse him of the heinous crime. To achieve his predetermined goal, he needed the support of religion and it was, in fact, during his reign that religion began making incursions into every sphere of life. He became a disciple of the Naqshbandiya school and made Sheikh Sirhindi's grandson a permanent fixture in his court.'

'He humiliated musicians and poets like us, though we were Muslims.'

'He banished astrologers like us from his court, because we were Hindus.'

'Mughal emperors were faithful to the tradition of participating in the festivities of Dussehra and Eid, but following the defeat of Maharaja Jaswant Singh of Jodhpur, Aurangzeb held himself aloof from such festivities.'

'More importantly, Your Honour, he abolished the prevailing

practice that required the emperor to bless the Hindu rajas who ascended the throne in their kingdoms by applying tilak on their foreheads.'

'Besides, learned adeeb, he did not even spare the Muslims. He issued an order that forbade Muslim men from growing their beards longer than the width of four fingers. Barbers went around the country executing this order, making life hell for ordinary Muslims like us.'

'Moreover, sir!' shouted a man, staggering about drunkenly, 'he banned alcohol! People like me were publicly whipped for partaking of our favourite beverage. Claiming that the *Diwan-e-Hafiz* was instrumental in encouraging the craving for alcohol, he banned the book from the madrasas. His lackey, Mohammed Fazil, even entered the estate of Ramsingh Gaur, the jagirdar of Rajnagar, and smashed all the vessels and leather bags that contained alcohol. For two whole days, gutters flowed with alcohol, while we sat gazing at it thirstily.'

'Peon, throw this drunkard out of the court!' the adeeb commanded.

'So, you too, have decided to behave like Aurangzeb, have you?' slurred the drunken man. 'But don't forget, it was this same man who allowed his foreign gunners to drink to their heart's content. On the other hand, his finance minister, Raja Raghunath, had imposed restrictions on the cultivation of the intoxicant, bhang. Just can't make sense of these strange, incomprehensible orders.'

'Honourable sir, we are Sufis. This deranged king forbade the singing of hymns on the birth anniversary of the Holy Prophet of Islam. Another of his lackeys, the daroga Mirza Baqar, launched a murderous attack on us at the shrine of the Sufi sage, Sheikh Yahya Chishti, in Ahmedabad. The emperor was a mere puppet in the hands of the ulemas and mullahs of his court and he regarded everyone, with the sole exception of himself, as a kafir.'

'Sir, we too, have a petition. We are impoverished potters who used to make clay toys during the festivals observed by all faiths. We moulded birds and beasts, men and women, out of clay. This king decreed that no toys should ever be made in his kingdom.'

'Honourable adeeb, we are Bohra Muslims. Most of us are Shias.

This king installed Sunni imams and muezzins in our masjids.'

'Apart from these measures, he also imposed restrictions on the rituals of Muharram. Even revered Sufis and sages were not spared. He had no qualms about humiliating holy men like Bengal's dervish, Syed Niamatullah, Kashmir's Mullah Shah Badakshi, a disciple of Miyan Mir, and Allahabad's Sheikh Muhibullah. He had dozens of Muslims beheaded. Sir, his was a reign of terror. Each day, we waited with trepidation for some utterly irrational proclamation to be issued. Ever-present in his court was a coterie of callow mullahs and maulvis, whose superficial interpretations of the scriptures guided the king. These men trapped the greatness of Islam within the walls of their selfish interests, with the king blindly following their dictates. He put his seal of approval on all kinds of torture and did not spare Muslims like us. We have little understanding, sir, of the kind of Islam he propagated.'

The court addressed the emperor. 'Aurangzeb!' it challenged, 'what have you to say to these allegations?'

'What do I have to say?' Aurangzeb retorted disdainfully. 'I choose not to counter any of these charges. I did what I believed was right. After all, I was the emperor. I know perfectly well that I stand accused of many crimes—the seven-year incarceration of my father, the assassination of my brothers, the downfall of the Muslim kingdoms of the Deccan, the persecution of Hindus and the wanton destruction of their mandirs as well as the downfall of the Mughal dynasty which I precipitated by waging war against the Marathas. I don't wish to advance any argument in my defence. Accompanying me are respected historians of my era. Ask them whatever questions you have in mind...let them corroborate the facts.'

'These men were historians at his court,' came the voice of a Rajput warrior. 'They were not given the licence to think or write independently. Whatever they placed on record was done under the supervision and patronage of the state. I served as Aurangzeb's mansabdar and in that capacity was given the command of four thousand men. I had to put up with the likes of historians such as these.'

'Who are you?' the court inquired.

'Sir, I'm Rao Chhatrasal Bundela of Malwa. At the beginning of the eighteenth century, the king had given me the mansabdari of four thousand soldiers, because I had fought battles for almost two decades. Force of circumstance had compelled me to take up this responsibility. But, that's another story. Don't trust his historians. *Alamgir-Nama, Mathir-e-Alamgiri, Muntakhabul-Lubab* and *Waqat-e-Alamgiri* are all accounts written by his slaves. These versions of history are thoroughly unreliable.'

'You can describe us as "state historians",' conceded Kazim Shirazi, 'but you cannot claim that Aqil Khan is one of our breed. His *Waqat-e-Alamgiri* was written clandestinely. Sir, you can rely on the authenticity of his account, at least.'

'No!' thundered another voice, as an impressive Rajput elder materialized before them.

'And who may you be?'

'Raja Jaswant Singh, the maharaja of Jodhpur,' came a disdainful reply. 'Even the maharajas of Jaipur did not render the kind of services I undertook for the Mughal Empire. It is I who took part in the major battles Aurangzeb led us into. All I have to say is that though Aqil Khan wrote clandestinely, he was part of the courtly retinue. How can you call him an independent historian?'

'All right! All right! I can see that this is a very complex issue.'

'It's not at all complex, sir,' Rao Chhatrasal Bundela countered. 'This man, Aurangzeb, imprisoned his father, killed his brothers and is responsible for condemning Hindustan's emerging history to the gallows. The death of Dara Shikoh marked the death of Hindustan.'

'Would you like to say something in your defence, Aurangzeb?' the court asked.

'No, I would not, because there is both truth and falsehood in all that has been stated here,' Aurangzeb replied.

'What do you mean by that?'

'What do I mean?' Aurangzeb smiled bitterly. 'I mean...today, people of little worth dare to challenge me and question my decisions. They would not have had the courage to do so in my era, when Time and Hindustan's future were my minions and I was slave to none.' Having said this, Aurangzeb laughed heartily like a man who enjoys in retrospect the import of his words.

By then, the emperor had become oblivious to his presence in the court of Time. Gathering his courtiers around him, he shouted like one deranged: 'Somnath Mandir, did you say? You mean the mandir is still there? The very same one which Mahmud Ghazni had destroyed? How is it still standing? Destroy it and Orissa along with it...What? Mandirs have come up again in Orissa? Order Asad Khan to demolish all mandirs built there over the past decade and to withdraw permission for renovation of others. The document sanctioning the execution of this order should be brought immediately to this durbar in the form of an undertaking, duly signed and sealed by the qazi. Mathura's Keshavrai Mandir should be demolished forthwith. The staircase built within it by Dara Shikoh should be razed to the ground. My commander at Mathura should be directed to inform this royal court as soon as the order has been carried out.'

Aurangzeb paced up and down as he issued these directives. His courtiers sat listening to him in silence. Soon after, whispers surfaced.

'What ails Alampanah Alamgir?'

'Such things were unheard of even in Shahjahan and Jahangir's time. Shahjahan too had many mandirs demolished. But even he did not issue such harsh and vengeful proclamations.'

'I heard that yesterday the emperor met some ulemas from Sirhind in the Durbar-e-Khas. They held discussions for several hours. The royal qazi, Abdul Aziz, was also present. They all offered the emperor advice on many issues, especially political and religious ones.'

'And how do you know about it all?'

'I was told by an informant, the *khabas* on duty there.'

'Did anything special transpire?'

'Just that it was decided that Hindus should be kept in check. While the traditions and rituals associated with Hindu–Muslim unity—carried over from the time of Akbar and Jahangir—were to be abolished, Hindus would be regarded as ordinary citizens. Moreover, the administration would follow the guidelines laid down by the Nizam-e-Mustafa as they had in the Holy Prophet's time. It was also agreed that after the demise of Jaipur's Maharaja Mirza Raja

Jaisingh, none of his successors would be granted royal favours or titles. As soon as the moment was ripe, the Hindu foreign minister, Raja Raghunath, would be replaced by a Muslim one. No Muslim would ever have to serve under a Hindu officer. The kafir Hindus, it was agreed, would be informed that they could no longer avail of the privilege of being treated on an equal footing with their Muslim victors. Their status would now be relegated to that of common citizens. The ulemas repeatedly addressed Aurangzeb as the Shahenshah, King of Kings, and described him as a great Muslim and the defender of Islam. This has, obviously, gone to his head.'

Then the year 1669 came roaring into the court. Terrified voices reverberated around the place. Fear permeated the atmosphere. Temples collapsed. Hours crumbled into fragments and scattered far and wide. The sculpted images of deities disintegrated. Chaos prevailed in towns and villages. The bejewelled idols of the gods were brought from the Keshavrai Mandir to Agra and buried under the staircase of the Jahanara Masjid. Damodarlal, the head priest of Ballabhacharya's Goverdhan Mandir, fled to Jodhpur, carrying the temple's idols with him. But the gods of Goverdhan Mandir did not find refuge in Jodhpur. For six long years, they would be in perpetual flight, moving from one place to the next. In the end, Damodar sent one of his priests to Rana Rajsingh of Mewar. The Sisodia ruler welcomed these homeless gods to his kingdom and offered them a haven in the village of Sihar. This little village would later became famous as Nathdwara, a centre for the Vaishnav sect.

Seeking a refuge for the idols of their deities, priests from all over the land—Mathura, Vrindavan, Kashi, Prayag, Ujjain and Puri—travelled with them clandestinely from place to place. The qazis exploited the situation to the hilt. In Gujarat, deals were struck and bribes offered to save mandirs. The strategy worked. Voices from Kashi exclaimed, 'The Kashi Vishwanath Mandir has been destroyed! It's gone! This Mughal king has attacked Hindus! He has waged war on us and on our faith!'

'Revenge! Retribution!'

'Har har Mahadev!'

'Allah-o-Akbar!'

Clutching his cane, Vishambarnath Pandey presented himself before the court and exclaimed forcefully, 'Adeeb! You seem to be a sensible man. What are you up to? Put an end to this bloodshed and hatred! Tell Hindustan the truth, the real truth that lies behind Aurangzeb's demolition of the Kashi Vishwanath Mandir. That was a different era altogether. In his book, *Feathers and Stones*, Pattabhi Sitaramaiah writes that in keeping with the royal tradition of the times, a large contingent of rajas and landowners, along with their retinues, served as escort for the Mughal emperor when he undertook a journey. It is a fact that the Mughal court consisted of a large number of Hindus. And when Aurangzeb passed by Benares, how could a Hindu from distant Delhi have proceeded further without paying obeisance at the Vishwanath Mandir and taking a dip in the sacred waters of the Ganga? So it was that all the Hindu courtiers and their families visited the mandir and took a holy dip in the river. When they emerged from the mandir, they learnt that one of their ranis, ostensibly a consort to several of the rajas, was missing. She had been observed entering the temple, but none had seen her emerge. Following an extensive search of the premises, she was discovered in one of the dungeons in a state of abject terror. She had been stripped, molested and robbed of her jewellery. When Aurangzeb came to know of this atrocity perpetrated by the priests of his kingdom, he was infuriated. He wrathfully declared that a place where rape and robbery could take place could never be deemed as sacred. The emperor issued an order for the building to be demolished forthwith and it was executed without delay. News of the demolition saddened the rani who had been abused by the priests. She sent word to the emperor, pleading for the temple to be rebuilt as the structure itself could not be blamed for what had befallen her. In his *Benares Farman*, Aurangzeb has mentioned his inability to accede to her wishes, because he was a Muslim and had issued a proclamation banning the construction of mandirs. To circumvent the problem, he had a masjid built on the spot instead, and thereby fulfilled the rani's wishes.'

The adeeb looked at Pandey with deference.

'So,' Pandey continued, 'this is an episode reported by Pattabhi

Sitaramaiah. There is no way we can authenticate it. Had it, indeed, occurred, any just ruler would have acted as Aurangzeb had. If, on the other hand, this incident was invented by certain persons looking for a pretext to demolish the mandir, surely Aurangzeb can in no way be held responsible for it.' Having spoken at length, Pandey leaned on his cane.

'You are an outspoken man, Pandeyji, and untouched by vices like deceit and overreaching ambition. But the more Gandhism has tried to simplify history, the more romanticized has it become. It requires courage to recognize and stand up to bitter truths, but your compromising statements belie all possible good intentions on your part. Anyway, let Pattabhi Sitaramaiah be summoned to the court.'

'Sir, here I am,' a voice announced. There stood before them a khadi-clad man, wiping the perspiration from his brow.

'Can you enlighten us about the source from which the incident was reported by Pandeyji a moment ago?' asked the court.

'Its source is a handwritten manuscript which belonged to a reputed Muslim gentleman of Lucknow,' Sitaramaiah replied. 'Owing to his sudden demise, the manuscript could not be duly examined and, therefore, was not published.'

'So, my dear man, how could you accept its authenticity?'

'This incident could very well be true!' Pandey interjected somewhat heatedly.

'My dear sirs, it is my humble contention that the principles of brotherhood and unity advocated by Gandhism are overly simplistic and might appeal to ignorant, illiterate Indians. With the broadening of intellectual horizons today, enlightened Indians would find it difficult to concur with your views. Such views alone are responsible for encouraging Hindu bigots and radicals to compile erroneous, misleading versions of history. Moreover, Aurangzeb was, obviously, a pessimist to the core and mentally unstable, because he conspired to have his own father thrown into prison and his brothers executed.'

'But there was a reason for it,' said a soft, cultured voice.

'And who are you?'

'Janab, I'm Shibli Nomani.'

'Please let Shibli Nomani Sahib have a chair, peon. And, allow me to pay my respects, sir,' said the adeeb, rising to his feet. The court remained on its feet until a chair was brought for Shibli Nomani.

Taking his seat again, the adeeb said, 'Honourable sir, we are waiting for your account.'

'Thank you so much, Your Honour,' came Shibli Nomani's reply. 'Many allegations have been levelled in this court against Aurangzeb. They are not entirely unfounded, but it is imperative that we understand the complexities of the context in which his decisions were made.'

The historian Sriram Sharma intervened. 'Honourable Court,' he said, 'Shibli Nomani Sahib has spoken up for Aurangzeb the way an indulgent father would for his son, because he is, after all, a god-fearing Hindustani himself. The fact remains that in Aurangzeb's time historical records were compiled to reflect the emperor's own perspective on every issue and Nomani Sahib has chosen to stand by them. Aurangzeb himself is present here today. If he has a conscience at all, he will explain why these historical records were written to conform to his point of view.'

'Your statement is neither true nor false,' the emperor declared, wiping his brow.

'What do you mean?'

'Simply,' replied Aurangzeb, 'that my actions could be deemed just or unjust, depending on the person who chose to interpret them. From Hindustan's point of view, I was guilty of wrongdoing. But from a different point of view, that of Islam, I was, perhaps, justified in doing what I did.'

'Actually, honourable adeeb, we must try and fathom the complex depths of Aurangzeb's psychology,' was Sriram Sharma's suggestion. 'When people feel they have sinned, they are inclined to turn to religion. Some veer naturally towards it; others pursue it in desperation. Aurangzeb had resorted to heinous crimes in his bid to seize the reins of power in Hindustan. The residual guilt burdened his mind with anguish and drove him to religion for spiritual salvation. Eventually, it transformed him into a rabid fanatic. Thus did Aurangzeb become the enemy of the Hindus in Bharat.'

'It could well have been the other way round,' said Shibli Nomani. 'Hindus may have turned hostile towards him. What followed was a saga of hatred in which the ruler clashed with the ruled, the victor battled the vanquished, and religion and sect were up in arms against each other—the perfect breeding ground for the rise of rebellious sadhus who formed their own sects and set up home on tracts of land surrounding important mandirs and places of pilgrimage. These places would gradually come to resemble fortified camps. With time, the sects established by these renegade sadhus would organize themselves into militias. It is possible that such developments were part of a reactionary movement triggered by the rampant Islamization that swept over the country during Aurangzeb's reign. And the emperor may well have issued orders for the demolition of mandirs in a bid to curb the sadhu militias.'

'But history offers no evidence to support this argument,' retorted Sriram Sharma. 'I'd also like to ask Pandeyji and Pattabhi Sitaramaiah why temples in Mathura, Orissa, Somnath and Ujjain were destroyed. Unlike the Kashi Vishwanath Mandir, none of these places of worship had witnessed anything remotely akin to the assault on the rani of Kutch.'

'I will answer that.'

All eyes turned to Hazrat Shibli Nomani.

'During that era,' he began, 'mandirs and masjids were no longer mere centres of worship and religious discourse. They had degenerated into hotbeds of intrigue and conspiracy. Iranian, Hindustani and English historians were mistaken in their assumption that the demolition of mandirs had incited rebellions. On the contrary, it was to quash rebellions that temples were pulled down.'

'Then why were Hindu *pathshalas* closed down?'

'In those centres of learning, Hindu pandits had started preaching their own religion to Muslim children. Dara Shikoh's active encouragement during the reign of Shahjahan had led to the meteoric rise in Hindu aspirations. Dara was anti-Islam and it was at his behest that the policy of appeasing Hindus had been introduced in Hindustan. After all, what purpose could have been served by teaching Hindu dharma shastras to Muslims?' Shibli Nomani's tone was emphatic.

'So,' retorted Sriram Sharma, 'you're trying to imply that it was Aurangzeb who adopted the policy of administering the country in the name of Islam and its ideals. It was he who levied the jaziya tax on Hindus.'

'It was unavoidable. The Hindus had been so pampered during the reigns of Akbar and Jahangir that they had quite forgotten their actual status as subjects of the Mughal conquerors of Hindustan. Shahjahan had tried to rectify this, but towards the end of his reign he had become a mere pawn in Dara Shikoh's hands. With Hindus developing notions of equality vis-à-vis Muslims, levying jaziya was a way of showing them their rightful place in society. Of course, the tax was also imposed to replenish the state coffers, exhausted by the construction of the Taj Mahal along with that of several other masjids and fortresses.'

'Which was the more important reason, Alamgir?' asked the adeeb. 'Did you want to put Hindus like us in our place or were you seeking to replenish your coffers?'

'Both,' came Aurangzeb's reply. 'Whatever has been disclosed about me—positive or negative—has two different aspects to it. And both are correct.'

'You are a strange man, aren't you?'

'How else could I possibly be? Every emperor, by virtue of being an emperor, is a strange man. All you scholars can do is sit in your study and churn out stories about them. I know only too well where you stand and what your limitations are.' Aurangzeb spoke with bitterness, a disdainful grimace of a smile on his face. His tone, though, was serious as he continued, 'Tell me, honourable adeeb—'

'Honourable adeeb! Is it really *you* addressing me in this manner? You, who spoke so disparagingly about adeebs not a moment ago?'

'Sir, I am neither Babar nor Akbar. I am a mere prince, a victim of Time. I aspired to the throne of Hindustan and tried every means—fair and foul—to seize it. As the Mughals had established no clearly defined laws of succession, I had to rid myself of my brothers and nephews. By imprisoning my honourable father, Shahjahan, I merely followed the precedent he had set. You should judge the misdeeds of each age in terms of the prevailing conventions of the time.'

Voices called out from the pages of history. 'You are a tyrant, Aurangzeb!' they exclaimed. 'You tried to murder Murad by giving him nothing for sustenance but water laced with the extract of opium, prepared by boiling sesame seeds in it. When the concoction failed to kill the robust prince, you had him assassinated by your jallads. And this, mind you, was the same younger brother you had acknowledged as your sovereign by swearing on Allah and the Holy Koran.'

'That is far from the truth,' interjected Shibli Nomani. 'The truth is that after defeating Dara's army—'

'But it wasn't Dara's army,' came the rejoinder from historian Sriram Sharma, 'those were Emperor Shahjahan's forces.'

'No, sir,' countered Shibli Nomani. 'Shahjahan's illness had given Dara the upper hand. It was on Dara's orders that the royal army had set out and been defeated by the combined military strength of Aurangzeb and Murad. The latter had fought like a lion and victory had made him arrogant. Assuming that the throne of Hindustan was his for the asking if only he could manage to defeat Dara, Shuja and Aurangzeb, Murad had embarked on a campaign to win over the officers in Aurangzeb's army by offering them extravagant rewards in the form of gifts or large grants of land. It was Murad's overweening ambition that drove Aurangzeb to seek revenge.'

'According to the historian Aqil Khan, Aurangzeb had asked Murad over to his camp by feigning a stomach ache,' taunted Sriram Sharma. 'He had plied his brother with such quantities of alcohol that he drank himself into a stupor. A prostitute was then sent in to divest him of his weapons. Overcome by lust and befuddled by alcohol, Murad was an easy target for Sheikh Mir who was sent in to manacle him. And so, he ended up as Aurangzeb's captive.'

'Yes, Aurangzeb certainly did as you claim...he did have his brother put in chains,' Shibli Nomani shot back. 'Had he beheaded Murad without preliminaries, it would have been better still. In that case, we would have appreciated Aurangzeb's far-sightedness.'

'Shibli Nomani Sahib!' the adeeb shouted, 'instead of being a rational, thinking human being, what you are, first and foremost, is a Muslim. That is your failing...'

'Yes, indeed it is!' retorted Shibli Nomani. 'I am a Muslim. Yes, I am!'

'But you were born a human being, not a Muslim,' the court interjected. 'You remained an innocent human being until the kalmah was recited in your presence and you were circumcised. And then you became a Muslim...'

Before the court could complete its statement, chaos erupted. People shouted, 'Our religion has been insulted, defamed! We will not tolerate it!'

'Silence!' shouted the adeeb. 'No religion is above human beings. Humans were born first; religion came later.'

Shibli Nomani tried to change the subject. 'Honourable adeeb, we were talking of Alamgir. Since he is here in person, let us resolve that issue. I wish to advance the argument that in spite of all the powers of the state being vested in him, Aurangzeb did not declare himself a caliph. It is also a measure of his greatness that he ruled as an Islamic sovereign. Had the traditions established by Akbar been perpetuated during Aurangzeb's reign, Taimur's dynasty would have been transformed into an un-Islamic one. When Alamgir took over the responsiblities of the kingdom, most of the latter's cultural and religious traditions had nearly become extinct. Courtiers had taken to presenting themselves in the royal court in shockingly inappropriate attire such as dhoti-like pyjamas and turbans. They exchanged greetings the Hindu way with a namaskar that involved joining the fingertips of both hands or by touching the feet of elders as a mark of respect. The un-Islamic tradition of jharoka-darsha.1, in which the emperor made a public appearance on a balcony, had become a ritual. Hindus had taken to marrying Muslim girls. Alamgir banned such unacceptable and un-Islamic practices. Policies that encouraged the appeasement of Hindus were abolished. He commissioned the writing of *Fatwa-e-Alamgiri* to ensure that his system of justice was henceforth based on laws of the sharia.'

'So, you're determined to prove that Aurangzeb was a better

Muslim than Akbar, Jahangir and Shahjahan put together, aren't you?'

'Absolutely! He was the one who sought his roots.'

'You mean to imply that his roots were not in Hindustan! Are you claiming that Taimur's blood did not course through the veins of Akbar, Jahangir, Shahjahan, Dara, Shuja and Murad?'

'It certainly did, but they ignored the demands of their faith. They took no advantage of their religious identity. This failure on their part corroded the sharp blade of religion. That is why I refer to Aurangzeb as Alamgir. When Alamgir reached Agra after defeating Raja Jaswant Singh and Dara, his father, Emperor Shahjahan, presented his courageous son with "Alamgir", the hereditary sword. If anyone had ever harnessed the power of religion for the first time, it was Alamgir.' Shibli Nomani's voice resonated with enthusiasm.

'I hope Aurangzeb did not hide his own failings and unjust acts behind the camouflage of Islam?' the adeeb asked.

An elderly historian rose to his feet.

'Honourable sir, allow me to introduce myself before you ask me who I am. Mohammed Habib is my name. I was a professor of history at the Aligarh Muslim University in Hindustan. My contention is that many sought to use Islam only when circumstances demanded it or they were keen to project themselves as the symbol of divine power. For centuries has Islam been thus exploited and the practice prevails even today. In the days of the Prophet Hazrat Mohammed, the sword served to bestow protection and mete out justice. Later, it was unfairly used in the name of Islam to exact revenge or propagate vested interests. Are you listening, Shibli Nomani Sahib? I also wish to submit that it would be a blatant distortion of the truth to describe the invasions of Hindustan spanning a millennium—from the time of Mohammed bin Qasim to Babar—as attacks targeting Hindus. We should, moreover, bear in mind that Islam came into being not merely as a religion, but equally, as a form of statecraft. And the norms of statecraft and religion are quite disparate. There isn't much more that I need say, but I do wish to counter Shibli Nomani's Islamic point of view by asserting that any invader who happened by chance to be a follower of Islam was but a Muslim and nothing more. He did not come to Bharat specifically to carry out a jihad against its Hindus.'

'How can you suggest that?' questioned Hazrat Shibli Nomani.

'All invaders who came to Hindustan—from Mohammed bin Qasim to Babar—were driven by the medieval lust for fame and riches. They were not crusaders of Islam. Their sole objective was to expand their kingdoms or line their purses. Don't drag Islam into this, please! Islam as a faith was far removed from such selfish compulsions, but many of its converts elected to be its flag bearers in their attempt to legitimize their plunder. Yet, there is no escaping the fact that the pillaging rulers who rose to prominence after the cultural evolution of Persia were Muslims. It was not Islam that attacked Hindustan, but Muslims who were driven to do so by their selfish medieval aspirations and feudalistic values. The complexities of the situation need to be taken into careful consideration. The country's Hindus were not attacked by Islam, but by converts to Islam. Recognizing the strength Islam lent to the power of the state, they felt that they could raise armies in the name of their faith. And yet, history is a witness to the battles that pitted Muslims against each other right from the seventh century to the sixteenth. If the court so desires, it can summon scholars and historians like Amir Khusrau, Burney and Farishta to verify the facts.'

Mohammed Habib sat down, exhausted.

The adeeb issued an order asking for Amir Khusrau, Burney and Farishta to be produced in court.

'But, sir, Dara Shikoh is keen to narrate his tale of woe,' the peon interjected.

'Bhawani Sengupta has been waiting here for a long time. Apart from the past, I do have to keep my finger on the pulse of the present. Or else, the future will simply be a repeat of the past. I only wish to analyse and understand that bit of the past which casts a dark shadow on the present, laying the foundations of hatred and revenge in many Pakistans.'

The adeeb stood up in the midst of the papers, books, petitions and histories that lay scattered around him. 'Speak to Dara Shikoh and Amir Khusrau, to Burney and Farishta. Bring to this court, with all due honour, whichever one of them wishes to relate his story first. They are all welcome here, especially, Amir Khusrau Sahib who belongs to Etah district near my home town Mainpuri. The two places lie in close proximity, their arms entwined about each other. Their free arm reaches out to Agra, the birthplace of Mirza Ghalib, Mir and Nazeer. I trace my lineage from the Vedic Aryans to Kabir, Amir Khusrau, Ghalib and Mir.' Then, looking towards Bhawani Sengupta, he asked, 'So, my friend, shall we call Dara Shikoh?'

'Along with Dara Shikoh, do please ask Kalikaranjan Kanungo to present himself as well,' suggested Professor Habib. 'Shibli Nomani has portrayed Aurangzeb as an upright Islamic ruler. I cannot bring myself to regard Aurangzeb as an advocate of Islam simply because he fasted thrice a week, copied verses from the Koran and personally stitched prayer caps for others. He merely used Islam for furthering his own agenda. Otherwise, what reason did he have for killing his brothers, Dara Shikoh and Murad, and compelling his elder brother, Shuja, to flee to Burma? He kept his own father incarcerated during the old monarch's final days and crowned himself emperor of Hindustan. Such conduct was hardly in keeping with the tradition of the royal Mughals or worthy of the descendants of Taimur. Can these deeds be described as Islamic and sanctioned by the sharia? Aurangzeb may well have been a Muslim, but he was not a faithful follower of Islam. He was simply a tyrant.'

Having heard out Mohammed Habib, the adeeb ordered the peon, 'Let Dara Shikoh, Murad, Dara's son Suleiman Shikoh, and historian Kalikaranjan Kanungo be presented before the court.'

The peon had just stepped forward to execute these orders, when Chris Hedges of the *New York Times* appeared before the court, completely out of breath. 'Do you know,' she asked, 'what blind bigots are up to in Egypt's Valley of the Kings? They've even made the Nile weep, apart from causing a wave of tears to well up in the eyes of the Egyptians. The latter now stand witness to the destruction of their civilization. Pharaohs who had slept peacefully in the Valley of the Kings for the past thirty centuries, now quake within their pyramids—the same Pharaohs whose association with divinity, unimaginable wealth and courageous exploits was known the world over, and who laid the foundation of one of the world's great civilizations along with India and China. Before their might and splendour, Central Asia and south-east Europe once trembled in awe. Today, this proud and historic civilization cowers before Islamic extremists and terrorists. Outfits like the Gamal–Islamiya and the Jihad are a scourge in the lives of the common people.'

'Hmm...you speak of scourges. Well, we shall unleash the scourge of Judgement Day! In Egypt, we shall destroy all that predates Islam! We shall rest only after we have ground it to dust!' The voice came from distant America and belonged to Mullah Sheikh Omar Abdul Rahman, an illegal immigrant and a rabble-rouser, who preyed on the sentiments of poor, illiterate Muslims in the name of Islam.

'Let Sheikh Omar Abdul Rahman be presented here,' the court ordered.

'But, sir, he is in the custody of the Americans,' the peon protested.

'Oh, I see. Right, but his voice mustn't be silenced. Let it be heard here,' the adeeb ruled.

So the voice of Mullah Sheikh Omar Abdul Rahman continued to reverberate in the court. 'Yes,' it announced loudly, 'we are followers of Islam. We were the ones to assassinate Anwar Sadat for striking a deal with the Israelis at Camp David. Now, we shall not spare the government of Hosni Mubarak and Hasan al Alfi either. What is so great about Egypt? We shall not rest till we seize power there. Then we intend to shake the very foundations of North Africa and southern Europe. We shall not pardon Algeria and Turkey who have nothing Islamic about them but their name. We must bring them back into the fold.'

'That is not the path of religion. In the name of Islam, you cannot wipe out our culture, civilization and history. I too am a Muslim, but I do not repudiate my history. Egypt has a centuries-old tradition of culture and philosophy. You have no right to obliterate the heritage of our Pharaohs, our believers in Hellenism and in Christianity. By doing so, can you prove that Islam is greater? It is only by comparing Islam with other religions that we can understand its bounty, its greatness and its immensity.'

Though this voice could be heard in the court, its speaker remained invisible. The peon cleared the confusion by explaining, 'Sir, the first voice you heard was that of Mullah Sheikh Omar from America. The second belongs to the qazi of Egypt—Judge Said Ashwami. I can see what kind of danger Said Ashwami's views have exposed him to. He is surrounded by a cordon of security, because the threat to his life by religious hardliners looms large. In fact, at this very moment, his house in Cairo is ringed by security men to ensure that the threat is not translated into reality.'

The court started at this piece of news. Then the *Al-Ahram* newspaper reported bomb blasts in the temples of the Pharaohs and at the pyramids in Giza. They had caused clouds of sand to rise like towers piercing the sky.

'That is exactly what is fated to happen, Adeeb!' shouted a hardliner of the Gamal–Islamiya. He was the man who had killed twenty white tourists as they sailed along the Nile, admiring the beauty and achievements of Egypt. 'It was bound to happen!' he went on. 'These Jews and Christians come here to watch cabarets. They roam half-naked in the bazaars of the flesh and visit the temples of the Pharaohs to worship through chants and rituals. Our Islam forbids it. From the tenth century onwards, we have committed ourselves to defacing and destroying all signs, symbols and cultural markers that are un-Islamic. It was in that spirit that our ulema, Sai Dahar, smashed the nose of the Sphinx and our sheikhs subsequently attacked the temples of the Pharaohs.'

Surrounded by armed guards, Qazi Said Ashwami gave his acerbic reply: 'But these very temples and pyramids have been providing the poor with stones to build their own homes! In the fourteenth century, those greedy sheikhs you call your flag bearers did not, as you claim, come to demolish the pyramids, but to plunder the wealth that lay within them. They were not the soldiers of Islam. They were bandits who concealed their real identity by pretending to be missionaries of Islam. I am a qazi. I try to dispense justice according to Islamic shariat and hadith. You insult Islam by asserting that these bandits in the guise of mullahs were the soldiers of Islam.'

As the debate grew more heated, Imam Wahid Mohammed Hanfi of the Abu Hajjaz Masjid in north-eastern Luxor peeped in apprehensively. There, in his masjid lay buried Abu Hajjaz, the greatest scholar of his time—Abu Hajjaz, whose boat procession was taken out even today, a procession that traced its origins to a similar one in ancient Egypt honouring the god Aman.

Standing among the stone pillars in the palace of Rameses with the sunlight falling on him, Imam Wahid Mohammed resembled a slender reed. He spoke out loud. 'Leave us in peace to lead our lives and cherish our beliefs,' he urged. 'These ancient pyramids and temples are symbols of our culture. How can you hope to achieve inner peace if you destroy them? If you negate your past, how will you claim credit for revolutionizing the world of the intellect by inventing papyrus paper? Listen, you can hear the voice of centuries here. Until you learn to respect what your ancient ruins stand for, you cannot save your future from decay. You sinners, do you know that Abu Hajjaz's masjid stands on that very soil which, from ancient times, has given birth to and nurtured churches and the temples of the Pharaohs? Look towards the Nile—you see before you the grandeur of Roman architecture. This country represents the confluence of many cultures standing in close juxtaposition. And our knowledge and thought emanate from that very confluence. Such is the message conveyed to us by our heritage.'

'The French dictator, Napoleon, had come here to explore this heritage,' Said Ashwami declared, taking up the narration. 'He had been overwhelmed by the architecture of the Pharaohs and of Rameses. He had gone back to his country only to return, accompanied by French cultural historians and intellectuals. He had wanted them to see for themselves, to marvel at this country's ancient civilization. The Romans and the Greeks too had visited this place. Herodotus, the Greek historian, had come here to obtain an insight into the miracle that was Egyptian civilization. It was he who had observed that the spirit of civilization breathed through the pores of all these ruins, these temples and pyramids.'

'Say what you will,' threatened Mullah Sheikh Ali Yahya, a small-time Egyptian terrorist, 'but we will have nothing to do with an un-Islamic past. The pyramids and the Sphinx symbolize idolatry. Our Prophet rejected idolatry and so do we. By desecrating the pyramids and the Sphinx, we destroy idols and earn divine salvation. The fragments of these monuments will lie buried, one day, in the sands of Giza. Do you hear? We will wipe them off the memory of mankind.'

'So you wish to establish another Egypt within Egypt, do you? You hope to create rifts among Muslims by establishing differences between the intensity of their devotion?' The adeeb's questions silenced Sheikh Ali Yahya. The voice of Sheikh Omar Abdul Rahman in America had also fallen silent.

The silence deepened. Not a sound was to be heard.

With great pride, the adeeb stood up and addressed the world. 'These voices have lapsed into silence of their own accord. Do not let your voices remain silent nor your feelings unarticulated. Place no curbs on them. Public opinion and sentiment alone can counter the powers that threaten mankind. It is necessary to recognize that each religion is different; but it is far more important to understand that all religions share the common message of humanity. Advocates of democracy should never allow themselves to forget that even the most useless, damaging and socially unacceptable opinions deserve a hearing in an ambience of freedom and transparency, unimpeded by restraints of any kind. This is the only way to counter and nullify brutally reactionary perceptions, even those that are needlessly provocative and have no significant impact.'

The peon sounded a note of caution: 'Sir, you've launched into a speech, yet again.'

'And why not? Don't judges and intellectuals in India deliver interminable concluding speeches? Anyway, I should certainly try avoiding such pitfalls. I would like to close my speech, however, by laying emphasis on the following point: the compulsions that drove ancient epochs were dictated by personal, military and economic concerns, not religious ones. In the name of religion, morality or tribal justice, issues were given a religious flavour. Thus, religion came to be fashioned into a weapon. In its name, massacres and forced conversions were carried out. Today, it is impossible to recreate similar conditions. Mankind has rejected these destructive tendencies of the past. But their remnants survive. From the ruins of memory, our times...'

'Sir, not again!' the peon exclaimed in exasperation.

'Oh...I'd quite forgotten...arrey, where's Bhawani Sengupta?'

23

Before corpses from Bosnia and Somalia could knock at the court's door or the innocent butchered in Brazil and Bolivia relate their experiences, Bhawani Sengupta spoke up. 'Chaos reigns supreme,' he declared. 'Human rights are being ground into the dust. The world is drowning in a deluge of violence, murder, suffering, deprivation, depravity and deceit. In Bharat itself, lotuses are being cultivated in pools of blood. Yet, despite it all, from this very situation springs a faint flicker of hope.'

'You're right,' agreed the adeeb. 'It is something that preserves our souls. The tragedy of our times lies in the fact that things happen, are heard of, are thought of, are understood, yet they all seem unreal, elusive. We are caught up in an effort to undermine the very values we have inculcated in ourselves.'

Bhawani Sengupta joined in enthusiastically. 'That is why I have returned here via South Africa, Israel, Palestine and Iran,' he stated. 'I met Yasser Arafat in Tunis. In Israel, I saw Rabin and Peres. The Jews and the Palestinians have levelled the walls they had erected earlier to preserve their respective "Pakistans". By doing so, they have afforded their people some respite, enabling them to recognize each other as human beings and learn to appreciate the fundamental freedom that is man's birthright. They have tuned in to the rhythm of each other's heartbeats. As a result, their guns have fallen silent, their missiles remain unlaunched and the stone-throwing episodes by the Intifadah have come to an end. This is a decisive step indeed. The Palestinians agree that the Jews have a right to live in Israel. The latter assure the Palestinians that they can set up and administer their state in the Gaza Strip and the West Bank. Jericho and Jerusalem will serve as the capital cities. The matter of the Golan Heights will be resolved later...'

Bhawani Sengupta paused briefly before continuing, 'Down in South Africa, the apartheid regime has come to an end after three hundred and forty years. Nelson Mandela has finally won. After a prolonged struggle, the whites have accepted defeat and conceded that their administrative policy of racial discrimination is now null and void. My last stop was Tehran. The West had declared Iran's Islamic revolution to be monstrous, horrifying and a mockery of all human values. Its propaganda machine had drawn attention to the murder of human rights in that country and to the dawn of a ruthless Islam. I went there to see for myself how blinkered the West's vision of the East could be. I discovered that its perception of Iran was warped, preventing it from coming to terms with Ayatollah Khomeini's Islamic revolution that has restored to his country the pivotal stature of an advanced civilization. From this vantage position, Iran has extended the hand of peace and friendship to two other advanced civilizations which are important regional powers—India and China.'

A man from the Shiv Sena interrupted: 'Do not let yourselves forget that Muslims are barbarians. They don't spare their own people. How could they spare us? Iran and Iraq—both Muslim nations—fought each other for eight long years.'

'Yes, but didn't the two warring factions of the Mahabharata—the Pandavas and the Kauravas—share the same faith? They too fought against each other. So don't drag religion into this argument. Listen to what Bhawani Sengupta has to say. We might derive some consolation from his words.'

The cries of Bosnian Muslims suddenly rent the air. Knocks thundered on the doors of the court. Screams and sighs rose to fill the atmosphere. Deceased Muslim women had arrived to narrate their harrowing tales of assault and brutality. The Serbs and Croats who had perpetrated these barbaric atrocities on Muslims, added to the din by shouting loudly.

Describing the plight of his country, a dead Bosnian Muslim asked, 'Is there no one to hear us? Can no nation give a fitting reply to the tyranny unleashed on us? We are dying of starvation in Bosnia. Our women are being raped and tortured. Our children are dragged out of our homes and murdered in cold blood. We are humiliated and rendered homeless as the world looks on in silence.'

'But the situation seems to have improved now. The Croats, Serbs and Muslims of Yugoslavia don't wish to live together any longer. So, they have accepted the partition of their country and prefer to exist as separate nations,' Bhawani Sengupta observed sadly.

In a voice tinged with sorrow, the adeeb sought further clarification. 'Do you mean to say that...that three "Pakistans" have been created in Yugoslavia?' he asked. 'The country used to consist of only two races—Serbs and Croats. The third is just a faith—Islam. Its followers are Muslims. They could be either Croat or Serb. It means that self-interest and hatred have swept over Yugoslavia as well.'

'But this time, it's the Christians who have brutally tyrannized Muslims and driven them away. Bombs have torn through the city of Sarajevo. It's well-nigh impossible for Muslims to carry on living there. Muslim women are abducted and subjected to such humiliation and torture that even the Pakistani army's maltreatment of Bangladeshi women during Bangladesh's war of independence pales into insignificance. Why, even the Japanese army did not perpetrate such horrors on Korean women! The bestiality endured by Muslim women in Sarajevo has no precedent. Everything has turned topsy-turvy there. Christian Serbs and Croats have compelled their Muslim compatriots to create their own "Pakistan". These acts deserve the severest condemnation. The refusal of people to live together in harmony is a crime against humanity. The course of history cannot be changed by religious conversions.'

The court was interrupted by the arrival of Om Prakash, a special correspondent, with a report from Dehra village in Ghaziabad. Overwhelmed with anxiety, the adeeb took a deep breath before asking him, 'So, my dear man, have there been any recent killings or clashes in Ghaziabad?'

'No,' came the reply, 'not this time. In fact, I bring news that will be a source of comfort for souls in torment. The world is aware of the perennial feud that existed between the Rajputs and the

Mughals. Maharana Pratap never accepted Akbar's sovereignty. Yet, Ghaziabad's Dehra village tells an altogether different tale of the very same Mughal period. The village is inhabited by Sisodia Rajputs, descendants of Maharana Pratap's family, who converted to Islam during Aurangzeb's reign. These Muslim Rajputs are installing a statue of their ancestor Maharana Pratap in the village. They firmly believe that religious conversion does not negate blood ties. They have forged a dual identity for themselves. They are not merely Muslims, but Muslim Rajputs. Out of the sixty villages in the region, eight-and-a-half are predominantly Sisodia Muslim. The rest are Sisodia Hindu. But they are united in their conviction that they share blood ties. They came here from Rajasthan to join in the battle their ancestor, Prithviraj Chauhan, was waging against Mohammed Ghori. Dehra village derives its name from *dera* or the encampment set up there by these Rajputs. For Hindu and Muslim Rajputs alike, Dehra is the centre of their existence. Each of the eight-and-a-half Muslim villages has a *numberdar mukhiya*—a village headman. They have names like Mehar Ali Rajput, and they say that should the need arise, they will build a masjid adjoining their mandir. Even today, when a Muslim woman performs the ritual of asking her brother to fetch rice for her child's wedding, the words of the same ancient song that Hindu women sing are on her lips: "Bhaiyya Raghubir, bring us our rice..." When she enunciates the word "Raghubir", it is not blasphemy; it is an intrinsic part of her culture. Honourable Court of Justice, the area between Delhi and Garh Mukteshwar is dotted with villages belonging to Rajputs descended from various clans. Residents of a few such villages converted to Islam. Adjoining those sixty villages are another eighty-four belonging to Tomar Hindus and Tomar Muslims. Nearby are twelve villages inhabited by the Nirvaan Rajputs. Six of those villages are Muslim. The other six are Hindu. In this region, the same can be said of the Tyagis, the Gujjars and the Chaudhrys. Despite their conversion, these Rajputs and Brahmins have not disowned their cultural roots. The same is true of the Mewati Muslims settled as far west as Alwar in Rajasthan. They may be Muslims today, but they retain their cultural ties and traditions.'

'No culture allows the creation of "Pakistans". Culture is not restrictive by nature. It is liberal, comprehensive. It celebrates not decay, but the continuity of life. Cultural assimilation is imperative, because it respects the value of life.'

'Sir, I had tried to achieve this,' a sombre voice rang out, as a handsome prince made his appearance in the court. Aurangzeb started at the sight.

'Is that you, Dara Shikoh?'

'Yes, it is I.'

A silence born of incredulity descended on the court. All eyes turned towards Dara Shikoh. Strange echoes reverberated in the court. Dervishes called, azaans summoned the faithful to prayer, Buddhist incantations resounded, Christian choirs sang, mandir bells tinkled and war cries rang out. They were interspersed with the groans of dying soldiers.

On receiving the news of his arrival, Babar had especially come to see his great-grandson Dara Shikoh. He looked lovingly at the young man. Many rainbows bloomed in the sky.

'Honourable Court,' said Dara Shikoh, 'in Bharat, I had longed for a new culture to bloom, based on wisdom and tolerance. It was the same culture that the Sufis and sants had dreamt of. I was the disciple of Khwaja Moinuddin Chishti, the patron saint of the Mughal dynasty. So was my sister, Jahanara, who even wrote his biography, *Munisul-Arba*.'

Aurangzeb interrupted. 'That is an utter lie! While on his way back from Kandahar, this man had become the disciple of Baba Lali in Lahore. Later, he became an apostle of the mendicant Miyan Mir. His wife, Nadira Begum, also became a disciple of this man. Miyan Mir was a Sufi of the Qadiriya sect and...a pupil of Abdul Qadir Jeelani! He joined the sect and believed that he had been transformed into a Qadri and a Hanfi!'

'True,' came the reply, 'but Sufis made no distinctions among themselves. And at the time, even my honourable father paid obeisance to Miyan Mir. I also endorse Sufi saint Abdul Qadir Jeelani's claim that the gates of hell will be closed for all and those of heaven thrown open, not only for Muslims, but also for kafirs and atheists. Abdul Qadir Jeelani sought the welfare of both Hindus and

Muslims. He wished to eliminate the differences that divided them. And, honourable sir, I have noticed that everyone in Hindustan has faith in monotheism. There is little difference between the Sufis who repose faith in one God and the Vedic faith's perception of unity in trinity. Harmony, mercy and understanding are the hallmarks of monotheism. They all reinforce our faith in one God. Yet, I share the view of Khorasan's famous Sufi, Abu Said Fazlullah, who declared that though God was one, the paths leading to Him could be many, running even into millions. That is so, because each believer in monotheism has the freedom to choose the manner in which he surrenders himself to God. Negating the concept of self and of the world as independent entities, monotheism stresses the existence of nothing but God; in other words, nothing in this world, including man, has an identity other than as a part of the Creator. Even as I understood this, my yearning for the Almighty remained unfulfilled. Here, I shall quote a couplet: What I searched the wide world for, I found within me/Being blind to its existence, I deceived none but myself.'

'This man was completely demented at the time,' remarked Shibli Nomani, 'and so he remains, even today.'

'Yes, those who seek the path of an all-embracing monotheism do pass through a trance-like phase before achieving their goal. To those who lack insight, these people appear deranged. That is why the pious Jew, Sarmad, had given your Alamgir the impression of being insane and was murdered on the steps of the Jama Masjid at his instigation. Today, Aurangzeb's metaphorical "Pakistan" appears to be poised on the foundation of hatred. My Hindustan acknowledges the rights of its larger Muslim population. The sons and daughters of its soil symbolize the foundation of integrated culture. There are many more Muslims in my Hindustan than in Aurangzeb's "Pakistan"!' Anger flared up in Dara Shikoh's voice as he continued, 'Islam is not the faith of barbarian conquerors. It is a religion that seeks to imbue the world with beauty and refinement through peaceful coexistence. Islam's Holy Prophet himself has acknowledged that before his own advent, Allah had sent many other messengers to light mankind's path to God.'

As the debate continued, the rainbows in the sky faded away. It started raining blood. The terrifying rat-tat-tat of Kalashnikov rifles swept the rocky landscape of Afghanistan. The anguished cries of the innocent tore through Central Asia, Turkey, Sudan and Egypt, eventually passing through Saudi Arabia and Pakistan to reach Kashmir where they wrought havoc.

'Who are these beasts?' the adeeb demanded, gathering in his arms the bloody corpses that had arrived from all over the world. Then a worried Nikhil Chakravarthy, the journalist, entered the court. The adeeb rose to greet him.

'Adeeb, do you know why the rainbows in the sky have disappeared?' the journalist asked. 'Can you imagine why it's raining blood instead?'

Trying his best to protect his paintings from the bloody rain, the artist, Prabhu Joshi of Dewas, spoke up. 'Adeeb...my brother,' he said, 'these paintings of mine have recreated beauty. They are compositions that represent the truth of nations. Does this shower of blood have the right to wash away my creations?'

'O Adeeb, you are a creative artist,' Nikhil Chakravarthy joined in, speaking in an anguished tone. 'It rains blood from Afghanistan to central Asia to the Kurdish regions of Turkey. Such showers also sweep across North Africa, Egypt and Saudi Arabia and are unleashed by the mujahideen who, having finished with Afghanistan, roam about in search of new battlefields. These warriors without a cause seek new frontiers for jihad. Heroes in their exploits against Russia, they have now been transformed into villains presiding over the Afghan civil war. It is a part of their strategy. Today, the very countries that fostered these rabid and unenlightened men have become their targets. It is the kind of situation in which the demon, Bhasmasura, had found himself in his time.'

'Yes, that's right. The Arab states responsible for creating these fundamentalists to liberate Afghanistan from Russia, now agonize over their nefarious activities, while the mujahideen, bereft of a cause, wander afar, seeking new battlefields, creating havoc in Egypt, Algeria, Jordan and Tunisia.'

At this point, some American soldiers emerged from the jungles in Vietnam, shouting, 'Where's the war? Where's the battlefield?'

'The war in Vietnam was over decades ago,' Prabhu Joshi explained to them. 'Just as the Vietnamese made you flee into their jungles, they compelled the American army to rush back home. They went back decades ago. The Vietnam War is finally over.'

'No!' the soldiers shouted back. 'War can never come to an end.'

'How can it when people like you never allow it to? Your guns and rifles have rusted. So have your minds. In this state, you can only wish for war...war and further destruction.'

'No matter what happens, we demand war.'

'Now, those who cannot go to war will become the scourge of society. They will turn into bandits and murderers. Honourable adeeb, why don't you try to understand our compulsions?' appealed a weeping Afghan mujahid. 'We were not bloodthirsty mercenaries to begin with. Like all children, we were born innocent, but self-interest and the lust for power transformed us into beasts. We have no skill to speak of other than those required for participating in the games of death. How I wish we had been trained to work in the fields and factories!'

His tears mingled with those of the American soldiers who had emerged from the jungles.

'What shall we do?' the soldiers all cried in unison. 'We are doomed to fight! We are accursed, honourable adeeb, accursed! All we can propagate is death!'

With these words, thousands of Taliban and American soldiers carrying arms from America, China and Russia, rushed towards Bosnia, Somalia, Jordan, Egypt, Libya and Tunisia. Soon, storms of death began to blow and rivers of gore flowed, as the ideologies of blood merged and the credos of Algeria's Islamic Front, Jordan's Mohammedi Army, Tunisia's Islamic Party, and Kashmir's Hizbul Mujahideen, JKLF and other such organizations became one. A cacophony of sound rose up, swept through the court and drifted towards the strife-torn countries of the world, wreaking havoc along the way.

The adeeb sat with his palms clamped over his ears.

The voice of Dara Shikoh spoke. 'Honourable sir,' it said, 'it was from those bloody storms that I wanted to save my land, my land which is the heart of the world's greatest culture. Our culture did not seek to invent weapons of war. Rather, its goal lay in gaining insights into the mystery of the Supreme Being and of the soul's spirituality. We did not give birth to mujahideen, blinded by their faith to all that was just and sound; we brought forth pirs, fakirs, Sufis, sants, dervishes and other pious men. From the depths of our jungles came sages with their message of peace, not brutes with war cries on their lips. Instead of aspiring to the throne, I sought a compassionate faith for mankind. And in my quest for a monotheistic faith, I wrote to the pious sant, Shah Dilruba, that a fakir like me had no use for the outward trappings of Islam. I saw myself as both believer and atheist. Through the worship of idols I sought the Supreme Being; indeed, in my endeavour to commune with my own soul, I became my own devotee. Within every idol is concealed the essence of life, just as faith lies awaiting discovery behind the façade of scepticism. There is no way I can destroy that faith. Should I do so, I will be depriving mankind of all semblance of trust and belief. Faith is the key to man's existence, because it is faith that binds us all to the Almighty One, the goal every true Muslim aspires to. Seeking the One in the many constitutes the core of the Wahidiya philosophy of tauhid or monotheism. The name of the Supreme Being will always differ from one faith to another, but no religion can deny its monotheistic spirit.'

As Dara spoke, cannons boomed and the foundations of buildings shook. Prabhu Joshi called out to Rajendra Mathur. Voices cried out, 'The civil war in Afghanistan has still not come to an end! The treaty of Jalalabad stands nullified. Villains fight each other, desperate to establish who among them is the greatest villain. The walls of each Afghan city tremble at the sight of these bloodthirsty men. The pawns in the country's bloody game of chess keep changing their positions. There's shelling all over the country. Rockets swoop down and the bombing continues without a pause. From every neighbourhood, innocent citizens flee with their families towards the country's border with Pakistan. Kabul has been defeated, destroyed.

The city of Mazar-e-Sharif groans in despair...'

'Oh!' a distressed Babar exclaimed. 'If Kabul has been destroyed, my grave, too, must have met a similar fate. Where do I go now for my eternal sleep?'

'That is no place for living men,' replied the voice of Rajendra Mathur. 'Fresh corpses lie there unclaimed. At least, you've slept peacefully for so many centuries...Actually, after the Soviet army retreated and the Najibullah government was overthrown, the influx of American dollars into the land dried up completely. The Afghan Pathans are yet to reconcile with the diehard Islamic extremists of Saudi Arabia and Pakistan, because the spirit of freedom flows in Pathan veins and their brand of Islam is more liberal than that practised in other countries.'

'Islam is free everywhere,' interjected Saifuddin Soz who had arrived from Humayun Road in Delhi. 'Kashmiri Islam is free in Kashmir as is Iranian Islam in Iran, Egyptian Islam in Egypt and Turkish Islam in Turkey. The greatness of Islam lies in its ability to absorb the culture of whichever soil it germinates in. That is why a Kashmiri Muslim is, first and foremost, a Kashmiri, and not a Muslim, irrespective of origin. It is the reason underlying a Kashmiri Muslim's problems in coexisting with a Punjabi Muslim from Pakistan. For centuries, a Kashmiri Muslim has lived with and shared his cultural traditions with the Hindu Pandits of Kashmir and will continue to do so. In Kashmir, Lalleshwari and Habba Khatoon cannot be treated as separate entities. Demanding a Hindu homeland in my region, Hindu Pandits of Panun Kashmir are actually harming the interests of Kashmir's Hindu Pandits. Ours is a confluence of the Sufi way and the tradition of the rishis. Far removed from religious extremism, ours is a new tradition of Kashmiri Islam that has reached us via Zainul Abidin, Lalleshwari and Habba Khatoon.'

At this, the adeeb pointedly inquired, 'Then why is it, Saifuddin Soz Sahib, that Kashmir's Hindu Pandits are demanding a Hindu homeland or their version of Pakistan?'

'Pakistan carries on giving birth to more Pakistans,' quipped Nikhil Chakravarthy. 'It is an infectious disease. As long as religion, race, caste and imperialist ambitions continue to hold mankind in thrall, as long as lust for power and supremacy thrives, this planet will continue to witness the birth and evolution of many such monstrous Pakistans. Yugoslavia is no more. Afghanistan is heading in that direction. The Taliban have no funds at their disposal. They can only be generated through the smuggling of drugs. Holding the reins of power in Kabul is essential for the control of drug routes. He who rules Kabul will be the beneficiary of the billions that drug smuggling rakes in. With this in mind, Pakistan's Inter-Services Intelligence actively connives with the Taliban to serve as the conduit and joint beneficiary of drug money. The Pakistani government lacks the resources to sustain the ISI. The agency has no option but to survive by seizing control of drug production. A cause for serious concern is the fact that the drug runners of Herat no longer operate through Meshhad. They prefer the cities of Kandahar and Quetta. Sometimes, they go as far south as the fringes of Baluchistan or the towns that dot the border between Pakistan and Iran. Also to be found in this region are tribes and clans that cherish their autonomy and are reluctant to submit to Pakistan's authority. These men are inordinately proud of their freedom, whether they belong to the Wazir tribe or the Masud, the Bhutani or the Mangal, the Bangash, the Orqazai, the Afridi, the Mohmand, the Otmankhel or the Tarklanari.'

Suddenly, a weak voice that seemed to issue from the lips of an ailing person rang out. 'Afghanistan's history cannot be determined if the Mughal dynasty and its legacy are bypassed,' it insisted. 'Even the history of Hindustan would be incomplete without it. That is why, honourable adeeb, you must give me a hearing.'

'Who are you?'

'I am Shah-e-Jahan, otherwise known as Shahjahan. I have come from the stony ramparts of Agra Fort in Hindustan. My daughter, Jahanara, has brought me here. I am gravely ill. Just yesterday, Hakim Bashi made me take his prescribed life-enhancing bath.'

'But...but if you are, indeed, Shahjahan, no one here shows any signs of recognizing you!' the adeeb exclaimed in some confusion. 'Even I can't recognize you.'

'How would you? Only Time can recognize me. Summon him

here. It is my illness that has brought about such a change in me, honourable adeeb. I no longer look the way I used to. I shall take you through history...the kind of history that is neither Shibli Nomani's version nor Kazim Shirazi's. This history belongs neither to Saqi Mustad Khan nor to Kafi Khan. And, if you bring up Aqil Khan's name, even his writings are fabrications. He might have written *Darbar ke Azaad Itihaas*, highlighting the spirit of freedom that marked the atmosphere of the court. But even so, he was a slave of his era, an era which itself stooped before the authority of the court.'

Shahjahan was out of breath after his long speech and Jahanara ministered to him. 'That era was a trial for me, Adeeb, a terrible trial!' As he stared sightlessly into the distance and uttered these words, tears welled up in Shahjahan's eyes. Jahanara wiped away the pearly drops with the edge of her chunni.

'How I wish I hadn't lived to see all that I did! While taking care of me during my illness, Jahanara kept many things from me. Had Dara's son, that is, my brave grandson, Shikoh, not visited me, I would have remained completely ignorant about the real situation.'

'But, honourable father,' Jahanara protested, 'it was your failing health that kept me from bringing you painful news! I could not bear to break your heart by telling you about the conspiracies hatched by Shuja, Aurangzeb, Murad and Roshanara. Your life was far more precious to me than the kingdom.'

'I know, beti, I understand it all. What really hurts me is the fact that Aurangzeb and Roshanara, my own son and daughter, conspired against me.' Shahjahan's voice cracked with emotion.

'You misrepresent facts, Alampanah,' Shibli Nomani interrupted. 'History does not bear out your allegations against Aurangzeb and Roshanara. Historical evidence of the time does not support your statements.'

'History is greater than the historian!' the adeeb rebuked Shibli Nomani. 'Whatever history might have to say about it, my heart tells me that Roshanara had not only conspired with both the Shahi Imam of the Jama Masjid and Qasim Khan, but had also ensnared them in a game of love. Play-acting all the while, she had exploited to the hilt her advantage as a beautiful princess. And, Nomani Sahib, a scholar's evidence that comes straight from the heart is of far greater worth than the evidence submitted by the historian to counter it.'

Before Shibli Nomani could reply, Shahjahan drew the adeeb's attention to himself. 'Adeeb, why do you allow yourself to be embroiled in this argument?' he asked. 'Some individuals are born for the specific purpose of ignoring reality and indulging in needless wrangling. Forget the debate. My request is that you travel to my era, equipped with the mindset and vision of your own age. Witness for yourself what transpired so long ago and strive to understand why it happened.' At Shahjahan's words, Time hurtled back into the past. The centuries staggered back in hasty retreat and came to a halt at Delhi.

24

Gasping for breath, Time's faltering steps led him to the stairs of Delhi's Jama Masjid where he sank down. A bhishti was passing by, carrying water in a leather bag. The adeeb called out to the man, asking him to quench Time's thirst. Pouring water out into a silver bowl, the bhishti handed it to Time. He drank from it and heaved a sigh of relief.

'Honourable adeeb,' he observed after taking a deep breath, 'time goes hand in hand with turmoil. On many an occasion have I been hounded by turbulent events. And I have emerged from them, drenched in blood. This particular moment, this century, does not belong to me. It is beset by upheavals, as the Mughal dynasty advances towards its downfall. This era is rife with conspiracies aimed at seizing the throne of Hindustan. The times of Akbar and Jahangir are gone and Shahjahan lies gravely ill.'

From far away in Delhi, the adeeb could see Shahjahan lying on a bed in the baradari of Agra Fort. Jahanara's hands gently stroked his forehead.

'Badshah Begum,' Shahjahan called out.

'Yes, honourable father?' came the reply.

'It is beyond my comprehension what destiny has in store for this kingdom! The fault is mine, Badshah Begum, for failing to give my four sons a sound Islamic upbringing. Perhaps, it is the reason why all four have chosen to head in different directions. In his pursuit of the monotheistic tauhid, Dara has turned to the Upanishads. Swayed by the influence of Wazir Saadullah Khan, Aurangzeb has become a fanatic. Shuja, I hear, is now inclined towards becoming a Shia. And the hapless Murad is prey to the lure of wine and revelry.'

The adeeb now watched intently, as Time receded even further into the past, metamorphosing into a golden swan, like the bird Babar had seen in Agra after ascending the throne. This bird rose and fell with the air currents. Its wings beat soundlessly as it soared across the sky. Specks of light trailed from its wings and were transformed into fragments of paper that blew about. Gradually, these fragments assumed the shape of books that could be seen flying about in the air—the *Badshahnama, Amal-e-Sualeh, Alamgirnama, Latiful Akhbar, Tarikh-e-Shujai, Muntakhabul Lubab, Masirul Umara, Dabistanul Mazahiboshi, Miratul Khayal, Waqat-e-Alamgiri, Faiyyadul Qawaneen* and the *Mathir-e-Alamgiri*. Pages from the accounts by Manucci and Bernier also fluttered about and a palace made of such manuscripts rose up before the adeeb's eyes.

On entering the palace, the adeeb was astounded by the wealth of documents that Hindustan possessed. An intoxicating aroma of ripe bel fruit pervaded the building. Mingling with it were other scents—of cities and people, nations and faiths. They wafted in from as far away as Turkey, Khorasan, Farghana, Samarqand, Andijan, Balkh, Bokhara, Ghazni, Kandahar, Kabul, Peshawar and Lahore. They emanated from Vedic religions, from Buddhism and Islam. Displayed in this palace were innumerable statuettes of thinkers and philosophers.

Suddenly, clouds of desert sand started rising in the air. Hot winds, interspersed with chilly ones, blew across the building. There was snowfall on the mountain ranges of the Hindukush, the Pamir and the Shivalik. Hailstorms lashed the plains of Andijan, Khorasan, Samarqand and Peshawar. Autumn swept through Ladakh, Kashmir and Tibet, turning the maple leaves scarlet, stripping the safeda trees naked and carpeting the forests with pine needles. It was peculiar weather indeed...

Time called out, 'O Adeeb, manuscripts from all civilizations lie open before you. Peruse them and guide the world down the path of peace.'

'O Lord of Time,' he replied, 'in its own way, each book paves the way to such a goal. But every epoch aspires to either write its own special narrative or have it written by others. Inevitably, each manuscript of truth is distorted into one of falsehood and each specious account comes to be acknowledged as the truth. What can I possibly do in the circumstances?'

'Given the situation, simply note the colour of tears in the universe...just the way you observed the tints of the water at the Dushrock Hotel in Mauritius. Those who do so, discover the real relevance of their times. O Adeeb, try to dam your ocean of tears, but bear in mind that a scholar dies if his tears come to an end. Life entreats you to undertake this important journey.'

The seventeenth century stood before him.

The adeeb issued a command: 'Emperors Babar and Aurangzeb, vacate your thrones. Time now wishes to weigh you in the balance of history.'

The messengers of Time rushed forth. Emissaries and spies came forward with their disclosures.

'In keeping with Emperor Akbar's policy of integration, Dara Shikoh has sent a proposal of marriage to Mirza Raja Jaisingh, asking for the hand of the raja's nephew for his own niece. Shuja and Aurangzeb, the second and third sons respectively, of Emperor Shahjahan, have arrived at a secret understanding—Shuja's daughter, Gulrukh Bano, is affianced to Aurangzeb's elder son Sultan Mohammed. Despite all efforts to keep this news confidential, it is spreading rapidly. By asking for Jaisingh's nephew's hand in marriage, Dara Shikoh has sought to compensate for the terrible misunderstanding that threatened to sour relations between the two during the third siege of Kandahar.'

The peon joined in with a remark: 'Do you see how even marriages in Mughal times were negotiated through carefully planned

moves like those in a game of chess? It is evident in the agreements
reached between Dara and Jaisingh, on the one hand, and Aurangzeb
and Shuja on the other. Ruling a kingdom as extensive as the one
over which the Mughals exercised their power, was certainly no
mean feat.'

An emissary arrived with fresh news. 'The maharana of Mewar
has begun a vicious campaign against Chittorgarh,' he announced. 'It
risks escalating into a major crisis.'

Another had yet more news to break. 'Honourable sir,' he said,
'momentous decisions are being taken right now in Emperor
Shahjahan's court. I have seen it for myself. When the subject of
Mewar came up, the emperor looked at his chief wazir Saadullah.
Although the man was frowning, his manner was calm as he
observed, "It is imperative that we look for the real motive underlying
this campaign. Rajputs, especially the Sisodias of Mewar, cannot be
trusted." Obviously, sir, Prince Dara was striving to discern Saadullah's
stance...'

'Yes, I have an idea of what must have been going through the
prince's mind,' said Time. 'Dara knew about Saadullah being a
devout Sunni who prayed five times a day as is mandatory for a true
Muslim. And deep down, the prince understood only too well how
important it was for the Mughals as conquerors of Hindustan to
maintain a distance with their subjects. In the past, relations had
been strained between the prince and the wazir on that score. I can
recall many occasions on which Saadullah had emphatically declared
in the court, "We should never lose sight of our lineage that can be
traced back to Emperor Babar who belonged to the family of
Taimur. We came from Farghana to Hindustan on the strength of
Babar's sword. Had it not been so, we would still be hunting wild
beasts in the forests today and preparing them for consumption the
way our tribal culinary traditions had taught us to." When Saadullah
had repeated this observation several times, Dara could bear it no
longer. In the emperor's presence, he had declared, "Honourable
Chief Wazir...that was a different era. Hindustan is now our
country, our motherland. We were born here and here shall we be
buried." Saadullah had made no reply, but it was obvious to all

present that the prince and the wazir were clearly divided over the policies pertaining to Mughal governance.'

Another emissary offered further details on the matter. 'But, sir,' he protested, 'this time the wazir quoted from an important document from the past. He also exhorted us to bear in mind the agreement between Emperor Jahangir and Mewar's Rana Amar Singh. The wazir contended that it was clearly stipulated in the treaty the two had signed, that no extensions to the fort at Chittor could be undertaken as part of any expansion plan. Nor could secret passageways be built without royal sanction.'

A man arrived to convey further news. 'The latest development,' he announced, 'is that the chief wazir has, with the permission of the emperor, dispatched Abdul Beg to the maharana of Mewar. Beg carries a farman directing Mewar to send a regiment of soldiers to the southern subedar, Prince Aurangzeb. However, Abdul Beg's real mission, sir, is to covertly gauge the maharana's military strength and to determine whether any expansion of the fort is being undertaken on the pretext of carrying out repairs.'

On his return, Abdul Beg presented a detailed report of his mission from which it was inferred that the intentions of the maharana of Mewar were clearly suspect. Wazir Saadullah set out with an army of 30,000 men in a bid to force the maharana's hand and engage him in battle. Eventually, however, Dara intervened and came out in support of the maharana. The prince arranged for another decree to be issued by Shahjahan that forbade an attack on Mewar. Saadullah rebelled against Dara's intervention and although he could not overtly disregard the royal farman, he lost no opportunity in teaching the maharana a lesson. By setting harsh terms and conditions for withdrawing his troops, he succeeded in wresting control of some areas of Mewar for his supporters. He also forced the maharana into an agreement which ensured that in future, the eldest son of Mewar's ruling clan would remain under the tutelage of the royal Mughal court.

Dara saved the maharana from a humiliation worse than outright ruin. But as irony would have it, the latter chose to interpret even this gesture of Dara's as a slight and preferred to align himself with

Aurangzeb. It was precisely what Saadullah had been hoping for. The wazir could foresee the battle for succession that lay ahead and planned his moves with the utmost caution. It was evident that he had little sympathy for Dara's patriotism and desire to keep his kingdom united at all costs.

Observing the rivalry between his dear friend, the wazir, and his favourite son, Dara, Shahjahan was as distraught as Akbar had been in his time on learning of the enmity between Salim and Abul Fazal. The intensity of Dara's hatred for Saadullah's authority matched that of his revulsion at the wazir's fanatical devotion to his Sunni faith. Moreover, the growing bond between Saadullah and Aurangzeb, who acknowledged the former as his mentor and teacher, was something Dara found hard to reconcile himself to. The spats between the wazir and Dara continued unabated. The spies and emissaries planted in Dara's court by Shuja, Murad and Aurangzeb carried back reports to their masters of the unrelenting animosity between the two. They also pronounced Saadullah to be an honest and intelligent individual who did not take kindly to the obstacles placed in his path. He was a competent and committed wazir, they reported, a radical Muslim and a man who always preferred to be on the winning side. They contended, however, that Dara was no devious schemer either, but a sentimental and persevering individual and a popular prince. The perpetual sparring between the two men was stoked by their pride and soaring ambitions.

Though internal conflicts and religious extremism surfaced during Shahjahan's reign, it was, on the whole, a progressive and humane period in Bharat's history.

And then there was the south—a matter of pressing concern. Aurangzeb was the subedar there. Over this issue, a split had developed between two camps—the fiery trio of Saadullah, Aurangzeb and Roshanara on the one hand, and the gentle duo, Dara and Jahanara, on the other. Eventually, it was this bitter factionalism that would lead to the battle of succession.

The adeeb was able to grasp the underlying compulsions of these historical events, but it was too late to change them. The princes had already planned their moves in the battle of succession and were impatient to put them into operation.

'O Time, where are you?' the adeeb called.

'Speak!' Time commanded.

'Since you have granted me the boon of travelling back through history, I seek your help once again…'

'Yes?'

'I wish to probe all the hidden histories that lie buried beneath History itself. I am keen to examine the blood that flows in its veins, to explore the intricacies of the minds that aspired and conspired to create situations of momentous import. Tell me how I can look upon this abstract, invisible, indefinable truth!'

'Adeeb, I am that invisible truth you call "eternity". You have made me omnipotent and immortal. Yet, for your own convenience, you have split me up into ages, epochs, centuries, decades, phases and moments. That history, through which you travelled back into the past as a historian, is a mere fragment of all these time spans. It shouldn't be difficult for you now to get to the heart of the truth.'

The adeeb realized that he had no one to rely on, but himself. So, he called out to Golconda Fort that had successfully resisted the onslaught of every invader through the centuries. The fort appeared and stood before him.

'What conspiracies have been hatched against you?' the adeeb asked it.

'Many,' came the reply. 'Some conspire against us, because my sultan, Quli Qutbshah, is favourably inclined towards Shias, not Sunnis. Other plots are hatched as Shahjahan's four sons engage in the battle of succession. Proclaiming his Sunni credentials, Aurangzeb conspires to defeat the Shia principalities of Golconda and Bijapur, with the intention of wresting control of their rulers' three-lakh-strong armies. Aurangzeb is not quite as intelligent, though, as he is made out to be. The mastermind of this conspiracy is actually his sister Roshanara. In the battle for the throne, she wants him to prove his military prowess and strength. Ably assisting Aurangzeb is Shahjahan's chief wazir Saadullah. It is the reason behind the prince's decision to lay siege to me for six months, during which all supply routes for my citizens and soldiers have been cut off. As far as we know, the Mughal Emperor Shahjahan has ordered Aurangzeb to merely flex his military muscle and facilitate the release of Mir Jumla's family from Golconda. The feeble pretext cited for justifying this attack is that Mir Jumla was a retainer of the royal court, not of Golconda. It is, obviously, a ploy on Aurangzeb's part to kill our ruler, Quli Qutbshah, and take over the principality. That is, in fact, what he did in Bijapur too. In implementing this scheme, he has the heartfelt support of both Emperor Shahjahan's crafty daughter Roshanara, and of his wazir Azam Saadullah, who believes Shias and Iranian Sufis to be the enemies of Islam. Actually, it is not Golconda– Bijapur, but the Peacock Throne of the Mughals that Aurangzeb has set his sights on. By defeating the two principalities, he aims to wrest control of our armies and put them to use in his future campaigns.'

Suddenly, amidst a rumbling of echoes, a pen, which looked brighter and more lethal than a sword, fell from the heavens. There was a crack of lightning and from the cavernous depths of the sky, fragments of light exploded. Knowing that the pen was mightier than the sword, the adeeb demanded to know the identity of the person it belonged to.

In a respectful tone, the peon replied, 'It belongs to Shibli Nomani, the eminent intellectual who already stands before you.'

'Shibli Nomani Sahib,' the adeeb asked gently, 'do you have anything to add to the account given by Time?'

'Indeed I do, Adeeb. So far, whatever has been said or thought of is incorrect—absolutely false. Actually, it is Dara who masterminded the conspiracy. It is he who persuaded Shahjahan to send a royal farman to Aurangzeb, commanding him to lift the siege of Golconda. For six months, Aurangzeb laid siege to Bijapur. Just when his victory seemed assured and defeat stared Bijapur's ruler Ali Adil Shah in the face, Dara's plans bore fruit. Shahjahan overturned his own farman and ordered Aurangzeb, Mahawat Khan and Chhatrasal Hara to return forthwith to Agra with the army. Aurangzeb was stunned by this royal decree. What a strange decision it conveyed! There is little doubt that Emperor Shahjahan was no more than a puppet in Dara's hands, the same Dara who wanted to undermine his brother's authority in the battle for the throne. So, without

Aurangzeb's knowledge, a treaty was signed by Dara on behalf of
Shahjahan and, ostensibly, at the "request" of Bijapur's ruler Ali Adil
Shah. Such was Dara's devious plot against Aurangzeb.'

'No!' protested the historian Kanungo, as the earth shook and
his pen raced over paper. 'That is certainly not true! In a bid to
consolidate his power in the south, Aurangzeb had taken it upon
himself to propose a treaty with the besieged and demoralized sultan
of Golconda. The terms of the treaty stated that the sultan's mother
would be held prisoner by the prince, his daughter would be married
off to the prince's son, and the sultan would execute a will allowing
none but the offspring of this union legitimate rights to the throne
of Golconda. Honourable adeeb, Aurangzeb made sure that the
terms of the will and treaty were never revealed to Shahjahan. Such
was the nature of Aurangzeb's conspiracy through which he hoped
to lay a strong foundation for his rule in the south. He chose Dara
Shikoh as a scapegoat for his endless scheming, because he knew that
he would be pitted against him during the final battle for succession.
Another factor played a role in these developments. Shahjahan was
greatly alarmed by Aurangzeb's ruthless machinations. He perceived
in this son the image of his own guilty conscience. Shahjahan too had
rebelled against his father and had had his elder brother murdered.
He feared that history would repeat itself through Aurangzeb. Beset
by apprehensions, Shahjahan felt that Aurangzeb was trying to realize
his dreams of ascending the throne of Delhi by wresting control of
the huge armies of Bijapur and Golconda and reinforcing his position
as subedar of the south. To circumvent this eventuality, Shahjahan
thought of transferring the subedari of the south to Shuja. He even
wrote to the latter in this connection. Unfortunately, the emperor
failed to pursue his plans further. He fell ill on 6 September 1657.
At the time, Dara Shikoh was only forty-two years old. With the
onset of Shahjahan's illness, the battle for succession had begun.'

An elderly ulema rose to his feet and sought permission to
speak. 'Sir,' he began, 'that was a different era altogether. All the
people present here now judge those turbulent, feudal times from
the progressive political perspective prevalent today. Where statecraft
was concerned, Islam never regarded the right of succession as a

ruler's divine prerogative. That is why succession in Islamic dynasties has always been decided at the point of a sword, never on precise, clearly delineated laws of inheritance. Moreover, there has been no condemnation of the violent opposition and bloodletting associated with succession in Taimur's family. The sword, not ethics, decides the issue here.'

Another ulema intervened. 'That apart, the individuality, character and religious inclinations of the princes had little to do with their mutual battles of succession. The battle between Dara and Aurangzeb was fought for the throne; it was not a conflict between the empire's Hindu and Muslim subjects. The question of religious beliefs was simply not relevant to the issue. Had it been so, the Syeds of Barha would not have cast their lot with Dara. Nor would Maharana Rajsingh of Jaipur have supported Aurangzeb. Furthermore, sir, I do not subscribe to Shibli Nomani Sahib's view that Dara had renounced his religion. He might have had his differences with the mullahs—in fact he did have them—but he was a Muslim who remained true to his faith until he died. Even the historian, Bernier, who was hostile to Dara acknowledges this.'

Shibli Nomani could restrain himself no longer. 'Whatever one might say to the contrary, the fact remains that Shahjahan wanted Dara to inherit the throne!' he burst out.

'That stemmed from Shahjahan's fear of Aurangzeb's rebellious ways and his passion for bloodletting,' Kanungo offered by way of explanation. 'He knew that Aurangzeb was quite capable of killing him, if it served his purpose.'

'But he didn't, did he!' Shibli Nomani retorted belligerently.

'Not at the point of a sword, perhaps. But by condemning Shahjahan to life imprisonment and thereby prolonging his humiliation, Aurangzeb forced upon him a slow and painful death,' Kanungo commented.

'Whatever may have transpired,' continued Shibli Nomani, 'there's no denying the fact that Shahjahan never allowed Dara out of his sight. During the twenty-year duration of his reign, Dara was rarely absent from the court for more than fifteen months. Though he had never proved his prowess on the battlefield, he was given the command of sixty thousand men. It was a far more important position than the collective responsibilities assigned to Shahjahan's three other sons. Dara's son, Suleiman Shikoh, was the subedar of Kabul in absentia. He was conferred the title of Bara Hazari— Commander of Twelve Thousand. Shahjahan had given Dara charge of the royal treasury, the army, the cavalry and the entire arsenal of ammunition. Much before the battle of succession was launched, Shahjahan had had a golden throne made and placed next to the Peacock Throne. He had made Dara Shikoh sit on it. Where was the need for a formal coronation?'

'What was wrong with that?' Kanungo countered. 'Firstly, Dara Shikoh was Shahjahan's eldest son. Secondly, by the time Shahjahan was in power, the Mughal dynasty had already ruled over Hindustan for a hundred and ten years. Shahjahan was familiar with the prevailing traditions of royal succession in the land. His conscience troubled him over the manner in which he himself had acquired the throne—by killing his elder brother. Perhaps, to prevent further bloodshed, Shahjahan wished to adopt the principles of succession that rulers in Hindustan and in other advanced civilizations had implemented. But that was not to be.'

The adeeb glanced at the peon who was taking down copious notes. 'What are you up to?' he asked.

'Like Ganesh, I am taking notes on this Mahabharata,' the peon explained. 'They will help you to compile your history, sir.'

Shibli Nomani intervened, 'Honourable sir, let no falsification of history be put on record.'

'So, shall we accept your historical insights, your explanations and arguments as the final word?' the adeeb asked.

'You must, because Emperor Shahjahan was a worshipper of Islam, not of Bharat. He was a true Muslim who—'

Shibli Nomani was interrupted by an elderly ulema who sarcastically asked, 'Is that why he was fonder of Aurangzeb with his zeal for Islam than of Dara Shikoh with his concern for Bharat?'

'This is hardly an argument worth considering!' Shibli Nomani retorted.

'It most certainly is,' the adeeb intervened. 'It is your manuscript, your perception which makes me infer that Shahjahan was more intolerant of Hindus than Aurangzeb ever was...that he had more Hindu mandirs demolished than Aurangzeb had, that he had tyrannized Hindus and was a more fanatical Muslim than Aurangzeb.'

'Yes, that is the truth.'

'Why, then, did Shahjahan not extend his support to the fanatical Aurangzeb who opposed Hindus, choosing, instead, to cast his lot with Dara, for whom Hindus were a greater priority than his fellow Muslims?'

'I have little to say about this issue,' Shibli Nomani remarked.

'I, on the other hand, have much to say. History written in blood and recorded under coercion can never be other than suspect. Such accounts are written by professional historians who are paid to do so. Far more authentic are accounts that record the thoughts, aspirations and remorse of the very people who actively participated in historical events. That is why Babar's *Babarnama* is an accurate and reliable historical record. No matter what Babar might have done to undermine the resilience of Bharat's Hindus, the fact remains that he never returned to Farghana. That is why he was buried in Agra. It is a different matter that he was later declared a Ghazi and his crumbling, maggot-infested bones exhumed and taken to Kabul for burial. Kabul was neither his birthplace nor his homeland.'

The peon noted this statement.

'I acknowledge Babar's role as an invader,' the adeeb continued, 'but no one seems to have appreciated his sense of remorse. Just think about it. Thousands of years before Babar, Orissa's Kalinga region was not ruled by its natives, but by an alien raja. When Ashoka attacked Kalinga, it was as an invader that he did so. The battle was so violent and left so many casualties that the waters of the Daya river itself ran crimson with blood. Ashoka sought redemption for his barbaric savagery in battle by evolving the principles of panchsheel and ahimsa. If Ashoka's act of repentance can be deemed patriotic, why can't remorse on the part of the Mughals who had embraced Bharat as their own country be regarded as such? The Mughals' search for absolution was, on each occasion, driven by a deep sense of remorse that sprang not from Arabic, Turkish, Tartar or Afghan soil, but was rooted in Bharat itself. Akbar is a shining example of the nobility of such a quest. Ruthlessly selfish rulers have, on several pretexts—of faith, race or fame sprung from unanticipated victory—omitted from the record of their tales of triumph, the fears that beset the human spirit. We are here to record those fears that history has overlooked, to lend expression, once again, to the feelings of compunction that overwhelmed medieval invaders and incorporate them into Bharat's folklore and songs of praise. Friends, I believe that Akbar was the human manifestation of Babar and Humayun's accumulated feelings of remorse. And in Dara Shikoh were manifested the compunctions that tormented Jahangir and Shahjahan. The problem, however, lies in the fact that regret and the need for redemption have no place in any religious institution or movement under a monarchy. For faith and religion rarely keep up with the realities of life and invariably lag centuries behind. It is the discrepancy between religion and reality that lays the foundation for the many "Pakistans" that have no grounds at all for taking root. It is men like Hazrat Shibli Nomani who pave the way for the rise of these grotesque "Pakistans". Do you know what's happening in Egypt, Tunisia, Turkey, Algeria, Somalia, Lebanon and Iraq? There, Muslims are pitted against Muslims! These conflicts, Shibli Nomani Sahib, are generated by fanatical zeal, not religion. A religion like Islam is battling its own zealots. Perhaps, all the religions in the world will be compelled to wage war on their own band of fanatics. With your bigoted vision and the arguments originating from it, you will continue to create one Pakistan within another. Caught in the web of such fanaticism, the world may only dream of a universal religion for all mankind. There never will be a world united by a single religion. Ours is destined to remain a repository of many faiths—where narrow-minded zealots are up in arms against each other forever.'

'You've launched into a speech,' the peon admonished, laying down his pen. 'We were recording history and you have digressed into philosophy. Time gave you the opportunity to be a historian and that's what you should focus on.'

At his words, Shibli Nomani took up his narrative again. 'Since childhood,' he related, 'there was ill will between Aurangzeb and Dara Shikoh. I now speak of 28 May 1637. Two elephants— Sudhakar and Suratsundar—were facing each other in combat on the sands of the Jamuna below Agra Fort. Such sport being a favourite regal pastime, the emperor and all the princes were present on the occasion. After trouncing Suratsundar, the enraged Sudhakar ran amuck and attacked Aurangzeb who was on horseback. The horse succumbed to its injuries, but the fifteen-year-old prince managed to escape with his life. Later, Shuja, Mirza Raja Jaisingh and Aurangzeb killed the mad elephant. Though Dara Shikoh was present, he had made no move to save his brother.'

It was Kanungo who presented the other version of the story. 'That happened because Dara was behind the elephant,' he explained. 'From his position, there wasn't much he could have done.'

Another ulema joined in the debate. 'Raising the subject of his narrow escape,' he began, 'Aurangzeb had told Shahjahan at the time, "Had I been killed by the enraged elephant, it would not have been a cause for shame. What was truly reprehensible, however, was the conduct of my brothers." Shibli Nomani Sahib, these are the exact words quoted by Aurangzeb's admiring historian Hamiduddin Khan. The incident highlights Aurangzeb's craftiness and the sharp edge of his sarcasm. Referring though he was to both his brothers, his actual intention was to draw attention to Dara. When Aurangzeb's official historian recorded this incident, he wrote, "Despite his eagerness to do so, Dara could not have helped Aurangzeb in his moment of crisis, as he was at the opposite end from the spot where the incident occurred. Besides, it was all over in a few moments." Moreover, Janab, another significant incident deserves mention in this context. Dara had had a new summer palace constructed for himself in Agra. Out of love and regard for his three brothers, Dara had invited them along with the emperor to survey his new palace. When they arrived, Shuja, Murad and the emperor entered the building, but Aurangzeb chose to sit by the doorway. Although Shahjahan repeatedly questioned the prince about his odd behaviour, Aurangzeb would offer no explanations whatsoever. For his unseemly conduct, he was even barred from the royal court for seven months. At the time, he had confessed to his sister Roshanara, "The summer palace had only one entrance and I feared that Dara, in league with the emperor, would have me assassinated along with my brothers. By killing us, Dara would clear the way for his own ascension to the throne. My suspicions prevented me from entering the palace and I chose to sit like a sentry at the door." The historian, Hamiduddin Khan, who enjoyed Aurangzeb's patronage, has recorded this incident in detail in *The Official History of Aurangzeb.*'

Waving some documents in his hand, Kanungo voiced his fears. 'Given its inherent psychological nuances, doesn't this incident clearly foretell that one day, Aurangzeb would be the one to kill his father and his brothers?' he asked. 'Otherwise, what made Aurangzeb reveal his secret apprehensions about Dara in the guise of explaining his reasons for wrecking the latter's supposedly heinous plans? From the very outset, it was Aurangzeb who had been anticipating the battle for succession. He had even chalked out his strategy for it. Dara Shikoh, a thorn in his side, had always been his chosen target. Aurangzeb knew that his machinations would serve him well in ridding himself of Shuja and Murad. It was his reason for swearing on the Holy Koran and assuring Murad, his younger brother and subedar of Gujarat, that after crowning the latter emperor of Hindustan, Aurangzeb would undertake the Haj pilgrimage. The rest of his life, Aurangzeb had claimed, would be spent as a haji and a dervish in the cities of Mecca and Medina. He believed that the most effective way of winning the battle he had geared himself up for, was to sharpen the blade of the weapon in his hands—the latent animosity towards Hindus. So, he wrote to Wazir-e-Azam, Saadullah Khan, claiming that Chhabila, a Brahmin from Bihar, had made disrespectful comments about the Prophet of Islam and proposed that the man be summarily sentenced to death and dispatched to hell. The intent of the manoeuvre was twofold: to convince Muslims that justice had been meted out, and to warn Hindus that swift punishment would ensue if they indulged in activities detrimental to Islam. Their cries of protest went unheard...'

The adeeb interrupted Kanungo. 'Look,' he said. 'I want to know more about this battle of succession.'

A weary Time came forward and offered, 'Allow me to narrate the true story. Apart from me, the only witnesses to it are the rivers and soil of Bharat.'

An expectant hush fell over the adeeb's court.

'There is no need to be so dejected, Adeeb,' said Time. 'I will tell you the truth. Which happens to be as follows: More fanatical Muslims were ranged against Dara than the number of Hindus who opposed him. During that era, people had faith in religion, but chose not to follow its dictates. The moment has come for you to travel back in time to that age marked by bloodshed.'

25

The adeeb gazed at the sky. Scarlet clouds billowed forth from every corner. Startled, he remarked to the peon, 'Black, brown, grey and white clouds have I seen...And the silver and gold which line the clouds at dawn or dusk. But never have I come across clouds like these, the colour of blood.'

'Sir, hasn't Time told you? We have now reached an era of history marked by showers of blood. These are vivid manifestations of what is about to take place.'

'Who will give us an account of it all?' the adeeb asked. 'These elephants and horses, those soldiers moving on horseback...these messengers, emissaries and spies...those palaces in distant Ahmedabad, Aurangabad and Bengal...these terrified people...those colonies of vultures waiting on the outskirts of cities...the gathering packs of mongrels. What does it all imply? Do these vultures, curs and eagles have an inkling of what lies ahead?' The adeeb could not stop striking his breast in anguish.

'Sir,' replied the peon, 'none other than Jamuna can relate what really happened in this century.'

'Who's Jamuna?'

'The river. All the rivers of this country are first-hand witnesses to its history.'

'Then summon the Jamuna.'

'Let us make our way there. You can rest on her banks and commune with her.'

The two men reached the banks of the river that flowed like an undulating green ribbon before them.

'What transpires here?' the adeeb asked uneasily. 'Why are those clouds the colour of blood? What does it all signify—this sense of impending doom, this atmosphere of collusion and conspiracy, these tense, silent people, the commotion of soldiers on horseback, those watchful hyenas, vultures and dogs, waiting, waiting...?'

The Jamuna launched into her narrative. 'Look, Surdas—' she began.

'What!' exclaimed the peon. 'My honourable adeeb's name is not Surdas!'

'The greatest adeeb I know of happens to be Surdas. That is why I look upon every adeeb as Surdas. When the windows of a person's mind are thrown open to the world, he is transformed into a Surdas. My own Surdas was a fortunate man, exposed as he was to nothing but the pure world of beauty and innocence. You, on the contrary, are unlucky. In search of beauty and love, you have lost your way in a world that seethes with deceit and fraud and is ruled by overriding ambition, clandestine alliances, secret conspiracies, weapons of destruction and violent death,' Jamuna observed sadly. 'But I will keep nothing from you. Look. The battle of succession has now reached a crucial juncture. It is winter. Slumbering in the embrace of wisps of rising mist, I was awakened by the thundering hooves of horses. I saw Prince Aurangzeb, who had been in the south until now, enter Agra. Then came Prince Shuja from the royal palace of Bengal. Both had arrived here without the emperor's royal authorization. The emperor was displeased, because the princes had breached royal protocol by failing to seek his permission before entering the city.

'During the same winter, it had taken Aurangzeb just three days to settle, amidst much revelry, the marriage of Shuja's daughter, Gulrukh Bano, with his elder son Sultan Mohammed. The episode distressed Shahjahan greatly. He was, after all, the emperor and family patriarch. Yet, no one had thought to consult him about the marriage of his grandchildren. His suspicions aroused, he imagined a conspiracy brewing. There even followed a long, bitter correspondence on the issue between the emperor and Aurangzeb. The former wanted the engagement called off. Attempting to create a rift between the brothers and win over Shuja, the emperor claimed that Aurangzeb had failed to administer the south ably and advised Shuja to relinquish the subedari of Bengal, of which he had hitherto been in charge, in favour of the subedari of five southern provinces. By then, Shuja, Aurangzeb and Murad Baksh had already struck a deal amongst themselves...And now, that epoch has come to an end, Adeeb.'

'And this ominous silence that bears down on us? This frenzied traffic of messengers, emissaries and horsemen? What does it all mean?' the adeeb asked.

'The storms of suspicion are brewing. The royal court has degenerated into a bazaar of secrets, spies and conspirators. These men, rushing about madly, carry information to the three renegade princes. Aurangzeb has established a network of informers. His allies inside the palace are Saadullah, the chief wazir, and Roshanara, his elder sister. The youngest sister, Gauharara, is intensely ambitious. She is the one who passes on all the inside information to Murad. Through letters and messages, the three princes keep in touch and plot their strategies. It is the horsemen here who help them do so. The plot against the emperor and Dara has already been set in motion. But shall I divulge a secret?' Jamuna asked.

'Do. What is it?'

'The mastermind of this entire plot is Aurangzeb. He rarely talks and is an attentive listener. His expression always remains impassive. Though there is tacit understanding and agreement between the three princes, Aurangzeb never allows himself to forget that after Dara, Shuja is the rightful claimant to the throne. After Dara, it is Shuja he regards as his enemy. And so, Aurangzeb strikes a separate deal with Murad and evolves a secret code for communications between them. The key to the code is sent to Murad on 23 October 1657, so that the two of them alone can decipher the real meaning of their missives. Conspiring with his three "dear" brothers, Aurangzeb has singled out Dara—the upholder of an Islam accommodating a multiplicity of religious tenets—as the common enemy. Taking Murad into his confidence, he has also targeted Shuja, describing him as a devious man and a heretic Shia. He has also convinced Murad into believing that he alone, among the three brothers, is the most eligible contender for the throne. To further his ulterior motives, Aurangzeb is trying to lend a religious slant to the battle for succession. It is now a certainty, Surdas, that the three brothers will unite in rebellion against the emperor and attempt to overthrow him. After defeating their eldest brother, Dara Shikoh, they will turn against each other and fight it out to decide on the successor to the throne.'

Armed with a telescope, the adeeb looked back in time...

Chaos prevailed in the city of Agra. Some declared that the emperor lay gravely ill. Others claimed he was dead. A strange restiveness pervaded the place. Merchants had deputed guards outside their warehouses, commodities were being hoarded, prices were spiralling rapidly and the sense of fear and insecurity was overwhelming. Traders who had come from beyond the borders of the kingdom were loading their merchandise onto camels and preparing to leave. The highways that came in from Bengal, from the south and from Gujarat were empty of traffic. The blood-red tones of the clouds had deepened...

Putting away the telescope, the adeeb asked the Jamuna, 'You must have seen it all.'

'There is little that I missed,' the river replied. 'Let us turn the pages of time and I will tell you what followed next. It is Hindustan's misfortune that Shahjahan fell ill while this conspiracy was unfolding. It was the summer of 1657. By the time September came around, the emperor was seriously ill. Regular reports of his failing health had been reaching the three princes who were bracing themselves for rebellion. While Dara Shikoh nursed the emperor, his opponents spread the rumour that Shahjahan was dead. Shahjahan foresaw the bloodshed that could ensue from this rumour. To disprove it and take his subjects into his confidence, the emperor appeared before thousands of people on the jharoka outside his living quarters. The date was 14 September 1657. A durbar was also held. Summoning his trusted courtiers and officers, Shahjahan wrote his will in their presence and directed them to obey Dara Shikoh's orders. Though there was no formal coronation ceremony, the emperor's subjects were left in no doubt that Dara was being invested with the full powers of a monarch. The emperor's health subsequently improved and it was felt that the environs of Delhi would prove more salubrious for his physical well-being. On 18 September 1657, the royal procession set out for the capital city. The news dampened the spirits of the rebellious princes for a while. But Aurangzeb was no ordinary man. Going to great efforts to achieve his goal, he fanned the rumour that Shahjahan was dead and that the man who had given an audience from the jharoka was merely an old Khoja Muslim who had been dressed in royal robes and made to play a part. When Aurangzeb's supportive sister, Roshanara, who was present in the palace, refuted this claim, another story was fed to the grapevine—that Dara Shikoh had abducted and imprisoned the old emperor and had taken over the reins of power. The three princes—Shuja, Aurangzeb and Murad—prepared for battle. That was not all. Shuja declared the emperor dead and crowned himself king. Then leaving his provincial capital of Bengal, he attacked Bihar, a region under Dara's jurisdiction. The emperor, who was still alive, could not bear to see what was happening. At the same time, he did not want any of his sons to suffer or be killed in the family feud.'

'What happened next?'

'No one can narrate the events that ensued except the rivers— the Ganga, Chambal, Narmada, Sutlej, Beas and Indus—or those who played a role in the internal feud of the royal family,' proclaimed the Jamuna before dissolving into the green ribbon that it had been earlier.

The peon called out: 'All the players, participants, protagonists and villains, along with the eyewitnesses of Bharat's seventeenth-century battle of succession, are required to be present in the court of the honourable adeeb!'

Within moments, a huge crowd had gathered. Dara Shikoh was there, along with Shuja, Aurangzeb and Murad. Also present were

Jodhpur's Raja Jaswant Singh, Jaipur's Maharaja Mirza Raja Jaisingh, Dara's sons, Suleiman Shikoh and Sipihar Shikoh, Dumrao's Rajput, Ujjania, Shahjahanpur's Rohilla chieftain, Sardar Diler Khan, Hissar's Daud Khan, the turncoat Khalilullah Khan, the Syed chieftains of Barha, mercenary sipahsalars from all over, Dara's Italian gunner, Manucci, the French physician, Bernier, and countless onlookers. Besides these people, the rivers mentioned by the Jamuna were also present.

The first to give a statement was the river Ganga. The peon took it down.

'I am a witness,' the Ganga reported. 'For a long time now, Shuja had been preparing for the battle of succession. Taking full advantage of the misleading news about the emperor's death, he had left his province and attacked Bihar. Shuja's naval vessels and Dara's armies clashed and trampled over me in their haste to reach Agra. Shuja was aware that Murad's army in Gujarat and that of Aurangzeb in the south had started marching towards the Narmada. The emperor tried to intimidate Shuja by sending him a stern farman, but it had little effect. Rather, it goaded the prince into commanding Dara to hand over Monghyr Fort in Bihar. Dara managed, somehow, to convince the emperor to send a large contingent of troops that would defeat and, thereby, halt Shuja's advancing army. Shahjahan accepted this suggestion with a heavy heart, as the downfall of the Mughal dynasty seemed imminent. Eventually, under the command of Dara's elder son, Suleiman Shikoh, the royal forces proceeded towards Benares. Though only twenty-two years old at the time, Suleiman was a courageous young man. Along with him, the Rajput army under Jaipur's Mirza Raja Jaisingh, who was appointed advisor to Suleiman, was also desptached.

'These armies reached my banks. Only later would it be known why Raja Jaisingh's forces had taken so long to reach Benares. Actually, Mirza Raja Jaisingh was Aurangzeb's secret ally. He was vigilant about ensuring that Shuja, Aurangzeb's accomplice, did not suffer any losses. For three days, the imposing Suleiman Shikoh camped on one of my banks in Benares. Then, using his boats as stepping stones, he built a sort of bridge and crossed over to the opposite bank. Shuja was in a great hurry to reach Benares, because it was easier to halt there and indefinitely delay the advance of the royal army. He also wanted the royal highway, which ran along my southern bank and passed through Chunar and Patna, to remain open. Suleiman had camped at Bahadurgarh. Shuja, in the meantime, was advancing with a contingent, but he had to find a place to halt. To set up camp, he chose an inaccessible area surrounded by hillocks, jungles and streams just behind my banks. He also established control over a stretch of my water by placing his artillery there. These measures facilitated the transportation of his supplies and munitions.'

The Ganga continued, 'The two armies camped for a while. Then, the Rohilla, Sardar Diler Khan, and Dumrao's Rajput, Sardar Ujjania, joined Suleiman with their troops. Mirza Raja Jaisingh had also reached the spot, but as military advisor, he held back the offensive. Finally, Suleiman was issued orders to attack. By then, his spies had furnished valuable information. On the morning of 14 February 1658, Suleiman launched a massive attack on Shuja's camp. Shuja was stunned. Astride an elephant, he called out to his commanders and soldiers, but by then, most of them had fled or been mowed down. Shuja was no coward and he bravely faced the royal army. Suleiman and Diler Khan cut off his paths of retreat. Mirza Raja Jaisingh and Anirudh Gaur approached Shuja's elephant. A fierce battle ensued and Shuja's mount was wounded. Despite this setback, the animal's skilled mahout was able to carry Shuja away to the boats anchored on my banks. The prince thus managed to escape imprisonment and death. Abandoning his wounded soldiers, he escaped to his provincial capital via Patna. Bereft of its commander and stranded between Suleiman's sword and my flowing waters, slaughter and pillage were all Shuja's hapless army could expect. I became the graveyard for those floating corpses. My water changed colour. Suleiman won a decisive victory and captured weaponry worth more than two crores.

'It took the fugitive Shuja five days to reach Patna. Mirza Raja Jaisingh, who was supposed to pursue and capture him, took twenty long days to reach the same destination. Unfamiliar with the terrain,

Suleiman had refrained from personally embarking on the mission of capturing the fugitive prince. Mirza Raja Jaisingh, on the other hand, was well acquainted with every inch of the ground. From Patna, Shuja fled to Monghyr. He sought refuge in Surajgarh, fifteen miles from Patna, and stayed there till the end of March. Eventually, Surajgarh was also captured by the royal forces, but Shuja managed to escape again. He was finally cornered between the hills of Kharagpur and my flowing waters. Even here, Mirza Raja Jaisingh's forces failed to capture the defeated prince. Despite the decisive victory won by Suleiman, Jaisingh was involved, all along, in peace parleys with Shuja's emissary, Mirza Janbeg, whom he entertained lavishly.'

'The tale of another fierce battle runs alongside this one,' said a voice. The adeeb recognized it as the voice of the river Narmada.

'What do you have to say?' the adeeb and the peon asked simultaneously.

'It transpired that Aurangzeb and Murad had learnt of Shuja's rebellion and attack in the east. From their positions in the south and the south-west, both the brothers set out for Agra. The news, relayed to the royal court by spies, left Shahjahan in no doubt as to the intention of all three princes to challenge the power and might of the empire. Immediate orders were issued to Rana Jaswant Singh of Jodhpur and Qasim Khan to advance rapidly and set up camp on my banks, so that Aurangzeb's forces could be prevented from joining up with those commanded by Murad. Both the Rana and Qasim Khan were outwitted by Aurangzeb. Putting his shrewd military strategy into operation, the wily prince managed to lead his forces to join up with those of Murad. On 15 April 1658, a fierce battle ensued on the plains of Dharmat, fifteen miles from Ujjain, situated on the banks of the Shipra river. Qasim Khan's Muslim soldiers betrayed him and the royal forces were routed in this crucial battle. Aurangzeb and Murad emerged victorious. Following his ignominious defeat, Rana Jaswant Singh fled towards Jodhpur. When he reached the city's fort, his consort, a proud Sisodia rani, refused to welcome back her defeated spouse.'

'Yes, that's right,' affirmed the Shipra. 'Mirza Raja Jaisingh

received news of the defeat when he and Shuja were engaged in
peace parleys at Surajgarh. He was ecstatic, and for two reasons.
Firstly, Aurangzeb had won. Secondly, it signalled the defeat of his
enemy, Jaswant Singh, who had claimed equal favour at the royal
court. Raja Jaisingh was also pleased that Jaswant Singh's patron,
Dara Shikoh, had been dealt a severe blow on the battlefield. That
evening, Mirza Raja Jaisingh celebrated his victory on the banks of
the Jamuna. He had already signed a peace treaty with Shuja on 7
May 1658. Honourable adeeb, had the royal forces not been defeated
at Dharmat, the history of Bharat would have taken a different
course altogether.'

'Even after the battle, the course of history could have been
quite different. Despite Jaswant Singh's defeat and Mirza Raja
Jaisingh's treachery, all hope had not been extinguished.' It was now
the river Chambal speaking. 'I happen to know...when the dark
clouds of war were hovering over Samugarh, Shahjahan had ordered
Mirza Raja Jaisingh to leave Bihar as soon as possible and join Dara
Shikoh's forces, so that they could put up a resistance against the
advancing armies of Aurangzeb and Murad. The battle of Samugarh
took place on my banks on 29 May 1658.'

'And what a tragically complicated situation it was!' the Ganga
joined in. 'Suleiman Shikoh had come to know of Mirza Raja
Jaisingh's machinations. On the way back to Agra, he wanted,
therefore, to keep his forces behind the raja's. Suleiman reasoned
that this manoeuvre on his part would ensure that in the eventuality
of an ambush, Jaisingh and his forces bore the brunt of the traitorous
attack. Honourable adeeb, it was during Akbar's reign that the royal
house of Jaipur had become a trusted ally of the Mughals. Mirza Raja
Jaisingh was now merely taking undue advantage of this trust. Such
was also the case with Gwalior. The Jamuna and the Chambal will
bear me out in my testimony that for a long while, the house of
Jaipur had, for the sake of political expediency, turned a blind eye
to all sorts of misdeeds and injustice. The house of Gwalior, too, had
only been lending its ear to tales of torment told by political
prisoners. The very same Gwalior had thrown in its lot with the
British in 1857 and cruelly betrayed Maharani Laxmibai of Jhansi.'

'Yes, indeed,' confirmed the Jamuna, corroborating the authenticity of the account, 'that's the historical truth. Dara learnt of his defeat in the battle of Dharmat when he was at Balochpuri en route to Delhi, where he was taking Shahjahan for medical treatment. On receiving the news, Shahjahan's royal procession returned to Agra.'

This revelation caused a sensation in the court and was followed by people whispering, 'Arrey, Emperor Shahjahan has something to say.'

A handsome old man stood up in the crowded court. Illness and the imminent possibility of civil war had made him despondent.

'Honourable sir,' he said, 'I had spoken up earlier but, in this crowd, I failed to make myself heard. I wish to state again that I am Shahjahan, the emperor of Hindustan. I can assure you that the world does not have a king or father more unfortunate than myself. I am a man broken by terminal illness. I...I have lost my mind. I find myself advising Dara to mount a campaign against my rebellious sons and, in the same breath, urging the vanquished Shuja to make peace with Mirza Raja Jaisingh. At the same time, I order Suleiman Shikoh and Jaisingh to return to Agra forthwith and am shaken by the realization that I am setting my own sons up against each other. Illustrious adeeb, I find myself unable to think or reason...my mind seems to have shut down. All I want is to save the Mughal dynasty from a bloody civil war.

'All manner of information is brought to me in the court. I am aware that my people are devoted to Dara Shikoh, but my lords, wazirs and mullahs are united against him. The god I worship knows that I am a devout Muslim. And now, having witnessed all the tyranny, the demolition of mandirs and the injustice meted out to Hindus, I have reached the conclusion that, in Hindustan, Islam must project a different, more tolerant image. Dara is involved in this endeavour. But now, he is up against the bigoted wolves of Islam. Some of my courtiers support Aurangzeb. So, occasionally, I tend to lean towards him. If, at times, I lend a sympathetic ear to Roshanara who openly supports Aurangzeb, at others, I am in agreement with Jahanara when she speaks of Dara's large-heartedness and the future of Hindustan. When my third daughter, Gauharara, enumerates Murad's virtues, I even begin to find merit in what she says. I have sent word to Mirza Raja Jaisingh and Suleiman Shikoh to come down to Agra as soon as possible, so that we can confront the forces of Aurangzeb and Murad. I can't imagine where they might have been detained. If we have to go into battle before they arrive, there will be no scope for a truce.'

Then the Chambal took up the narrative. 'Yes, that is precisely what happened,' she said. 'Shahjahan's court was in an uproar because of heated exchanges. In the end, recognizing the danger posed by the advancing armies of Aurangzeb and Murad, the emperor ordered Dara to take on the renegade forces and halt their progress. On 22 May 1658, Dara reached Dholpur and busied himself with the fortification of the lines of defence along my banks. That was when I had a close look at him. He looked just like a Sufi dervish. On 23 May, before Dara could organize his soldiers into proper formations, Aurangzeb attacked his forces at a place forty miles from Dholpur and turned the tide of destiny. From my banks, the defeated Dara fled towards Agra, halting only at Samugarh to establish a garrison. It was in Samugarh that the fierce, decisive battle between Dara and Aurangzeb would take place. Thanks to the treachery of Khalilullah's forces, Dara was defeated.'

'Let Khalilullah be produced here!' the adeeb ordered the peon.

Khalilullah made his appearance, his hands clasped together in a gesture of supplication.

'Sir, circumstances compelled us to betray Dara. The fact is, Jaipur's Mirza Raja Jaisingh had, by sending missives and emissaries, turned all the Hindu rajas into Aurangzeb's staunch supporters. Besides, we were Turanis who did not get along with the Hindu and Muslim recruits in the Hindustani army. The Hindustani soldiers did not look upon us as compatriots, but as mercenaries. All these reasons conspired to turn us, deep down in our hearts, against the forces of Hindustan. Honourable adeeb, there was no premeditation in our treachery towards Dara. In Samugarh, Aurangzeb's forces swooped down on us. With defeat staring at us in the face, we chose to align ourselves not with Dara's losing side, but with the Sunni

Aurangzeb's victorious forces. We are mercenaries. We earn to live, not to die. We put up an honest fight, but when we face defeat, our lives lie in the hands of the victor. Dara Shikoh's army with its Iranians, Turanis, Rajputs, the Syeds of Barha and native Muslims, was not without its differences, its misunderstandings and its petty jealousies. Dara had lined up his army on the dusty plains of Samugarh. Barqandaz Khan and Manucci were handed charge of the artillery. Behind the artillery were placed impressive contingents of foot soldiers carrying guns that had to be loaded with dynamite sticks. Following them were five hundred camels, bearing revolving cannons on their backs. They were followed by rows of elephants especially trained in warfare.

'The entire army had been divided into five units before being given its field placing. In the forefront were the contingents of Rajputs and Pathans under the command of Rao Chhatrasal and Daud Khan. In the middle were ten thousand soldiers led by Prince Dara on an elephant. Six thousand of the most loyal soldiers surrounded the prince. With my fifteen thousand men, I was on the right flank. The battle began, the cannons boomed. For a while, Aurangzeb's artillery retaliated, but then fell silent. It seemed that Barqandaz Khan and Manucci had rendered the prince's artillery ineffective. That assumption was our first mistake. We attacked, a fierce battle ensued and Aurangzeb's soldiers in the frontlines were mowed down.

'At this point, Dara himself chose to advance and attacked the contingent in front of Aurangzeb. As the men scattered in the onslaught, the drummers signalled victory. That was our second error. Aurangzeb's fury was aroused and he turned the tables on us. Rao Chhatrasal was killed, along with his son, his brother and his three nephews. When Rustam Khan was killed, Sipihar Shikoh had no option but to flee with those of his men who had survived Aurangzeb's vicious backlash. The camels mounted with cannons and the elephants trained for warfare were abandoned. Dara was surrounded by the enemy forces. Only Daud Khan remained to defend him.

'Then the third mistake was committed. Dara descended from

his elephant and mounted his horse. Now, his wounded and battling soldiers could not see him. A sudden sandstorm blew in from the direction of the Chambal. Everyone was scorched by it. Dara was shaken by the desperate cries of the injured and dying soldiers who had been loyal to him. When he heard the cries of Sipihar Shikoh, it broke his spirit. What could I have done then? I, too, fled. Sir, it is unfair of you to claim that I fled to save my life just when Dara sought the assistance of his right flank and Aurangzeb's son, Sultan Mohammed, launched a frontal attack. The truth, sir, is that Dara was not a seasoned warrior. He lacked the leadership qualities, military expertise and fortitude essential on the battlefield and failed to stand up to Aurangzeb's greater combat experience and superior strategic skills.'

'Whatever be the reason,' shouted the Chambal, 'the battle of Samugarh was not fought for the throne! Its goal was to decide the future of the country. It marked the end of Akbar's era. It was he who had created a nationalistic empire, not an Islamic one. It was in the interest of that empire that Dara had wished to rule over and sustain a united realm, that he had sought the path of unity—unity of faiths, minds and people. He did not believe in confining Islam to the believers of the shariat alone. The unifying spirit of the shariat, he felt, transcended all religions, and aspired to transform it into an infinite faith without boundaries or borders that would be relevant for all men, including non-Muslims.

'It is true that when Dara returned from the failed siege of Kandahar, he spent three weeks with Baba Lali, a Sufi familiar with the Vedas who lived in Kotal-Mehran near Lahore. Dara had the Upanishads translated into Persian, but he remained a disciple of the Sufi sage Mullah Shah. He had met Sheikh Muhibullah Allahabadi and kept in constant touch with Shah Dilruba, Sheikh Mohsin Fani and Sarmad. But you couldn't describe that as a sin, could you?'

'His only sin lay in being the crown prince and heir to the Mughal empire and in trying to write a new chapter in the annals of human history,' said the adeeb, beginning to pace the floor. The peon looked at him in alarm.

Darkness descended. The adeeb looked around and shouted,

'This is the darkness of the seventeenth century! The same gloom that hung over the sandy plains of Samugarh! The blood-laden clouds now turn black and craters have formed in the sand because of the blood it has soaked in. Vultures descend on the field and dogs tear at the bodies of dying men. Look! Cast your eyes over this horrifying scene and see if you can find Dara Shikoh.'

A rumbling voice spoke from the heavens: 'Dara Shikoh is only a short distance away. He stands under a tree, divesting himself of his armour.'

The adeeb looked closely at the spot. There, under the dense, shadowy foliage of a tree, was Dara with a few soldiers for company. Having flung away his armour, he sat reclining against the tree. Snorting horses, foaming at the mouth, stood around. Then came the increasingly loud noise of drumbeats.

A wounded soldier suggested, 'Your Honour, let us move away from here. The drums and soldiers of the enemy are headed in this direction.'

'No, I shall not go anywhere,' Dara replied. 'Whatever has to happen, let it happen now.'

'You must leave. This is just the first battle. Many more lie ahead.'

'The course of this very battle could have been different,' Dara mused. 'If only Mirza Raja Jaisingh had hastened from Bihar to reach this place with the royal forces in time! It was because of him that Suleiman Shikoh was held up. He could not run the risk of allowing his forces to march ahead of Jaisingh's. Perhaps, it was Allah's will.'

The adeeb then watched, as Dara heeded the advice of his loyal soldiers and mounted his horse. He proceeded in the direction of Agra.

'Dara reached his palace at about nine in the evening,' reported the Jamuna, wiping her tears, 'and locked himself in. The sound of weeping rose from every nook and corner of Agra. A feeling of bereavement swept over the entire city. The Emperor Shahjahan sent a messenger summoning Dara to him immediately, but the prince found it impossible to heed his father's command. He wrote back to the emperor saying that the latter would never again need to set eyes on his shamed, dispirited and vanquished son. Describing himself as an unfortunate, half-crazed man who had been robbed of his very reason for living, Dara merely sought his father's blessings for the long journey he would be undertaking. Then, at about three in the morning, he left Agra with his wife, Begum Nadira Bano, his children and his grandchildren. Taking along with him the few loyal soldiers who remained, he set off in the direction of Delhi.'

The voice from the heavens spoke again, 'On the morning of 3 June 1658, Aurangzeb's forces surrounded the capital city of Agra.'

The heavenly voice became a shadow, the shadow assumed a form and the form moved towards the adeeb. As the adeeb and the peon looked on in amazement, they realized that it was Dara Shikoh who stood before them.

'Is it you, Dara Shikoh?' the adeeb asked in surprise.

'Yes, illustrious adeeb, it is I, that unfortunate prince who could not prevent Aurangzeb from creating his Pakistan.'

'What happened after Aurangzeb surrounded Agra?' the peon asked in a respectful tone.

'When Aurangzeb's forces surrounded Agra, I was already on my way to Delhi,' Dara replied and came to sit near the adeeb. 'I did not want to abandon the emperor, but circumstances compelled me to leave the city. Look, Adeeb, the story of my flight is a long one. Homeless, I roamed all over the land. There were only two safe havens for me—Allahabad and Lahore. I thought it better to go to Lahore. Like a vagrant, I wandered endlessly. The tale of my wanderings is a truly pitiable one.'

26

'The tale of my aimless wanderings is a truly pitiable one,' Dara reflected. 'Like a rudderless vessel was I tossed by storms of uncertainty, raked by the thorns of fate, lacerated by the cruel force of circumstance. I was reduced to being a threadbare pennant...a mere skeleton of my real self.'

Sitting nearby, the sorrowful Jamuna whispered, 'Dara, never did you seek to serve your own interests through guile or manipulation. You know only too well that, when you lost the battle at Samugarh, Shuja had already started harbouring suspicions about the means Aurangzeb had deployed to attain his decisive victory. By then, he had become Aurangzeb's foe. You should have resorted to the strategy of befriending Shuja and jointly mounting an offensive from the east. The outcome would have been a crushing defeat for Aurangzeb. Both of you were not the kind who would let ideological malice influence your judgement. Nor were you religious fanatics. Shuja and you could have convinced the people that yours was a concerted effort to simultaneously protect the Emperor Shahjahan and break the siege of Agra. Had you signed a treaty with Shuja, you would have won the support of your subjects for any course of action that you decided on.'

'I had, in fact, tried doing so. It was why I ordered Suleiman Shikoh to return the city of Allahabad to Shuja's officers,' Dara answered.

'Even so, you demonstrated neither shrewdness nor political foresight. You did not repose as much faith in Shuja as you should have. Had you done so, the whole of Hindustan would have opposed Aurangzeb. Shuja was in the east and Murad was almost ready to sign a treaty with him. In Rajasthan, Raja Jaswant Singh was present in Jodhpur. Aurangzeb had no standing in Punjab or Kabul. In the south, Golconda and Bijapur were hostile to him. Had you been astute in planning your military strategy, Aurangzeb would have found himself in a dangerously critical situation. Your decision to proceed to Lahore offered him the chance of dispatching his enemies, one by one. Your greatest blunder was to order Suleiman Shikoh to join you in Lahore via the Terai instead of striking a military deal with Shuja.'

'Perhaps, it was a mistake,' Dara admitted with a deep sigh. 'And once things go wrong, they cannot be set right. The saga of my misfortunes begins here. On 12 June 1658, I set out from Delhi and reached Lahore on 3 July. There I met Raja Rajrup of Jammu. He vowed to help me. To seal our agreement, my wife, Begum Nadira, sent him milk drawn from her breasts, eager to establish a mother–son bond between them. With Daud Khan and Izzat Khan's help, I surrounded Ropar, situated on the banks of the Sutlej. While we were thus engaged, I was being pursued by Aurangzeb's commander-in-chief Bahadur Khan. His forces crossed the Sutlej during the night and the crisis reached its height.'

'I had seen Dara,' the Sutlej testified. 'He felt unsafe on my banks. By then, Aurangzeb had dispatched Mirza Raja Jaisingh and Khalilullah to assist Bahadur Khan against Dara.'

'Yes, this was the same Khalilullah who had betrayed me in Samugarh!' Dara shouted. 'I could not bear to see my wife and children being slaughtered before my eyes, so I set off towards Multan.'

'But escape wasn't easy. Aurangzeb's forces wanted to capture Dara alive. Then it was my sister, the Beas river, who did all she could to help Dara. She stretched herself wider and overflowed her banks. Now, all that stood between Dara and the forces pursuing him was the breadth of the Beas.'

'Yes, all that separated us were the waters of the Beas. The proximity of Aurangzeb's forces made even my most trusted sipahsalar, Daud Khan, fearful about his family's safety. Although Manucci, my Italian gunner, and Sipihar Shikoh had joined us at Bhakkar, Daud Khan sought my permission to leave and returned to his home in Hissar via Jaisalmer. Only misfortune lingers by the side of a defeated warrior. My soldiers forsook me and my officers deserted me to return to their fiefdoms. And that vile man, Raja Rajrup, to whom Nadira had sent her breast milk, crossed the Beas and joined Aurangzeb. It was this traitor Rajrup who would later crush the vanguard of my forces in the battle of Devrai. But that was later...Somehow, I managed to reach Multan on 4 September 1658.'

Time intervened. 'Honourable adeeb,' it began, 'Time is neither Hindu nor Muslim. History stands witness to the fact that rulers and dynasties were either Hindu or Muslim. It was their vested interests and ambitions that turned them into bigots. Each time they failed to realize these overriding ambitions, they sought refuge in religion. Tell me, how many subedars, rana-maharanas or emperors have given up their thrones for their faith? The truth is that till today, not a single ruler has ceded his throne for the sake of fulfilling his religious yearnings. How else does one explain Aurangzeb's habit of copying verses from the Holy Koran and stitching prayer caps for his sustenance? If he were, indeed, a true believer, he would have stood by his claims and crowned Murad the emperor of Hindustan before proceeding on Haj and spending the rest of his life as a haji-dervish in Mecca and Medina. I reiterate my conviction that people cling to religion to serve their vested interests. But no one is willing to abide by its principles!'

As Time uttered these words, a strange silence descended on the place, a silence loaded with questions, as people scoured their conscience... 'O Time, whenever mankind gropes for its conscience, the heartbeats of this revolving universe seem to come to a standstill,' the adeeb observed. 'But tell me, what happened next?'

Time continued with the narrative: 'Dara made the mistake of fleeing towards Lahore.'

Dara's eyes confirmed the statement.

'To escape Aurangzeb's forces, Dara Shikoh moved away from the Beas towards the south of the Indus and reached Bhakkar. Fifty miles downstream from here, the way led to Iran via Kandahar.'

'What else could I have done?' asked the despondent Dara.

His remark angered Time. 'You have chosen to tread the same path as your ancestor Humayun. And, honourable adeeb, when Dara Shikoh, fleeing in terror, sought refuge in the court of Iran's ruler, Shah Abbas, the women in his entourage rebelled. They protested that they preferred a living death in their homeland, rather than their fate as objects of lust in Shah Abbas's harem. They added that they would rather emulate the jauhar of Rajput princesses and immolate themselves, than be presented before the Shah of Iran.'

A fragrant breeze wafted in, wiping the perspiration from foreheads before coming to a halt. 'Who are you?' the peon asked this breeze.

'I am Hindustan's Culture.'

'What have you got to do with history and its chronicles?' the peon reprimanded it. 'Can't you see that Time, Dara Shikoh and our adeeb are deeply involved in investigation and analysis? I resent your intrusion!'

In a soft whisper, Hindustani Culture replied, 'Listen, O Peon of the Illustrious Adeeb! The deference and respect accorded to women determine the level of a society's culture. Cultures that showed little respect to women were wiped out, like that of Rome, Greece and Egypt. Though we deem it barbaric, we know that women in Hindustan chose to commit suicide when their culture failed to live up to expectations and protect their honour and chastity. By doing so, they brought glory to their own culture. Dara Shikoh's wife, Nadira Bano, and the womenfolk in his officers' families were prepared to embrace death for the very same reasons— protection of their honour and the perpetuation of their cultural tradition. If, in these harsh times, women rebel for the sake of their honour, they have every right to do so! The tradition of jauhar is, undoubtedly, a barbaric one, but the violation of a woman's honour is infinitely worse. So, do you understand, Peon Sahib?'

Suddenly, a number of black- and white-winged centuries flew by, saluting Hindustani Culture. The lines of the poet Iqbal's 'Tarana' echoed all around:

O, spirited Ganga, do you remember the day
When, beside your waters, our caravan came to stay?
Tho' Greece and Rome and Egypt
Have all been swept away
Our name and our identity
Live on even today...

Before the words could die away, Akhtarul Iman arrived, speaking in a deep, gloomy voice. 'You talk of yesterday,' he observed. 'The same is happening even today.'

Greeting him, the adeeb asked, 'And so, brother, how are you?'

'I sail in the same boat as the rest of you—you, Adeeb, and your peon...Dara Shikoh, Time and our Culture.'

'What do you mean "in the same boat"?' the adeeb inquired.

Akhtarul Iman's reply came in the form of a poem:

'We were just sitting around, Bhaiyya on the right,
Badi Apa with Shabana,
Regaling us with stories—serious and lighthearted—

Of her spouse's household,
Making us all laugh.
Before us sat Ammi, her sewing-box open before her,
Her mouth full of paan,
Listening to the antics of her daughter's in-laws,
Peevish, at times; caustic, at others.
We sat, herded together by Naima and Shahnaz,
Listening to their intermittent tiffs.
Deep as ever in domestic chores,
Majhli Apa came and went.
Far away in a corner sat Abba,
Perusing the papers of his property.
All of a sudden, pandemonium—a new nation was born.
In an instant, the gathering went helter-skelter.
The eyes opened to see the earth, splattered with blood...'

Akhtarul Iman could read no further. His eyes welled up and he
was racked by sobs.

'Don't weep, Akhtarul Iman,' said Time, offering him solace.
'How I wish it were your mother's paan that had stained the earth
instead of the fountains of blood that drenched it when a new nation
was created! But that was not to be.'

'It was exactly what had happened when the trail of bloody
events shadowed Dara Shikoh on the battlefield of Devrai. I am a
witness to them all,' confirmed Culture, 'a witness to the fact that
Aurangzeb defeated his brother, Dara, in 1659 by conspiring with
Hindu traitors, and created his own Pakistan within this land. In
those days, the names of nations did not change; the names of rulers
did. The change of rulers ushered in new developments in the
political scenario along with a shift in perspective. This is what sets
off the chain that creates innumerable Pakistans.'

Culture was in full flow now.

'I do not allow the winds of change to alter the emotional and
sentimental disposition of my offspring. I cannot bear to see the
spark of life being extinguished in mankind, of heartbeats fading
away, of blood ceasing to course in the veins of humanity. That is
why I have survived these five thousand years.'

At these words, windows began to open in the sky. At each, there appeared a face, gazing out. These were the writers of the entire world.

The adeeb looked at Culture in amazement.

'Adeeb, it is your brethren who have kept me alive. Politics has split me in two, but I am no territory to be cut up and parcelled off by anyone!' Culture philosophized. 'The form in which you see me is not the only one in which I manifest myself. I had appeared in a different guise in Mohenjodaro and Harappa. When the Vedic Aryans arrived here, they did not come bearing weapons; they carried grain and the implements to cultivate it. They were not invaders. Why should they have been? The earth lay invitingly bare before them. Everyone was free to settle wherever they chose to. That was when my form changed. Adeeb, I evolve constantly; so, I am eternal. I know that in these times, Jinnah has created political walls, segregating one man from another; but no wall can ever still my voice or confine my spirit.'

The peon passed a note to the adeeb. The message it contained said that on hearing the voice of Culture, Joginder Paul, Krishnaji and Wazir Agha had arrived to listen to the exchanges. The adeeb acknowledged them with a glance. They sat down in silence. More painful than their inner anguish at the partition of the country was the burden they had to bear of those many centuries their pens had never touched upon.

'Wazir Agha and I were not there,' Joginder Paul observed softly, 'but, in the ages gone by, there were Sufis and sages who put a stop to religious feuds. They sought, instead, to evolve a path that would bring about the confluence and unity of religions.'

'That was my goal as well,' Dara Shikoh declared forcefully. 'Was I wrong in pursuing it?'

Time looked at Dara sadly and replied, 'Dara Shikoh! Your biggest mistake was to pay no heed to the vested interests and overweening ambitions of your time; you chose, instead, to look to the future of Hindustan.'

The historian Kanungo intervened. 'But Aurangzeb chose to disregard the country's future,' he protested. 'He thought solely of

his own future and as a result, even reached Multan in pursuit of
Dara. Shuja, in his quest for kingdom and throne, advanced as far as
Allahabad. Like a relentless hunter in pursuit of his quarry, Aurangzeb
was determined to seize the Mughal throne. On coming to know
that Shuja was advancing towards Agra, he turned back from Multan.
Aurangzeb knew that Dara, moving along the Indus, would reach
Kutch. He saw his older brother as a prey in flight, a hunted rabbit
whose days were numbered. So, he set Safshikan Khan the task of
pursuing Dara Shikoh while he himself set off in the direction of
Allahabad to confront the renegade Shuja.'

Having given his statement, Kanungo asked Hazrat Shibli Nomani
a pertinent question: 'If Aurangzeb, or Alamgir, as you call him, was
not interested in occupying the throne of Hindustan, why was he
bent on going after Shuja, once Dara had been taken care of?'

Seated on his cemented chabutra and puffing on his hookah,
Shibli Nomani listened to the question before thundering, 'Who
dares ask me such a question!'

Time stepped forward to inform him that successive centuries
had the right to ask questions relating to the facts contained in the
pages of history and demand answers to them.

'And who has given them this right?' Shibli Nomani shot back.

'It is Culture who has earned this right for herself,' Time
replied, 'because she has always been in step with the changing
times.'

'You are out of touch with reality!' Culture shouted at Shibli
Nomani. 'You cannot claim to speak for Aurangzeb and the philosophy
that lay behind his scheming. Why don't you answer us? Tell us why
your Alamgir turned back from Multan towards Allahabad to confront
the forces of Shuja!'

'I do not know the reason. I cannot comment on it,' Shibli
Nomani replied and lapsed into silence.

Time spoke up. 'Honourable adeeb,' it said, 'the history of
Hindustan bears witness to the fact that the invaders who attacked
the country were foreigners, only so long as they were involved in
a military offensive against it. Once that was past, each of them
assimilated themselves with Hindustan's culture and concerns. Even

Islam took on a Hindustani identity as Sufis and sages came from beyond its borders and preached its message. The soil of this land has immense strength and powers of absorption. I strongly support the argument that Hindustan's soil was as much a part of Dara Shikoh's being as it was of Alamgir's. Both belonged to this land.'

'I am also a son of this soil!' a loud voice resounded.

All eyes turned towards its source.

'Who are you?' the peon inquired.

'I am Raja Rajrup of Jammu.'

Dara Shikoh recognized him at once. 'Yes, Adeeb, he is, indeed, Rajrup, the ruler of Jammu,' he said. 'He was the one to give me his word that he would raise an army of Rajputs from the hills for me. On that occasion, I was proceeding to Lahore from Delhi following the defeat at Samugarh.'

'I had done so because Dara Shikoh had always been a staunch supporter of the Hindus and someone they could turn to in times of distress,' explained Rajrup.

At these words, Dara retorted in anguished tones, 'I placed my trust in this ungrateful wretch with whom my wife had sought to establish a symbolic tie by drawing the milk from her breasts and sending it to him. She believed that if he drank it, the gesture would sanctify the bond of mother and son forged between them. This Hindu Rajput, I had imagined, would then swear allegiance to me and united, we would go on to write a fresh chapter of history once the crisis had passed. Yet, having drunk the milk, this Rajput violated the world's most sacred bond. I even gave him a huge quantity of gold, but just a year later, his treachery came to light during the decisive battle of Devrai. Rajrup chose to break his oath and join hands with Aurangzeb against me.'

'Shame...shame...shame!' exclaimed the voices of Joginder Paul, Krishnaji and Wazir Agha.

'Silence!' shouted Rajrup. 'I have nothing to be ashamed of. I am a Rajput, a Hindu, and proud of the fact that, in my time, each Hindu adopted treachery as the basic principle of his life. Whatever significance "homeland" or "realm" might have had for Dara Shikoh, we Hindus from the Middle Ages lived solely for ourselves. The notion of "country" or "nation" did not exist for us.'

'Shame! Shame!' the same voices echoed in unison.

'Silence!' roared Rajrup once again. 'You scholars have risen above faith and religion. You have caged human values. That is why you remain forever mired in poverty and suffer humiliation and betrayal. Lacking insight, people like you can never understand the faith that great rajas and maharajas like us have in their craven ambitions. With great pride do I emphatically reaffirm that, in my time, we Hindus did not believe in such concepts as "country", "nation" or "Hindustan"! Why me alone, even Jodhpur's Maharaja Jaswant Singh who swore by the ideals of friendship and patriotism in Dara's presence, betrayed him. In fact, Mirza Raja Jaisingh very openly joined forces with Aurangzeb. Mewar's Maharaja Jaisingh whom Dara had defended against Aurangzeb and his chief wazir, Saadullah, turned against his erstwhile protector by bribing the rulers of Banswara, Dungarpur, Basawer and five other parganas.'

'Rajrup is right,' the historian Constable intervened. 'I wish to present before this court a document mentioned by Bernier in his travelogue.'

'What document is that?' the adeeb wanted to know.

'Sir, this is a letter written by Aurangzeb's friend and Dara's foe, Mirza Raja Jaisingh of Jaipur, threatening and cajoling, in turn, Jodhpur's Maharaja Jaswant Singh into withdrawing his support to Dara Shikoh.'

'Let this letter be read aloud,' the adeeb directed.

The peon began reading it. 'Here is Mirza Raja Jaisingh's letter to Jaswant Singh, maharaja of Jodhpur: "What do you hope to gain by helping Dara Shikoh, a prince disowned by destiny? By persisting in this vein, you are merely ensuring your own downfall and the ruination of your family. Nor will this course of action benefit the wicked Dara. Prince Aurangzeb will never forgive you for it. Being a ruler myself, I formally appeal to you to refrain from shedding Rajput blood. Do not harbour any hopes of garnering support from other rulers, because I have the means to quash any such efforts on your part. Such a course of action will adversely affect all Hindus and I cannot allow you to incite them to violence. Once ignited, their inflammatory feelings would spread rapidly over the realm and be impossible to douse. If, on the other hand, you forsake Prince Dara and leave him to his fate, Prince Aurangzeb will forget the past, refrain from demanding that you return the wealth you had acquired in Khajwa, and hand over the governance of Gujarat to you right away.'"

'Stop!' Kanungo intervened. 'The subedar of Gujarat was Prince Murad Baksh. How can Mirza Raja Jaisingh put forward the suggestion that this region be handed over to Jodhpur's Maharaja Jaswant Singh? This letter could not have been written without Aurangzeb's active connivance!'

'It is Hazrat Shibli Nomani alone who can give us an appropriate response,' the adeeb declared.

'I have no concrete knowledge of this issue,' Shibli Nomani retorted like a true intellectual.

Then, Subhash Pant snatched away from the peon's hands a Document that had come to meet the adeeb all the way from Dehradun. Seeking the court's permission to read it, he began, 'I must read a few lines from this letter, because the poet Raghupati Sahai Firaq, a respected elder, always claimed that to attain the truth, time should not be fragmented into past, present and future. It is true, sir, that whenever the norms of honour are violated, it is culture and civilization that decline and disintegrate. Should this happen and culture fragment into many separate units, a time will come when every man will have evolved his own brutal, private version of culture. That is when he will find himself entrapped in isolation, rue the absence of human bonds and shed bitter tears. Man's existence is counted in years; he can die at any moment. But culture's song is eternal. It breathes spirituality into every man's soul, awakens him to the aesthetics and worldliness within him and carries him beyond the threshold of mortality.'

Tears brimmed in Culture's eyes as she sat in silence. Wiping them away with her chunni, she looked in the direction of Wazir Agha and Joginder Paul. The latter's lips trembled with emotion on observing Culture's plight, and he called out to her, 'Ma! Our own mother nurtures us in her womb and gives birth to us, but you become a part of us and accompany us beyond the portals of death. You are the human mind's greatest strength. Had it not been so, you could not have transcended barriers and given birth to Hegel and his path-breaking thesis. Marx saw Hegel's formulations as a form of antithesis and later, Mahatma Gandhi, the world's great spokesman for culture, gave us the philosophy of synthesis which arose from that antithesis.'

Time rose to his feet and said, 'Dara Shikoh had also propounded this philosophy and provoked Aurangzeb into describing him as a heretical kafir who gave credence to a multiplicity of deities.'

Wishing to summarize the argument, the adeeb raised his eyebrows and announced, 'Deriving his strength from culture, man can inculcate within himself the qualities of tolerance and forbearance and succeed in working towards unity. But all mankind can never worship one god. This can only come about when the suffering borne by all men is similar. In a world beset by exploitation, injustice and inequalities, a thousand kinds of suffering are spawned every moment. There is no parity in the kind of torment men endure, no balance in the happiness allocated to each individual. The feeling of oneness that grows from sharing pleasure and pain in equal measure is absent from man's experience. Only when the burden of suffering is equally apportioned to all human beings will the inhabitants of this planet worship one god. This god will come to mean far more than the imageless, final arbiter of disputes. He will become the everlasting core of happiness for all mankind. Transcending the confines of a visual form, he will evolve into a manifestation of benign Truth. Like the family elder from whom all seek advice, this god will be an integral part of every household.'

'Sir,' the peon admonished, 'there you go again, giving a speech. If you don't curb this tendency of yours, your cross-examination will never yield a concrete and convincing conclusion.'

'What exactly do you mean?' the adeeb inquired.

'Just this, sir: the centuries stand waiting. Time and Culture are present in the court to assist you. Instead of deriving important lessons from the blood-soaked centuries of the past that will be of help to the future, you go off on a tangent into these philosophical digressions.'

'I beg your pardon, my man. Why just scholars like me, practically everyone has used the pretext of principles and values and referred to art in their bid to skirt the truth.'

'Then, honourable sir and illustrious adeeb, expose the fraud being perpetrated on the common man. Tell us where and when the fundamental rights of the masses were brutally violated, so that the nexus between legislative and executive power can be challenged and the future safeguarded against repression and tyranny. After all, it is these blood-soaked centuries that have inflicted gaping wounds on our psyche. It is we, along with our descendants, who have paid a heavy price for the savage and bloody feud between Aurangzeb and Dara Shikoh.' Pain scarred the peon's words.

'You, too, have taken to delivering long speeches,' the adeeb quipped, 'but tell me, at which juncture does history await us now?'

'In the seventeenth century,' said Subhash Pant, thrusting forward Mirza Raja Jaisingh's letter, 'the same year that Jaipur's Jaisingh wrote to Jodhpur's Maharaja Jaswant Singh.'

'Please read further,' the adeeb instructed.

Before beginning to read the letter, Subhash Pant made a comment: 'Honourable sir, even though Aurangzeb was not the subedar of Gujarat, he used Mirza Raja Jaisingh to convey to Jaswant Singh the assurance that Gujarat would be taken away from Prince Murad Baksh and placed in his charge. This devious and wicked plan of Aurangzeb succeeded with the connivance of Hindustan's traitorous Hindus.'

'How so?' the adeeb asked.

'Listen to this,' began Subhash Pant. 'One Rajput Hindu of Hindustan, Mirza Raja Jaisingh, writes to another Rajput Hindu of Hindustan, Raja Jaswant Singh: "By agreeing to take over Gujarat and administer it under Aurangzeb's protection, you can surely perceive the advantages of the situation." These are Jaisingh's words. Listen to what he writes next. There's another assurance: "It is there that you will have complete peace and security. I wish to affirm that whatever assurances I have made here will be executed to the letter."'

Everyone was stunned. The adeeb took Bernier's document

away from Subhash Pant and thoughtfully observed, 'One fact is crystal clear—no matter how cowardly or treacherous the Hindus were, in the battle for power and the crown, neither Aurangzeb nor Dara Shikoh were above reproach. Another point that emerges clearly is this: Though stories abound of Kshatriya valour and Rajput courage, Shivaji and Rana Pratap alone are its true symbols. Other than that, Kshatriya courage has been feeble and vacillating. Besides Shivaji and Pratap, has there been a single warrior or ruler who swore by his Kshatriya faith and succeeded in winning a battle? The extent of Maharana Pratap's valour can be gauged from the resistance he put up against imperial power till his dying day. The Rana was a fearless martyr who, unlike other Rajputs, was no opportunist craving for pelf and power. By the time his age dawned, the Muslim inheritors of the Mughal Empire were seen as belonging to another faith, but were not regarded as foreigners.'

'And, sir,' the peon intervened, 'another fact emerges here. Though Hindus were in a majority in the country, Hindustan was never a Hindu state. No visible or religious evidence of a Hindu nation existed at the time. Power politics in Hindustan was never grounded in Hinduism. There was no state religion as such. Hindus revered their faith, but were free from the politics of religion.'

The objectivity of the peon's conclusions had everyone looking on in amazement. This filled him with confidence and thus inspired, he continued, 'Sir, Hindustan's history—even the Puranas—testify that crusades were frequently undertaken here for the cause of truth or civilization. But no epic battle was ever fought to establish the pivotal primacy of any one religion or faith. This is not the land of religious crusades. Even the battle between Ram and Ravana was not fought over religion. It was just an epic confrontation—the forces of morality pitted against those of misconduct, injustice, incivility and tyranny.'

The echoes of 'Bravo!' resounded, as Subhash Pant, Joginder Paul, Wazir Agha and Krishnaji applauded to acknowledge the soundness of the peon's argument. Greatly encouraged, he went on. 'Even the Mahabharata was not fought for religious reasons. That was another epic battle fought against sin, exploitation of women, falsehood and greed. Ashoka's Kalinga war was not a religious crusade either. That too was undertaken to quash duplicity and greed. Chandragupta did not fight Alexander for the sake of religion; it was a ruler's courageous attempt to defeat a foreign invader's craving for territorial expansion.'

'What conclusion do you wish to draw?' the adeeb inquired.

'Just this, Your Honour: The territory of Hindustan has never been an arena for religious warfare. But our Shibli Nomani Sahib has tried to make the history of Hindustan lean on the crutches of religion by declaring the Aurangzeb–Dara Shikoh feud to be the battle of a believer against a "kafir". By proving Dara Shikoh to be a *mulhid*—a man subservient to many gods—Shibli Nomani has elevated Aurangzeb to a status that makes him a greater Muslim than all followers of Islam and bestowed on him the role of the defender of Islam. History stands witness that Shahjahan surpassed his son, Aurangzeb, in his blind and extreme devotion to Islam. Yet, in the battle of succession, despite his religious inclinations, this same Shahjahan chose to support not Aurangzeb, but the liberal Dara Shikoh.'

'Earlier, I had sought the answer to this question from Shibli Nomani, but he had no reply,' said the adeeb, looking at Raja Rajrup. 'You were giving a statement. Will you continue, please?'

'I shall only repeat what I was saying, honourable adeeb. In those days, we Hindus had no nation, no homeland, no Hindustan! If anything concerned us at all, it was our kingdom, our power and our army. The Hindu feared no one. If there was one thing that did terrify him, it was the authority of the powerful, and he grovelled and wagged his tail before it. What other reason could there have been for the Rao of Kutch to cast his lot with Aurangzeb and become an adversary of Dara Shikoh when the latter's son, Sipihar Shikoh, was engaged to his daughter? The Rao feared Aurangzeb's power. When Dara hadn't a soul to turn to after his defeat at Samugarh, it was the Rao of Kutch who manifested his ingratitude by turning against him.'

'What do you have to say for yourself?' Dara Shikoh asked him bitterly. 'Despite your vow to respect the bond Nadira had established with you, you chose to desert me in my moment of crisis!'

Rajrup proudly justified his actions. 'In the decisive battle of Devrai,' he declared, 'I betrayed the trust you had reposed in me. I ascended the steep hills of Gokla and attacked your forces from the rear. Your sipahsalar, Shahnawaz Khan, was roundly defeated and died in combat. What could I have hoped to achieve by supporting you? Since political power was coming within Aurangzeb's grasp, I preferred to align myself with him.'

A storm was brewing over the salt marshes of Kutch. A wall of quicksand rose up to the sky. Out of its fissures grew brambles. Suddenly, the brambles turned into birds in flight. Their fluttering wings spanned the sky and eclipsed it completely, casting a giant shadow over the earth.

'What could this be?' asked the startled adeeb.

'This, janab, is Kalyug, the epoch of darkness!' the peon replied heatedly.

27

'Sir, I am Kalyug.'

The adeeb was taken aback. He could not believe his eyes. 'You are Kalyug? But you were Time…the keeper of hours and moments.'

'To suit their convenience, men of wisdom changed my name. Today, I am known as Kalyug and I am waiting to tell this court the story of Hindustan's unfortunate son Dara. A more inhuman and barbaric tale is yet to be told! May I, with your permission, relate how Pakistans were created in the hearts and minds of people, many centuries ago?'

'Permission is granted.'

Kalyug took a deep breath and began. 'On the evening of 14 March 1659, following his defeat in the battle of Devrai,' he said, 'Dara fled towards Gujarat–Kutch with his sole surviving general, Feroz Mewati, and his son Sipihar Shikoh. The women in Dara's family and entourage waited on elephant-back on the shores of Anna Sagar lake—with Dara's trusted Khoja, Maqbool, guarding them. They, too, were awaiting their turn to flee.'

Dara gazed at Time with sad eyes. The latter took another deep breath and continued, 'Honourable sir, I can now see everything clearly before me. It is night. With just two thousand troops left under the command of Feroz Mewati, Dara is moving in the direction of Merta. The whole night goes by...then another day. From Merta, Dara moves south towards Gujarat.'

'Yes, sir, I hoped to be given shelter by the Rao of Kutch, my son's father-in-law. Then an emissary arrived with the news that Aurangzeb had issued a farman. It ordered Mirza Raja Jaisingh to set out with twenty thousand men, capture me and produce me before Aurangzeb, dead or alive. My old friend, Jodhpur's Maharaja Jaswant Singh, was ordered to help Mirza Raja Jaisingh in the execution of the farman. Honourable sir, I don't wish to level any charges, but I will say one thing today: In my endeavour to evolve a composite culture along the lines laid down by my great-grandfather, Akbar, I was frustrated, not by Aurangzeb, but by the Hindu rulers of my homeland. Shameless ingratitude and deceit mark this terrible saga of Hindustan's cultural decline.'

Listening to Dara's words, Culture sighed. 'Though I could not be severed,' she observed, 'the Alamgiri sword of power and ambition slashed through the lives of thousands of people who had been living in the shelter offered by my shade. As a result, people walked about clutching their decapitated heads in their hands. In the cavities of their gouged-out eyes, flames flickered on burning wicks of cotton. This, honourable sir, was an era when wicks produced more gloom than light, when the slumbering head of a debauched century had left its imprint on the pillow of politics. This wanton century in Hindustan warmed its body on the embers of politics and, sprawled on royal beds, abandoned itself to indolence and sensuality. Each Hindu ruler would auction his daughter like a fragrant bouquet in the kingdom's bazaar. In exchange, he sought ease and pleasure through bargains that brought him additional estates and freedom to indulge his whims. For the sale and trade of Hindu girls, a Hindu merchant was always present and engaged in protracted bargaining.'

The adeeb gave Culture a piercing look, but she continued unfazed, 'So, in those materialistic and amoral times, who would spare a glance, sir, for the vanquished Dara? Who would deign to look at the centuries to come? The period preceding Aurangzeb's era was one in which every man in Hindustan had become a nonentity as far as courage and integrity were concerned. Hindustan during that epoch had no human beings, just living shadows.'

'Yes, honourable sir,' Dara joined in, 'as I fled from place to place, desperate to save my life and preserve my self-respect, I failed to come across genuine friends or people with the courage of their convictions. All I encountered was their shadows...shadows that had no ties with the past.'

'Sir, even these shadows of memory and gratitude did not sustain Dara for long,' Time interjected. 'For such shadows have no will of their own. They are inconstant, changing with the individuals they are attached to. I see Dara's two thousand troops dispersing before my eyes. Dara, wearing a muslin waistcoat and worn-out chappals, is moving from Virgaon towards the barren Rann of Kutch. The small band of soldiers accompanying him is barefoot now, and assailed by hunger and thirst. The inhospitable Rann of Kutch nurtures no wildlife that can be slaughtered to provide them with meat. The only vegetation that grows here is the thorn bush with its poisonous stems. These can offer no succour, only death. There is no drinking water. Sucking the moisture from the broken fragments of their earthen utensils to quench their thirst, this despondent band of men is making its way towards Sindh.'

Dara explained, 'The person responsible for this situation is Mirza Raja Jaisingh who has hemmed me in from all sides. A vicious trap has been laid to prevent my escape. The only option left for me is either capitulation or death. They have cordoned off all possible routes of escape—Sirohi and Palanpur in the south, Derwara in the south-east, Kathiawad and Kutch in the north...'

'At this time, sir,' intervened Kalyug, taking up the thread of the narrative, 'all Dara has is the protection of his four hundred soldiers who are being relentlessly pursued across the salt marshes by Mirza Raja Jaisingh's twenty thousand men. To escape death, Dara had been planning to cross the Indus and flee to Iran via Kandahar. But the plan is much too risky. So, Dara hopes to reach Afghanistan's borders and seek the shelter of the tribes living there, the reason being his faith in the ruler of Afghanistan's Dadar principality, Malik Jivan, whom he had once saved from a death sentence passed on him in anger by Emperor Shahjahan. Dadar lies just nine miles from the Bolan Pass. Malik Jivan is not just a debauch; he has been fathered by a Hindu. Dara is confident that this Hindu–Pathan ruler will not have forgotten the debt of life he owes him!'

All those present in the court were listening to this account with great attention. And so, the narrator continued: 'Honourable sir, whatever I have said so far is also recorded in *Tarikh-e-Shujai.* Clutching at shadows in search of a refuge, Prince Dara Shikoh advances towards the safety afforded by the region under Malik Jivan's jurisdiction. Such is the accursed nature of Dara's fate that on 6 June 1659, his wife Nadira breathes her last just a short distance from the borders of their chosen haven. Dara is insane with grief. Nadira's last wish is that her mortal remains be taken back to Hindustan for burial.'

'That moment was the nadir of my grief and despair. I had been robbed of everything I had ever held precious. Nadira had been my wife, my advisor and disciple, a shareholder in my destiny...she was everything to me. My numbed body was but an empty grave. Only my breath coursed through it.' Dara broke down and sobbed helplessly. Amazingly, his tears flowed like waves to his eyelashes and, without falling, receded back into his eyes.

Culture comforted Dara. 'Hoard your tears, Dara,' she urged, 'for the centuries will weep for you. If all your tears are spent now, the centuries too will harden their hearts against your misfortune. Hindustan's civilization, though not its emperors and Alamgirs, will remember you forever with tears of remorse.'

Kalyug wiped clean the blurred mirror of time and continued, 'Now, all that Hindustan's Prince Dara Shikoh is left with are Sipihar Shikoh, seventy soldiers, four Khojas and his dead wife's body—that too in an alien land. And he is wearing the same waistcoat, the same worn chappals! Crossing the frontiers of his land, Malik Jivan comes forward to pay obeisance to Dara and condole Nadira's death.

'"Your Excellency," he says, his voice full of commiseration at

Dara's plight, "I am greatly beholden to you. It was you who had saved me from the wrath of the emperor when the subedar of Multan arrested me for a small misdemeanour and sent me to the royal court for punishment. Had it not been for you, I would have been trampled to death by elephants on the emperor's orders. It was you alone who interceded on my behalf and saved my life!"

'Hope shimmers in Dara's moist eyes.

"'Today, you wander about looking for refuge. You have left your home far behind. And now, in this foreign land, a tragedy of such dimensions has befallen you!" Wiping away his tears, Malik Jivan continues, "Malik Jivan's land is now yours."

"'I wish to send Nadira's body back to Lahore with full honours. It was her last wish to be buried in her own country, not on alien soil. It is my desire that she sleep forever in the vicinity of Mian Mir's sacred resting place in Lahore."

"'That is no problem at all," Malik Jivan reassures him. "All arrangements will be made. You cannot go back to Hindustan. Danger lurks there. I know that Aurangzeb's mercenary flunkey, Bahadur Khan, and his troops are pursuing you relentlessly."

"'Once I have fulfilled Nadira's last wish, I will proceed to Kandahar and try to reach Iran," Dara reveals.

"'Everything will be arranged according to your wishes. But we cannot just leave Nadira Apa's body lying here...In my heart of hearts, I cannot bring myself to accept it. I merely suggest that till suitable arrangements are made to take her body to Lahore, all of you rest here in Dadargarh."

"'So be it, Malik Jivan," Dara agrees. "It is now time for namaz. Once the prayer is over, we shall proceed to your land with Nadira's body."

'As Dara sits down near his wife's mortal remains in preparation for prayer, the loyal Gul Mohammed speaks up. "Sir," he asks, "are you going to be facing the east as you pray?"

'At these words, Dara warns Gul, "Don't let such trivialities bother you. This is a burial service for Nadira. From where I sit, I have a clear view of her face. Don't differentiate between east and west and remember that Allah's messenger, our revered Prophet

Mohammed, had chosen to face the Kaaba instead of the holy city of Jerusalem while offering his prayers. The Christians and Jews had not taken kindly to this deviation from the norm, because their own faith revolved around such trifles which they revered as the touchstones of truth and falsehood. When these people raised objections and asked the Holy Prophet why he had chosen to face a direction other than the conventional one while praying, he had quoted the *Surah-e-Baqar* in reply: 'Both east and west belong to Allah. Whichever direction you face, there will you find Him. Faith or virtue is not served by the particular direction one faces when offering namaz. What truly matters is one's faith in Allah, the conviction that judgement for one's deeds awaits in the afterlife, and respect for all sacred texts, prophets and angels.' Such was the Holy Prophet's message."'

While Dara is preoccupied with the rituals of namaz, the narrator continues. 'Honourable sir, while Dara is offering his prayers, Malik Jivan returns. He has made arrangements for Nadira's body to be sent to Dadar with full honours. Reassured that his beloved wife's remains would not lie abandoned and dishonoured on alien soil, Dara feels deeply grateful to Malik Jivan and blesses him for the refuge he had been offered in these tragic and trying circumstances.'

Gazing silently at Kalyug with a sad expression, Dara heaved a sigh. Detecting the sorrow that lay behind that sigh, the adeeb asked the narrator to continue.

'Illustrious scholar, by now Dara is a broken man. Two days later, when it is time to carry Nadira's body to Lahore, Dara summons the few loyal retainers who had remained with him and says, "I cannot return to Hindustan. Neither can I compel others to forsake their homeland. While I am sending my soul back to Lahore, I grant each of you the liberty to return to your homeland. Acting as escort for Nadira's remains as she makes her journey home, will be Khwaja Maqbool who brought her up and served her selflessly. To provide protection along the way, Gul Mohammed will accompany Khwaja Maqbool to Lahore. Those who wish to return home to Hindustan can travel back with the funeral cortège. Those who choose to remain behind will accompany me to Iran."'

'This account is authentic,' Dara testified, 'and so, apart from Sipihar Shikoh, half a dozen Khojas and a few servants, everyone returned to Hindustan. Gul Mohammed left for Lahore with Nadira's funeral procession.'

'And...and the next morning, that is on 9 June 1659, when Dara, along with Sipihar Shikoh and a few trusted retainers, leaves Malik Jivan's Dadar and moves towards the Bolan Pass...'

An earthquake shook the ground. The rocky cliffs of Bolan rumbled and disintegrated into a million fragments that flew up towards the sky. In the scorching heat of June, a snowstorm blew across the landscape and made the rocks underground shiver with cold!

'Kalyug, what is this I see before me?' the adeeb shouted.

'Honourable sir, the blood that courses through the rock cliffs has suddenly turned cold,' came the reply.

'The reason?' the adeeb asked balefully.

'Sir, just as Prince Dara Shikoh was traversing the Bolan Pass en route to Kandahar, Malik Jivan and his barbaric men encircled him, cutting off all routes of escape. This was the most heinous betrayal of all! Just two days after offering him hospitality and showing him due deference, Malik Jivan had not merely obstructed Dara in his flight to safety, but had arranged to have him arrested. Malik Jivan next dispatched two of his fastest riders to Aurangzeb's two sipahsalars who had, by then, crossed the river Indus. The two men were none other than Jaipur's Mirza Raja Jaisingh and Bahadur Khan.'

Screaming, the seventeenth century went into convulsions. The cliffs averted their gaze in shame. The sky turned yellow and the cadavers of thousands of birds littered the way from the Bolan Pass to Delhi.

'And...and then, on 23 June 1659,' the narrator continued, 'Malik Jivan handed over his prisoners, Dara and Sipihar Shikoh, to Aurangzeb's sipahsalar Bahadur Khan. For this treacherous act, Aurangzeb would reward Malik Jivan with many jagirs and titles and much wealth.'

'Yes, honourable sir,' commented Dara, 'that ungrateful wretch,

Malik Jivan, on whom these honours were bestowed, went on to betray his own Hindu–Pathan lineage by converting to Islam. He became the Muslim Bakhtiar Khan!'

'Now, remember,' reminded Kalyug, 'it is Malik Jivan that we shall henceforth be referring to when we speak of Bakhtiar Khan.'

'Let Malik Jivan alias Bakhtiar Khan be produced here,' the adeeb ordered his peon.

'Step forward, Malik Jivan alias Bakhtiar Khan!' the peon called.

When the man appeared, Dara looked at him with utter contempt and turned away.

'Your treachery led the history of Hindustan to take a self-destructive turn. Do you have anything to say to justify your actions?' the adeeb asked, offering Malik Jivan a chance to defend himself.

'Honourable sir, what you describe as "treachery" today was, in our time, no treachery at all. Rather, it was an established practice, a tradition that allowed overriding ambitions to soar. Man did not live for religion then. He lived and fought for his kingdom and territory. Conversion was only a matter of convenience. Just as we swiftly replaced wounded horses in the battlefield, so we wasted no time in converting to another faith. The only battles we aspired to win were those that yielded wealth and territory!'

Once again, Dara looked at him scornfully, but made no comment.

'When I learnt that in the battle of succession, Dara had defeat staring him in the face and was fleeing to Kandahar, I realized that a more opportune moment would not come my way. I was lying in wait for Dara to enter my territory. You will not find a cannier and more dangerous opportunist than this Kalyug who speaks so boldly in your presence today. It was Kalyug who was my greatest friend and supporter in those days. It was with his assistance that I was able to take advantage of the circumstances—Nadira's death and my success in winning over Dara and Sipihar Shikoh with my hospitality and graciousness.'

Greatly perturbed, the adeeb shouted, 'From where emanate these stifled, heart-rending wails of lament? Why does this river of tears advance in my direction? I observe the leaves on the trees growing along its banks withering and drifting to the ground. Where am I and what is causing these unnatural phenomena?'

Kalyug gently intervened. 'Illustrious adeeb, the stifled wails of lament resonate in human hearts only when human values have been brutally slain. The river of tears overflows its banks only when culture is in danger of withering and dying out. In such circumstances, man's helpless tears are never visible. Swallowed by the earth, they gush forth wherever a new civilization is about to take birth. Honourable sir, these very tears feed and nourish new cultures. If they dry up, it marks the lonely death of a culture.'

'But I have still not received the answer to my question—where is this place in which the river of tears wells up and trees suddenly shed their leaves?'

'Sir,' Kalyug explained, 'this is the city of Delhi. The scene before you symbolizes the decay of culture, set into motion with the arrival of Mirza Raja Jaisingh and Bahadur Khan and their prisoners Dara Shikoh and Sipihar Shikoh. The treacherous Pathan ingrate, Malik Jivan, is accompanying them to Delhi. As the city cries its heart out, Dara and his son are placed in the custody of the eagle-eyed Nazar Beg. The date is 23 August 1659. Nazar Beg is Aurangzeb's trusted servant. He has kept Dara and his son confined in a haveli in the Khwaspura locality, three miles south of the road that runs between Delhi and Shahjahanabad.

'Presenting himself before Aurangzeb on 25 August 1659, Nazar Beg apprises him of the condition of the two prisoners. Four days later, Aurangzeb decrees that the kafir, Dara, and his son be subjected to public humiliation. On that day—29 August 1659—Dara is paraded in disgrace along Shahjahanabad's main thoroughfares in the custody of the vast royal army. The endeavour is to prove to the citizens of Delhi that this is, indeed, the real Dara Shikoh. The prisoners are made to wear coarse and filthy clothes. Ordinary turbans have been substituted for the ones they had worn earlier as a mark of their royal status. They are forced to wear tattered Kashmiri cotton shawls that the menials in the palace use. Two aging cow-elephants are adorned with stinking garbage. Sipihar Shikoh is made to sit in the howdah of one of these beasts. Behind walks Nazar Beg with an unsheathed sword. Alongside Dara's elephant ride Malik Jivan alias Bakhtiar Khan and a troop of soldiers on horseback. Leading this humiliating procession is Bahadur Khan on elephant-back. They pass through Lahori Gate that holds many memories for Dara. His eyes downcast, he endures the intense humiliation of his predicament. Grief-stricken crowds line every road along which the procession moves. Witnessing the humiliation of their beloved prince, the people are sad, helpless and full of despair. The earth has swallowed their tears.

'As the procession passes through Lahori Gate, a beggar yells out, "Prince Dara Shikoh! You always gave us alms, but wretched souls like us have nothing to repay your kindness with."

'Tears course down Dara's cheeks as he looks at this man. He can only mumble, "I have nothing but a few tears left. I have preserved them for those of my countrymen who are unfortunate like me. Here, I offer you my tears. If you can preserve them with care, never allowing them to dry up, you can ensure that some day, somewhere, another Dara will be born."'

'I am the eyewitness who testifies to the authenticity of this episode,' pronounced a man who looked like a foreigner.

'And who are you?' the peon asked.

'I am Bernier. I am a traveller who also happens to be Dara's friend and personal physician. I have lived with Dara through his trials and tribulations. When he was paraded in that humiliating procession through the city, a huge mass of people had crowded Saadullah Bazar in Chandni Chowk. Loud lamentations rent the air, as though a marquee of lamentations had sprung up. It was the first time in my life that I had witnessed anything like it. Having wended its way around the ramparts of the fort, this degrading procession returned to Khwaspura via Khizrabad. Once again, Dara and Sipihar Shikoh were confined in the haveli.'

Kalyug took up the narrative once again.

'A storm of fury raged in the eyes of Delhi's ordinary citizens as they beheld this procession. In their sighs of lamentation brewed a tempest that threatened to overtake the city. The news reached

Aurangzeb. The silent sympathy of the masses made him tremble with apprehension. He feared rebellion and believed that the people might be ready to sacrifice their lives in order to save Dara and secure his freedom. This frenzy of fear gnawed at him relentlessly and robbed him of his sleep. Gazing out from his chamber into the pitch-black night, he saw his future stretched before him, as dark as the night, while his present crumbled into pieces. He saw himself lying buried in the mound of its shattered fragments. "Ya Allah!" screamed Aurangzeb, wiping his perspiring brow and drunkenly colliding with the chamber's walls.

'It was Roshanara who came to help him get a grip on himself. "O, my fortunate brother," she said wryly, "this is no time for confusion, uncertainty or restlessness. It is crucial to strike when the iron is hot. This is a moment history has gifted to you and none other. So, do wipe the sweat off your conscience and wage a decisive battle against Dara Shikoh."

'"Apa…Apa," whispered the shaken Aurangzeb, "what can I do now? My conscience trembles at the very thought of inflicting punishment on my elder brother. The entire populace of Hindustan loves him. The news I have received of what transpires behind the scenes is earth-shattering—at any moment, the people of Delhi may rise in revolt against me."

'"There's only one way of quelling such a rebellion," Roshanara asserted.

'"And what way is that?" Aurangzeb asked.

'"Given the rather delicate situation," she replied, "exploit your Hindustani subjects' deeply entrenched faith in their religion."

'"How…how do I do that?" Aurangzeb croaked.

'"All you have to do is get the ulemas to issue a fatwa. They have to declare Dara Shikoh a kafir for worshipping multiple gods. And then, they must sentence him to death."

'"How is it possible to get such a fatwa issued?" Aurangzeb wanted to know.

'"I know these mullahs, maulvis and ulemas through and through. This is not Arabia or Iran. This is Hindustan, where these spineless men have always behaved like curs wagging their tails before royal authority. Summon them to a meeting and apprise them of your wishes. Using great tact, put the onus of the decision regarding Dara's death sentence on them. Then, wait and watch—their final decree will be no different from the one the two of us desire!"

'The terrified Aurangzeb did summon these clerics. They gathered in the Diwan-e-Khas that evening. Roshanara's whispered injunction to her brother had been, "Remain silent, but use your guile to ensure that Dara is given what we desire—the death sentence. This will also guarantee our absolution from guilt in the eyes of history. In future, it will be said that the decision was arrived at by common consent, that Aurangzeb was compelled to defer to the collective wishes of his priests and courtiers. There was no way he could have disregarded the opinion of such fine intellects."

'The atmosphere pervading the Diwan-e-Khas that evening was far from the righteous satisfaction that accompanies the dispensation of justice. It was gloomy and despondent, as though a condolence meeting, rather than one to discuss the affairs of state, had been convened. It lasted just a short while—the crucial decision had been taken much earlier; only the seal of the ulemas was required to ratify it. Even though the courtier, Danishmand, had been a bitter opponent of Dara, he had voiced his objection to the death sentence. "There is no justifiable reason whatsoever for sentencing Prince Dara to death," he had declared. "It would be better if the prince and his son were imprisoned for life in the fort at Gwalior and kept there under strict supervision."

'Danishmand's intervention created ripples in the court and Roshanara realized that her plan might come to nought. She proffered Aurangzeb further advice. "If Dara is sentenced to life imprisonment," she said, "he should be fed a concoction of arhar dal and opium so as to ensure his eventual death from slow poisoning."

'This time, Aurangzeb refused to go along with her advice. He remembered that after dealing with Dara, he would have to settle scores with another sibling—the debauch Murad Baksh. Roshanara's suggestion would come in very handy for dispatching Murad, Aurangzeb decided. Danishmand's recommendation was, however, overturned by three vociferous opponents of Dara—Khalilullah

Khan, Shaista Khan and Tabbarruk Khan. This development was only to be expected. From the very outset, the ulemas, mullahs and maulvis had been against the ways of the supposed heretic Dara. Learned in the shariat and the scriptures, these clerics had long perceived Dara to be a danger to their faith. He infuriated them with his beliefs and practices. With hardly any deliberation preceding their decision, they rejected Danishmand's suggestion and issued the fatwa of death against Dara.'

Kalyug continued with his tale. 'Both Roshanara and Aurangzeb sighed with relief. It was the ulemas themselves who had proposed the death penalty for Dara whom they saw as an enemy of Islam. Conveniently, the diktat of these clerics was successful in concealing from the masses Aurangzeb's lust for power and his designs on the Mughal throne. Had his true motives come to light, the country would have erupted in a bloody civil war. In fact, it nearly happened, though on a small scale. All Aurangzeb ever acknowledged was his powerlessness in the face of a religious fatwa.'

Having said this, Kalyug looked towards Hazrat Shibli Nomani. The latter seemed listless and deeply upset. The adeeb too was pained by the man's dismay. Shibli Nomani was not only his senior, but also belonged to the adeeb's own community of intellectuals. Moved by his silence, the adeeb said, 'Honourable sir, your feelings of dismay cause us concern, but what are we to do? Each century has the freedom to forage for the truth. And you are aware, sir, truth is a dream that embodies the soaring aspirations of mankind. That is why, in each passing century, truth is purified in the furnace of culture for the betterment of mankind.'

Shibli Nomani gazed at the adeeb, almost as if he concurred with most of the testimony presented in the court. After giving it a thought, he declared, 'Honourable adeeb, whatever I have written about Alamgir is the truth about that man; and it is a truth that determines the fortunes of the seventeenth century.'

Tucking in his cummerbund with one hand and juggling a cigarette and a walking stick in the other, Raghupati Sahai Firaq made an appearance. His large, watery eyes took in the assembly at a glance. He took a puff at his cigarette, exhaled a cloud of smoke and said, 'Sir, no matter how great an individual happens to be, his perception of truth cannot determine the future of a nation. Even emperors and dictators cannot be granted this right, because *Destiny is bound to nations, not to the fortunes of one man.* Your Alamgir, Shibli Nomani Sahib, was just an individual, a prince; not a statesman of his time.'

Another puff at the cigarette and Firaq was gone, gone the way he had come. Culture did try to detain him, but he would not be stopped. The assembly was left gaping after him.

The peon then gestured to Kalyug to carry on with his account. And so, the narrative continued...

'Illustrious adeeb, as soon as the fatwa decreed that Dara be put to death, the session involving the conspirators who had devised it, came to an end. The next morning, on 30 August 1659, a special function was held in the Diwan-e-Aam to honour Malik Jivan. For his treachery to Dara Shikoh and his loyalty to Aurangzeb, Malik Jivan's name was changed to Bakhtiar Khan and his place was assured in the Mughal hierarchy by making him a Hazari, the commander of a thousand men. When Malik Hazari Bakhtiar Khan was returning from the court with his Afghan soldiers after being rewarded for his treachery, the people of Delhi could no longer contain their wrath. As he passed through Chandni Chowk, they attacked him and his soldiers. As a bloody riot broke out, chaos ensued. Women heaped abuse, garbage and sewage on him. The offal of animal cadavers was hurled at him and he was attacked with burning logs and embers pulled out from stoves. In this revolt, a few hundred of his men were killed. Had the Kotwal of Delhi not quelled this uprising in time, Malik Hazari Bakhtiar Khan would not have escaped alive. By evening, the desolation of death hung over Delhi. This incident brought Dara Shikoh even closer to the common man during the last days of his life.'

Bernier nodded in agreement. 'I can vouch for this incident. I witnessed the gruesome bloodshed first-hand. I also challenge the historical veracity of the *Alamgirnama* which claims that Dara was put to death purely to respect a religious fatwa. The latter was merely a pretext, as Aurangzeb had decided much earlier that Dara had to be disposed of. If Dara's execution was not premeditated, what could have been the motive for bestowing a new name and title on Malik Jivan? This was his reward for betraying Dara.'

Kalyug picked up the narrative once again. 'That night, the aura of death hung over Delhi's desolate townscape. And on that fateful night, Aurangzeb summoned his trusted executioner Nazar Quli Beg. When the hunchback bowed before him, Aurangzeb ordered, "Go to the haveli in Khwaspura. Remove Sipihar Shikoh from his father's presence. Then slice off the kafir Dara's head and bring it to me. To execute this mission, Shafi Khan will accompany you."

'On the night of 30 August 1659, Nazar Beg and Shafi Khan entered the darkened room of the haveli in Khwaspura where Dara and his son were being held. At the time, Prince Dara was cooking masoor dal. For him, the arrival of the two men foreshadowed his doom. All he asked was, "Why are you here at this hour? What for…?"

'Nazar Beg replied, "The order is to take Sipihar Shikoh away from you." These words alerted Sipihar Shikoh to the true intentions of the two men.

'"Have you been sent to kill us?" Dara asked them sternly.

'"To that, I have no answer," the hunchback replied. "Now, get up."

'The frightened Sipihar Shikoh clung to his father. Shafi Khan and Nazar Beg pulled him away. Unable to restrain himself, Dara shouted, "You will have to pay the price for insulting men of royal blood!" But the two executioners paid no heed to Dara's wrath nor to Sipihar's cries. They were merely bent on carrying out their emperor's orders. In that dark room, there was no weapon at hand that Dara could use to protect himself. Concealed in his pillow was a small knife used to sharpen his quills. Pulling it out, Dara attacked the two assassins. Nazar Beg then unsheathed his dagger and slashed through Sipihar Shikoh's arm. The boy screamed in pain. Using all the strength he could muster, Dara wrenched his son away from the grip of the two executioners. "Go and tell my heartless brother," he cried, "that this innocent boy has done him no harm…he should not be taken away from me."

'"We are not messengers!" the hunchbacked butcher exclaimed. "We are here to carry out Alamgir's orders."

'"And that's exactly what we're doing." With these words, Shafi Khan once again seized the injured boy. Dara now had no doubt that his death had been decreed.

'As the two men were dragging his son away, he stabbed Shafi Khan with his small knife. The weapon ended up embedded in his ribs. Sipihar Shikoh was handed to the soldiers waiting outside the room. The blood spurted from Sipihar's arm and formed a rivulet. The sight of it jolted Dara. There was nothing he could do. Through the wall he could hear his son's terrifying screams, as if the child were being drawn and quartered. "Spare my son this torture!" Dara implored. "Go and tell that ruthless Alamgir that he is no pious namazi, but a traitor. Tell him that he is a sinner in the guise of a devout worshipper. I may not have been a pious worshipper, but I have always held myself above sin. Remind him of what the holy Jabir had said—a worshipper cannot be the equal of one who is above sin. Tell him...tell him that the fatwa issued by his mullahs is a serious breach of faith. It is heresy." By then, Sipihar's screams had taken their toll on Dara. All he could mutter was, "Spare my son...whatever be your orders, execute them on me..."'

Darkness enveloped the court. The adeeb looked around in amazement at the eerie atmosphere.

Half the stars in the sky seemed to have lost their glow. The rest had disintegrated into slivers of glass that fell from the sky. Clouds that had covered the moon blew away like shattered fragments. With an unearthly sound, the moon itself cracked like shards of glass. Startled by all he saw, the adeeb asked the peon, 'What is going on? What is happening?'

'Sir, Time has turned back. It is the final hour of the night of 30 August 1659. But 31 August finds it difficult to dawn, because the sun is in mourning and clad in a black robe.'

'The sun is in mourning?' the adeeb asked in disbelief.

'Yes, sir. In that haveli at Khwaspura, the boiling dal is down to a simmer. For Dara is now being slain.'

'He is being slain? But why do I hear the recital of the kalmah?'

'That is Dara's voice, sir. He has now finished reciting martyrdom's kalmah-e-shahadat...and now...now his head has been severed from his body.'

The darkness grew ever deeper. Silence reigned supreme. Garbed in the colours of mourning, the sun peeped out from a corner of the earth.

'Honourable sir, as the sun rose, the severed head of Dara was taken to Aurangzeb,' Kalyug carried on, 'but he could not muster the courage to look at it. Yet, he had to glance at it to confirm that it was, indeed, Dara and put his fears to rest. When he finally did so, an uncharacteristic scream escaped his lips as he cried, "O Wretched Kafir, I cannot bear to look upon your face!" Then, averting his gaze, he ordered that the head be wiped clean and placed on a large tray. Roshanara arrived to dispense further advice. "Get Dara Shikoh's head perfumed, enclose it in a box and dispatch it as a gift to our honourable sire," she suggested. To comply with the order, Nazar Beg and Shafi Khan set out with Dara's bloodied, decapitated head. The news of Dara's death had spread like wildfire.'

Then, a strange scene was enacted before the adeeb's eyes. A quartet of silver wings lay on the ground before him. Startled, he asked to whom they belonged.

'Sir, they belong to the angels who had come to carry away Dara's soul. But these heavenly creatures could not bear the pain of Dara's death and their beautiful wings just fell off.'

The adeeb was overcome by sadness as he looked in Dara's direction. Their eyes met and the prince murmured, 'The last I remember of the incident was the moment I was reciting the kalmah. After that, I was overcome by a strange spiritual inertia. What transpired after I was beheaded is a thought that fills me with revulsion.'

'The vilest aspect of this sordid episode was its aftermath—the day of Dara's beheading marked the dismemberment of Hindustan's newly emergent composite culture,' Culture observed in a deeply sorrowful tone. 'What Dara had envisioned as a new culture, had been spoken of, centuries ago, by the Holy Prophet.' With these words, Culture withdrew and sat down, murmuring, 'Since then, I am only half-alive.'

From the two ends of Chandni Chowk there emerged a pair of processions. One of them was especially strange to behold. It consisted solely of headless torsos beating their breasts. From their severed necks spurted fountains of blood. The other was a procession of royal soldiers, unsheathed sword in hand.

Along with Dara, the adeeb observed the scene, then asked, 'Kalyug, what is this meant to be?'

Kalyug replied: 'Honourable sir, the mourning procession of headless torsos represents the ordinary citizens who loved Dara Shikoh. The other one consists of Aurangzeb's soldiers.'

'I can understand the mourning procession, but why are the soldiers out in a procession?'

'I can understand and see it all now,' Dara intervened. 'Look closely at the soldiers. In their midst is an elephant.'

All eyes turned to see a headless man tied to the animal's back. This corpse had been taken through the streets of Delhi. The procession was now entering Chandni Chowk.

'Dara, do you recognize the decapitated man?' the adeeb asked.

'Yes, Your Honour, I do. That is my headless corpse.'

28

Apart from the headless torsos, another horrifying sight unfolded before the adeeb's very eyes. It spanned the centuries...

Before him lay a land called Hindustan, whose citizens had no heads on their shoulders. Wherever the eye travelled, it beheld these decapitated people. Bazaars, mandirs and masjids had their gates thrown open. Shops in Chandni Chowk displayed their wares, as these torsos walked about, speaking, haggling over prices, shopping. They even visited places of worship. Headless though they were, devoid of lips that could move and eyes that could blink, their voices were audible everywhere.

This horrendous scene was not confined to Hindustan alone; it spread across Central Asia, all the way to Turkey. The face of the entire human race seemed to have undergone a metamorphosis. Even nature seemed to have lost its vibrancy. Flowers bloomed devoid of fragrance. Dates grew, but tasted insipid. Honeybees shunned date palms. The skies were bare, with not a bird to be seen. Darkness descended, but no stars shone in the heavens. The moon looked sere like the shrivelled leaves of autumn. Rivers followed their course, but not a wave rippled across their surface.

The sun rose, shrouded in robes of mourning. The swallows, impatient to be out and about, failed to comprehend why day was refusing to dawn. Alarmed sparrows perched on walls. The fish stopped swimming in the waveless Jamuna. Even now, tremors shook the historic haveli at Khwaspura...

The adeeb's eyes fell on the Red Fort at Shahjahanabad. He noticed that the sentries on guard along its ramparts, balconies and gates, were headless. He could make no sense whatsoever of this strange phenomenon and shouted for the peon.

'Coming, sir,' came the reply.

'Tell me,' the adeeb asked when he appeared, 'does my torso have a head?'

'It does, sir.'

'I can see that you have yours, too. But do explain to me why the people around us are headless.'

'Sir,' the peon replied, 'history contains many such epochs where people lose their heads...when the processes of thought and understanding, of the exploration of truth, comes to a complete standstill. Honourable adeeb, we are merely passing through one such era.'

'Do the eyes lose their power of vision at such times?'

'No, sir, the eyes observe whatever takes place.'

'But where are the eyes of these headless torsos?'

'Sir, their eyes, millions of them, have congregated at another place to witness yet another shameful episode in history. Do you see those mountains of eyes in the distance?'

The adeeb was shaken at the sight and cried out, 'What is it that these millions of eyes are so curious to witness?'

'Honourable sir, Aurangzeb and Roshanara have changed their minds. Dara Shikoh's headless body will now be strung up at Lahori Gate and his severed head will be displayed at Chandni Chowk.

Look...Nazar Beg has taken over the responsibility for this task.'

The adeeb saw Dara's body dangling from Lahori Gate. The prince's head sat impaled on a spear at Chandni Chowk. At both places, huge mountains of eyes gazed at the spectacle.

Suddenly, the impaled head burst into peals of laughter and a terrifying earthquake sent tremors rumbling through the ground. As their master laughed, Dara's Shirazi pigeons turned to look sadly in his direction. His pet African lions, too, looked at him in surprise. Never had they heard the illustrious Prince Dara Shikoh, crown prince of the realm and scion of the dynasty of Taimur and Changez, laugh quite so raucously. As his head continued to laugh, the mountains of eyes stared at it in amazement.

A hush prevailed in the Diwankhana-e-Ilm, the chamber of scholarship. Erudite men of learning—the Sanskrit scholar, Kubatrai; the poet, Ranjan Das; Kashinath and Dwarkanandan who had translated the Vedas and the Upanishads respectively into Persian and many others—sat around dejectedly. Strangely enough, the silver flowers in the Chandni Khana from which fireworks were set off, drooped and withered. The chandeliers, holding a thousand lamps that banished darkness and trapped the afternoon sun's radiance in their flames, refused to light up. The comely slave girls, who flitted about carrying camphor lamps, had chosen to discard them. They stood in silence, clad in robes of mourning. All the cannons in the realm stood overwhelmed by shame. Dara Shikoh's steed, Falakpaima, stood next to the prince's headless body at Lahori Gate, its eyes brimming with tears. The eyes of his favourite elephant, Fatehganj, were also moist. The breeze had dropped and the pennants on the royal fleet, the *Uqab-e-Surkh*, drooped like corpses.

Another loud burst of laughter from Dara's spiked head at Chandni Chowk, another rumbling earthquake...and then, the head spoke: 'Patriotic service to one's homeland is the greatest virtue and the best way to revere one's faith. That is what I have accomplished...'

The loud voice resounded through the heavens...

In the shallows of the Jamuna, the lotuses opened their eyes. The river fronds attuned their ears to the sound. A million voices chorused, 'Long live, Sultan Dara Shikoh Alam, the Crown Prince of our Realm! Long live the Bright Star of the House of Taimur and Changez, the Monarch of High Fortune, our beloved Prince!'

'Zindabad! May he live forever!'

The corpses of some of Dara's sympathizers still lay rotting in Chandni Chowk, but the crawling maggots in their wounds had become still. Aurangzeb's spies, moving about in the guise of sadhus, fakirs and dervishes, were stunned to hear these voices. Where did they come from? To whom did they belong? After all, Dara's head hung all alone at Chandni Chowk. Not a soul was around. Yet, the voices showed no signs of falling silent.

When the voices reached Aurangzeb's ears, he set off for Roshanara's apartments. Bowing to greet her when she appeared, he proceeded to tell her about his fears.

'How is that possible?' she retorted. 'These voices are simply the figment of people's imaginations. Thanks to the Almighty, the beacon of your good fortune shines over the entire kingdom.'

'But, Apa, my spies will never bring me incorrect information!'

'Then summon your astrologers and palmists at once and have them trace the source from which these voices emanate.'

It did not take long for these men to arrive. After great deliberation, the palmist, Dhananand, ventured, 'The point, Your Highness, is that even after Dara Shikoh's assassination, his sympathizers' feelings for him live on. Their wounded hopes float about his head, creating all that commotion.'

Manjam Shafiullah seconded this view. 'Your Highness,' he said, 'the wise Dhananand is right. What is more, the dead Dara Shikoh's head is holding its own court, attended by his headless ministers, mansabdars and chieftains. This invisible court is in session all the time.'

Aurangzeb was incensed by what they had told him. 'This is dangerous!' he exclaimed. 'This tumult among the dead should be stopped sooner rather than later.'

'There's one way to achieve this, Jahanpanah,' the astrologer, Ashfaq, suggested with some hesitation.

'And what is that?'

'Every Muslim commoner in the kingdom must be told that Dara Shikoh had become a Hindu. The ulemas and the muftis should be made to issue a fatwa like the one you had decided on the night Dara and his son were imprisoned in the haveli at Khwaspura...the night you stared out into the inky darkness.'

'Ashfaq's suggestion is a sound one,' remarked Roshanara.

'What if another courtier like Danishmand stands up and challenges it?' Aurangzeb asked Roshanara.

'Alamgir,' came the reply, 'wise courtiers like Danishmand are few and far between. Every kingdom has many men like Tabbaruk Khan who overrule and overturn the advice of men like Danishmand. There will be many who vie to fulfil our aspirations.'

*

The night was pitch dark. Even the stars had snuffed themselves out.

The adeeb had arrived and was sitting under the peepul tree near the intersecting roads at Chandni Chowk. The scene remained the same—Dara Shikoh's head stood alone on the point of a spear; yet the sound of a million voices continued to reverberate.

Then, in the depths of the night, the adeeb noticed a lean figure, regal in a sherwani, emerge and come to a halt at the crossroads. The man walked along, pausing from time to time. His every step seemed to be accompanied by the sound of a brass gong being struck. Yet, nothing was visible around him, save for Dara's decapitated head, impaled on a spear.

For a while, this regal personage walked on. Then he sat down on a boulder, clutching his head in his hands. The adeeb rose and went over to him. He stopped in amazement as recognition dawned—this was his contemporary, the novelist Qazi Abdus Sattar!

'Is that really you, Qazi, my brother?' he asked, unable to believe his eyes.

'Arrey, bhaijaan, it's you, is it?' came the Qazi's equally incredulous rejoinder.

Both looked in the direction of Dara's head. Qazi Abdus Sattar declared, 'Brother, no historian will ever return here again, but writers of every century will perforce retrace their footsteps to this place. For Dara Shikoh had accepted the challenge of creating a new culture, a new way of life. Destiny, however, snatched the pen from his hand and a blood-smeared sword sullied the horoscope of an entire nation.'

At his words, a laugh rang out from Dara's head and the ground shook with its vibrations. When the laughter died down, raindrops fell on Chandni Chowk, almost as if the clouds were weeping. But no, this was no shower; these were Dara's tears raining down on them. Flowing with them were tears that welled out from the mountains of eyes nearby. As the tears became a deluge, a strange voice exhorted, 'Centuries to come! Heed what I say! The hand of tyranny will drive emerging cultures to sob and whimper in this manner. People with a vision like Dara Shikho's will continue to be hanged at the gallows. Their tears will be the dewdrops that glitter on blades of grass. And human destiny will never change till mankind learns to recognize the tears in those dewdrops.'

Qazi Abdus Sattar and the adeeb tried in vain to locate the source of the voice. But there was no one around. Suddenly, the peon materialized and announced, 'Honourable sir, this is the voice of the Future, seized by apprehension over its own future.'

The voice echoed again. 'Wait and see,' it declared. 'Victory will forever elude the tyrant, bigot and emperor who is fanatical about his faith. Yet, the battle between the forces of tyranny and humanity will never cease to rage. In every century, an Aurangzeb will be born, along with a Dara Shikoh. This cycle must be disrupted. Or else, like my own, your future too, will be bleak. If I should die, all your dreams will come to nought.'

To these words, the adeeb's spontaneous reply was: 'No, Future, that won't happen. We have begun to understand the significance of dewdrops on blades of grass...we will never allow you to die; nor will our dreams ever perish.'

The Future remained unseen.

*

With a beating of drums, the fatwa issued by Aurangzeb's Islamic ulemas was being publicly proclaimed. 'O Brothers in Islam, the danger that threatened the Islamic caliphate of Hindustan has now abated. Dara Shikoh, the patron of Hinduism with his deep-rooted abhorrence of namaz, Ramadhan, Haj and zakat, had been wrongfully conspiring to ascend the Peacock Throne. He had flaunted his defiance of Allah by incorporating the likeness of Hindu deities into the royal insignia. Enlisting the help of Hindu yogis, sants and Rajput warriors, this man had plotted to banish Islam from the face of the paradise that is Hindustan. The qazis and muftis of this city have issued a fatwa, my brothers, proclaiming Dara Shikoh's execution by the sword to be the noble act of the most glorious jihad of all—the Jihad-e-Akbar!'

Dara's head smiled at these words. The universe was rent by an earthquake. Near the Jama Masjid, the declaration of the fatwa, preceded by drumbeats, was made many times over. The namaz prayers had been offered at sunset. The market place at Chandni Chowk, usually ablaze with the light of a myriad lamps and torches, was dark and silent. The streets and pathways that usually spilled over with people, and were redolent with the scent of attar and flowers, were now deserted. Nowhere to be seen were the flashily dressed *kahars* who carried palanquins to and fro. The shops near the Jama Masjid, where stories used to be read aloud, had closed their eyes. Also missing were the elderly men who usually reclined against bolsters laid out on white sheets and puffed on their hookahs, exhaling the fragrant smoke. No silver glasses, filled with faluda and sherbet, were being passed around.

Then a few liveried soldiers made their appearance. Preceded by a roll of drums, another announcement was made: 'The world is Allah's and the following order is our emperor's—the Shahenshah of Hindustan, Alamgir Aurangzeb, Monarch of the World! You are hereby warned that not a single headless one will be spared! All torsos are ordered to fix their heads back on their shoulders. Neither bazaar nor shop must, henceforth, remain closed. Life and work will go on as usual!'

As the soldiers and drummers moved on, the frenetic activity in Jumman's kitchen resumed—the stoves were re-lit with charcoal fires, huge cooking pots bubbled with fragrant meats and their delicious aroma wafted around the place. Scores of shoppers reappeared; conversations were struck up once again. Sweetmeat shops threw open their doors, their halwas, murabbas and mithais resplendent as a bride. Huge grinding stones were washed with rose water. Well-muscled men, silver bells tied to their forearms, began grinding intoxicating bhang on them. The tinkling sound of their bells drew people to them. Hookahs were readied once again. Fumes of Moradabad tobacco floated in the air. Gossip and hearsay resurfaced.

'Thanks be to Allah! Had Alamgir Aurangzeb not taken over the reins, the seven-hundred-year-old legacy of Islamic rule would have come to an ignominious end in the hands of Daraji Maharaj!'

At Jumman's eatery, someone sowed the seeds of an argument. 'Arrey mian, be grateful for small mercies!' he said. 'Had Dara succeeded in wearing the crown, you wouldn't be here eating *harisa*! The consumption of meat would be prohibited and you'd be left craving for it!'

'Oh, yes...His Highness must've been counting the final hours before ascending the throne, while the other three princes in their respective provinces remained oblivious of his plans. Daraji Maharaj had made concrete plans for his ascension. All that remained to be organized was the royal procession that would precede the coronation!'

'It had gone this far!'

Such comments and bickering were audible everywhere. Certain individuals would initiate these debates by provoking their audience, then move on, leaving dispute and disagreement in their wake.

'Arrey, it's an established fact that intellectuals well versed in the Vedas and the Upanishads were ever-present in Dara's court. Munshi Chandrabhan was prominent among them. The ones closest to Dara were Kashinath, who translated the Vedas into Persian; Dwarkanandan, who translated the Upanishads; Pandit Kubatrai, the Sanskrit scholar; and the court poet Ranjandas.'

'I've heard that in the shadows cast by Dara's bedside candelabra, there lay a golden tripod. On its shelves were volumes of Vedas, Upanishads and Sufi treatises, all written in letters of gold.'

'Heresy! That's what it was!'

'Arrey, when he'd gone to fight in Kandahar, not only had he taken along a huge army of battle-hardened elephants, cavalry, cannons, archers, foot soldiers, labourers, water-carriers, stone masons and his sycophantic retinue, but he also had five camels tagging along, loaded with Hindu scriptures and Sufi texts. On the backs of five different elephants, sat scholars of Sanskrit, Arabic and Persian, intellectuals, poets, linguists, astrologers, ascetics and yogis!'

'Apart from this, his personal Diwankhana-e-Ilm was a library in which the Hindu deity Shankar's image overshadowed everything else. The image of god Shiva was engraved on the diamond pendant he wore. On the ring he wore on a finger of his right hand, was etched the Almighty's name in Sanskrit. Is there a soul who wasn't aware of his conversion to Hinduism?'

'No, that wasn't quite the case. Essentially, he was a Muslim who'd leaned a little too far in the direction of Hinduism. Had he ascended the Peacock Throne and worn the emperor's crown, the Hindu influence would've pervaded every walk of life and the Mughal dynasty would've come to an end!'

Dara's suspended head burst into loud laughter...so loud, that the pigeons sheltering in the ramparts and domes of the fort fluttered off in alarm.

Alamgir Aurangzeb was filled with apprehension as this laughter reverberated through his palace. A frown creased his forehead. His eyes narrowed. He rose to his feet abruptly.

Voices were audible from the gateway to Roshanara's palace. The sentry at the gates, Khwajasara Fahim, was startled. A servant ran by and announced that Aurangzeb was approaching.

The golden-haired, voluptuous Uzbek women who guarded the palace, stood at attention. The African slave girls, dressed in white, prepared to carry messages from one person to another. When news of her brother's arrival reached Roshanara, she came down to wait for him by the flowing stream that ran along its marbled, man-made course within the palace. Aurangzeb entered. At a signal, all the guards and servants withdrew, leaving Aurangzeb and Roshanara to themselves in the chamber. The two conversed for a while in private. It was decided that Dara should be buried to prevent his severed head from repeating the misdemeanour it was guilty of—laughing aloud in public.

Accordingly, the prince's body was buried, unwashed and unshrouded, in Humayun's mausoleum. Amazingly enough, people continued to see Dara's face at Chandni Chowk and his laughter still rang out. In fact, the peepul tree standing at the spot now joined in the laughter by clapping its branches together. Slowly, all the peepul trees in the kingdom joined in the chorus of laughter. It was, indeed, a terrifying sight to behold!

In this ominous atmosphere, the mournful strains of a song were audible:

It's rare in this world
To find a soul
Who values humanity,
Transcends caste and creed,
Rises above fear and greed,
And breaks free
Of the past and bonds of the heart...

The disturbing lyrics echoed around the place over and over again. Then a man appeared and announced, 'People of the world! I am the representative of bygone centuries and the narrator in the drama being enacted before you. The underlying causes of whatever you have witnessed today lie within me. The Hindu caste system is on the verge of extinction. Its four main varnas have split up into small sub-castes that regard themselves as superior to one another. Caste discrimination is rife. Hindus have fallen prey to unwarranted arrogance. No wonder Guru Nanak's words float about like wandering gypsies, constant reminders that in this epoch not a soul is free from the guilt of discrimination, greed, ambition or arrogance. Aware as they are of their indispensability in the matter of rituals, it is the Brahmins who keep the rest of society in their stranglehold.'

29

The peepul trees continued to laugh. The situation was rather strange, however, because others of their species—the banyans, which were almost 2500 years old, were shouting slogans. It was an eerie sight indeed! While the mature trees laughed, the old ones raised slogans and the young peepuls brought their branches together in applause. For once, youth and old age were united in a common cause!

The adeeb listened to them attentively. It took him a while to decipher their message. The old banyans were shouting:

'Vedic culture, murdabad! Down with Vedic culture!'

'Down with the caste system! *Varnavad* murdabad!'

'Down with Brahmins! Murdabad!'

'Root of all suffering—Varnavad, Varnavad!'

The startled adeeb called for the peon. Before the man could arrive, a young tree approached the adeeb and stood before him.

'Was there something you wanted to know?' it asked.

'Yes, there was...what does this mean? What kind of dissent is this supposed to be? Why are the older trees shouting slogans, while you young ones applaud?'

'Janab, it so happens that the Vedic Aryans had brought about a schism in society for their own vested interests. Our elders, the banyans, do not accept it. Unlike the Aryans, we do not claim to have been born from the soles of the god Brahma's feet. The Aryan perception of divine creation has no rationale...'

An ancient banyan tree stepped forward. 'The caste-ridden Varnavad established by the Aryans is not based on the laws of nature,' it declared. 'It overlooks the fact that even Brahmin women menstruate, bear children, suckle and nurture them. Despite it, Aryan Brahmins, born from the womb of woman, claim that they came into being from the mouth of Brahma. And Brahma's mouth has no uterus...'

Then came Gautama Buddha's voice from Gaya, 'Break it! Disrupt the cycle of Varnavad created by the Vedic Aryans! I am an Aryan, but the Varnavad and Brahminvad established by the Vedic

Aryans have made us all exiles within our own culture. We refuse to be counted as such. We do not acknowledge the Creator's omnipotence. We reject the belief in reincarnation. It may be irresistibly appealing, but it goes against nature. We consider the Aryan perception of Brahma in the Upanishads to be of little value. Written after the Brahminical scriptures, the Upanishads are examples of Aryan arrogance. We deny the necessity of priesthood by declaring that no being is omnipotent. Reincarnation is a myth. Every individual is the means to his own enlightenment; he alone can liberate himself from the compulsions of the material world. No divine voice ever comes forth from within a human being. Gods do not exist and the writings celebrating their exploits are but manifestations of a slave mentality. What fails to stir the mind or impress the intellect is best cast aside. Accept the new, not the reinvention of the old. Intelligence alone—not some magical force—has always presided over the transition from the old to the new. It is said that a powerful force created us. Well, listen. The worldly and the mortal are inferior to Creation. Only he who acknowledges the reality of death can be a creator. Until that moment when Gilgamesh of the Sumerian civilization returns with the antidote for death, liberate yourself from the fear of death by acknowledging its inevitability. That is nirvana! It can be achieved in this birth and on this planet. Nirvana germinates within each and every individual. That is why it is universal—it belongs to the entire human race. It is a way of severing the ties that bind death to suffering. Do not allow yourself to be the cause of death...therein lies ahimsa, the pinnacle of compassion.'

'Yet, even after so many centuries, Delhi witnesses the macabre dance of death. Just observe these storms, adeeb!' Qazi Abdus Sattar said breathlessly, as he came running in from Chandni Chowk. 'Guru Tegh Bahadur has cast off his fear of death. Now, not only does Dara's head laugh in Chandni Chowk, even the severed head of Guru Tegh Bahadur refuses to fall to the ground. Their blood has turned to dynamite and spins about like an explosive cannonball. The sight has caused armies of dust storms to break loose.'

'Has Aurangzeb murdered someone again?' the adeeb asked his friend.

'Yes, indeed he has. He is now possessed by the demon of religious conversion. Kashmir has been chosen as the new arena for religious suppression and conversion, because it is home to the intellectually evolved Pandits. The ignoramuses here are oblivious to the fact that much before their time, those who wished to embrace Islam in Kashmir had already done so. They are unaware that Kashmir had been visited, long ago, by Muslim preachers and the Sufi, Syed Ali Hamdani, a sage from Persia.'

'But sir, he was a Sufi, not a Bahawi. Emperor Aurangzeb and the subedar of Kashmir, Sher Afghan, cannot abide the idea of unity among the different Islamic sects,' the peon answered.

Qazi Abdus Sattar agreed wholeheartedly. 'Adeeb, your peon is absolutely right,' he declared. 'The Sufi sect recognizes neither ruler nor caliph as the intermediary between Allah and itself. In Kashmir, the worshippers of Shiva harbour similar sentiments. Till this very day, the *mutawalli* or caretaker of Lord Shankar's Amarnath Cave is a Muslim. He is simply a mutawalli, not a maulvi, mullah or purohit—a point of view sanctioned even by Kashmiri Buddhists. It is what makes Kashmir so special, what defines its essence— Kashmiriyat. The tantric significance of Shiva worship had greatly appealed to the Sufis. There is a marked difference between the rituals practised by Kashmiri worshippers of Shiva and the rites established by Hindus who worship the same god elsewhere in the country. Kashmiri Buddhism differs from the Buddhism practised in Tibet or in any other Buddhist country. Even Islam practised in Kashmir is more liberal and tolerant than it is elsewhere. It is the reason why Shah Hamdani's masjid stands within a Buddhist vihara by the Jhelum. People of all faiths pray and worship at Dastgir Sahib's shrine at Khanyar and at Nand Rishi Nooruddin's sanctuary at Charar-e-Sharif. Whenever a boat or a shikara is launched, the pious rishis are always remembered. It is this particular tradition that Sher Afghan and Emperor Aurangzeb are bent on abolishing.'

'Sir, that is why when Kashmiri Pandits could no longer endure their tyranny, Pandit Kriparam gathered together a band of his brethren and called upon Guru Tegh Bahadur Sahib. These men had complete faith in Guruji's power. Having heard their accounts of torture and forced conversion, Guruji made it clear that saving a faith from extinction was possible only if some great soul was prepared to lay his life down in its cause. While the gathering pondered over the issue, Govindrai, Guruji's nine-year-old son, spoke up. "Revered father," he said, "at this moment, is there anyone greater than you in this land? You alone can preserve our faith."'

'What...what was Guruji's decision?' the adeeb wanted to know.

The peon replied, 'He advised Pandit Kriparam to go and inform Aurangzeb that he was the disciple of Guru Tegh Bahadur, Guru Nanak's successor. Kriparam was to tell the emperor that if Guruji were to embrace Islam, all the kingdom's Hindus would willingly embrace it too. Aurangzeb was immensely pleased with the idea. He immediately issued a farman calling for the arrest of Guruji Maharaj. Orders were also issued for the temporary suspension of all forced conversions and oppressive measures in Kashmir.'

'What happened next?'

'In keeping with Emperor Aurangzeb's decree, Delhi's qazi, Abdul Bahawi, was assigned the task of converting Guru Maharaj to Islam.'

'No, that's untrue! Quite untrue!' protested an old man, coming to stand before the adeeb. 'All the riff-raff stand here, hurling accusations at Alamgir, trying to sully the name of this eminent and benevolent man who happened to be the last emperor. The history of Hindustan is not about to tolerate the bad blood born of these unfounded allegations.'

'Your name, please?' the adeeb inquired.

'I am Abdul Bahawi, the qazi of Delhi, whom your kafir peon referred to not a moment ago.'

'Qazi Sahib,' the peon replied, 'I am no atheist. I am a true Hindustani Muslim who offers his namaz five times a day! It is narrow-minded Bahawi mullahs like you who have unleashed the real kufr on us. Centuries before either you or your Alamgir, Aurangzeb, appeared on the scene, men of superior intellect and liberal outlook like Moinuddin Chishti, Nizamuddin Auliya and Amir Khusrau had transformed Islam into a world religion. Ever since you bigoted

Bahawis handed religion over to the sword, people like us have had to answer for your acts of tyranny and oppression! You have committed the crimes, but we Muslims, the people of Hindustan, Pakistan, Afghanistan, Daghestan, Sinkiang, Chechnya and Tajikistan have had to pay for them.'

'Silence!' the qazi roared. 'I was asleep as I awaited the Day of Judgement, but kafir Muslims like you have snatched away my peaceful repose! That is why I am present at this accursed assembly!'

'Qazi Sahib,' the peon remonstrated, 'this is no assembly. This is the court of Time, the court of those centuries that weigh heavily on the human spirit. It is here that cases, centuries old, are given a hearing, so that the ultimate truth is laid bare before us all. It ensures that no spirit is restive and that in this serai of the world, each one of us can live without fear.'

'Illustrious adeeb, if this is, indeed, a court, not an assembly, I request you to have the history of my time summoned here,' the qazi suggested.

'Ask History to appear before this court,' the adeeb ordered.

Smeared with blood, the history of the seventeenth century made an appearance.

'Honourable sir, did you summon me?' it asked.

'That's right,' the adeeb replied, 'but you are so stained with blood, it will take you centuries to wipe it away.'

'It is something from which I seem to have no reprieve. Whenever people were killed, it was my blood that flowed. It is I who died with every civilization and my bloody seed gave birth to the next one. Just as Nature is manifest in the earth, mountains, seas and heavens, the roots of my being lie in mankind's sorrow, his aspirations and dreams and in his quest for happiness. Honourable adeeb, I can vouch for the fact that selfishness, religious fanaticism and lust for power have made us brutal and intolerant. Anyway, let us put this aside for the time being. Tell me why I have been summoned here.'

'To confirm the truth behind Guru Tegh Bahadur's murder,' the adeeb replied.

'The truth is crystal clear, sir. The psychological impact of the fatwa and of the announcements proclaiming Dara Shikoh to be a patron of Hinduism was impossible to reverse. Even Aurangzeb had to grudgingly accept this reality. Though he was emperor, he was also rendered powerless by the diktat of this fatwa. Guru Tegh Bahadur's martyrdom was the outcome of a powerless emperor's limited vision.'

'No!' interrupted Qazi Abdul Bahawi. 'History is distorting facts. Alamgir was not a slave to any failing. If he was a slave at all, it was to Islam.'

'Do you mean to say that Babar, Humayun, Akbar and Jahangir were not Muslims?' History inquired. 'Honourable adeeb, to grasp the seat of power in Delhi, Aurangzeb had used religion as his weapon. After having Dara assassinated, he had grown despondent. His depression caused converted Muslims in the kingdom to suffer from a sense of emotional alienation. Two centuries later, it would become the root cause of the country's partition. Allama Iqbal would fall prey to it. It was during this phase that his Kashmiri Pandit ancestors, the Kauls, converted to Islam. In his early poetry, Iqbal spoke of his roots. Later, however, he used it to confine the universal relevance of Islam within demarcated boundaries by proclaiming the religion to be the exclusive preserve of Muslims. It was this mentality that would make the country's Muslims aliens in their own land.'

'I can't understand why everyone is given to long speeches these days,' the peon whispered in the qazi's ears.

Overhearing him, History came back on course. 'My apologies, honourable adeeb,' he murmured. 'You were interested in knowing how and why Guru Tegh Bahadur was killed. Well, this is the way it happened: By the time the farman ordering Guruji's arrest reached Anandpur Sahib, he had already left the place, having named Govindrai as his successor. Travelling through Ropar, Saifabad, Samana, Kaithal, Rohtak and Palwal, Guruji had reached Agra. He was arrested there and brought to Delhi. In Delhi, it was through Qazi Abdul Bahawi that the proposal of his conversion to Islam was put forward. Very firmly, Guruji turned it down, whereupon Aurangzeb decided to sentence him to death. The executioner, Jalaluddin, was summoned from Samana.'

Once again, Qazi Abdul Bahawi heatedly intervened. 'That's an utter lie!' he exclaimed. 'Emperor Aurangzeb never took any such decision. In fact, His Highness was not even present in Delhi at the time. He was in Hasan Abdal.'

'So, was it you who decided on the death sentence?'

'No, I might have been the qazi of Delhi, but I was not empowered to take such decisions.'

'In that case, don't try to shield the emperor! I was a witness to all that happened. It is, indeed, true that Aurangzeb behaved like a coward and left for Hasan Abdal after issuing the fatwa. The decree of death was read out before the crowd under that peepul tree at Chandni Chowk. It bore Aurangzeb's name and official seal. As for you, Qazi Abdul Bahawi, you were the one who stood there like a royal representative!'

These words caused the qazi of Delhi to bow his head in shame. The narration continued: 'But Guruji Maharaj had not averted his gaze the way you have. He had looked proudly ahead. Honourable adeeb, the hands of the clock were striking ten in the morning. It was Thursday, 11 November 1675. This qazi here signalled to Jalaluddin to behead Guruji. But Jalaluddin had a problem. He was accustomed to striking at bowed heads. He had never come across one that was held so fearlessly upright. The qazi realized where the executioner's problem lay and instructed the man to carry out the beheading by positioning his sword under the prisoner's chin instead of on the nape of his neck. So, forced to use his left hand to draw the sword from its scabbard, Jalaluddin severed Guruji's head from his body...

'Then a strange new spectacle presented itself. Even after the execution was over, Guru Tegh Bahadur's torso stood upright like a tree trunk in Chandni Chowk. His head did not tumble to the ground. It revolved in its original position like a blazing cannonball. Instead of blood, sparks flew from it. The city was engulfed in the darkness of a fierce storm. A terrible earthquake shook the land. Buildings rattled as a pall of darkness spread over everything. In the blinding storm and chaos, Bhai Jaita saw his opportunity. Risking his life, he seized Guruji's head and made good his escape. Crossing the

Jamuna and passing through Baghpat, he made his way to Anandpur Sahib.

'As the storm raged and chaos ensued, Lakhishah, the owner of a cart used for transporting building material into the Red Fort, managed to escape detection and carried Guruji's torso away to his own shack by concealing it under sacks of earth and limestone. Once home, Lakhishah busied himself with preparations for the funeral pyre. Piling together everything he had in his house, he consigned Guruji's torso to the flames. Eventually, the storm abated, the tremors ceased and light shone through the darkness. Mughal soldiers arrived to fetch Guruji's mortal remains, but found nothing— neither head nor torso!

'Meanwhile, Bhai Jaita had reached Anandpur Sahib with Guruji's head. Guruji's widow and disciple, Mata Gujri, took it from him and proceeded to Kiratpur. There, along with his other disciples, she performed the last rites for the martyr...Another contingent of Mughal troops came looking for Guruji's remains, but returned empty-handed.'

The peon looked around in amazement. The court was overflowing with people, but the adeeb had disappeared.

30

The peon was anxious. The adeeb was nowhere to be seen. Yet, his voice could be heard from different directions. When the peon turned to listen to the adeeb's voice issuing forth from one direction, the same voice seemed to hail him from another. This left the peon bewildered—how many directions could a single voice possibly call out from? In the end, it was he who called out, 'Illustrious adeeb, where are you?'

'I am right here, within the refuge offered by my life!'

'But where is that? In which place?'

'There are many places at which I am present simultaneously. I was with Zainab and Buta Singh in the deserts of Rajasthan not a moment ago...I was also at Quetta, where I'd gone looking for Salma...While I was looking for her, Vidya's handkerchief floated down to the railway platform at Kanpur...So, I set out in search of Vidya...'

'Did you meet Vidya?'

'No, but I learnt a great deal about her.'

'What...what did you find out?'

'Simply that whatever she had hinted at before abandoning her studies was true. Her father, Babu Ramnarayan, had arranged her marriage to a man from a family living in the Ramnagar area near Sadar in Delhi. Ramnagar is the place near the railway station where the city's garbage is dumped and from where garbage collection vans set out on their rounds. The groom's people had asked for the girl to be taken to Delhi. So, Babu Ramnarayan had set out for Delhi from Fatehgarh.'

The adeeb sifted through the details. 'Vidya was brought to Delhi. A number of relatives were present to participate in the ceremonies preceding the wedding. These included the rites relating to the agreement over auspicious dates, the *ladki dikhai*—the bride's formal meeting with her prospective in-laws, the *tipna milvai*, when the horoscopes of the couple would be compared, and the *saeet nikalvai*, during which the auspicious moment for the actual ceremony would be decided on. People who had not met for years came together on this occasion, bringing their families with them. And even the elders joined in the activities. Vidya's was a small family comprising her parents and a brother. A distant relative—a brother-in-law—lived in Karol Bagh. It was at his house that Vidya's family had put up. It had, initially, been decided that the ladki dikhai ceremony would be held in the compound of a mandir in Ramnagar. Later, however, the groom's family had invited Vidya's family over.

'Vidya was dressed for the ceremony. Being indisposed, her brother-in-law could not attend it. He had, however, escorted the group to the Rohtak Road junction and helped them hire a tonga for Ramnagar. Where this tonga eventually disappeared, is something I have never been able to find out.'

'Why, what was the problem?'

'The day it happened was 3 June 1947.'

'You mean...?'

'I mean that when Vidya's small family set out for Ramnagar, a meeting had just ended at the viceroy's house. Present there, along with Mountbatten, were Nehru, Jinnah, Sardar Patel, Acharya Kripalani, Sardar Baldev Singh, Liaquat Ali Khan and Abdul Rab Nishtar. And the viceroy of India had taken a decision. Actually, the decision had been made much earlier.'

'Which decision was that?'

'The decision to partition India.'

'That can't be true!' the peon interjected in surprise.

'My dear fellow,' replied the adeeb's voice, 'the history that is on record or has been recorded under duress, the views expressed during interviews for public consumption and the "reality" that is created by so-called "documentary evidence", can never represent historical truth. Authentic history is that which is engraved on hearts and minds and erased the moment it is put in writing, lest it be read by those for whom it is not intended. The worth of those erased words is appreciated solely by scholars who understand the language of Socrates, Gautama Buddha, Christ and Gandhi.'

'Then why do you fight shy of reading such history? Come forward and read what this one has to say,' the peon challenged the adeeb.

'Dear sir,' the voice of the adeeb rang out, 'allow me the liberty of enjoying the asylum my life has granted me. Since all the tales of my life remain incomplete, I seek your indulgence so that I may see them through to their denouement. I must find out where Vidya was spirited away in that tonga of hers which seems to have sprouted wings. Salma had abandoned me to the tender mercies of khuda after bidding me "Khuda hafiz". But I need to be sure whether she is enjoying the Almighty's protection herself. Without that reassurance, carrying on with my life is well-nigh impossible. There is no Mountbatten, Attlee, Cripps, Churchill, Nehru or Jinnah to enlighten me about the way one should lead one's life in the centuries to come. It is Salma alone who can reveal the way for me...for Salma was a story...Shahin was another such story...Buta Singh and Zainab's is a living legend...Surjit Kaur who fled from Multan to Amritsar is yet another tale. Still another is that of the mendicant, Kabir, who fled from Punja Sahib and now begs for alms around Mount Mary Church in Bombay. Give me but one chance to live with my stories!'

'Time has not given you the right to indulge yourself in this manner. Emerge from your cocoon and address the questions raised by history. It is imperative that you do so, because historical manipulations have spread their tentacles around the humane finales of all your stories. If you wish to provide spiritual succour to mankind in the centuries to come, you must put up a fierce resistance against these manipulations and rescue your stories from their clutches.'

'So you're not about to give me any peace, are you!' retorted the adeeb's voice in defeated tones. 'Won't you, at least, allow me to spend time with my stories and lead my life?'

'No, that is out of the question now. This is not the moment for going to Rajasthan to complete the saga of Buta Singh and Zainab, nor for making your way to Quetta to seek out Salma. Neither, for that matter, is it the moment to locate Vidya's winged tonga. Illustrious adeeb, now is the time to step out from the protective cocoon of your stories!'

A silence filled with anticipation hung over the place for a while. Then suddenly, the adeeb appeared from nowhere and stood before his peon.

'Sir,' he said, 'here I am, present in your court. I shall do whatever you expect of me...But what do I do about Kabir? One of our famous poets, Nida Fazli, tells me that Kabir, a beggar in Pakistan, has come down to Mount Mary Church only to solicit alms there. According to Nida Fazli, when the month of Ramadhan comes around, Kabir returns to Pakistan to beg for alms there. That is how he earns his living. If the need arises to cross the border again, he will have no qualms about paying merchants of death like the Kashmiri mujahideen to facilitate his return to India. Once here, he will earn his keep again, begging for alms either at Mount Mary Church or at Mahalaxmi Mandir. If the situation so demands, he will even contribute to the welfare of the families of jawans killed in the Kargil conflict. Sir, after the country was partitioned, nothing remains but begging and hunger—the legacy bequeathed to mendicants like Kabir, and the fate to which politically sundered nations have been doomed.'

As the peon stared at the adeeb, the latter sadly continued, 'How can I ever forget that exquisitely beautiful woman, Surjit Kaur of Multan?'

'Which Surjit Kaur is that?' the peon asked.

'The very same, whose son lies in a coma from the day the country was divided! To this day, Surjit Kaur, now an old woman, tends to her comatose son and couldn't care less about freedom.'

'This is, indeed, an enigma!'

'It's no enigma at all—just reality. In the viceroy's house in Delhi, Clive's portrait in the room had smiled the moment Mountbatten raised the issue of partition as a precondition for granting the country its independence. At the same time in London, the sleeping Churchill had awakened in his mansion, lighted a cigar, and taken a deep puff. This was 3 June 1947—the same evening on which Mountbatten announced over All India Radio, the liberation of the country from colonial rule...and its partition. The voices of Nehru and Jinnah had supported that announcement.'

'History is well aware of it.'

'But history is not aware of what Aurangzeb wrote to his son, Azam, from his grave in Aurangabad. "My son," says the letter, "I wrote this for you a few days before my death. But I am sending it to you three centuries later, having made some additions to the original message. I came to this ephemeral world alone; and alone shall I leave it. Today, I heard voices reverberating across the skies and my soul was awakened to the consequences of my excesses. I am guilty of many sins. Earlier, I had imagined myself leaving this world anonymously, like a stranger. But having heard these voices and the inferences they have drawn about my conduct, I realize that I cannot escape the burden of my sins. I have no way of knowing what kind of punishment awaits me on the Day of Judgement. Whatever I did in the name of religion was undertaken in the belief that it would unite the country. I realize now that I had erred. But never would I allow the country to be divided. I did not regard myself as a foreigner. I conceded there were differences in faith, but ensured that no breach would ever divide national sensibilities.""

'But that is precisely the objective the British succeeded in attaining on 3 June,' murmured a soft voice from Rajghat. 'At a prayer meeting in May 1947, I had argued that unless the British were eager for it themselves, Jinnah Sahib would never obtain his Pakistan. I had appealed to the British, indeed, begged them to hear me out. Leave us to our fate, was my earnest plea, abandon us to God's mercy. There will be discord, violence, civil strife...we will handle it. From massacre and destruction will we emerge stronger by far. Ours is a civilization that has survived the battle of the Mahabharata. It is from the perplexing dilemmas inherent in this epic battle that the principles of the Gita have evolved, emphasizing action devoid of the passionate quest for rewards. Those principles have endeavoured to undermine the Brahmin stranglehold on the caste structure. Eklavya's humiliation was avenged in Dronacharya's bloody death...I beseech you, yet again! The British have no right whatsoever to bind our freedom with terms and conditions. You are not doing us a favour by liberating the country from your rule. If at all a favour is involved, it is in the courtesy that we Indians extend to you in according you a traditional send-off. Had we not done so, none of you would have left this country alive. The civil war would, as a matter of course, have followed later. But ahimsa makes me reject the very notion of such a massacre.'

As the voice from Rajghat died away, another incident took place. Someone attacked Gandhiji with a sword in Bhangi Colony. His body was slashed in two; but hope sustained each part. Gandhiji lived on with his divided body, his blood seeping out from each part. Yet, his life did not flow out with it.

Christ looked down from the cross. Even the Holy Prophet, Mohammed, surveyed the scene. In Bhangi Colony, Gandhiji's severed body remained erect.

Even Mercenary History looked on...History that sought to evade the truth underlying Gandhiji's dreams and Mountbatten's devious machinations. History turned to look at the adeeb.

'Produce Mountbatten before the court,' the adeeb ordered, putting his tales on hold.

31

Mountbatten was produced before the court.

It was spilling over with people from places that had once been a part of the British Empire, an empire on which the sun never set. It was a secure realm, this empire, in which the colonizers established themselves without fear, where as the sun set on one colony, it rose simultaneously in another. This empire ruled over a quarter of the world. It included people from India, Gorkhas from Nepal, Pathans from Afghanistan, Hussas from Africa, Sudanese, Cypriots, Jamaicans, Malaysians and Chinese. There were others who came from Hong Kong, Borneo, Canada, New Zealand and Australia.

The British Empire had collapsed, but its last royal representative, Mountbatten, was present in the adeeb's court. Questions flooded the minds of the people assembled there. Hostile eyes stared, ready to cross-examine the witness.

The peon turned some pages of recent history. 'Honourable sir,' he began, 'Britain and her allies have heaved a sigh of relief after defeating fascism. Yet, no sense of elation seems to stir the British at the approach of Christmas, 1946, and the advent of the new year. Hitler has devastated most of London. There is no electricity. Milk is in short supply and so is morning tea. Beset by these hardships, the brave and disciplined Londoners, mired though they are in gloom, try their best to celebrate Christmas and usher in the new year. In the minds of British citizens hovers a single prayer—the prayer for peace. They pray in darkened churches for the safety and well-being of mankind. Instead of the thousands of candles that lit up churches before World War II, a solitary candle illuminates whatever is left of life. There has been no change, however, in the arrogant attitude and regal traditions of Queen Victoria's descendants. In Buckingham Palace, as in the mansions of British aristocracy, turkeys procured with much effort and at great expense from as far away as Finland and Egypt are being roasted to celebrate victory and bring in the new year.'

As the adeeb looked in the direction of Buckingham Palace, the peon, Mahmood, sought to catch his attention once again. 'In

London, many bodies are yet to be given a burial,' he told him. 'In Trafalgar Square, just below the shattered visage of Nelson's statue, innumerable corpses and thousands of dead pigeons mourn their deaths, while turkeys are prepared and celebrations planned in palaces for the new year.' Having said this, he rustled the questionnaire in his hands.

A man from the Congo intervened with his grievance: 'Illustrious adeeb! These whites from England and Belgium abuse us as "niggers". But the moment they needed uranium for their atomic bombs, they came to the Congo, accompanied by the Americans, and hailed us as their honourable brothers! They carried a letter from the world's great physicist, Einstein, to Belgium's queen, begging her not to allow the sale of uranium to Germany. It was from this point onwards that the ancestors of Mountbatten—the man who now stands in your court—began hatching their conspiracies...'

'What exactly is it that you wish to convey?' asked the adeeb, interrupting him.

'Just this, Your Honour: don't trust these Englishmen. They have no royal lineage to speak of. They are nothing but thieves and robbers. Their pillaging ancestors in Europe were the ones who laid the foundations of dynasties. Ask Mountbatten here where his blue blood comes from.'

Mountbatten looked in the direction of Lord Ismay and his political advisor, Conrad Corfield, expecting them to answer the question about his lineage. Lord Ismay was silent. Conrad Corfield, the son of a missionary, looked around in embarrassment. Mountbatten knew the answer well enough, but hesitated to articulate it.

Noting the man's silence, the peon made his disclosure. 'Honourable sir,' he declared, 'he is the last of a dynasty of fugitives. His ancestors were expelled from Russia. So, they settled in Germany. When things became difficult for them there, they made their way to Britain where they lived as ordinary citizens. Ask him about his lineage and identity before his ancestors settled in Britain.'

'My father's German family name was Battenberg,' Mountbatten informed them.

'Why did he need to change his German name?'

'Because World War I had broken out. Anti-German sentiment had risen to such a fevered pitch in Britain that my father had to resign as the First Sea Lord because of his German ancestry. To prove his loyalty to his adopted country, he was forced to change his German name, "Battenberg", to the more English-sounding "Mountbatten".'

'So, these are Europe's infamous blue-blooded looters and profligates! It was their ancestors who had converted Europe into their personal fiefdom. In their greed for wealth and power, they had changed their names and identities at the drop of a hat. All the royal houses of Europe were related through blood or marriage. Whether it was the Kaiser, Russia's Tsar Nicholas, Spain's Alphonso or the Greek, Constantine...whether it was Romania's Ferdinand, Sweden's Gustav, Norway's Hakkon or Yugoslavia's Alexander—all were involved in the brutal oppression of the masses as they indulged their lust and their taste for luxury. By cohabiting with the women of the lands they ruled, they produced a line of titled heirs. While royalty politically reined in its titled descendants, it gave them a free hand to indulge in the plunder and repression of the masses.'

'The peon, Mahmood, is right,' declared an imposing individual.

'And who are you?'

'I am Todarmal, Emperor Akbar's finance minister.'

Everyone present in the court stared in amazement at this grand personage—the most valued of Akbar's navratnas, his nine advisors.

'Is there something you wish to say?' the adeeb inquired.

'Yes, there is. I demand to know from the last representative of British rule in India why his ancestors felt the need to change the Mughal system of land revenue and replace it with zamindari and ryotwari?'

'I know nothing about it,' Mountbatten replied.

'But surely you knew that your country had neither minerals nor raw materials to speak of? Poverty stared your nation in the face. Your farmers faced ruin, as their labours yielded diminishing returns. The poorest among them organized the Diggers' Movement and rebelled. It gave your landed gentry many sleepless nights, the same gentry who had connived with royalty to brutally put down the rebels. So tell us, isn't it a fact that you evolved the zamindari system to crush the farmers? And that is precisely what you later implemented in India?'

'I cannot answer your charges. I am no economist. I am an admiral in the Royal Navy...I am viscount of Burma.' There was a tinge of bitterness and arrogance in Mountbatten's reply.

'But you will answer for the misdeeds of your ancestors. You say you are an admiral of the royal fleet. Surely, you have heard of William Hawkins?'

'I don't recall having done so. I am not familiar with his name.'

'You claim to be an officer of the Royal Navy and yet you've not heard of your naval ancestors?'

Mountbatten decided that in the presence of Todarmal, discretion was the better part of valour.

'Illustrious adeeb, along with Raja Todarmal, I wish to ask Mountbatten a question,' the peon intervened. 'Do you remember, honourable sir, how I had come looking for you at the Dushrock Hotel in Mauritius when you were there with Salma?'

'Yes, I do remember,' the adeeb retorted bitterly. 'You are forever intruding in my personal life. You have snatched my peace away from me and robbed my stories of it too. You have flung me repeatedly into the debased, brutal and conspiracy-ridden world of kings and kingdoms.'

'Honourable sir, I understand your anguish and resentment. But when a society based on human values metamorphoses into one driven by material compulsions, man's tranquillity, happiness and dreams are trapped in the vault of commercial profit, and when a mighty civilization is caught in a web of deceit woven by treacherous merchants, Time stands at a crucial juncture. At such moments, not only do the hubs of commercial markets change, the values by which human behaviour and interaction are judged undergo a transformation as well. There is a shift in emotional perspectives and even the complexion of stories acquires a different shade in ways that remain undefined and unarticulated. Just think about it, sir—hasn't the partition of the country irrevocably changed the climax of all our stories?'

The peon's words impelled each person present in the court to look within himself for answers. The situation filled Mountbatten with a feeling of unease. Though raging inside, he calmly stated, 'I can't waste my precious time here, I'm afraid. I can spare you just another half-hour or so, no more.' He glanced at his watch.

Raja Todarmal stepped forward and said, 'Honourable adeeb, before I ask a single question, I would like to turn back all the pages of Hindustan's history. Read every page—in the entire span of this nation's history, has the country ever been partitioned? The Aryans never divided it into sections and called them, say, an Indus zone, a Saraswati region or a Ganga province! All their writings refer to the Indian peninsula as a subcontinent. They always acknowledged this great land as a unified whole.

'To vanquish Ravana, people from every corner of this country joined hands with the Aryans. Even after emerging victorious from the battle described in the Mahabharata, the Pandavas did not break up the kingdoms of their vanquished enemies into separate regions. India continued to be regarded as one vast country, as it had in the past. Friends and foes living here remained an inseparable part of its soil.

'In 3 BC, Alexander swept in from Mesopotamia and defeated Maharaja Porus. But he did not seek to divide the land he had invaded into separate fragments. The Tartars and Huns who attacked it, refrained from doing so as well. When Mohammed bin Qasim arrived, he ruled over the region of Sindh. He too never thought of breaking up this land to create another nation out of it. Even Ghori, Nadir Shah and Abdali did not change its contours. Turks and Afghans came here as well. Had they sought to do so, they could very well have created another Turkestan or Afghanistan in this country. The Mughal dynasty always acknowledged and accepted India's unity and integrity. They did not create their own separate nations on its soil. Had Aurangzeb so desired, he could well have used his power and his sword to banish non-Muslims from this land and declare it an Islamic state. He could have named it Islamistan. But as long as he lived, he fought, won or lost for this land and this land alone.'

Todarmal paused and looked at the assembly. Then he asked, 'So, honourable sir, how did this country fall prey to partition—for the first time in its five-thousand-year-old history—at the hands of the merchant race of Britishers? Does this naval man, Mountbatten, have an answer?'

'I have no answer for this question, nor for any others of its kind!' Mountbatten replied testily.

'Why ever not? Why don't you have an answer? After all, it was you who came to partition this land!' the peon declared.

Mountbatten was incensed, but restrained himself and calmly countered, 'I came to give India its independence.'

'Independence!' the peon laughed mockingly. 'Who were you to grant us independence? You had not conquered this land in the usual way. You had seized control of it through devious treaties and conspiracies. You are not even familiar with the name of your naval ancestor William Hawkins. What would you know of the others who accompanied him? At the time, your country was as impoverished as ours is today. Your family members weren't royalty then. They were a criminal clan that harboured pirates and looters!'

'Shut up!' Mountbatten's façade of civility had crumbled to reveal his fury.

The adeeb admonished the peon, 'My dear man, we mustn't dispense with civility ourselves, must we? I don't quite follow—which era are you referring to?'

'Illustrious adeeb, I talk of the age when Mahakavi Bihari was composing couplets on the rituals of feminine adornment and you were at the Dushrock Hotel in Mauritius, rapt in Salma's embrace, counting the kisses that had bloomed like blue blossoms over her body. I had arrived there, looking for you...'

Memories of the scene swam before the adeeb's eyes...the peon anchoring his boat at the hotel's jetty.

'Do you remember?' the peon asked. 'Salma's presence had not deterred me from cautioning you that an adeeb who assumed the responsibility of probing and understanding the wounds inflicted on culture, automatically forfeited personal freedom and was not at liberty to count the blue flowers blooming in his private life!'

'Yes, my dear man, I do remember that moment!'

'That was when I had informed you about the pirate vessels from Spain, England, France and Portugal sailing towards the East. The West knows about the history these vessels have written. As the heir to this history, I want Mountbatten Sahib to cast off the arrogance he so proudly wears as united India's last viceroy and divided India's last royal Governor-General. I want him to look deep into the true nature of his pillaging forebears like William Hawkins and Thomas Roe.'

Directly addressing Mountbatten, the peon said, 'Do you know that in comparison to Emperor Jahangir's kingdom, the worth of your royal family was that of a lowly village *lambardar*'s? When Dutch merchants raised the price of black pepper by five shillings a pound, it left your ancestors in a terrible quandary. Then, in 1599, your bania-like merchants set up the East India Company and that pirate, William Hawkins, embarked on his voyage with the permission of Elizabeth I.'

'I am not interested in hearing about it!' Mountbatten exclaimed in irritation.

Before the adeeb could intervene, the peon shouted, 'You will certainly have to hear it all—you who are responsible for the world's biggest and bloodiest migration! It is you who callously presided over the ocean of tears flowing in the country at that moment in history. You are the scoundrel guilty of disrupting the harmony of this land! Are you aware that in 1600, when your ancestor, Hawkins, disembarked at Surat, he had a list in his pocket? It was a list of what he had come to take back from India. Besides black pepper, indigo, cumin seeds, cloves and ginger, it included emeralds the size of eggs and elephant ovaries to bestow eternal youth and strength on the person who consumed them!'

Mountbatten's face was suffused with anger. Raja Todarmal calmed the peon down. 'Mahmood Sahib,' he said, 'don't dwell on his family tree. It torments him. Even we have misdeeds and failings to answer for. It would be better if you sought from him an explanation of how he succeeded in enforcing a partition that even Aurangzeb had failed to bring about. I shan't interrupt again. All I want is to sit in a quiet corner and listen to the arguments on the issue, as I have to report back to Emperor Akbar.'

'So, Mountbatten Sahib, you are a naval officer. You have heard about the exploits of your naval ancestors. All those men who set out for the New World from Britain, France, Spain and Portugal were not discoverers or scientists. They were, essentially, pirates out to plunder the world's wealth.'

Masking his embarrassment, Mountbatten glanced at the adeeb.

'Admiral Mountbatten,' said the latter, 'when you go back, do investigate the following point: At a time when the Mughal administration was granting peasants and farmers freedom and ownership rights on the basis of economic policies devised by Raja Todarmal, why was your infamous queen, Elizabeth I, investing money in companies run by Portuguese smugglers involved in the slave trade from Africa?'

Mountbatten's throat had gone dry. He was immediately offered a tin of Coke.

'So...let us continue with the discussion. When did you come to India as viceroy?'

'In March 1947.'

'What brief were you given?'

'That India be granted independence.'

'Before setting out to grant her this freedom, who were the persons you met?'

'Obviously, I met Prime Minister Attlee.'

'And...?'

'My cousin, Emperor George VI.'

'And...who else?'

'And...' Mountbatten reflected, 'I also met Winston Churchill, the former prime minister who had led Britain to victory in World War II.'

'Had any of these men given you a separate brief?'

'No, I was invited to 10 Downing Street by Prime Minister Clement Attlee. He asked me to come down to India, grant it independence and return home.'

'In what circumstances did your imperial government arrive at this decision?'

'I really can't say much about the circumstances, but following our victory in World War II, it was clear to us that we could not hold on to our colonies much longer.'

'So, you decided to teach India a lesson before leaving it. You knew that once India gained its independence, the sun would set on the British Empire. You conspired with Churchill to blame Mahatma Gandhi and the Indian freedom movement for the collapse of the British Empire. You made Gandhi the victim of your base imperial vanity. Since he was to be honoured, the "naked fakir", Mahatma Gandhi, had been invited to Buckingham Palace. But Churchill, your arrogant former prime minister who was smarting from his electoral defeat after the war, refused to meet him. Hadn't you come to India wearing Churchill's arrogant attitude?'

'No, I had not!'

'Then why was it that Lord Ismay, who had worked closely with Churchill during the war, accompanied you as your assistant on your mission to grant India its freedom?'

'That was the decision of the Labour government. I had nothing to do with it.'

'Do not lie, Admiral Mountbatten! If you had managed to persuade the Labour Prime Minister Attlee to accede to all your demands, why did you fail to bring someone of your choice to India to assist you in place of Lord Ismay? What kind of compulsion dictated your choice of an assistant who had served in the same position under Churchill—the man who vehemently opposed independence for India and vowed to teach the country a lesson?'

'These questions have to do with administrative decisions. They involve the world's biggest empire. It would be advisable if your court did not interfere in such matters.'

'Mountbatten, this is a court of mankind's soul and conscience. There is no escaping it! Here, answers will emerge to those very questions you avoid addressing. You might choose to remain silent, but this particular court is attuned to the sound and meaning of the language of silence.'

Loud knocking reverberated through the court. Anxious, the entire assembly turned in the direction of the noise. Those who knocked were licking the blood that had dried on their bodies. Some of them tottered, their shattered bones refusing to support them. Others carried corpses of children on their shoulders.

The peon stepped forward to establish order and inquire as to where they had all come from. A corpse replied, 'We come from East Timor, Indonesia. Are you listening? For centuries, we have been demanding our right to freedom. We acquired it partially, but it was accompanied by death and exile. The Indonesian army and private Muslim militias have cracked down on us. We are being brutally slaughtered. Our shacks have been set on fire, our homes razed to the ground. Thousands of our people have sought refuge in West Timor. Our capital city, Dili, is now a ghost town.'

'If this was inevitable, where was the need for demanding independence from Indonesia? If the people of East Timor ended up as refugees in Indonesia's West Timor, why did you seek freedom at all?'

'For the sake of our religion.'

'Your religion?'

'Yes, illustrious adeeb, we are not Muslims, but Christians!'

'You mean...that you too are victims of colonization! In the name of religion, you too became pawns in the hands of Portuguese colonialism...just as Hindus and Muslims had served as pawns for British colonialism! I would like to know whether you are Indonesians or not!' the adeeb asked bitterly.

By then, the peon had reached Dili and started reporting from there. 'Honourable sir,' he began, 'I speak from Dili which used to be inhabited, once upon a time, by large-hearted people. Easter, Christmas and New Year were celebrated here, along with the Prophet Mohammed's birthday. The month of Ramadhan too was faithfully observed. Furthermore, plays were performed here by contextualizing themes from the Mahabharata. At this moment, however, the city lies utterly devastated. Following bloody riots, President Habibi has declared martial law. The Muslims of Indonesia are against the idea of East Timor's Christians establishing their independent state. Scores of corpses lie rotting on the roads of Dili. Following the declaration of martial law, Muslim militias have ganged up with the army to evict the Christians forcibly. I can hear Muslim militiamen screaming, "You Christian dogs! Leave East Timor! If you want an independent country, go and create one in the Pacific. Only the ocean can give you refuge!"'

There was a pause and people in the court exchanged worried glances. Then the peon's narration from Dili resumed: 'Yesterday the bishop's house was torched. A short while ago, Australian ambassador John McCarthy was viciously attacked at his consulate. He was hit by three bullets, but is now reported to be out of danger. The militia has taken over the United Nations building. Foreigners are leaving East Timor because of security risks. Seven thousand terror-stricken Christians have sought refuge in the bishop's compound. More than two thousand people have sought shelter in the compound of the Red Cross. Militiamen have taken over the city. Some of the people fleeing towards the port in East Timor pass through Muslim-majority areas where the severed heads of Christians, impaled on stakes, line the road. Their staring eyes contemplate the desolation of the land that has been liberated. The hamlets along the seafront are full of living corpses. Each one attends the funeral of its dead companions. It is difficult to differentiate the living from the dead here. From what I see around me, it is apparent that in the name of freedom, Portuguese colonialism has succeeded in establishing the world's largest cemetery. East Timor will be a free country, inhabited only by the dead. The light from the candles burning on their graves will forever darken the centuries ahead with murder and mayhem!'

As the crowd swelled in the court, Mountbatten's restlessness grew. The scholar noticed that four of his stories were present. It was another matter that they did not know or recognize each other. Every time his eyes came to rest on them, he was overcome by anxiety.

Salma's expression seemed to be bidding him 'Khuda hafiz' over and over again. Vidya had arrived from Rohtak Road in a tonga, the very same tonga whose horse appeared to have sprouted wings and disappeared with her after the declaration of independence and partition. Surprisingly, Buta Singh had come alone...Zainab was nowhere to be seen. Present in the court was Surjit Kaur, who had left her Multan home earlier, dressed in all her finery, with her innocent, opium-drugged baby in her arms. She now carried on her shoulder her unconscious fifty-year-old son, shrouded in a sheet. Also standing quietly in a corner was the beggar Kabir. Truly distressing, however, was the sight of Buta Singh's mangled corpse using its own hands to brush off the flies buzzing around it.

The adeeb was lost in thought—why had all his stories come here? After all, it was not the imperialist colonial Mountbatten who would be writing their denouement! If time permitted, he would do so himself...or, perhaps, some other writer would take up these heart-rending tales.

Then Mountbatten's stentorian voice rang out. 'Why have you detained me?' he asked.

'To ask you: when did you decide on India's partition?'

'This is an unfounded accusation,' Mountbatten replied, wiping his sweaty brow. 'I had repeatedly recommended that India stay united.'

'Do you know how Jinnah Sahib had responded in 1933, when the idea of Pakistan was proposed by Rehmat Ali for the first time in a London hotel?'

'I do not.'

'Then, allow me to tell you—Jinnah Sahib had said that it was an impossible and ill-considered dream...'

Mountbatten stared at the young adeeb, a student of history, who was interrogating him.

'Are you, perhaps, aware,' the adeeb continued with his cross-examination, 'that around the year 1934, Jinnah Sahib was so repelled and disheartened by politics that he sailed for London, abandoning an immensely lucrative practice at the Bombay High Court? He had, at the time, renounced politics and declared his intention to give up his burgeoning legal career in India and settle in England where he would practise law.'

'I have no knowledge of Mr Jinnah's decision,' Mountbatten replied.

'In that case, what sort of specialized knowledge or administrative credentials can you claim that qualified you for the position of viceroy of a country like India with its vast cultural wealth and diversity? Who bestowed on you the right to grant it its freedom? Had you any inkling at all of where inconsequential riyasats like Merta and Balsar lay? Were you even aware of the existence of the five hundred and sixty such riyasats in the land, with each of which your imperialist government had signed treaties governed by unfair terms and conditions? Had you bothered to read the terms of those treaties before coming to India or even before you granted the country its independence?'

'No, I had not.'

'Were you aware of the discord fomented by your forefathers between Hindus and Muslims in India?'

'No, I was not.'

'Then you would, obviously, be unaware of what Jinnah Sahib did in England after his departure from India in 1934. You would be ignorant of his political, social and professional activities at the time.'

'I have no knowledge of them.'

The adeeb launched into a speech. 'I seek your attention, gentlemen,' he said. 'Twenty pages are missing from Emperor Babar's *Babarnama*...the very pages that would have served as proof of Babar never having visited Ayodhya. He had ventured as far as the Ghaghra River in pursuit of Afghan rebels. Having chased them away, he had hunted in the jungles bordering the river till news reached him of the arrival of his begum and daughter from Kabul. He had set out immediately for Aligarh. Despite the barbarism associated with his era, finer feelings and sympathy coursed in the veins of emperors, rendering them human. Babar had turned back from the western jungles of the river to meet his wife and daughter. He had never crossed to the eastern side of the river to reach Ayodhya.'

'What exactly are you trying to imply by offering me a piece of information we have no way of verifying?'

'I am trying to convey the message that politicians like your Churchill had already laid the plans for India's partition. You were sent as viceroy merely to execute it!'

'This is a baseless allegation!'

'Then, could you enlighten us further about the grave situation that developed when Jinnah went into political exile in England? Could you tell us about the people he met there, the politicians and statesmen he secretly interacted with during his three years of exile?'

'Secret interactions?'

'Yes,' the adeeb affirmed. 'Listen, Mr Mountbatten. Just as your agents made twenty pages of the *Babarnama* disappear, your nation and its historians connived in obscuring those three crucial years of Jinnah Sahib's sojourn in England. Could you throw light on the policies and strategies adopted by the British government when it found itself unequal to the challenge posed by Gandhiji's andolans and Bhagat Singh's martyrdom?'

'I have nothing to say about the situation.'

'In 1933, Rehmat Ali had consigned his own vision of Pakistan to the dustbin. Try and recall the ambience of those days in India...try and remember the role played by the country's revolutionary history. Go back to those powerful words uttered by Shaheed Bhagat Singh on the last Sunday of July 1930: "They think that by destroying my body, they will consolidate their position in this country. They delude themselves. They can kill me, but they can never kill my principles. They can crush my body, but they cannot crush my ideals which will loom over the British government like a curse, until it leaves my country!"'

'I have never had anything to do with Shaheed Bhagat Singh,' Mountbatten countered.

'But you were, in fact, in Britain at the time. And you have royal lineage...you should be having some knowledge of the India-related activities of the time. Jinnah Sahib had, ostensibly, gone to London to practise law, but there is little evidence to suggest that he fought a single case during his stay there! Why was it that during those years a number of important leaders of the Indian Muslim League, along with big landlords, small nawabs and taluqdars from India, were frequently travelling to London?'

'There were no travel restrictions on Indians wishing to visit London,' Mountbatten retorted.

'That's all very well, but why were these people meeting members of the Tory establishment in particular? And why did they need to have such secret meetings and parleys?'

'This is pure conjecture, unsubstantiated by British documents,' was Mountbatten's acid retort.

'In that case, there is no question of any records existing in the secret files of Britain's intelligence agencies of the three meetings Jinnah had with Churchill?'

'I do not consider myself under any obligation to answer such ill-advised questions. In any case, I personally have no knowledge of such meetings taking place.'

'Well, one may take your word for it...But, perhaps, you should be informed that India's freedom fighters and its non-violent movement for independence had already clearly established that the country could not be kept enslaved for long. Between 1934 and 1937, many devious political policies were evolved to sustain British rule in India. World War II followed and put a temporary hold on their implementation. As soon as the war was over, General Wavell was suddenly removed from his post and you were appointed India's viceroy, so that the strategies already chalked out for perpetuating British rule in India could be enforced. You were sent here for that very purpose. The plan was to stall India's liberation indefinitely. When this became an impossibility, the decision was made to divide the country into fragments.'

'This is a completely false allegation...you are sadly mistaken! All through, my endeavour was to preserve India's integrity. I failed because of Mr Jinnah's obduracy.'

'Jinnah Sahib had become your trump card. The truth is that you Englishmen deliberately made him your trump card.'

'What do you mean?'

'I mean that in keeping with your nefarious plans, Jinnah Sahib had been projected as the leader of the country's Muslims. Otherwise, god-fearing, pious Muslims in India would never have accepted this pork-eating atheist as their leader. This is the miracle of imperialism that you people wrought! It is, indeed, incredible that in the name of religion, a man who was so far removed from his own and had

never read the Koran—since he knew neither Arabic nor Urdu—
was appointed the leader of the Muslims! He did not even know how
to say his prayers during namaz! About Jinnah Sahib it can be said
that in spite of being a "Muslim", he never really was one. All of
northern India's taluqdars, small nawabs and landlords had been
insidiously won over by dangling before them the tasty morsel of
their own homeland—a country named Pakistan!'

'You are at liberty to infer whatever you please,' Mountbatten
announced with supreme indifference. 'I have no desire to discuss
this issue. I know my version of the truth...my conscience is my
witness. And the statement that I had come to India to postpone
granting the country its independence is an entirely erroneous one.'

'Listen, Mountbatten Sahib, it is true that the Tories lost the
election after the war, but the reins of government were still in
Churchill's hands. Churchill could well have kept the Labour
government's decision suspended in the House of Lords where your
kind was in the majority. After the war, Britain was devastated and
starving. By delaying Independence, you could have prolonged your
period of exploitation by a few more years.'

'No!' Mountbatten shouted. 'We had enough wealth in the Isle
of Wight to feed ten more generations and live comfortably!'

'Your riches on the Isle of Wight were not earned by the honest
sweat of your brow; this wealth came to you from the exploitation
of your colonies. You cannot claim it for your own!'

The words came from Kabir, the beggar, who had stepped
forward to have his say.

'I am not prepared to argue with a beggar!' Mountbatten
declared arrogantly. Before the adeeb could respond, Kabir exploded
in fury.

'Mountbatten!' he thundered. 'It is looters like you who have
given birth to beggars like us. Nowhere in the world were beggars
like me to be found until the advent of your Industrial Revolution.
The poor and the rich had always coexisted, but it was only after
colonization that the phenomenon of soliciting alms came into being.
Colonization itself has introduced the trend of deviating from the
norms of economic equity and justice and given birth to ruthless,

exploitative materialism and competition. It is your colonial agenda that has disrupted the world's economic equilibrium and reduced its victims in India and Pakistan—vulnerable people like me—to begging. Even our prayers are directed against each other's interests, as we address the same god.'

The other beggars in the court were listening to Kabir with rapt attention and approval.

'Let's put aside these serious issues, Mountbatten Sahib, as you seem to regard the prospect of addressing them as a personal affront. The fact remains, however, that I am not merely a beggar; I am also a citizen of my country. You shouldn't try to evade a citizen's questions. You might have been India's last viceroy, but I'm not its last beggar! My tribe, in fact, is flourishing after your departure. And I am proud to declare that it is not just oppressed people like me who have now taken to begging. Scores of countries in Africa, Latin America and Asia have joined our brotherhood. We now enjoy international citizenship. Those countries solicit alms from the International Monetary Fund and the World Bank. People like me beg at the Jama Masjid in Lahore, join the queue outside Mount Mary Church or Mahalaxmi Mandir in Bombay and even stand outside a church in Buenos Aires, South America, to arouse people's compassion. But men like you, with your rank materialism, have made even compassion redundant. Listen, Mr Mountbatten! Genuine human justice emerges from compassion. Civilizations that lost their compassion for their fellow beings became extinct...'

Those assembled in the court appeared to have momentarily forgotten their grief, despair and pain. There was something in Kabir's words that seemed to appease the pain of emotional wounds inflicted over the centuries.

'Just give me an answer to my last question,' he said. 'Did you know nothing about Jinnah's terminal illness?'

'I did not,' came Mountbatten's reply.

'How is this question relevant?' a voice called out from the crowd.

'Not only is it relevant, it also has a vital link with the tragedy of Partition. Over and over again, Mountbatten has held Jinnah responsible for insisting on Partition. By putting the onus of the decision on Jinnah, Mountbatten has acquitted himself. It is now alleged that had the news of Jinnah's terminal illness got around, the Congress leaders of the freedom movement would have curbed their haste for Independence. After Jinnah, there was no leader of stature in the Muslim League who could, as successfully, have justified the need for a separate Muslim state on the basis of the two-nation theory. Wasn't this the truth, Mountbatten Sahib? Had Jinnah's illness been publicized, the tragedy of India's partition could have been averted, couldn't it?'

'Yes,' Mountbatten conceded.

'Jinnah's X-ray reports were with Dr Jal Patel of Bombay. The doctor had predicted that Jinnah had just over a year to live.'

'Yes...and Dr Patel had kept the news of Mr Jinnah's terminal illness confidential.'

'But what were his reasons for doing so? Dr Patel was no politician...Are you suggesting that had this secret been leaked, the country could have been spared the trauma of Partition?'

'Yes.'

'In other words, Dr Patel was keen on the partition of India?'

'I cannot comment on that.'

'So, your secret service and allied agencies which had so successfully ferreted out the innermost secrets of invincible dictators like Hitler and Mussolini, had no inkling at all of Jinnah's disease? Anyway, Jinnah had never really looked robust; he always seemed to be ailing. And he had already crossed the age of seventy. Then how was it that his tuberculosis was such a well-guarded secret?'

'It could well have been the outcome of some devious ploy on the part of the Muslim League,' Mountbatten replied. 'Its members were only too aware that they had no other leader who could either match Mr Jinnah's stature or measure up to Jawaharlal Nehru or Sardar Patel's fine intellect so as to be in a position to rationally justify the two-nation theory based on religious and cultural differences. However, it is equally true that neither my government nor I had any inkling of the terminal nature of Mr Jinnah's disease.'

'That's incredible! Jinnah already had pleurisy. He was prone to frequent attacks of bronchitis. He had always suffered from asthma. He was so ill on the train on his way back from Shimla in May 1946 that his sister, Fatima Jinnah, had to urgently summon Dr Patel to attend to him midway through the journey. In spite of this, your government had no clue about the serious nature of his illness?'

'No, I'm afraid not.'

'We are truly overwhelmed, both by your powerful and scheming government and by your unblemished innocence,' was Kabir's mocking reply. 'Though it is monstrous to use Jinnah's terminal illness for scoring political victory or inflicting political defeat, it is true, is it not, that driven by your imperialist compulsions, you had made vital decisions about India's independence much before it actually came into being?'

'For god's sake, stop playing cheap games with history!' Mountbatten answered agitatedly.

'Mountbatten Sahib, real history is not the version written by the imperialist powers,' was Kabir's stinging retort. 'It is that which has come to be engraved down the years on the souls of oppressed nations. Our history courses down the centuries like mighty rivers. Yours flows like canals...canals you have dug with spades of distorted logic and self-interest. So, don't you sermonize to us about history! You have written your history and we have lived it!'

There was commotion in the court. People raised slogans as they triumphantly hefted Kabir onto their shoulders. Mountbatten surveyed the scene with alarm.

The adeeb intervened to restore order. 'This court is merely the purveyor of truth,' he declared. 'All truth stands here as the outlines of stories—Salma cannot live in peace anywhere with the truth hidden in her heart; since Partition, Surjit Kaur roams about, carrying her comatose son on her shoulder, a son who is more than fifty years old; Buta Singh is a mangled corpse; Vidya's tonga has flown into oblivion, no one knows where. These are not solitary figures; there are millions like them. Kabir here is the living symbol of two nations. He has the right to—'

Kabir cut him short. 'That is why I am here, illustrious adeeb. I only seek a few specific answers from Mountbatten Sahib. What was the pressing reason or insurmountable hurdle that made him want to grant India independence in such haste?'

'That wasn't my decision. It was Britain's Labour Prime Minister Clement Attlee who was in favour of independence for India. It was entirely his decision.'

'You're right when you say that it was Attlee Sahib who decided to grant India her independence. But history tells us that the manner in which it was granted was determined by your royal family and by Churchill. Before setting out for India, had you not met Churchill as well as the king?'

'Those were just courtesy calls required by protocol.'

'So, was it protocol that dictated you bring along Churchill's former assistant, Lord Ismay, and that infamous conspiring imperialist, Sir Conrad Corfield, as your own assistants and advisors? Was it?'

Though filled with rage, Mountbatten thought it prudent to remain silent.

'And now—my last question,' said Kabir. Everyone eyed him expectantly.

'What explains your indecent haste in choosing to grant India independence in August 1947, when your parliament's House of Commons had decided to do so in June 1948?'

Mountbatten could contain himself no longer. 'It was because the threat of civil war loomed large over India!' he replied. 'All the conditions were ripe for it. At the instigation of the Muslim League, Bengal had already witnessed the consequences of Direct Action Day.'

'You had shown us this horrifying spectre many a times, and, wearying of it, Gandhi had appealed to you to leave us to God's mercy. He had affirmed our willingness to face whatever came our way. But you had arrived here with a well-defined notion of how to grant this country its independence, if it became absolutely imperative: Nehru and Patel were to be handed a crippled India and on Jinnah would be bestowed a termite-infested Pakistan.'

'No! This is a gross untruth!' Mountbatten roared.

'No, it is not! Driven by your colonial imperialism you sought to exact revenge for the unity that was demonstrated by the country in 1857!' The words seemed to come from the universe. Their source could not be located, but their echoes reverberated around the place.

It was Kabir who recognized the timbre of the voice. 'That is the martyr Bhagat Singh,' he announced.

32

1857...But preceding it was 1757!

A resonant voice echoed across the universe: 'Moments had erred, centuries were punished...'

'It was Jahangir who erred,' the peon screamed like a madman, 'when he granted permission to the English traders to cast anchor at Surat and build a warehouse there. Do you remember those pirate ships, sir, making their way round the southern tip of Africa and sailing towards the East, when I'd come looking for you at the Dushrock Hotel? At the time you were involved in a quest for beauty and personal happiness. And bearing the brunt of it is 1857. Honourable sir, happiness and beauty are for those who truly embody the freedom of their times. Vanquished civilizations alone choose to make do with no more than a warped semblance of happiness and beauty instead of aspiring for them in all their wholesome purity. Just observe, illustrious adeeb, how the representatives of the East India Trading Company have misused the Hooghly river's estuary. In exchange for indigo, opium, black pepper, cloves, cardamoms, ginger and cinnamon, they have offloaded scores of European prostitutes on the shores of Bengal. This is the perverted version of beauty blighting India's shores. Robert Clive has just made a gift of fifteen such women for the harem of Mir Jafar, the sipahsalar of Bengal's Nawab Siraj-ud-daulah. Clive's scheming continues unchecked...'

While speaking, the peon seemed to have created a stage where a historical spectacle would unfold before the eyes of the assembled court. In his hands, he held the curtain ropes while assuming the role of the narrator. As the curtain rose, the story began to unfold...

'Having obtained the royal licence through Empress Nurjahan, the East India Company set about consolidating its own position in Hindustan and discovering ways to undermine the regime's power. The Mughal Empire was in decline and minor rajas and nawabs squabbled with each other. Driven by the ambition of taking over the zamindari and subedari of the land and using their trade activities as a front, Englishmen exploited the situation to the hilt. In addition to establishing a foothold in Bengal, they built forts on the pretext of constructing warehouses and raised an army, ostensibly, to protect those warehouses. These illegal activities were unacceptable to Bengal's Siraj-ud-daulah...'

Blazing with fury, Siraj-ud-daulah materialized on the stage and exclaimed, 'No! Under no circumstances will we tolerate this situation! We will not have this firangi company run by foreign merchants erecting forts on our soil and maintaining an army here. We know that they are lying about the royal licence—the emperor has issued no farman whatsoever sanctioning the construction of forts in the name of warehouses. We will expose the deception they practise and their fraudulent schemes to usurp our land. We are the representatives of the emperor in Bengal. We will lay siege to the illegally constructed fortresses and mansions of these firangis and wrest them away from their control...'

The curtain fell.

The narrator took up his commentary: 'Robert Clive, the once-petty representative of the East India Company, now heads it. He is perennially hatching conspiracies of one kind or another. He has reduced Mir Jafar, Siraj-ud-daulah's commander-in-chief, to being his lackey by supplying him with whores of foreign blood. Clive has also dangled the bait of Siraj-ud-daulah's throne before him...Now look! There stands before you 1757 and the battlefield of Plassey, awash in blood. Mir Jafar has become a turncoat. He has ganged up with Clive against Siraj-ud-daulah, taking along with him his most trusted soldiers...'

The curtain went up again to reveal the battlefield of Plassey. Cannons were fired. Dynamite exploded. Clouds of smoke rose up. The cries and noise of battle were audible. Bullets whizzed by, horses' hooves thundered and the groans of the dying reverberated around the place.

The curtain descended again and the peon continued with his narrative: 'A victim of conspiracy and treachery, Nawab Siraj-ud-daulah has lost the war...Seven years later, in 1764, the English win the Battle of Buxar and firmly establish colonial rule in India. They conspire against independent principalities and force them to sign treaties whose terms are unfavourable to the latter...In faraway Deccan, the ruler of Mysore, Haider Ali, refuses to bow down to the sweeping ambitions and nefarious schemes of the English...'

The curtain rose. Haider Ali and his begum were engaged in conversation. 'No!' Haider Ali exclaimed. 'You cannot imagine the havoc wrought in northern India by these scheming firangis. Clive, the sipahsalar of the East India Company, bribed Nawab Siraj-ud-daulah's seniormost wazir and sipahsalar, Mir Jafar, into betraying his ruler. This treachery resulted in the nawab's defeat. After the battle of Plassey, the English have gone on to win the battle of Buxar.'

'But, my noble liege, the French firangis have an encampment here at Pondicherry. As foes of the English, they can be our allies!'

'Never, Begum! Foreigners can never be our allies. Be they French or English, they are both enemies of our freedom. The only difference being that the French are here in the south of the country and the English are present in the north.'

'May the Almighty keep my liege in His protection!'

'Begum, the protection and freedom of our land is by far more important than I am. Inshallah, as long as Haider Ali is alive in Hindustan, his country shall never be conquered and enslaved!'

The curtain came down once again. The narrator took up his account. 'Haider Ali's constant skirmishes with the English had made life very difficult for them,' he went on, 'but on 7 December 1782, the ruler of Mysore passed away at Chitoor, sixteen miles from Arcot. It was left to Haider's son, Tipu Sultan, to carry on his father's mission against the English.'

Up went the curtain.

'Listen! Today, Tipu Sultan, a son of Allah and a servant of his motherland, knows that in certain parts of the country, the firangis have succeeded in furthering their nefarious plans. They are trampling underfoot the plains of the Ganga and the Jamuna. We have no access to those areas, but I vow that those unprincipled men of the East India Company shall not set foot in the region of the Cauvery basin! It is both shocking and lamentable that our compatriots, be they Maratha peshwas, Hyderabad's nawabs or the rulers of riyasats, have become helpless puppets in the hands of these firangis and have taken to exterminating their own people. And, taking full advantage of these dissensions in the land are the firangi pirates themselves!'

The curtain closed again and the narrator picked up the thread of the narrative. 'As the plunder carried out by these pirates of the East India Company continued unabated, it was met with stiff resistance from people like the Chenamma, Rani of Chitoor, Travancore's Velu Thimpi, Tilkha Manjhi, the adivasi chieftain of Santhal Parganas, and sanyasis of various mutths.'

'Peon Mahmood Ali!' The voice rolled in like the eerie rumbling of a tornado. The peon recognized it as the voice of the adeeb.

'Illustrious adeeb, from where do you call?'

'I speak from the port city of Canton in southern China.'

'How did you get there?'

'Why...you were the one to intrude into the private core of my stories to inform me that the firangi pirates were headed eastwards. This caused Salma to be overwhelmed with guilt and she left after bidding me farewell. Shahin's tormented, incomplete saga ended up abandoned somewhere. The tale of Vidya's flying tonga remained to be drawn to a close. Surjit Kaur went about carrying her eternally comatose son on her shoulder, full of questions as to why he was in this condition. Buta Singh, whose body was crushed under a train, waits to have his story written. Mahmood Ali, it was you who had condemned my stories as inconsequential. Since then I have been wandering about, bearing the burden of your criticism. Like a nomad, I have moved from one country to another. If you hadn't cursed me, I would have been writing stories that ought to have been written, reflecting the beauty, compassion and sensibilities of my era. You are the killer of my compassion, my aesthetic sense and all my sensibilities. You are the one to have reduced me to this state— that of a homeless wanderer.'

'When and how did you reach Canton? Why did you need to go there?'

'Mahmood Ali, let's not get into these issues and arguments. In each nation, I have my own country. One country of mine is in Pakistan, another in Kosovo...I have my countries in Albania, Russia, Daghestan, Afghanistan and even in East Timor. In China, too, I have a country. That is why I am here.'

'But what for?'

'Because those merchants who once colonized India are on the prowl again. With their colonial mindset, these firangis are seeking to make inroads into China's markets. It was the reason for my coming here. And listen! It is for the sake of markets that imperialism is born. Conversely, it is to keep imperialism alive that markets are created. An umbilical chord binds the two. Imperialism manifests itself in different ways. There can be democratic, economic imperialism that needs to subsist on the markets that generate profit...Markets! Markets! Markets! Markets alone define the principles and parameters of industrial progress. This is known as capitalism. Imperialism is another name for it. As is colonization. And it will acquire some new name in the century that knocks to announce its arrival. The capitalist system cannot survive without the tapping of natural resources and the opening of new markets. In the midst of the world's torment, inequality and debasement, capitalism creates a superficial feeling of well-being. The decaying emblems of capitalism are human cadavers that spray themselves with perfumes by Christian Dior and Chanel. Their slit throats are adorned with Lanvin ties or fabulously expensive necklaces. Enclosing their shattered wrists are watches manufactured by Rado or Raymond Weil. In their smashed fingers, they hold Mont Blanc or Waterman pens.'

This long diatribe by the adeeb left everyone stunned. The peon breached the silence. 'You are right, illustrious adeeb,' he admitted. 'Even today, Coke and Pepsi have reached villages in India that have no facilities for potable water.'

'So, what's wrong with it?' called out Bina Ramani's voice from Tamarind Court in Qutub Colony. In the courtyard of this restaurant lay the body of Jessica Lall. Patting it with affection and gratitude,

Ramani declared, 'She is the very first martyr of our culture of wine, women and song. Immediately after she was born, she must have been suckled on her mother's milk. She never did taste it again. It has always been beer ever since, because beer contains more proteins than milk and fewer calories than apple juice. This is the secret of Jessica Lall's allure and tempestuous beauty that had driven Manu Sharma out of his mind.'

'Stop this nonsense at once! Our stories of happiness and sorrow lie incomplete, and here you are getting involved with Bina Ramani!' a story reprimanded the peon. 'Call back the adeeb! We need him here to complete our lives.'

'The adeeb is busy in the Chinese port city of Canton. I have no idea why he is there. It is not possible to call him back from there.'

'No, you are mistaken. Right now, I am strolling in the poppy fields of Mandsaur–Jhabua in central India. It is springtime...a sea of poppies in brilliant colours dances before me. And Lu-Xun is with me.'

'Lu-Xun...who is he?'

'China's greatest writer.'

33

While the beauty of the poppies dazzled Lu-Xun, it also aroused in him deep feelings of disquiet. 'The more delicate and beautiful these flowers,' he murmured, 'the greater is the degree of intoxication and violence associated with them. Adeeb, perhaps you aren't aware that after consolidating their position in India, the men from the East India Company had begun smuggling opium into China. These pirates would load their steamers with cartons of opium that had been produced in Calcutta. On reaching the island of Macao, they would hide among the sand dunes. From there, these men would smuggle out opium via either Wangxia or Kuancha. Stealthily, their steamers would glide up the Pearl river estuary, eventually reaching Canton, Linting or Whampoa. The routes of these smuggling vessels were charted very carefully so as to allow them to enter the mainland undetected. It is from there that this narcotic was smuggled to every corner of the country.'

'Even prior to this development, opium was exported from India to China,' the adeeb remarked.

'Yes, you are right. In the Ching dynasty, opium was used as an ingredient in medicines. Its annual production was limited to two hundred cartons. On the other hand, the British government had given the East India Company a free hand in this contraband trade that now involved two thousand cartons of opium, not two hundred. The entire supply was auctioned off, at ten times the amount, in Calcutta itself. It was then smuggled into China, offloaded at ports and sent on to the mainland.'

'O Scholar from China, your country's failing, along with that of the Ching dynasty, is evident in your inability to curb this smuggling.'

'That's because the opium habit has now become a status symbol among the nobility and bureaucracy of China...Here, take a look at my country.'

The adeeb turned to see an ancient civilization drowning in the fumes of opium addiction. Black smoke wafted out of people's eyes and nostrils. The Pearl river had turned black. Millions of individuals tramped like zombies through the streets of port cities like Shanghai, Canton, Nanking, Amoy, Fuchow and Ningpo. What was really intriguing was the absence of shadows cast by these hordes as they moved about! As they walked on, the only question on their lips was, 'Where are we? Which city is this?'

'This is truly horrifying!' the adeeb exclaimed. 'Your entire civilization lies in a state of stupor. Even their shadows seem to have deserted them!'

'The shadows are not lost. These pirates have snatched them away from us by enfeebling our will. We are now a people bereft of a culture. Culture is the living shadow of the world to which our ancestors belong. Like shadows, they are ever-present beside mankind. These foreign pirates have found a way of sapping the life-force of civilizations like ours. First, they snatch away the shadows of ancestry; then...' Lu-Xun paused as the peon cut in.

'You are quite right!' remarked the latter. 'First, they slay the shadows of ancestors. Then, they lay culture to waste. Finally, they uproot and cast away the ancestry of civilizations. In their overwhelming greed for power and material gain, almost all European countries—Spain, Portugal, Holland, England and France—have unleashed bloody conflicts based on religious differences. They have transformed religion into a lethal weapon!'

'I am a witness to it!' shouted Salim I, ruler of the Ottoman Empire. 'They have dispensed with the Christian virtues of compassion, non-violence, remorse and mercy, only to replace them with barbarism, violence, ethnic arrogance and cruelty. Not in the entire history of mankind have so many killings taken place in the name of religions, as they have in the span of the barbaric history of western imperialism.'

Francis I of France challenged this allegation. 'Your Islamic history,' he retorted, 'is far more barbaric than our Christian one. You cannot deny your own brutal oppression and persecution of the Shias, your brothers in faith. You invaded and forcibly occupied parts of Persia. You ravaged Tabrez and Kurdistan. You wrought havoc in Mesopotamia and Egypt and eventually seized control of them. You spurned Islamic tradition and declared yourself the caliph. You are the one who has destroyed civilizations, not the Christians!'

'Wasn't the Spaniard, Hernando Cortez, a Christian? Wasn't he the one to lay waste to Mexico's prosperous Mayan civilization, first betraying, then killing the Aztec ruler Montezuma? How callously you depleted the population of America's indigenous natives! Are you aware of this? Your illiterate chieftain, Pizarro, stormed into Peru and sent back to Spain tons of silver mined in the Potosi mountain ranges—silver that would sustain Europe for another three centuries! You are a Christian pillager! On the pretext of defending your faith, you created the Crusaders!'

'And you created jihadis!'

'In the name of Christianity, you gave birth to that fanatic Ignatius Loyola!'

'In the name of Islam, you bred the murderous jihadi Hasan bin Sabah!'

'Your Ignatius Loyola killed thousands of Muslims!'

'Your own Hasan bin Sabah was responsible for the death of millions of Christians!'

'Will you stop hurling accusations at each other and degrading yourselves by wrangling in this undignified manner?' Lu-Xun asked in his placid manner. 'The fact remains that Asia is the cradle of all faiths and civilizations. To further industrial progress and prosperity, Europe was on the lookout for foreign markets. It was the reason for materialistic Westerners like you to begin encroaching on ancient civilizations. You had no idea of what lay beyond your shores. All you had heard of was the name of the "golden bird" called India. In the quest to exploit it, your pillaging forebears had touched down on India's Malabar coast. And your Columbus had reached America on the same mission.

'Do not overlook the fact that the New World came into your hands in the course of your quest to discover India. You had no religion; you merely wore the mask of one. Hypocrites that you are, you claimed that these explorations were undertaken for the spiritual salvation of the people who inhabited the countries you set foot in. You certainly didn't venture forth with horses and explosives to save souls; your actual intention was to enslave them. The lust for profit drove you to destroy ancient civilizations. Read the pages of history and find out for yourself.

'Born in India, Buddhism had spread to the rest of Asia, but not a single drop of blood was shed when that happened. Buddhist preachers did not go about their business like warriors on horseback, carrying explosives as baggage. They crossed the sacred Himalayas on foot. When they chose sea routes, they did not carry weapons of war. Their hands did not bear spears, swords or guns; their sailing vessels were not fitted with cannons. All they carried in their hearts was the message of peace, ahimsa and compassion; all they held in their hands, the bodhivriksh, a banyan sapling. That was a time when even the highest mountains bowed before faith, when the waves of vast oceans carried the message of a faith's peaceful principles from one shore to another. Trade and markets existed even then. Need determined the volume of imports or exports. The economic structure of our ancient civilizations complemented and sustained each other instead of fomenting rivalry and exploitation driven by the compulsion of reaping profits. The evidence lies in the three thousand years of peaceful coexistence between India and China, unmarred by conflict.'

'But a war between the two countries did take place in 1962!' a bitter voice cried out.

'That was the outcome of a flawed legacy—an improperly demarcated border—left behind by the British imperialists,' Lu-Xun replied.

Suddenly, the sky darkened. The sun disappeared. Anonymous voices called out. Blasts and explosions occurred. Startled, the adeeb asked, 'Mahmood Ali, what has become of the sun? To whom do these voices belong? Why has the sky turned black?'

'Honourable adeeb, Vasco Da Gama has trained his cannons on Calicut and launched an offensive. The New World discovered by Columbus nurtured many civilizations. They are now enduring the depredations of Portuguese and Spanish pirates. Involved in the ensuing rapine and plunder are scores of barbaric, illiterate social outcastes like criminals and assassins. One-fifth of their booty is handed over to their own country that proclaims them to be great warriors and patriots. These bloodthirsty looters have the support not only of their king and members of their aristocracy, but also of their corrupt and fabulously wealthy clergy. They have devised their own interpretations of Christ's compassionate credo of sin and penance. For them, sin is no more the reason for penance. The price of penance can now be paid in gold or silver, washing away the taint of sin. Mayan civilization has been laid waste by Hernando Cortez. Thousands of young men from the Aztec tribes have been slaughtered. Jungles have been razed. Colonies are now being established in America, Trinidad, Mexico, Cuba, Panama, Brazil, Peru and other regions. The indigenous Indian tribes are being systematically exterminated. Black slaves are being imported from Africa by men who auction them off, as though they were beasts...As millions of birds flutter out of the burning jungles in panic, the sun is eclipsed and darkness engulfs the land...'

At this moment, a groaning voice called out, 'Since you have lent us your ears, listen to the tale of how our civilization was devastated and met its tragic end.'

'Who are you?' the adeeb wanted to know.

'I am Montezuma, the ruler of the Aztec empire. I had welcomed Cortez as an honoured guest when he arrived in Mexico. But, in return, he unleashed havoc on our clan. As a result, my council and my people turned against me. In spite of it all, I tried to save the Spanish conquistadors from the offensives launched against them by our newly elected King Coahetomac. Fearing that violence would beget further violence, I did not oppose my clan or the new king. Instead, I advised Cortez on how he could escape from the new ruler's army by taking the royal route down south and from there, return to the safety of Spain.'

'Though I don't deem it absolutely necessary, I would like to interrupt Montezuma's account here,' a calm voice called out.

'And who are you?' the adeeb asked.

'I am Bernal Diaz, a royal historian from Spain. Now that you oppressed peoples have established your own court, I have come to caution you against distorting history that is already on record.' Diaz's voice was tinged with colonial arrogance and bitterness.

'Honourable Bernal Diaz, by analysing the history you have chronicled, we are attempting to explore the realities underlying the history of mankind,' Lu-Xun stated. 'There is no reason why this endeavour of ours to better understand the past of oppressed peoples should upset you. The truth, as you know, is indestructible. You have succeeded in masking it with your words. By cleansing your words of their blood, sweat and tears, you have tried to purify your writings and make them more palatable for posterity. You have camouflaged the stench of slaughter, of rotting corpses, with the fragrance of your words, so that your writings do not reveal a hint of the atrocities perpetrated by you on peoples and civilizations. Colonial and imperialist powers tom-tom the news of how they have civilized "savages". They seem oblivious to the fact that it is the skins of those savages that are tautly drawn across the very tom-toms they beat upon!' Lu-Xun angrily declared, wiping his perspiring brow.

'Lu-Xun Sahib, please don't do that,' a strange voice entreated him. 'I wish to analyse and study your perspiration.' A stranger, carrying several bottles in his hand, strode towards Lu-Xun. All eyes in the court turned towards the man.

The adeeb recognized him at once. 'Arrey, aren't you the ashruvaid who makes a study of people's tears? I met you a few centuries ago! Perhaps you were the gentleman involved in analysing the tears of mankind, trying to understand the causes of its physical and spiritual suffering, weren't you? Your mission, I believe, was to locate and remove the causes of this suffering!'

'Yes. I am the same ashruvaid, adeeb. But the world has changed a great deal since. We are now living through the epoch of murder, slavery and weapons of destruction. Entire tribes lie exterminated within their own territories. And, as you are surely aware, invaders and corpses have no tears to spare. So, I am now engaged in the study of the properties of perspiration. By slaughtering one tribe after another, colonialism has created a situation whereby it no longer has access to cheap labour. Its representatives now resort to forcibly transporting slaves from Africa and Asia. Come along with me to see for yourself the flourishing slave trade that operates on the island of Gori near Dakar. From here, it's a straight sail across the ocean to Columbus's America.

'On the foundations of this slave trade, men have built countless mansions. In the stables and enclosures below these mansions, you will find slaves from Senegal and central Africa chained like cattle. The physique of the male slaves determines their price; the condition of the teeth, the price of the slave children. As for the price of female slaves, it is decided by subjecting their breasts to a humiliating physical scrutiny. These women are sexually violated in their cattle pens. They are then transported by boat to the huge vessels that lie off-shore and are finally shipped across to America. On their way back, the ships bring back the treasure looted from the New World. Perhaps you know that during the past one year, these invaders have carried back sixteen thousand tons of silver and a hundred and eighty tons of gold. The metals have not been mined; rather, they have been melted down after being looted from the treasuries of the natives or from the wearer's person. Now, since there's also a shortage of honey, sugar has come into vogue. As a consequence, indentured labour is being brought in from Africa, India, China, Sumatra and Ceylon. The coolies are made to work on the sugar plantations of the West Indies, Cuba, Brazil, Java, Fiji and Mauritius. Sugar is being sold at exorbitant prices in European markets. While opium is smuggled into China, silk and tea are smuggled out. Silk-spinning wheels lie idle in China, because the smuggling of opium—not a taxable commodity—is a hundred times more lucrative.'

'This ashruvaid speaks the truth,' Lu-Xun interjected. 'William Jordan, the linchpin of the smugglers, became a member of the British Parliament in 1841. James Matthieson, another smuggler, returned home to buy a huge island off the west coast of Scotland. James spent three lakh twenty-nine thousand pounds just on repairing and damming this island's shores. And I am not at all surprised that Queen Victoria rewarded him with a knighthood! The royalty and historians of Spain, Portugal, France, Britain and the Netherlands referred to these smugglers and looters as great explorers and discoverers! And why not? Not only did royalty get one-fifth of the loot as their share, they also obtained unilateral rights to establish their colonies. Involved in this trade were British and American companies like Perkins and Russell who brought with them gunboats to assist the smugglers. The latter were followed by preachers who eroded our traditional beliefs and robbed us of our faith. Within our own societies and countries, our souls wandered like refugees. That is when our shadows rebelled against us.'

'This is precisely what happened to our civilization!' shouted the Aztec ruler Montezuma, 'But a still more lethal game was played against us. Honourable intellectuals! Each civilization, race, community and century awaits the arrival of a saintly prophet. This expectation keeps alive cultures and civilizations. Our tribes too waited in hope that our god would visit us one day. These invaders exploited that hope. Their preachers studied our language, faith and customs. Then they deceived us into believing that they had become like us. Their leading priest, Alvarez, spoke to us in our language, conveying the miraculous news that our long-awaited god had arrived...that he had assumed a human incarnation. We all believed him. This priest then persuaded us to believe that our god was Hernando Cortez, the man who had appeared before us on horseback. Since our tribesmen had never seen a horse before, it seemed a strange, exotic beast to us. Soon, we began regarding it as a divine creature. We couldn't believe our eyes when we beheld our god, Cortez, on horseback. He looked so different from the way we had expected him to be. We believed that god and horse were one, and knowing that gods could assume any form, none of our tribes had any reason to doubt what they saw...'

The royal historian from Spain, Bernal Diaz, glared at Montezuma with anger and contempt. Lu-Xun, the head of the jury, stared balefully back at Diaz. Then, he gave the adeeb and Montezuma a meaningful glance. The latter continued his account.

'The Aztec council had already removed me from office. Our new king, Coahetomac, had refused to acknowledge the divine origins of Cortez. To teach my tribe a lesson, Cortez first used me, then had me imprisoned. I advocated peace. We Mayans had a legend—if birds stopped roosting in our realm, we were to look into our souls and release them from spiritual bondage. Just as a bird trails no shadow in the sky when it flies, we were told the Mayans would be freed from all shadows.'

Montezuma's words left the entire assembly dazed.

'Cortez wanted me to intercede on his behalf and speak to the new king about a treaty. But that was impossible. I also realized that it was just a ruse on Cortez's part to gain enough time to prepare his army for war. I did not wish to deceive either my new king or him. Cortez was no more my god; he had become my friend. And I could not betray either. So, I rejected his proposal for initiating peace talks. It was for this reason that Cortez killed me. That was how he repaid my friendship. Since then I have been wandering about in search of the true principles of friendship. Can friendship not transcend ambition and become the basis of peaceful coexistence?'

The court now turned to look at Bernal Diaz. 'Let him have his say,' Diaz offered. 'Later, I will reveal the truth as history records it.'

So, Montezuma continued with his narration. 'Honourable gentlemen,' he went on, 'had Cortez been civilized and merciful the way a god is merciful, our tribes would have agreed to accept him in our society. What didn't we have at our disposal—land, jungles, mountains, rivers, seas, the sky? There were our plains, our fields and our grain. The soil gave us everything—there was nothing that we wanted for! After killing me, Cortez threw my body into a shallow ravine. To protect himself, he began moving away with his army. Suddenly, the sound of thousands of conch shells being blown startled him. Cortez discovered that he had been surrounded. Our warriors rained arrows on him. In panic, his men jumped into the waters of a nearby gulf. They could neither swim forward nor step out of the water, as they were weighed down by the large quantities of gold, silver and precious stones they had stuffed their pockets with. Every one of them drowned.'

'Is this an authentic account?' the adeeb asked Bernal Diaz.

'Yes, it is,' came the calm reply.

The adeeb was reminded of Garcia Lorca's prophecy, even though the man was born towards the end of the nineteenth century. 'What has transpired since?' the adeeb inquired.

Montezuma carried on with his account. 'Honourable sir,' he continued, 'since then the spirit of friendship has wandered, our jungles have smouldered and our birds have fled, leaving behind a curse. They have cursed this race of fierce alien invaders, cursed their cities, towns and houses and have vowed never to go there. Observe the skies and cities of Europe, America, New Zealand and Australia—you will never see our exotic birds there.'

Total silence descended on the court as Montezuma went on with his story. 'And then there was Francisco Pizarro—an unlettered, crass individual who had been conceived out of wedlock and was ostracized by his own society. Like Cortez, he too had deceived South American natives by pretending to be a god. He too came along with the preachers on horseback. This barbaric tyrant was responsible for destroying the last vestiges of the Inca tribes and, along with them, their civilization that had worshipped the sun. His brutalities had not only bloodied the rivers and creeks in Brazil and Peru, but had also choked them with the rotting corpses of the Incas. The river waters had tired of pushing these corpses into the sea. The seas had refused to accept them, as the habitat of marine life would be polluted. The stench of these corpses was so overpowering and widespread that trees and shrubs stopped flowering and producing fruit.'

Kabir's eyes were sad as he gazed at Montezuma.

'In Pizarro, King Charles V of Spain had seen another Cortez. Even before the adventurer had been successful in his quest, the king had made him a captain-general and declared him governor of Panama. Have you ever heard of such honours being bestowed on a bastard in any civilized society? In fact, the king had equipped Pizarro with steamer warships, soldiers and steeds to loot, kill and invade our land! And it was this brutal army that would utterly destroy the Inca civilization.'

Unable to contain himself any longer, Bernal Diaz shouted, 'That's enough! Put an end to this nonsense! The Inca civilization, for which paeans are being sung, was no civilization at all! It was just a congregation of wild, illiterate tribes with neither culture, nor language, nor script, nor even the most primitive mode of transport! These people were worse than animals!'

Montezuma's reply reverberated around the court. 'Are you aware,' he thundered, 'that before your arrival, these Inca tribes cultivated potatoes and maize on a large scale? That theirs was an agrarian society with its own granaries? They had turned the vast valley of the Andes mountains into arable land. They had a king, a council of ministers, a bureaucracy and an army. Their granaries overflowed with grain that sustained the royal household, officialdom and the army. Each one of the Incas worshipped the sun as soon as they awoke in the morning. Can you deny any of these facts?'

'I don't deny them—to a large extent they are not wrong.'

'You've got a rather philosophical way of acknowledging the truth, I must say,' the adeeb told the royal historian.

'But didn't I say that this was a congregation of wild tribes—unlettered and ignorant?' Diaz repeated. 'For transport, they had nothing but their feet. Their roads were no more than the most primitive of paths and they had no vehicle worth the name! They were so uncivilized in every respect!'

'We had a language that served our specific needs. From our close communion with nature we had evolved a language composed of signs. As an agrarian society, we had borrowed the sounds and inflexions of birdsong. Ours was a language that expressed compassion, joy and sadness and served as a means of communicating with nature. Our tribes had also invented a script based on the principles by which a spider wove its web. Like the spider building its home, we would knot skeins of yarn into meaning. Your assumption, born of ignorance, that they were fishing nets, drove you to consign our hymns to the flames—our hymns, woven in skeins to honour the sun and the seas. Is this what your own civilization taught you? We trusted our own feet, rather than wheels, to take us wherever we wished to go.' A weary Montezuma wiped his perspiration and sat down.

Questions now flew thick and fast in the crowded court. To restore order, Lu-Xun asked Diaz a question, 'What are your norms for differentiating between the civilized and the uncivilized?'

The royal historian angrily retorted, 'I have no desire to quibble over the parameters defining what is civilized and what is not! I just wish to have the final word on the matter by asserting that each member of Montezuma's tribes was a cannibal!'

At these words, the entire court seemed to hold its breath.

'Is there a witness or evidence to corroborate this?' asked Lu-Xun, echoing the sentiments of the court.

'Ask King Montezuma here!' Diaz answered. 'He was the one to lead Hernando Cortez and me to the kingdom's main temple. Its floor and the path leading up to it were awash in blood. Human blood smeared the walls at the entrance. In the sanctum sanctorum itself was a vessel full of blood. The stench of blood and putrefying flesh permeated the place. In the temple's innermost chamber, five human hearts were laid out before fearsome-looking idols. The hearts' last feeble convulsions were visible, as blood pumped out of them. Neither Cortez nor I had ever set eyes on a more barbaric and macabre scene.'

Bernal Diaz's words provoked a tumultuous reaction in the court. Voices were raised in condemnation, horror and anger.

A Spaniard present in the court aimed a dagger at Montezuma. The weapon lodged itself in his chest. Drawing it out, Montezuma remarked, 'My friend, though this dagger has found its mark, the dead do not lose their lives twice over. Ask your historian how many more untruths he needs to tell!'

'These are facts!' Diaz shouted back. 'The Aztec priests swaying before the idols did not appear to be in their senses. They had picked up these feebly palpitating hearts and consumed them to appease their deities. The gods of their civilization accepted human sacrifice and sanctioned their cannibalism. The stench emanating from their main temple was more overpowering than the collective odours of Spain's abattoirs!'

'Hear me out, historian Bernal Diaz! You were a meat-eating race and so were we. You slaughtered your animals in abattoirs, because you did not owe your gods an account of the animals you slaughtered. We, the Aztecs and the Incas, were, on the other hand, bound by an oath. We had to account for the number of animals we slaughtered for our own livelihood. It was why we preferred to sacrifice our animals before our gods. What you claim to be human sacrifice was, in reality, animal sacrifice. By sacrificing beasts in our temples, we sought to earn the benevolence of our gods. Such were the fundamental differences between our two civilizations.' There was a decisive edge to Montezuma's words.

'But the Aztec and Inca civilizations have not been absolved of the crime of cannibalism,' remarked Lu-Xun. 'It is among the most heinous of crimes against humanity. It needs to be investigated.'

His words led the adeeb to ask Spain's royal historian, 'Honourable sir, you have given us an account of the blood-spattered temple and its priests who ate beating human hearts to appease their deities. You have accused the Aztecs and the Incas of cannibalism and human sacrifice. Is there another witness to corroborate your account?'

'I happen to be the lone witness and that should suffice!' Diaz exclaimed.

'No, the testimony of a single witness is hardly enough when the reputation of two civilizations is at stake!'

'And that too,' interceded Lu-Xun, 'when it happens to be a matter of evidence against civilizations which were highly evolved from both the spiritual and the philosophical point of view. Not so long ago, I had been listening to Montezuma's account of the advanced civilization he had ruled over. He had claimed to being opposed to violence and was aware of its self-perpetuating character. To avoid bloodshed, he had revealed to Cortez the safe way out of their kingdom. Had his tribe been uncivilized or cannibalistic, it would never have sought the benevolence of its gods. Did you hear what Montezuma had to say about birds fleeing a nation? How that nation was expected to introspect and thereby liberate its spirit? Did you mark what he said about birds not trailing their shadows in the skies and how we, too, could be released from the ties that bound us to our shadows? Besides, you do know how Montezuma wanders in quest of friendship's true principles even after meeting a brutal end?'

'In much the same manner,' the adeeb intervened, 'Prometheus wanders in search of fire and Gilgamesh pursues his goal of finding the antidote for death. Likewise, Kabir moves from place to place, seeking blessings in both India and Pakistan. Surjit Kaur carries her son on her shoulder, hoping he will regain consciousness. Dear Mr Bernal Diaz, it is the white races that have caused this perennial meandering. Your campaigns harboured death and were targeted against civilizations! You have tried to absolve yourselves of guilt by tarnishing the reputation of tribal civilizations, accusing them of cannibalism. To arrive at the truth, we need further evidence.'

The adeeb then called Mahmood Ali, the peon.

Mahmood Ali summoned prospective witnesses. As he called out to them, the curtain rose on a scene of centuries-old cemeteries. As everyone looked on, the gravestones moved aside. From within them emerged intimately entwined naked corpses engaged in sexual intercourse. A crowd of these corpses was seen making its way to the court. It was a titillating sight, mesmerizing, yet obscene, like a documentary on unbridled lust. It depicted every perverse variation of sexual positions. The fair-complexioned Pandava men were engaged in copulation with the dark-skinned women of their tribes. Leading them all was Hernando Cortez, coupled with the dark Marina.

Montezuma squeezed his eyes shut, as did everyone else in the court. They cried in unison, 'What is the meaning of this?'

'We are in the process of civilizing them,' came Cortez's answer in his harsh voice.

'But if one goes by your account, these are all women from the cannibal tribes! And, with them, you...!' the adeeb exclaimed, his eyes still shut.

'Oh, let accounts remain in books,' was Cortez's rejoinder. 'The greatest truths are half-truths. Empires are not built on truths. Don't deny us our pleasure.' With that, he lost himself again in the arms of the native girl he had named Marina. They clawed at each other in a fury of unrestrained passion.

A terrible earthquake rumbled through the earth. Rocky cliffs clashed in subterranean regions. Fissures appeared in open fields and the trees swayed wildly. As the adeeb surveyed the scene with terror-stricken eyes, he saw Hiroshima approach, gasping as it ran. Its skin was scorched. Like the eyes of a crab, its own started out of its sockets. Its nails were burnt and pus dripped from its flesh. The sight left everyone shocked.

'What happened, Hiroshima?' the adeeb inquired. 'Why do you look so perturbed?'

'It is the same tragedy all over again!'

'Where?'

'In Tokiyamura, a hundred kilometres from Tokyo!'

'What kind of tragedy is it?' asked a worried Montezuma.

'Another one caused by a nuclear explosion. The atomic bomb unleashed on me was by no means an accident. A meticulously planned and efficiently executed experiment set in motion on the pretext of ending a war, it was nothing short of a heinous attack on the human race. You beasts, just look at my mutilated body and the devastated contours of Nagasaki! Look at the disabilities that have hit children still in their mothers' wombs! Observe how millions of people melted like wax in the intense heat and disappeared into thin air like vapour! Others were ripped apart and burnt down to tiny fragments! Listen to the screams of death that rose in the throats of victims, never to be heard! Imagine the helplessness of the dying whose breath was slowly choked out of them—the death rattle as their lives were snuffed out! Look at me! If you have the courage to

take your next breath, look at me! I am Hiroshima...Hiroshima!
Gaze upon my bloody sores oozing pus that runs down in streams!
This sticky pus that has held my scorched body together! I have
borne the annihilation of mankind! I have endured death! If you can
summon the courage to do so, look at me! In 1945, Nagasaki and I
were cities. But today I am the symbol of protest!'

'We are all with you, Hiroshima!' Montezuma swore over the
handful of pus he held in his palm reverentially, as though it were
the sacred waters of the Ganga. 'Our tears are a token of the agony
we share with the five lakh people who died and with those who
melted into nothingness in their mothers' wombs. Our hearts go out
to the twenty lakh individuals who were so severely crippled that
they surrendered their wish to live and begged for death!'

'Centuries ago, this is exactly what had transpired on the plains
of Kurukshetra,' said the adeeb, looking beyond the centuries. 'The
era in which the Mahabharata is set embodied the rise and fall of
Vedic civilization. In this age dawned the sublime moment of truth,
along with Krishna's principles of karma and life. For eighteen days,
in the midst of combat, truth was repeatedly slaughtered. On the
first day of battle, the great archer Arjun had ridden into the
battlefield in his fiery chariot. His charioteer, Krishna, had passed on
to him the knowledge of the paramount truth of life. Then Krishna
devised a rare new way of conquering death, snatching death away
from death itself! It was necessary to do so because their foes, the
Kauravas, had created death. The effectiveness of Krishna's new
invention manifested itself on the very first day of battle, when
bonds and affinities between men were ruthlessly massacred! On the
second day, honour and fellow feeling were brutally assassinated! On
the third, compassion died! On the fourth, all ethics and norms of
religious faith passed away. What remained? Only a battle to mark
the onset of war! It was inevitable that on the fifth day, the insanity
of war would be unleashed. On the sixth, violence and bestiality had
replaced strength and courage. The seventh day witnessed the birth
of hatred. Murderous rivalries broke out on the eighth day, and the
ninth day saw the suppression and collapse of all human values. It
was at that moment that Bhishm Pitamah assumed awesome powers,

grievously wounding the heroic Pandavas. This so enraged Krishna, the neutral protagonist of the Gita, that he picked up a broken chariot wheel from the battlefield and dashed towards Bhishm. The battle lasted eighteen days, but by the tenth day, the large number of wounded and crippled had surrendered their will to live. Just the way the twenty lakh Japanese victims of the atomic bomb craved for death after being maimed by nuclear radiation.'

Everyone in the court sadly gazed at Montezuma.

'Surveying this scene,' Hiroshima reminisced, 'Gilgamesh had called out to me from the depths of the ocean. "Till I return with the antidote, keep battling death," he had exhorted. He had also urged me to resist the very desire for death. Since then, I have followed his advice.'

'Amen!' interjected Montezuma. 'The Vedic Aryans were instrumental in causing the decline of their own lineage. Christ's compassion killed the compassion of Gautama Buddha. But no one can destroy an Aryan whose birth preceded the writing of the Vedas, a Jew who arrived in this world before Jehovah, a Parsi who predates Zarathustra, a Buddhist whose birth preceded the advent of Buddha, a Christian who came to this world before Christ did or a Muslim who predates Prophet Mohammed!'

'But death still refuses to concede defeat,' Hiroshima intervened. 'Uranium has adversely revolutionized Tokiyamura—the radiation level in the atmosphere has gone up twenty thousand times. After the bombs were dropped on me, this is the fifth most dangerous development in the world.'

'I hope these radioactive rays will not reach Korea and China after crossing the borders of Japan,' a worried Lu-Xun asked.

'I do not think so,' Hiroshima replied. 'Officials claim that the situation has been brought under control and there is no danger. The same thing had happened in Windscale in the United Kingdom, in America's Three Mile power station and in Russia's processing plant at Chernobyl. And now, the possibility of another such occurrence looms large—one that registers seven on the danger scale. Since these demoniacal atomic powers pay no heed to it, I have vowed not to let the inventors and perpetrators of nuclear tragedies rest in peace. I shall not spare Truman or the scientists who worked on the Manhattan project. Brigadier-General Graves who supervised the project shall have no peace. Einstein too doesn't deserve to be forgiven. Robert Oppenheimer, Fermi, Hans Bethe, Edward Taylor and all those who worked for them—be it France, Germany, Britain or Russia—are to be condemned as criminals, enemies of humanity! They have no right to the privilege of peaceful repose as they lie in their graves! No! Never!' Screaming and shouting, as it wiped away the pus oozing from its wounds, Hiroshima rushed eastwards.

34

Time ran after Hiroshima, but failed to catch up with it. Then, another scene began to unfold before Time—a nation that refused to come to terms with the mutilation of its spirit and its partition along religious lines, had stood up and challenged the world's greatest colonial power! It had looked upon its mutilated parts and had recognized them as fragments of its very being.

As words waited in anticipation of being read, the soft scratch of a pen writing on paper was audible. The pen, moving across paper in a haveli at Delhi's Kucha Ballimaran, belonged to Asadullah Khan, a soldier of the nation. The same Asadullah Khan alias Mirza Nausha, who bore the pseudonym Ghalib, and whose grandfather, Qauqueen Beg Khan, had come to Delhi from Samarqand and chosen to serve in the court of Emperor Shah Alam. A proclamation was issued to this effect and the man was given fifty horses. Asadullah Khan was born in his grandfather's Akbarabad–Agra house. His uncle, Nasrullah Beg Khan, was the Maratha-nominated subedar of Akbarabad. His position underlined the desire to forge a spirit of brotherhood and national identity. At the time, Asadullah Khan Ghalib had chosen to go to Delhi following his marriage with Umrao Begum.

It was the best of times. It was the worst of times. When he became subedar, Nasrullah Beg Khan endeavoured to transform the misgivings Hindus and Muslims harboured about each other into an abiding bond of trust and friendship. But the British did not quite approve of his efforts. And when General Lake of the firangi army took stock of the situation, he was deeply shocked.

He had seen the headless corpse of Dara Shikoh, buried without ceremony after his assassination, turn and sit up in his grave at Humayun's mausoleum. Dara's severed head, impaled on a spear in Chandni Chowk, had opened its eyes and smiled in anticipation. The headless corpse had broken through the grave and made its way to Daryaganj. The severed head had descended from the spear and moved to rejoin the torso.

11 May 1857...

At Delhi's Red Fort, the voice of Emperor Bahadur Shah Zafar, the last of the Mughals, could be heard wafting along in the breeze. 'The announcement to wage war for Hindustan's freedom has been made,' it proclaimed. 'The time has now come to avenge the ignominy of defeat at Buxar and throw off the yoke of servility! History has taken a new turn. Our purpose is to overthrow the rule of the firangis. This statement of ours should not be issued in Persian; rather, it should be couched in Hindustani, so as to be easily comprehensible to the man on the street.'

Drums were beaten at street corners, as the town criers made their announcement. 'Pay heed, O Subjects of our Emperor! Listen! Listen to this proclamation! Be you of high rank or low, lend us your ears! Obey the farman of our legitimate ruler, our emperor! He asks you to drive out these foreigners, these alien firangis from our land...The emperor has taken over the reins of our united and victorious Hindustan. Chase the firangis out of the land! This is your emperor's decree!'

Voices were audible from the east. 'People of Lucknow and Avadh, war has been declared...' Standing under the protective gaze of his mother, Begum Hazrat Mahal, the fourteen-year-old Nawab Birjees Qadar read out the announcement. 'All Hindus and Muslims are aware of the four things dear to every human being. The first is one's religion. The second, one's honour and pride. The third, one's life and the life of one's loved ones. And the fourth, one's freedom and one's ancestral property. Entitled to every one of them in the past, every one of them did we enjoy. The state interfered neither with our religion nor with our rights. But these firangis have flouted our traditions. Their political conspiracies have been directed against social harmony. So, whether you are a Muslim Syed, a Sheikh, Mughal or Pathan, whether you are a Hindu Brahmin or a Kshatriya, Kayastha or Mahajan, drive these firangis out of your land, once and forever! The war for our liberation has been declared!'

Sparks of freedom flew from Lucknow to Bareilly. The Afghans of Rohilkhand also declared war. In Kalpi, Nana Sahib and Tantia Tope girded their loins for battle. To oppose the unilateral decisions of the British, Maharani Laxmibai of Jhansi embarked on the road to rebellion with the words, 'I shall not give up my Jhansi!'

And then the cannonade was launched. The rani assumed charge. 'Cannon expert Ghulam Ghaus Khan,' she commanded, 'you will man the southern tower. Kunwar Sagar Singh will defend the Khanderao Gate. Khuda Baksh will defend the Syed Gate and Dulhazu Sahib will be posted at the Orchha Gate. During the daylight hours, every one of you is responsible for the protection of the armoury and all the battlefronts. At night, their charge will be handed over to Sundar, Munder, Kashibai, Bakhishan, Juhi and Motibai.'

Then, the battle drums rolled.

The forces of Tantia Tope and Nana Sahib clashed with those of the British. War was also declared in Arrah, Bihar, by Raja Kunwar Singh of Jagdishpur.

From Faizabad came the war cry, 'Throw out these tyrannical firangis! Let this be each man's war of independence! Though I am a maulvi, I must affirm that the freedom of our people transcends all faiths and theology itself!'

From Delhi, Emperor Bahadur Shah's voice announced: 'Hindustan has been awakened! In this spirited nation, there are no Hindus or Muslims—we are all Hindustanis and nothing but Hindustanis! We are also aware, however, that some of our people have turned traitors. The firangis have managed to win over to their side a number of disloyal maulvis and mullahs, some hypocritical pandas and mahants and even certain members of the royal family! The Englishmen, Commander Lawrence and Finance Commissioner Martin Givens, have lured away these turncoats with promises of land, jagirs, titles, unimaginable wealth and even the throne!'

Time echoed these sentiments: 'Gwalior avoided lending Laxmibai its support against the British. Later, it skirted the issue of offering her refuge. A traitorous jagirdar of Kalpi–Bithur betrayed Tantia Tope just as Malik Jivan alias Bakhtiar Khan had deceived Dara Shikoh. One of Emperor Bahadur Shah's sipahsalars opened the Kashmiri Gate for the English forces. In Lucknow, a meeting was held at Martin Givens's residence to bring together old enemies of the ruling clan as well as members of the royal family who had fallen out with their more powerful kin. Present here were former nawab, Ahmad Ali Khan, former wazir, Mohammed Ibrahim Sharfuddaulah, and their aged uncle, Sahib Nawab Mirza Hussain Khan—all counted among Hindustan's most depraved aristocrats. It was to people like them that Emperor Bahadur Shah owed his arrest and imprisonment in Humayun's mausoleum before he was exiled and sent to Rangoon. Babu Kunwar Singh became a martyr. Tantia Tope was hanged. In Gwalior, the Rani of Jhansi had to commit suicide. Begum Hazrat Mahal and Nana Sahib were forced to seek refuge in Nepal. They were never heard of again. Hindustanis alone were to blame for their defeat in the country's war of independence in 1857. To save his own skin, Emperor Bahadur Shah had fled to the dargah of Hazrat Nizamuddin Aulia. He seemed to regret having taken over the reins of this battle. Actually, Emperor Bahadur Shah was no poet; he was just a coward.'

'How can you possibly make such a claim?' the peon, Mahmood Ali, asked Time.

'You can hear all about it from the Sufi sage and dervish Khwaja Hasan Nizami Sahib of Nizamuddin Aulia's dargah.'

'He is right here.' The peon gave Hasan Nizami Sahib a questioning glance.

'Allow me to tell you about it,' Hasan Nizami Sahib offered. 'My late mother had heard the story from her own father Hazrat Shah Ghulam Hasan, when he was still living. On leaving the fort, Bahadur Shah had headed straight for the dargah. My grandfather saw him seated on the ground, leaning against the gate that faced the tomb. The emperor hadn't eaten all day. His snowy beard was bedraggled, filthy with grime and sweat. The emperor had admitted at the time that he had no doubts whatsoever that he would be the last of Taimur's descendants to occupy the throne. He admitted his lack of judgement in relying on those wretched soldiers in Meerut with whom his fortunes had sunk. Bahadur Shah had explained that it was his reason for leaving the fort. Noticing that the emperor was hungry, someone had invited him to eat. The emperor had thanked the man, nibbled on a few morsels, then announced his plan of taking up residence in Humayun's mausoleum, leaving everything in the hands of destiny. He was arrested at the mausoleum and sent away to Rangoon.'

When the narrative came to an end, the peon looked around. The adeeb had disappeared. The peon called out, 'Illustrious adeeb, where are you? Time waits for you. The war of independence of 1857 has ended in a humiliating defeat. History has paused and stands waiting. You are nowhere to be seen. Are you lost, honourable adeeb?'

35

The adeeb was lost in Salma's arms.

'Do you know, adeeb, your body and mine serve as both temple and crematorium. Diyas light up both. Whether you light one in my body or I do so in yours, it is the glow that lives on forever. Some people live on in memories; others are chapters that wind up. In neither case, do they light up our lives. Before I met you, my body was a receptacle for snuffed-out diyas. You brought it light and made it come alive with radiance and fulfilment. I now stand at that crossroad of my life where I need a diya with an eternal flame.'

Salma's words were a steadying influence on him. Before him stretched a turbulent sea. A maelstrom of waves rose from its depths. A torrent of unrestrained waters flowed. An entire world of oysters opened and shut their shells. And in the ebb and flow of the waves, shining through the core of its being, was a lighted diya.

Gathering her languorously in his arms, he asked, 'What was all that about, Salma? On every occasion we meet, something new seems to transpire. These diyas that lend your body light—where do they come from?'

'Adeeb, when positive thoughts take root in our minds, the oysters shed a pearl. It becomes a diya that transforms love into worship. Perhaps, this is the lamp symbolizing devotion and the ritual of aarti...or the eternal flame that burns in a masjid on a moonless night, reminding the faithful of Allah's all-pervasive presence.'

'Salma, whether your mind echoes with the chants in a mandir or the azaan in a masjid, both are sacred. You are the one to have opened my mind to the azaan's spiritual appeal. The cries of oppressed peoples the world over—be they from Kosovo, Iraq, Daghestan, Chechnya, East Timor or Kargil—are nothing but a form of azaan, a call to prayer. Each of them calls out to his god and all their gods are but One, the Supreme One, responsive to every plea.'

'You're right, adeeb. But today, I am here to take a decision,' Salma stated.

'A decision? What kind of a decision?' the adeeb asked anxiously.

'That I will absorb the radiance of the lighted diya and set you free.'

'What do you mean?'

'I mean that my son has grown up now. Should he ask me about you, I will not be able to give him an answer.'

'You mean...?'

'I mean that I must choose between my son and you.'

'Salma, you have made me whole, fulfilled. You have delivered me from the sense of displacement and isolation that threatened my entire existence. But your son is yet to mature. It is imperative that he be helped to forge his identity and define the parameters of his life. So, don't choose me. He needs you more.'

'And, if it is you I want?'

'Then what will happen to your son?'

'He can live either with his maternal grandparents in Patna or with his great-grandfather in Quetta, Pakistan.'

'You mean we will be subjecting our progeny to another partition? No, Salma, that would mean betraying history all over again. It is immaterial whether he stays in India or in Pakistan. What matters, above all, is that he should be able to realize the full potential of his life and that alone must serve as the fulcrum around which all our decisions are made. Now, it is up to you to decide which of us you will choose!'

'Adeeb, it is you who brought radiance to my life. You alone have seen the light burning in my womb. Sohrab is its enduring flame. But if it comes to the crunch...' Salma lapsed into silence.

'Yes...?'

'...I wouldn't choose you. I would choose my son Sohrab.'

For a moment, he looked at Salma in amazement. Had she wished to, she could very well have lied just to please him. When a woman is lying, she looks beautiful. But when she speaks the truth, she looks ravishing. The adeeb gazed at Salma, having his fill of her beauty. She gazed back at him with the same passion.

'Amen!' he prayed, and then asked, 'How will I survive without you, Salma?'

'I have found an easy way out for that.'

'And what is it?'

'That in the company of a rival you look at me with the same intensity that you manifested when you took me in your arms. Let intimacy smoulder in your gaze as you imagine me sharing your bed. This is the only way you can release yourself from the bondage of love.'

'Salma! Have you any idea as to what you're suggesting?'

'Yes, I do. This is the only way you can stop loving me and begin life anew.'

As the adeeb looked at her intently, she continued, 'You are the only light in my life. Isn't it better for us to take the momentous decisions of our lives ourselves rather than allow death to have the final say? This is not a matter of faith or spirituality. It is a matter of conviction that ennobles the mind. There can be no dispute about it.'

'Amen!' came the adeeb's instinctive response.

'Farewell,' Salma murmured in a tearful voice. She wiped away her tears and rushed out.

The adeeb simply could not make sense of what he had just experienced. It was in this bewildered state that the peon found him. Mahmood Ali angrily erupted, 'I'm quite familiar with your habits · by now. Whenever you get a chance, you escape into your stories!'

'Please, Mahmood Ali! Do let me live in peace within these unfinished stories...please! Give me just one day to live with my tales.'

The peon noticed the bleakness in the adeeb's eyes and was deeply disturbed. 'Honourable sir,' he murmured, 'if the era itself cannot survive, what will become of your stories? If you insist, I will try and arrange a day's reprieve for you.'

The peon left the adeeb there, still struggling to come to terms with his separation from Salma.

A little later, the peon returned to announce, 'With the greatest difficulty have I managed a day's reprieve for you! This epoch has granted you a single day, during which you may remain oblivious to the world's massacres, the agonizing screams of restless spirits, the horrific sagas of bloody conflicts, and the terrible sighs of those in the throes of death. Neither tear nor scream nor sigh will trouble you today, if your literary conscience allows you to sit in peace and write your stories. But do emerge from your cocoon that represents no more than a semblance of humanity. Build a "Taj Mahal" of stories inspired by contemporary man's depravity and immorality!' As the adeeb looked at the peon, the latter observed, 'But, honourable sir, you have always been the voice of the common man.'

'Buta Singh and Zainab are ordinary, innocent people, Mahmood Ali. Shahin is a girl from the lower middle class. Kabir is a beggar. Surjit Kaur too is an ordinary woman who has carried her comatose son on her shoulder all these years. Not only has she been praying for the well-being of her son, but she has also prayed for Hazrat Rukne Alam's dargah and for her home town of Multan!'

'That's very strange, honourable adeeb!' the peon remarked.

'Mahmood Ali, my heart had raced when I was living through and writing that story. Surely, you remember? Surjit Kaur had stepped out of her ancestral home in Multan after giving her son a dash of opium. She was dressed for the occasion, resplendent in all her jewellery. She knew the rioters would target her jewellery and thus diverted, they would spare her son. When the jewellery was gone, they would rape her. Once again, they would leave her son alone. She had assumed that in the course of these incidents, she would be able to cross the border of the newly created Pakistan and her son would be safe. That was why she had given him opium, so that he wouldn't fret and cry, but remain listless in her arms. Once she had administered that dose of opium her son never opened his eyes again. Whenever war breaks out between India and Pakistan, she always comes to me asking about her Multan, hoping that it hasn't been bombed. I have tried my best explaining to her that she has nothing to do with Multan now, that it is no longer a part of her country, but a city in Pakistan. That demented woman just refuses to understand!'

And the adeeb narrated the next part of her tale...

'She came in 1948, carrying her unconscious child. She knew about the Indo–Pak war and wanted to be sure that Multan had not been bombed. I had reassured her that the hostilities were confined to Kashmir and that her Multan was safe. In 1965, she was back again, screaming, "I hope our forces have not attacked Multan to teach Ayub Khan a lesson? I hope no bombs have fallen on my Multan?"

'With great difficulty, I had managed to reassure her on the subject once again and sent her back. She returned in 1971, carrying her now-adult son on her shoulder. Yet again, she asked, "War has broken out. I hope my Multan is safe?"

'"Surjit Kaur," I had replied at the time, "the place where Multan is located is no longer a part of either your country or your town. You now live in Rajouri Garden, Delhi, India's capital city. You are an Indian citizen. Delhi, not Multan, is your city now. You have to try and make this city your own."

'"I do acknowledge this," she had said, "but tell me—has Multan been bombed?"

'"No, Multan is safe and the Shimla Accord has been signed," I reassured her again.'

While the peon gazed at him, the adeeb went on. 'Then she

came back in 1999,' he continued, 'carrying her fifty-two-year-old comatose son. "A conflict rages in Kargil," she announced. "I have heard that this might escalate into a full-fledged Indo–Pak war. I am ridden with anxiety. I do hope no bomb has been dropped on Multan?"

'And this time, I yelled at her. "Surjit Kaur!" I shouted, "Multan is not your town any more!" She stared at me, stunned. She just could not understand the import of my words. It was beyond her comprehension—just as Cyril Radcliffe's demarcation of the boundary between India and Pakistan eludes my own comprehension.'

'Cyril Radcliffe? Who the hell is he?' the peon asked.

'He is the man who finalized the demarcation of the border dividing India and Pakistan.'

*

It was a terribly sultry day in July. Cyril Radcliffe was in Mountbatten's study. He was neither a sociologist nor a geographer. Yet, Mountbatten had assigned this lawyer the task of drawing up the boundary lines between India and Pakistan. Radcliffe had been tersely told: 'You are to divide both Punjab and Bengal into two separate parts, following which you will demarcate the international boundary separating India and Pakistan.'

'But I am not suited for this task,' Radcliffe had protested. 'Where are Punjab and Bengal located?'

'You can find them on the map,' was Mountbatten's reply.

'If I am to follow your directives, I must undertake an extensive tour of the region. I have to visit all these places.'

'That's not possible. We have no time for that. It's July now. By 15 August, all the formalities of partition have to be complete.' Mountbatten's tone was crisp.

Suddenly, Kabir barged into the viceroy's study and shouted, 'Lat Sahib! This barrister, in whose hands you've thrust the butcher's knife, cannot even distinguish between wheat and barley! And this butcher is going to divide Punjab?'

Before either Mountbatten or Radcliffe could respond, Kabir went on, 'This butcher here cannot tell the difference between rohu and hilsa fish! And he's going to partition Bengal?'

Kabir had vanished before the viceroy's guards could react. That evening, a perturbed Cyril Radcliffe paced about on the Ridge, the point from which soldiers of the British army under the command of Brigadier John Nicholson had set out in 1857 to attack the Red Fort. From there, Radcliffe could see Raisina Hill, the location of Viceroy House, a powerful symbol of imperialism and the residence of the man who was ready to divide India. The country was ultimately divided—not just its land, but also its innocent people. Their corpses littered the land—corpses that were consumed by carnivorous creatures congregating in India from all over the world. In the history of the planet, it was a unique occasion indeed.

'We could not even administer the last rites to thousands of those corpses,' Kabir went on, standing before the adeeb and the peon, a twisted staff in his hand, 'but Corfield, the viceroy's advisor who admired Churchill, was busy extracting a promise from the new bureaucracy he had created in India, to ensure that the ancestral burial grounds of the British, scattered throughout the country, would be accorded due respect and taken care of.'

'Oh, is it you, Kabir?' the adeeb asked. 'Weren't you in the viceroy's study a moment ago, reprimanding Cyril Radcliffe?'

'That was quite some time back,' Kabir replied. 'Anyway, let's put that out of our minds. Tell me, instead, the story of Buta Singh who was so happy after his marriage to Zainab. It was, perhaps, their first real taste of happiness after Partition.'

'Yes, Kabir, you are right,' the adeeb answered. 'Buta Singh and Zainab were Adam and Eve, born from the bloody massacres and the rape and plunder that ensued during the country's partition. They alone had dared to eat the apple of love. But for such events, love would never have flourished and the world's gutters would have been choked with the bubbling blood of lust and hatred.'

'Yes,' Kabir affirmed, 'I was in Pakistan at the time. I had seen Buta Singh with a little girl, but hadn't been able to talk to him. I can't imagine why he went to Pakistan.'

'Don't you know about it?' the adeeb asked. 'Allow me to tell you. Buta Singh's brothers had just not been able to reconcile themselves to his newfound happiness. According to an agreement reached at the time, on both sides of the new border, lists were being drawn up of women who had been raped during the upheaval of Partition. Buta Singh's nephew took it upon himself to carry information about Zainab to the special unit of the army assigned this task. That very evening, soldiers arrived to whisk Zainab—now a married woman and a mother—away from her home. She was taken to a refugee camp in Delhi. To Buta Singh, it seemed as if fate had buried him under an avalanche of misfortune. He just picked up his little daughter, Tanvir Kaur, and set out in search of her mother.'

The peon, Mahmood Ali, interrupted him. 'Honourable adeeb,' he reminded him, 'you have been granted just a day's reprieve and the sun is about to set. If you don't mind my doing so, may I quickly go through the rest of Zainab and Buta Singh's story before twilight sets in?'

'But I wish to complete this story with all its nuances of searing beauty and pain,' the adeeb protested. 'If this unique story can acquire the aesthetic form of an epic poem, it will live on through the centuries. Just give me enough time to complete it.'

'Please don't insist on this point, sir. The times are not right for epics. Be done with what you have to say as quickly as you can. Otherwise, your stories will suffocate and die a premature death.'

'Fine. Just dig a little grave here and bury my pen,' the adeeb said in a voice full of anguish. 'Once that's done, you can continue with the narration.'

'So, Kabir, this is what happened,' the peon said, picking up the thread of the narrative...

'Buta Singh was just an illiterate farmer, but he managed to overcome all the obstacles that stood in his way and reached the camp to which Zainab had been taken. When he approached the office of the camp's in-charge, Mridula Sarabhai, he heard her interrogating Zainab.

"'Your religion?" Mridula asked.

"'Islam," came Zainab's reply.

"'After marriage?"

"'Islam."

"'It didn't change?"

"'No."

"'Did Buta Singh abduct you?"

"'No."

"'Did your family cross over to Pakistan?"

"'Yes, half of its members went over...the rest are here."

"'Why didn't you accompany the half that went to Pakistan?"

"'It wasn't necessary. I had met a man I liked here."

"'But you're a Muslim and Buta Singh is a Sikh. You shouldn't have stayed back in India."

"'Why not? Crores of Muslims have chosen to stay back in India. Is it necessary for every Muslim to go to Pakistan? I don't need Pakistan."

'As Zainab uttered these words, Buta Singh wiped his eyes and placed Tanvir Kaur at Mridula Sarabhai's feet. Then he pleaded, "This is our daughter. Zainab and I are man and wife. I want her back—my wife, the mother of my child! I love her passionately! I want justice!" Buta Singh broke down in tears.

"'I'm sorry. We have no faith in love professed by corpses!" Sarabhai exclaimed.'

'Yet another love story begins to unfold here,' the adeeb interjected. 'Mridula Sarabhai happened to be in love with India's then prime minister, Jawaharlal Nehru. This incarnation of beauty lived in an ivory tower, far from the world's travails. But it was not to her that the sensitive and idealistic Nehru turned when the deluge of blood released by Partition soaked his bed at Teen Murti to such an extent that he could no longer bring himself to sleep in it. At the time, Nehru had sought the emotional support of Edwina Mountbatten, knowing only too well that he could not expect from Mridula the kind of spiritual solace he needed. The latter had come to regard Edwina as a rival and Nehru as an unfaithful lover! It explained her lack of faith in Buta Singh's protestations of love. Her contempt for the fickleness of men had led her to avenge herself on Nehru by using Buta Singh as a scapegoat!'

'That's right,' agreed the peon. 'But the sun is about to set and you need to wind up the story fast.'

'What happened next?' Kabir asked.

'Since she was a Muslim, Zainab was handed over to her people in Pakistan. To get her back, Buta Singh recited the kalmah and converted to Islam. He changed his name to Jamil Ahmad and his daughter, Tanvir Kaur, became Sultana. When he could not procure a visa to visit his wife in Pakistan, Buta Singh illegally entered the country by crossing the border in Rajasthan. At this point, like so many other stories, this one too becomes a saga of love and sacrifice, union and separation, trust and dishonour, a devotion bordering on the insane—'

'Mahmood Ali, your narrative should be more specific,' the adeeb chided him. 'The greatest of mankind's stories generate compassion, because they are born out of human torment and passion.'

'Honourable adeeb, the time for narrating stories is drawing to a close. The sun is on the verge of setting. Let me narrate to Kabir the climax of this story, or it will remain incomplete.'

'Well, all right...go ahead. You have a knack for murdering stories,' the adeeb commented before sinking into silent despondency.

It was left to Mahmood Ali to complete the story of Buta Singh alias Jamil Ahmad. 'Despite his best efforts, Buta Singh could not bring Zainab back. Her family did not accept his conversion to Islam. Zainab was prevented from giving her statement in court. Sir, this is an agonizing story about the partition of the country and the fragmentation of its soul. Jamil Ahmad, earlier known as Buta Singh, lost his case in spite of converting to Islam. When he died, there was no permanent place for him in the cemeteries of Pakistan. His body was exhumed and left unattended. The railway station where he had jumped onto the tracks with his daughter to commit suicide is still there. Buta Singh's corpse, with Sultana in its arms, wanders about like Manto's Toba Tek Singh. It is present in this court today to hear your verdict.'

'Well, Mahmood Ali, you've finally dragged the story of Buta Singh and Zainab to an end. But Vidya's story still remains untold,' the adeeb reminded him.

'Now, which Vidya is that?'

'The same one who was travelling in a tonga from Rohtak Road to Ramnagar for her engagement ceremony, when rioting erupted at Qasabpura, causing the tonga's horse to fly away with her. Till this day, I wander about in quest of this story, the most silent of them all.'

'The sun has set, Your Honour. The time to visualize or write your stories is over.'

'Don't!' Kabir begged. 'I am eager to hear every one of the adeeb's stories.'

'Kabir, this is not the time to narrate or to listen to these stories. Now, you may only look upon them—'

'That is precisely the problem, Mahmood Ali, my friend,' Kabir replied. 'The light has gone out of my eyes. I have gone blind, begging for alms. My income has, no doubt, increased, but I can only listen to stories now...I can't see them! I can hear voices filled with joy or pain. I can no longer witness happiness or suffering.'

36

So, India witnessed the agony and ecstasy over the massacres and festivities engendered by its partition. Many a marriage procession and funeral cortège was seen making its way to its destination, without ever reaching it. There were no wedding mandaps or crematoriums awaiting such processions. All around the country, rituals of celebration and mourning were being observed. No one knew where exactly Cyril Radcliffe's line had ripped the land in two. But for those who mourned or celebrated, this line was clearly visible. The area littered by the corpses of Hindus and Sikhs was Pakistan; the region strewn with the corpses of Muslims was India. The corpses alone determined where the borders lay.

What had not been decided, however, was the fate of 565 illegal colonies established by the hand of British imperialism. The viceroy's advisor, Corfield, was ensconced in London, busy explaining to Britain's political elite that treaties between the British crown and all the Indian riyasats had been drawn up and signed. Under the India Independence Act, these riyasats could not be left to the mercy of either India or Pakistan. The British Crown could not forsake its responsibilities. The former British prime minister, Churchill, had agreed and declared, 'The rajas and maharajas, the nawabs and the Nizam have been our friends and allies. We have signed treaties with them. It is our duty to grant them their freedom!'

Unwilling to tolerate these rulers who were like festering wounds on the country's body, Nehru, Patel and Jinnah had opposed Churchill on this issue. Eventually, the British government was forced to acknowledge their point of view. By then, however, the partition of the country was well under way. British officers were engaged in preparations to return home. The Indians serving as officers in the army were being divided according to their choice of country. And the process of change and interchange was in full swing. In the cantonment at Delhi, Hindus and Sikhs were bidding farewell to their Muslim colleagues. The space in the army mess being inadequate, the formal dinner that had been organized was being held in the open area around it. And, across the border in Rawalpindi, a teary Colonel Idris declared to his departing Hindu and Sikh soldiers, 'My friends, my officers and my jawans! Together, we shed our blood in World War II! Together, we were victorious on many fronts! Together, we saluted those of us who were martyred at the battlefront! Wherever you are, these blood ties will remain indestructible. We shall forever remain brothers and cherish our shared memories!'

All those present embraced each other, wiped away their tears, bade each other farewell and moved on. But Muslim soldiers leaving their cantonments in India were beset by the greatest dilemma of all. In India, they were free to choose between the armies of either country, but the situation in Pakistan was somewhat different. That nation had been created in the name of Islam and for the Muslim brotherhood. The question of non-Muslims living there simply did not arise. In India, there were no such preconditions. The country had been declared a secular state. But the dilemma remained. The Indian Army was non-aligned as far as religion was concerned—all its soldiers were simply Indians. It did not matter whether they were Hindus, Muslims, Sikhs, Christians or Parsis. But the ones in a quandary had to come to a decision about who they were, where their faith lay and what they should opt for.

This great dilemma had weighed on the minds and hearts of soldiers in all the garrisons of the country. It was not an easy decision to make. No human being in the world has memories more intense than those which a soldier's heart nurtures. It is because he fights for life and for honour—his own and his country's. He also fights in the name of his memories. He is the first and last disciple of peace. Just as a soldier's step forward propels him towards the battlefront, the very next one longs to turn homewards. Thoughts like these swept through Inayat Habibullah's mind when he surveyed his Lucknow. It was in this city that some of his ancestors had been martyred in 1857. He could visualize the smouldering fires in the buildings that had borne the brunt of dynamite. He could imagine how the blood spilled during the massacre had taken ages to dry. It was in this city that Habibullah had decided to live with his memories.

But in the riyasat of Rampur, the wazir's two sons had made decisions diametrically opposed to one another's. The elder son, Major Yaqub Khan, who was just an officer in the viceregal bodyguard, chose to go to Pakistan in search of better opportunities. The younger son, Captain Yunus Khan, could not leave behind his memories and chose to stay on in India.

The words of Colonel Idris bidding an emotional farewell to his officers and soldiers, had reverberated again and again in the ears of his men who had, along with him, sought and wrought victory in World War II. They had all kept the flag flying high.

But in 1965, the Indo–Pak war had lent another dimension to the painful tragedy of Partition. A fierce battle had raged in the hills of Poonch in Kashmir. Commanding the Pakistani troops was Yaqub Khan, formerly of Rampur. And, facing him was the Gorkha Regiment led by Rampur's Yunus Khan! Two siblings, ranged against each other, had met in battle. Both were paying the price for the partition of the land. And now, it was a matter of life and death, a question of defending the honour of one's country. As India's Major Yunus Khan led the onslaught, he had shouted, 'Bhaijan, defend yourself!'

But Yaqub Khan of the Pakistani army had not been able to save himself. He had died in combat and it was left to Major Yunus Khan to bury the 'enemy', his elder brother. With a heavy heart, Yunus had prayed at his brother's grave and returned to base camp. But his heart had rebelled and he had taken early retirement and returned to Rampur.

Jinnah Sahib could not, however, have returned to Delhi. He had created his Pakistan. Before leaving for it, he had stood for the last time at his wife Rati's grave in Bombay. But for how long could he have continued to stand there? From Bombay, he had to go to Delhi, and from there, he would proceed to Pakistan. He would not be returning to India, ever again!

It had been decided that 14 August would be marked down as Pakistan's independence day, while India would commemorate its own independence on 15 August. No great deliberations were involved in deciding these dates. They were actually the result of Mountbatten's haste and idiosyncrasies. When a journalist had asked him whether a date had been decided on for India's independence, he had replied off the cuff, without giving the question serious thought. He had mentioned the first date that came to mind, the date of the Japanese surrender to British forces in Burma under Mountbatten's command. Such was the manner in which the date for India's independence came to be decided!

In just five months, Mountbatten, Churchill and Radcliffe had rent asunder a 5000-year-old civilization! And the birth of Pakistan had been part and parcel of the same conspiracy. Jinnah Sahib had set out from Delhi for Karachi to take over the reins of a Pakistan that existed, to all intents and purposes, on paper only. No land demarcations had been made till then. People had no idea where the border lay. It was only the corpses littering the land that indicated where one country ended and the other began.

Jinnah Sahib's DC-3 aircraft had taken off for Karachi from Delhi's Palam airfield. He had been gravely silent, even though his sister, Fatima Jinnah, sat beside him. His silence affected flight pursers and attendants so greatly that even they dared not utter a word. Fatigue and sadness marked Jinnah Sahib's face. When Fatima looked at him, he took a deep breath and said, 'What had to happen, has happened...This had to come about...'

When the aircraft was about to land in Karachi, Fatima had observed the sea of people waiting to welcome Jinnah and remarked, 'The ocean has swept in to welcome you...'

Jinnah Sahib had remained silent. It was difficult to tell whether he was tired, despondent or out of tune with the times. On 14 August, a number of official functions had been organized. Besides, Eid was being celebrated on the very historic day that Pakistan had been created. When his advisors suggested arranging an official dinner to commemorate the occasion, Jinnah Sahib had asked them to organize a lunch on 13 August instead. His trusted aide-de-camp had politely interrupted with the words, 'Your Excellency, 13 August is the last day of the month of Ramadhan. It would, perhaps, not be appropriate to schedule an official lunch on that particular day.'

Eventually, the luncheon engagement had been shelved.

But along the borders, the corpses celebrated Eid. They wore new clothes and embraced the corpses of the Hindus and Sikhs that lay around them. This unusual phenomenon had stunned the world. No one could believe that it had actually happened. The large portrait of Robert Clive which had once hung in the study of India's Governor-General, Mountbatten, and been consigned to a storeroom that very morning, erupted in anger, 'How is this possible?' it raged. 'In 1757, we had laid down, in principle, the foundation of two separate communities...'

Gilchrist stepped forward with, 'By hiring both Munshi Sadasukhlal and Maulvi Mir Amman at Fort William College, we had shattered the spine of the language they shared.'

Macaulay intervened. 'By making English education compulsory,' he declared, 'I had marginalized Persian and reduced Hindustan's intellectual and cultural elite to being illiterate ignoramuses.'

Brushing the mud off his body, Lord Curzon emerged from his grave. 'What Mountbatten has achieved today,' he proclaimed, 'is the culmination of what I had initiated in 1905. Through the partition of Bengal, I had divided the Hindus and the Muslims. I had created a Pakistan for these Muslims at the time! But Bengal's Muslims failed to foresee their future. They turned down the proposal of partition I had offered. I eventually revoked the order and advised the nawab of Dacca to counter Hindu influence by forming his own separate party of Muslims. That party is the Muslim League. And today, it has created Pakistan!'

Macaulay added, 'To destroy the Hindu–Muslim unity witnessed in 1857, I had established boarding schools for the debauched offspring of India's rajas, maharajas, nawabs and taluqdars. I had ensured that the natives receive compulsory religious instruction on their respective faiths in those elite schools. You talk of the Taliban in Afghanistan. In each Indian principality and riyasat, I had succeeded in creating Hindu, Muslim, Sikh and Christian "Taliban". To bring about the partition of India on the basis of religion and community, these riyasats served the purpose of our imperialistic designs. On the one hand, we successfully nurtured Muslim resentment in riyasats ruled by Hindus; on the other, we succeeded in our policy of fomenting Hindu resentment against Muslim rulers. The spirit of unity that marked 1857 was unacceptable to us. That is why it became imperative for us to change the course of history...'

While Macaulay was still speaking, there rose a terrible din. In the sky appeared flying machines made of beaten gold. Seated in them were twenty-four wealthy men who had reaped their harvest of prosperity from the starvation and death marking Ireland's devastating famine. These men bore a grievance, however, against Dutch merchants who exercised monopoly over the spice trade with the East and had raised the price of black pepper. It was what drove those twenty-four men to band together on the afternoon of 24 September 1599. It was on that occasion that the East India Trading Company was created in a dilapidated building on Leadenhall Street.

It should come as no surprise that India's viceroy was selected with the tacit approval of the British royal family. The governors of Indian principalities, however, were appointed from among the descendants of the proprietors of the East India Trading Company. On 14 and 15 August 1947, these governors would welcome the arrival of their ancestors in their golden flying machines.

Their advent was marked by the lowering of the Union Jack
from thousands of places that had symbolized colonialism and
imperialism—British military barracks, government buildings, navy
headquarters, monuments of imperialism, Fort William in Calcutta
that had witnessed the conspiracies of Clive, Fort George in Madras,
the viceregal lodge in Shimla, the Residency in Lucknow and
countless others. An air of sadness prevailed. The flags being lowered
were not made in India. A particular family of English tailors had
been granted the monopoly of making them. In the many colonies
of the Empire, these flags were replaced twice or even thrice a year.
So, making these flags involved a business that ran into hundreds of
thousands of pounds. Greatly perturbed by the possibility of this
lucrative monopoly business coming to an end, an elderly member
of the family of tailors had a heart attack. And it was the men in the
flying machines who came to his aid. Then began a round of
allegations and counter-allegations. Remarkably enough, it was the
Aztec ruler, Montezuma, who countered the allegations levelled
against India. Charges and counter-charges flew thick and fast.

'We have granted you independence, but you are incapable of
managing it!'

'And who are you to grant India independence? Every individual
is born free. Five thousand years ago, it was this same Bharat that had
invented the guiding principles of spirituality and justice. This
civilization had liberated itself from the fear of nature by evolving
principles of devotion. Faith had replaced fear. Have you ever heard
of faith, spirituality and justice? You don't even possess words in
your vocabulary that might stand for them. All you have is
individualism. This civilization, on the other hand, has unity!'

'At this juncture of independence, Hindustan has millions of
Dalits and Muslims, thousands of Christians, Parsis and Jews. Apart
from them, the country has a sizeable population of uncivilized,
illiterate tribals. Among them are the cannibals of the North-East.'

'These are the gifts of your own brand of colonialism. Bharat has
granted each citizen the right to life, whereas you don't allow
foreigners to settle in your land, even today. For centuries, Bharat
has offered shelter and the means of livelihood to its people. You

have all created your own Pakistans. And when our civilization successfully withstood the numerous attacks by your barbaric forces, we paraded the heads of those barbarians to broadcast our victory. You then slandered us by describing us as cannibals. It is the very same accusation that you level today against the people of the northeastern states of Bharat. They are not cannibals. They are warriors who can cut you to shreds.'

While Montezuma grappled with the questions that came his way, the adeeb took advantage of the respite to get back to his stories. He made a dash for Delhi's Rohtak Road, where Vidya's tonga had disappeared en route to Ramnagar. No one knew where it had vanished, taking along its occupant, a young girl...

On the way to Ramnagar, Vidya's tonga had to pass through Qasabpura, where the killings had started. The butchers of the locality, armed with their knives and cleavers, were engaged in the 'pious' act of slaughtering the kafirs. Vidya's tonga was caught in the midst of it all. A sudden explosion had started a fire. A pall of smoke hung over everything. Several pedestrians were set on fire. Their screams rent the air. Vidya had seen a shining dagger plunge like lightning into her babuji's ribs. After that, nothing registered. Her parents and younger brother had been killed. The terror-stricken horse drawing the tonga had been injured by pellets from the explosion. The tonga was on fire and trapped inside was a half-swooning Vidya. After a long while, she heard a voice call to her. 'Beti,' it said, 'hold my hand. Don't worry. Be brave. Try and get away from the fire. Try...try and escape...'

The semi-conscious Vidya had found herself with a family of Mewati Muslims who were on their way to Pakistan after having crossed many rivers of blood. She owed her life to them. At Qasabpura, they had encountered another bloodbath. By the time dusk fell, they had reached Nuh, a town in Mewat, and sought shelter in the house of a distant relative. Though Vidya was virtually in a state of shock, she had felt a strange affinity with the house. There was no rioting here. No one talked of India or Pakistan. The conversation veered around the scanty rainfall in the past two years that had led to ponds and ditches drying up. There had been a poor harvest of peas, barley and chana. Hopes had risen in the month of Baisakh, only to be dashed. Not a drop of rain had fallen and the arhar crop had withered away...

Vidya was lulled by this conversation into a feeling of relief. It reminded her of Fatehgarh where similar exchanges took place, where her neighbours talked of retailers and her babuji's lawyer friends discussed the same issues that were being deliberated over in this house. In her home town, the heat used to be just as intense and marriages took place during the summer months as they did here.

Whatever be the faith of Hindustan's farmers, the seasons were common to them all. It was the month of Baisakh and the auspicious time for marriages in Mewat. The fourth day of the lunar month had dawned. Yasin had told Syed Siraj who was bound for Pakistan, 'Syed Sahib, we've refused to go along with Jinnah Sahib. We won't be going to Pakistan. After all, what is there in Pakistan that we don't have here?'

'Bhaijan, Pakistan is a dream and we're going there to realize it,' came Syed Siraj's reply. 'And now that we've set off, there's no way of turning back.'

At that moment, Mushtari arrived to give her father, Yasin, the news that the ceremony of *chaak pujan* was to take place and that her four maternal uncles were about to arrive with the rice. She asked her father to change into fresh garments.

At this, Syed Siraj gave his wife, Ruqaiyya Begum, a look that questioned the Muslim credentials of Yasin, his brother from Mewat. The latter did not improve matters by remarking, 'This girl that you've brought along with you...she can become a liability.'

'But what could I have done? I couldn't possibly have left a destitute like her to die in the burning tonga.'

Vidya felt that death on that terrifying day would have been better than having to hear such exchanges. Fear stalked her from every corner. She felt trapped. The memory of a particular evening swam up before her eyes...

She was on her way back from the Christian basti of the dark-skinned lady doctor, the Kali Mem, as she was known. Vidya went to the basti to give tuitions to children there. For the past few days, she had observed some Hindu boys following her, the same ones who congregated every morning, ostensibly for a workout, in the park facing her house. They had stopped her one day and asked, 'Are you a Hindu?'

'Yes…why do you ask?'

'Then why do you go to the Christian basti every day?'

'I teach at the primary school there.'

'She's lying!' one of the boys snarled. 'She doesn't let on that she has become a Christian. She goes to pray at the church there.'

To this, Vidya had angrily retorted, 'The Kali Mem is a doctor. She goes to the basti to treat people, not to convert them.'

'Whatever it may be,' Vidya was told, 'if you're a Hindu, stop going there from tomorrow.'

Little had she known what was in store for her. Her memory brought back another evening, when two of those boys had abducted her. In a godown filled with potatoes, they had used her to satisfy their Hindu lust. Out of shame and fear, she could not bring herself to utter a word about it to her babuji. The two boys had raped her repeatedly. Since then, she had become prone to fits. Her hometown had begun to terrify her…

She was brought back to the present by Yasin advising Syed Siraj, 'Why don't you marry her? Grant her the status of your second or third wife. Or else, you will find it impossible to cross the border to Pakistan. Military men conduct a rigorous search for women who are being forcibly taken across.'

At this Ruqaiyya Begum, Syed Siraj's wife, had cast an oblique look in her husband's direction, prompting him to reply hesitantly, 'This girl's a Hindu. I don't want her being raped or knifed. As soon as I reach Pakistan, I will find a suitable bridegroom for her and marry her off.'

Yasin's wife, Naghma Bi, had hastily thrust a burqa and a brightly coloured wooden box into his hand.

'What's this for? What's inside?' Syed Siraj had asked.

But Naghma Bi had been in a tearing hurry, as the sounds of singing could be heard at her doorway. The women singing and dancing away were Hindus. They had come to collect the *neg*, the money distributed to singers who invoked divine blessings that would bring the groom good health and prosperity. Naghma had to see to a hundred little details—the chaak pujan ceremony had to be completed; she had to observe the ritual of waiting for the groom near the wall of the well; she had to cajole and convince him that she would keep her daughter in hand, so that his mother would never be driven to suicide by the antics of a wayward daughter-in-law; and she had to promise that her daughter would never offend her in-laws by making insolent remarks or ripostes. In the midst of all these preoccupations and tensions, Naghma Bi had found time to advise Syed Siraj, 'Make her wear a burqa when you take her away from here. If her face is not veiled, the Hindu–Muslim question may come up. If she travels dressed as a Muslim, chances are that she'll get through without difficulty. While crossing the border, she must not betray any reluctance or regret at leaving India. She must seem very eager to be in Pakistan. Once you're safely across, put sindoor in the parting of her hair. It's there in the coloured box. On the other side, Pakistani soldiers will notice the sindoor in her hair and ask about it. Tell them she's a married Hindu woman you've abducted. This will please those soldiers and they'll let you through.'

Syed Siraj could only say, 'You've been very practical about the whole thing, bhabhiji!' By then, Naghma Bi had disappeared once again to supervise the ceremonies.

Trying to find a way out of this vexing situation, Ruqaiyya Begum had suggested, 'Why don't you leave the girl in Naghma Apa's care? I'm sure she knows the name of the town she belongs to. When the situation improves, Naghma Apa could send her home.'

'Begum,' Syed Siraj had replied, 'in these trying times, no one has a home any more...everyone has been rendered homeless. Though we've set out, we don't know where our home is going to be in Pakistan, do we?'

Vidya could not remember much about that journey. Snatches of memory came back to her—the call of the azaan, when the hired lorry arrived to transport them across the borders of Nuh...those Hindu boys in Fatehgarh...that dreadful potato godown...the absence of Amma and Babuji. Whenever she thought of these things, her mind seemed to freeze. She had heard someone say, 'Let's go, beti,' and she had boarded the ramshackle lorry with her new family. For a while, they had waited for some other passengers. In the meantime, Syed Siraj had performed his ablutions and said his prayers in the masjid nearby.

The journey began. The black shadows of depression lifted. The sun seemed to have come out once again. Except for the keekar, they saw no other trees on the way. A couple of ber trees went by. Hanging from their branches were empty nests of the weaver bird. Then came the border, where they met other people. Nearby was a small tea shop. After drinking tea and making a few inquiries, they were advised by the soldiers to 'go towards Lyallpur'. They were told: 'There are vast tracts of empty land there and many houses lie vacant. You might find a few occupants around.'

'Occupants? Then why would they give us their houses?'

'Dispose of the corpses. Get rid of the cobwebs and clean up the place. The area has ample water resources, as the Sutlej canal runs through it. Go via Jaranwala. The town has a mandi, a huge grain market where you can buy provisions. If you're short of cash, you can earn some by transporting grain from one part of the town to another. You won't have any problems. This country offers you an easy life.' The soldiers' words had been reassuring.

Syed Siraj's small family had eventually reached Lyallpur. They had found a house for themselves. Some mohajirs—migrants from India—had reached there before them and set up their homes. A few signs remained of the house's former occupants—twigs of cotton near the broken tandoor, a string of dried turnips hanging from a nail.

The neighbours came over to give Syed Siraj's small family an effusive welcome. It turned out that these neighbours had migrated from Old Delhi—from Kucha Saadullah in Daryaganj. They had lived in the Naharwali Haveli there. Nearby was another haveli, the Gul-e-Rana, formerly the home of Nawab Liaquat Ali Khan, now prime minister of Pakistan. Sir Syed Ahmad Khan's haveli was situated in Tiraha Bairam Khan. It was the place where Sir Syed always stayed, whenever he came over from Aligarh.

'Allah be praised!' said Nadeem Sahib, the neighbour who had arrived and settled down in the area before them. 'I did not get a chance to study at Aligarh. I was educated in the Anglo-Arabic School at Ajmeri Gate. When I crossed over, I got a job in the Foreign Office. Our government desperately needs mohajirs like me who have sound knowledge of a foreign country like Hindustan. My life was made. You should also try and land a job like mine.'

'I will have to take up some trade. I don't have the competence—the liaquat—to handle a job,' Syed Siraj had replied.

'I think it's enough for us in this country to have the liaquat of our Prime Minister Liaquat Ali Khan! Do you know Urdu?'

'Yes, I'm familiar with it.'

'Then, Bhaijan,' suggested Inayat Ali Khan, another neighbour, 'tell us in Urdu a little more about that girl in your household who applies sindoor in the parting of her hair.'

The words aroused the suspicions of Syed Siraj's wife. The future, though hazy, seemed to take shape before her eyes. One never knew when it would be clearly revealed. But one thing was evident—it took no time for a man to be aroused. Once that happened, it did not take him long to undo the cord of his pyjamas. Ruqaiyya Begum's house had many rooms, but only one charpai. If the cord came undone, she knew she would never be destined to sleep on that charpai again.

It was a mercy that Syed Siraj had to spend several days travelling to the mandis nearby to get a feel of the grain trade. He even had to visit the huge mandi at Jaranwala. During one of his absences, Ruqaiyya Begum summoned a maulvi and made Vidya recite the kalmah. She then kissed the girl's forehead and gave her an exotic new name. 'You're now the *pari*, the fairy Parveen Sultana!' she told her.

Syed Siraj was immensely pleased to hear this when he returned home. Lovingly putting his arm around his wife's ample waist, he declared, 'Begum, you've done a commendable job. This deed of yours is born out of your goodness and piety.'

The next time Syed Siraj left town, his wife did something else that was born out of her goodness and piety. She had, in fact, been making preparations for it for weeks. Nadeem Sahib's gaze had made her conscious of how alluring her ample waist was, with its many folds. One day, she had adorned her waist with a silver belt and noticed how Nadeem Sahib's eyes were glued on her. Ruqaiyya Begum had coquettishly declared, 'The folds around a woman's waist are the signs of a man's enduring passion and virility. They appear on her only when a man drowns in the deep waters of love.'

Nadeem Sahib had given Ruqaiyya Begum a meaningful look. A restless impatience had seized him, as he became lost in thought.

'What are you thinking of?' she had asked.

Nadeem Sahib had gazed at her again. A surge of desire had coursed through him. To test the waters, he had hesitantly whispered, 'The problem is…'

'All problems get solved if one has the determination. This one too can be resolved in no time at all. You know, the pari is always there…'

Pari! Pari! The word resounded in Nadeem Sahib's ears and he found himself drowning in its notes. To ensure that he did not drown alone in the deep waters of love, Ruqaiyya Begum made her move three days before Syed Siraj was due back. Apprehensions about her spouse taking a second wife drove her to escort Pari and Nadeem Sahib to the masjid. There, the nikaah was performed, declaring Pari and Nadeem Khan man and wife. Ruqaiyya Begum's only condition was that her 'daughter' be sent off to the groom's home with much fanfare the following Thursday. That was when Syed Siraj was expected to return, bringing along some good news about the new business that he planned to venture into. Despite all manner of objections, Nadeem Sahib had chosen to wait till Thursday evening.

37

Thursday evening arrived. Wedding songs were sung in the homes of the bride and the groom. Some frenzied dancing had also taken place. Then, the inevitable transpired—Parveen Sultana alias Pari alias Vidya became Begum Nadeem Khan.

Begum Pari had no complaints about life. Everything seemed acceptable now—the horror in her home town of Fatehgarh, death standing before her on Rohtak Road...and now, her future in Lyallpur. Everything seemed safe and secure.

Nadira Begum, a neighbour, had joined in the wedding festivities. She had cracked her fingers against her forehead to ward off bad luck and had prayed that soon, the umbilical cord of another male child would be buried in the soil of Punjab. She wore a turquoise ring on her finger; turquoise earrings hung from her ears; a matching nosepin adorned her face and her turquoise silk gharara swished against her hips with her movements like a grinding machine. When she observed the frenzied rituals being conducted, she gave vent to her irritation. 'Arrey, what're you up to, you lalas, you unrefined louts! At least, now you can sober down! I'd come to join the celebrations and convey my good wishes. So what if I didn't get to eat nurpulao, sheermaal and korma? Remember, this is a day when honour is bestowed on a woman...always remember that.'

At that point, Nadeem Sahib's first wife had tearfully erupted, venting her feelings in curses and abuse. 'She's a Hinduain...!' she had exclaimed. 'Impure! Unclean...!'

'No, a horse's mouth, the flames of a fire and the womb of a woman can never be impure, unclean...'

For many years after the wedding, Pari alias Vidya had thanked Allah for her womb. Though her waist had not expanded, Nadeem Sahib had given her all the love and regard she could have hoped for. She had given him three children. Then, he had had a stroke. The government had been kind enough to offer his eldest son, Parvez, a job in the Foreign Office.

Most of Pari's time was now devoted to taking care of her husband. She would wash him in the morning and give him breakfast. For lunch, she served him khichdi. From the magazines that came to the house, she read him poetry or fiction. For dinner, she made him sip meat broth. Then, she put him to bed. In one of those magazines, she had read a translation of one of the adeeb's stories and her curiosity had been aroused. 'Is he the same person I had left behind at the railway station at Kanpur?' she had asked herself.

That evening, Parvez had given her the news. 'Ammi,' he had told her, 'I've been posted to India, at our embassy there. Next month, I have to leave for Delhi...'

'Delhi!' Nadeem Sahib had exclaimed in a slurred voice. His eyes shone. 'Delhi?' he had asked. 'That's where our houses used to be, in Kucha Saadullah Khan...Naharwali Haveli.'

'And, if you get the chance, do visit another place...'

'Which place is that, Ammi?'

'Kanpur Station.'

'Kanpur Station?' exclaimed Parvez in surprise. 'What a strange thing to say, Ammi!'

'Oh, there's nothing strange about it. I've read a translation of an Indian story in which Kanpur Station figures frequently. I felt there must be something special about it. But anyway, it was just a stray thought—there's no better city than our Lahore.'

'All right, Ammi. I'll visit Kucha Saadullah Khan—and Kanpur Station.'

'Yes, beta,' his father had urged him in a faltering tone, 'take a good, fond look at our houses. And yes, in Kucha Chelaan at Ajmeri Gate, there used to be a hakim—Ashraf Ali Khairati Sahib. He had a cure for strokes—the Ramban powder. If you have the time, visit his pharmacy and send me some of that medicine. Perhaps, this medicine from my homeland will prove more effective. There's a masjid there. On my behalf, buy oil worth eleven paise and pour it into the masjid's diya. When you come home on vacation, get a ber sapling from the Qutub Nursery. We don't get bers here.'

'Abba, have a list prepared for me...a list of all that I have to see, all those I have to meet and all that I need to get for you. I'll bring back whatever you ask for. Just don't ask me to get the Taj Mahal or the dargah of Aulia Moinuddin Chisti! Those I won't be able to ferry across!'

His words had made a smile flicker across Pari's ruby-red lips. Nadeem Sahib had merely looked depressed. She had caressed his forehead and murmured, 'You should now put your memories on hold, the way I have. Look there...outside the window...how beautiful that palm grove looks! When the trees flower, what a swarm of buzzing bees will be drawn to them...!'

Nadeem Sahib had looked at Pari and said, 'Begum, the biggest hives were to be found at Sikri's Buland Darwaza. If you're ever there, do go and see them. These days the tesu must be blossoming along the banks of the Jamuna and the Betwa. Forests of dhaak must also be blooming there...'

Pari could only gaze at his sad eyes.

'Begum,' he had said tremulously once again, 'it takes centuries to rein in memories. We only remember those who are really close to us...Begum, half my body is paralysed, because half my memories are lost...'

Pari had drawn him into the warmth of her soft arms. Kissing his inert body, she had said, 'My lord, I will make you well again...Allah will then give us more pleasant memories to cherish.' It was then that she had seen Qurratulain Hyder's metaphorical river of fire flow by before her eyes.

Suddenly, the sounds of mourning swelled from a basti nearby. Pari and Nadeem Sahib had looked at each other inquiringly. The sounds rose to a crescendo. Pari approached the window and looked out. From the other side of the palm grove, the sounds of mourning grew louder. Her heart beat in terror. A calamity had befallen someone. She looked up at the sky and saw a swarm of swallows fly past.

A man passing through the lane informed her, 'War has broken out. News has come from the border—Abdul Ghani's son is dead.'

Pari's heart sank.

From behind her, she could hear Nadeem Sahib's quavering voice, 'What is it, Begum? Is another Pakistan being created?'

Pari looked straight ahead. There were no swallows in the sky now, only millions of butterflies. In a few moments, the details of the scene came into focus. These were not live butterflies. They were just broken butterfly wings, floating on a blast of hot air. They came to rest on the palm trees. Those that did not get lodged in the branches, wafted down to the stony ground below where they lay still.

She looked at the broken wings and then at the palms. Her gaze moved to the listless Nadeem Sahib who resembled a broken butterfly wing himself. Silently, she asked herself, 'Who knows whether the honeybees will ever come or not?'

The silence replied, 'Perhaps they wouldn't want to come when war clouds gather.'

'Begum, find out why this war has broken out,' Nadeem Sahib urged her from his bed.

'Abba, don't worry,' Parvez had come back to reassure him. Nadeem Sahib was surprised to see him.

'You were going to Hindustan, weren't you? What happened?'

'Flights have been suspended because of the war. I've just returned from the airport.'

'But this war...'

'The Bengalis want their own Pakistan.'

'What is Hindustan doing about it?'

'It's helping the Bengalis to acquire their Pakistan.'

'So, how many more Pakistans are to be created now? How many Pakistans are to be born within Pakistan itself? The saraikis of Punjab are demanding their own province. The Sindhis who have lived in Pakistan for generations want their own Sindhu Desh. Just as a contentious Punjabi–Urdu debate has been triggered by some people here, the Sindhi–Urdu conflict has been precipitated elsewhere. The Pakhtoons now clamour for their own Pakhtoonistan. Ataullah Mengal demands a free Baluchistan. And, our mohajir brothers in Sindh Karachi want to create another Pakistan for themselves. I've heard that Hindus in Hindustan are demanding from their countrymen a Hindu Pakistan. The Tamils in Sri Lanka want a separate Lanka for themselves.'

'This is happening all over the world, Abba. Palestinians are killed on the borders of Israel. A massacre is taking place in Rwanda—the Hutus have killed five hundred thousand Tutsis. The Sindhis have even gone to the extent of describing Quaid-e-Azam Jinnah Sahib as a mohajir. They have even defaced his portraits. Killings now take place on the border. The hills and plains around Chhamb-Joriyan and Khemkaran are bathed in blood...'

Parvez was still speaking, when the sound of crackers erupted.

In the Bengali bastis near Karachi, secret festivities were on. Bangladesh had been created.

On the Quaid-e-Azam's tomb, some Toba Tek Singh had written: 'Quaid-e-Azam, we've repaid half your debt...'

From the bunkers in Bangladesh, there emerged long lines of young women whose wombs bore the bloody traces of rape. These women were soon transformed into walking corpses.

Observing them, another Toba Tek Singh, this time from Lucknow, had screamed, 'You savages! These are the symbols of your victory and defeat! When there is war—in whichever place it may break out or for whatever reason—this is what happens!' He had then handed the adeeb a manuscript of his story. 'Read this! Read it aloud, so that everyone in the world can hear it! This is what happens on all borders...'

The adeeb made a place for himself and settled down to read the manuscript...

*

The wife combed her hair. Then, she carefully applied lipstick. On her soft cheeks, she rubbed the traces of the lipstick that had stuck to her fingers. Suddenly, a series of explosions took place. The glass panes of the window in the room shattered. More explosions followed and screams rent the air. The sound of bombs, bullets and mortar echoed. And then followed the hush of death. The basti had emptied out—those who could escape had fled; those who could not, sought places to hide in...

Then, more explosions occurred.

The husband commented, 'Even though our forces are not resisting them, I can't understand why they're bombing us.'

'It's what they want,' the woman replied indifferently. 'Perhaps, they're bombing us just to announce their arrival. After all, you can't expect them to land here accompanied by music and revelry!'

Several hours later, the silence was broken by a commotion.

The man said, 'They've come...'

Shadows fell in the doorway. Uniformed officers came in. They told the husband, 'There's no need to be afraid or to flee. If you are really cooperative, we may even give you a reward.'

A sudden turmoil broke out among some soldiers. Perhaps, many more people had arrived. Someone shouted, 'Hey, there's a woman here! A woman!'

The wife had become somewhat anxious, but composed herself. In a measured tone, she asked the officer, 'Are these your men?'

'That's right.'

'In that case, can't you control them?'

Her words infuriated the soldiers. They advanced menacingly towards her, but the officer's stentorian voice ordered them to hold back. The soldiers resented his intervention. 'We have captured this area. Everything here belongs to us...and we shall claim it!' they shouted.

'Get out!' the officer shouted back.

Gradually, they retreated, then left. Once outside, one of the soldiers showered obscenities on the woman and the officer. At this, the officer rushed out. But the men had all vanished. He returned to the room. It now struck him that there was a woman in the room and that he was a victorious army officer. He stared at the woman closely. Her face was impassive. Not once did she blink. Her hair and clothes were dishevelled, but her beauty shone through...

The officer approached her and started brushing away the dust from her hair and clothes. The woman's face and body betrayed no reaction. Then his glance fell on her husband and he burst out, 'You idiot! What the hell are you staring at me for? Go and fetch whatever there is to eat in the house.'

The husband moved quickly, as if to carry out the order, and the officer warned him, 'Don't try to escape! This basti is surrounded by soldiers. Any false move and you will be shot!'

The husband went into another room. The moment he left, the officer noticed, the frozen woman came to life. Suddenly, she made a dash for the door. The officer lunged out and caught her by the waist. When she dug her teeth into his wrist, he slammed his fist into her waist. The woman neither screamed nor moaned. She clawed at his face with the nails of both hands. Somehow, the well-built officer was able to subdue her. He tied her hands behind her back. Her panting caused her breasts to heave in a manner that drew his attention to them. The officer now tore off her clothes, so that not a shred of cloth remained on her body. He was already greatly aroused. Straddling her, he thrust himself deep into her naked flesh a couple of times, then with a jerk, pushed her away. Slowly, the woman sat up where she had lain on the floor.

That was when her shaken husband entered, carrying a plate of food. The officer picked up his stengun and placed it in his lap. Then, he fell on the food. Just as he was drinking water after the meal, there was an uproar. The same group of soldiers had returned, shouting, 'Sir! Sir, in this entire basti, we could find only four women. They're so old that even a dog wouldn't deign to sniff at them...'

'Sir, you've finished with this woman...now hand her over to us!'

Without any hesitation, the naked woman rose to her feet. In a trance, this beautiful creature walked towards the soldiers. A tumult broke out. They fell on her. In the melee that ensued, glimpses of her rosy flesh could be seen amidst the tangle of arms and legs. It looked like a child's toy being tossed and turned in the murky waters of a flood...

The next morning, the officer returned. He was accompanied by a group of silent men. Some of them were journalists. The officer told her, 'These men are highly respected journalists writing for English-language publications in our country. The world reads what they write and listens to what they say. They want a statement from you. Understand?'

A tape recorder was switched on and she started to speak: 'We had never imagined that soldiers from an enemy nation could treat us with such consideration. We're deeply indebted to them.'

Then, they were gone—the tape recorder, the journalists and the officer who left after expressing his thanks.

The night was dark. The wind could be heard whistling. The silence was rocked by explosions as bombs rained down. Machine-gun fire rattled against walls and windows. Then a massive explosion shook the very foundations of the house. Despite his tension, the husband heaved a sigh of relief and said, 'It seems our forces have arrived. We shall now be free.'

'From whom?'

'From enemies and misfortune!'

The sound of machine guns drew nearer. The explosions grew louder. The husband looked out of the window and noticed that the soldiers belonged to his own country. They had won the war and wiped out the enemy. Now, they were raiding houses to liberate their land from foreign occupation.

They eventually found the house—the one where the woman lived. Now, the officer who belonged to her own country ordered his troops to leave the premises. Then he repeated exactly what the enemy officer had done to her. This was followed by the same orgy in which she had been forced to participate by the enemy soldiers. And finally, like the enemy forces, these troops too fled into the night.

Then, the English-language press of her country turned up. The woman stood before them, stark naked, having withstood the sexual assaults of her own countrymen who had used her to satisfy their lust and instinct for savagery. The tape recorders were switched on, once again. And yet again, she said, 'I welcome the soldiers of my land. They have defended us so courageously. They have protected our honour. Their conduct, their humanitarianism and their values deserve praise...'

After recording her statement, the press and the army dispersed. They left behind a battered, naked woman who repeatedly asked herself, 'Who, after all, was the real enemy?'

38

It is always difficult to identify the real enemy...

From the darkest recesses of creation, Hiroshima came roaring, its body a mass of wounds. 'It is hard to recognize enemies! Now, they have all banded together to conspire against human dignity and destroy it! They have taken an oath: Henceforth, they will settle all disputes that relate to the right to life. After defeating the Titans, Yamraj, the Aryan god of death, had called a council. Present on the occasion were Hades of the Sumerian–Akkad civilization, Pluton from the Roman civilization and Zeus's brother Poseidon.'

'Who's Poseidon?' asked Mahmood Ali, the peon.

'The third brother of Zeus…the one to whom he handed over the realm of the oceans. Poseidon is also the stepbrother of the debauched Aryan god Indra. After defeating the Titans, the gods were all in a state of intoxication, as was customary following every great battle. While returning with Poseidon after their victory, Ajax had behaved like the uniformed officers who had raped the young wife. He had dragged Cassandra away from the idol of the goddess Athene to which she had been clinging and violated her. Athene had regarded this rape as a violation of her own person, since Cassandra had been clinging to her image when she was forcibly taken away. Just as the Aryan Ahilya had been sacrificed by being turned into a stone idol, Athene had chosen to become an image made of wood…'

'Since then, the entire pantheon of deities is bent on destroying peace on earth,' Montezuma explained. 'Even Apollo had wanted to possess the eternal virgin, Cassandra, but could not for want of an opportunity. The tradition of plunder and mass rape following a war continues to this day. It was what the so-called "civilized" Spaniards had carried out in Brazil. And the women of our civilization had to endure it. It is the convention of these white races that call themselves "civilized". Anyway, let's be done with this. We are all aware that these tyrannical ancient civilizations had split up their empires. Zeus had chosen to rule over the skies. He had handed Poseidon the charge of the oceans and to Hades the netherworld. But do bear in mind the agreement these cruel beings had endorsed— that they would exercise equal rights over the earth. In their bid to conspire against the earth's inhabitants, the modern descendants of these gods hark back to that agreement as they consolidate their hold over the world.'

'I am referring to that agreement,' Hiroshima affirmed. 'When Yamraj had called his council, he had not only invited the gods of death belonging to different pantheons, but had also summoned

Hitler, Mussolini and the Japanese Tojo. Invitations had been sent as well to atomic scientists who despised racism, but had no qualms about developing weapons of murder and mass destruction. They all belonged to one clan. Though legislation was responsible for building up a climate of anti-Semitism, and Jews had been deprived of higher education, this group of scientists harboured no racial or ethnic resentment. Their abiding preoccupation was the search for a formula that could destroy the whole of mankind.'

At Hiroshima's words, a butterfly which had escaped alive, fluttered her wings and declared, 'Here is another dark age in the history of mankind. To bring death upon others, the entire community of scientists in America, Germany, England and Russia has undertaken a mission. They have all become servile minions of the purveyors of death like Yamraj, Poseidon and Hades. These men have pawned their souls. They have placed weapons of wanton destruction in the hands of tyrants, while they themselves go about collecting awards and benefits...'

'The butterfly is right,' asserted Hiroshima. 'In their laboratories today, this brotherhood of scientists and researchers works towards evolving the most horrifying instrument of death. They should never be forgiven! These merchants of death cannot be allowed to operate in the name of progress! For the divinities and dictators who attended Yamraj's council were joined by scientists like von Weisecker, Werner Heisenberg, Edward Taylor, Robert Oppenheimer, Rutherford, Rabi, Enrico Fermi, Lyozelard, Niels Bohr, Rudolph Perls and Einstein.'

'Allow me,' offered Montezuma, stepping forward. 'Let me narrate the tale of how these scientists reached the pinnacle of unrivalled fame. Let me lay before you that brutal past, where scientific knowledge was harnessed to bring about the destruction of mankind. Unfolding before you is the history of fame and of infamy...There was a time when scientists dedicated all their efforts to the welfare of mankind and were absorbed in the study and discovery of nature's precious secrets. Their only goal was the good of mankind. Marie Curie had discovered radium. She had showered praise on Rutherford, one of her peers working at Cambridge, with the words, "He is the only physicist who will enrich the world with his discoveries." In Rutherford's research, Marie Curie had seen hope for the entire human race. In his laboratory, Rutherford was engaged in efforts to fathom the unsolved mystery of an atom's energy...'

A man who looked like a scientist, interrupted. 'Not only did he do so, Rutherford actually succeeded in splitting the atom. He also discovered the atom's pivotal "nucleus" which was a thousand times smaller than the atom itself. Rutherford was aware that the potential energy of a nucleus was a thousand times greater than that of an atom...'

Everybody looked at the man in surprise.

'And who may you be?' Hiroshima asked curtly.

'I am Piotr Capizza, a Russian,' came the reply. 'I am one of Rutherford's students.'

'Scientists like you who work for the destruction of mankind are not allowed here,' Hiroshima retorted angrily. 'It would be better if you left at once.'

It was Montezuma who calmed Hiroshima down. 'I understand the agonizing pain of your wounds,' he said, 'but we should welcome scientists like Capizza.'

The onlookers wore expressions of dubious inquiry.

'I am not wrong in making such a claim. However unbearable our sorrow and suffering might be, we should not forget our conscience. Try and remember...this is the same Piotr L. Capizza who had worked with Rutherford in Cambridge. He was one of the few scientists who had a conscience. After discovering the secret of splitting the atom, Rutherford had felt both guilty and sad. He had confided in the Curies. "We have to keep our findings a secret," he had urged. "They must never fall into the wrong hands. If they do, the power of nature could be used to destroy mankind." It was then that scientists like Capizza and Maxbourne, who worked in Edinburgh, had refused to divulge the secret of atomic power to any political establishment.'

As Montezuma spoke, fragments of History started to make their appearance. Fierce storms of ambition swept through Europe.

The demons of racism and nationalism raised their ugly heads. The revolutions in France and Russia alerted the citadels of capitalism to keep their armour and arsenal in readiness.

Suddenly, Mussolini's loutish volunteers descended into the political arena. In Italy, they terrorized the workers and the poor. They became the self-appointed guardians of priests and worshippers in Italian churches. They hijacked institutions, asserting their power and superiority. They seized control of trade unions. Infiltrating the bureaucracy and the police, they let loose a reign of terror. In this environment of anarchy, Mussolini emerged as a centre of power and a symbol of cultural nationalism that was not endorsed by his people. He began meddling in the established norms of administration. And his first move in his bid to do so, by hook or by crook, was to reach an understanding with the Church, prompting the Pope to declare, 'We have given Italy its God, and to God we have delivered Italy.'

Elsewhere, racial hatred and blind nationalistic fervour had given Hitler to Germany and Germany to Hitler!

'Stop!' Montezuma called to History. 'Just wait!'

So, History stopped in its tracks. And the flow of a 300-year-old cultural, aesthetic and humanistic tradition was arrested. Colonialism and industrialization killed the sensibilites that had earlier characterized romanticism. The creative arts descended from the pinnacle of artistic taste, thought and feeling to drown in the depths of meaningless romanticism. In place of the artists and writers who had been committed to high aesthetic values, there rose a new crop of successors who were unable to reconcile to the trauma of their displaced predecessors. For the sake of their own survival, they declared each other geniuses. The economic depression in America and Europe dealt a severe blow to the art market. Beethoven's avant-garde music was lost in the world's pandemonium. Instead of exploring the beauty and pain of life, art sought recognition and acclaim for its warped representations. Picasso's Cubism was driven by the urge to break away from traditional representational art and explore the aesthetic perceptions of the human mind. Reality was overturned and replaced by abstract forms symbolizing a terrifying angst-ridden supra-reality. Dali and Dadaism sought to portray through their distortions the truths of their extraordinary world. Dali conceptualized time as a melting watch, but could not hold back the hands of time. Benito Mussolini's forces paused momentarily after capturing Ethiopia. Hitler's forces took a break after trouncing Austria, Poland and the Rhineland.

Montezuma's gaze travelled over a rocky, uneven plateau, fissured with excrutiating pain. In places, flames appeared through the fissures. Along with them rose a hissing toxic vapour in which semi-conscious people writhed and choked.

Hitler's fierce dog stood guard behind him as his master fed the pigeons and proclaimed, 'The sun and the world's empires exist for none other than Caucasian Aryans like us. We have our own knowledge, our own perceptions and our rationale. We can do without the petty knowledge of the Jews!'

Once again, the rocky plain spouted hissing jets of steam and people succumbed to the poisonous fumes.

In other parts of the world, people gasped in horror at what was happening in the laboratories of Berlin, Leipzig, Gottingen and Munich.

'Look, Hiroshima,' Montezuma called out, 'the story of your suffering begins here. It is from this point that the history of the split atom takes a horrifying new turn. A race richly endowed with intellectual ability, knowledge and scientific acumen will never put up with humiliation. The atom exists in the womb of all matter. Within the atom lies the powerful nucleus that constitutes the crucial centre of energy. However well-guarded the stages of splitting the atom may be, the fact cannot be concealed that the process releases energy far exceeding that conserved in scores of suns. This energy is capable of meeting the earth's energy requirements for many centuries to come. It can also deliver man from death and disease, pain and tragedy, fear of sin and penance. Unfortunately, the channelization of this energy veered away from positive goals and took a negative turn. And the reason was the exodus of the Jews.

'Hiroshima, you and Nagasaki have had to live through the tragedy of the atom bomb. The real targets of this destructive

weapon were Hitler, Berlin and Munich. Most of the atomic scientists
were Jews who had been emotionally uprooted, dispossessed and
treated like lepers. Never had such humiliation been heaped on a
race in the annals of history! It was the effect of racial discrimination,
along with the fear, oppression, humiliation and sense of betrayal it
spawned that would fuel Jewish outrage and sow the seeds of a
meticulously organized form of revenge. The quantified principles of
mankind's progress would be replaced by strategies that yielded
nothing but despair and pessimism. Hitler's arrogance, emanating
from a sense of racial superiority, had heaped great humiliation on
Jewish scientists. He had justified the extermination of their entire
community. And see what happened as a result!'

Hiroshima with its battered form turned to look. In the
laboratories, the sages of science were undergoing a metamorphosis,
changing into demons of destruction. Feeling faint, Hiroshima covered
its terror-stricken eyes with its hands. And History, which had
paused for a while, began marching forward...

And so, Hitler went back to the ethnic cleansing of the
laboratories. One by one, he terminated the services of the non-
Aryans. Man's indestructible intellect became the target of racial
violence. Jewish scientists began their exodus. Albert Einstein left
Berlin and proceeded to America. Other scientists fled to Copenhagen,
Paris, Zurich and Cambridge. Enrico Fermi, the father of the atom
bomb, was forced to flee because of his Jewish wife. Even Edward
Taylor, nicknamed the 'Fat Man' of the hydrogen bomb, could not
stay on. He joined Oppenheimer at the Los Alamos Laboratory in
America. World War II laid the grounds for another conflict—that
between Aryans and non-Aryans. Utterly crushed, the Jewish spirit
sought revenge and...

'And at four a.m. on 16 July 1945, my soil in the Alamagordo
desert of New Mexico was witness to an event that should never
have been allowed to take place!' groaned Montezuma, as if he were
grievously wounded. 'The first test of the atom bomb! Far away,
Oppenheimer performed a macabre dance on witnessing the success
of the Trident experiment. Familiar with the Sanskrit texts of the
Hindu Aryans, he remembered an uplifting line from the Gita. "I am

Death," he quoted, "and I am Life!" and then, he exulted, "I am now the incarnation of Death...I am here to lay waste to the earth...I am now Death itself..." The mushrooming cloud of radioactivity obliterated the sky. That day, the sun refused to rise. Even in the subterranean regions of the earth, the blast had its impact. The underground waters boiled. Fish writhed in the heat, as corals and aquatic life perished. The delicate skin of mermaids broke out in boils and blisters. Even Gilgamesh, burrowing into the depths of the sea for his antidote, started to boil in the heated waters. He began to suffocate. I had descended to the depths of the sea to rescue my friend Gilgamesh. And what did I see—boiling waters, sea foam aflame, shoals of dying fish, crumbling palaces of coral, charred sea anemone and mermaids writhing in the scalding waters. Somehow, I was able to help Gilgamesh. We were lucky to have discovered a tulsi shrub growing by the River of Fire. Its dark leaves and buds sheltered Gilgamesh from the fiery waves.'

From somewhere in the universe, came the sound of clanging chains. The voice of Prometheus rang out. 'Protect Gilgamesh,' it exhorted. 'Tell him...tell him that to the right of the tulsi, in the direction of the deepest stratum of the sea, there lies a sea path leading to the forest of fire. This flaming forest is flanked on one side by the mythical mountain that shelters the setting sun; on the other side lies the hamlet of dreams. Hidden in this hamlet is the divine physician, Shurupak—the sole purveyor of the elixir of life. It is this elixir alone that can liberate us from death!'

39

'Honourable sir, you must do something to free us from the clutches of death!' the peon implored the adeeb in anguished tones. 'While Shurupak sits guarding the elixir of life, a mad race is on in the world's laboratories to produce the most horrifying weapons of death and destruction. After successful testing, war-mongering political establishments produce weapons of mass destruction on a large scale. Do something, honourable adeeb; otherwise, the planet Earth will vanish from the face of the universe!'

'You can't be serious!' the adeeb exclaimed in concern.

'I am, sir. I've just returned with information from Montezuma's council. Atomic and hydrogen bombs are being manufactured in Los Alamos. Oppenheimer, John Manley, Taylor and Fermi are involved in manufacturing bombs that will destroy all creation.'

'But Germany is on the verge of losing the war,' the adeeb countered. 'The Russian forces have brought the Germans to their knees. Their surrender is imminent. So, why do we need bombs?'

'Anything is possible in the insanity of war. Though the German physicists, Weizecker and Heizenberg, do not see eye to eye with Hitler, they're staunch nationalists who would willingly die for the sake of inventing a German bomb!'

'And the Soviet Union?'

'There, Kurchatov has been assigned the task of manufacturing death. The Russians fear Weizecker and Heizenberg's invention. Piotr Capizza has refused to work on the bomb and has been sentenced by Stalin to seven years of hard labour. His passport has been impounded and he is under house arrest.'

'And Britain?'

'Most of Britain's scientists are foreigners. They have Fritz and Perls, joined by two assistants sent over by Joliet Curie from France—the Austrian, von Holborne, and the Russian, Kovarsky. Like Capizza, another exiled scientist, Max Bourne, has refused to work on the bomb. Both Capizza and Bourne believe that these bombs are detrimental to human existence.'

The adeeb heaved a sigh of relief. At least, there was someone to defend the forces of life, he was thinking, when bloodied History returned...

There was a violent explosion. The earth shook as if hit by a massive meteor. Dust and smoke swirled around the place. Chaos prevailed. Flames shot up. A scorching wind raged. Temperatures vied with the heat of the sun, as radioactive rays spread far and wide. And then, from the fissures in the earth, spurted streams of blood.

The world stood stunned.

Newspaper headlines screamed helpless outrage across the globe:

AUGUST 6—ATOMIC ATTACK ON HIROSHIMA

AMERICA ATTACKS CITY WITH ATOMIC BOMB

ENTIRE TOWN DESTROYED

DEVASTATION ON EARTH

Standing 150 miles away from the devastation, a blind girl claimed, 'I saw the sun burning.' Unaware of the destruction, a man on his way home was struck by the changed landscape. 'There's no place I could call home,' he volunteered, 'but my Hiroshima had the biggest railway station in southern Japan...can't imagine where it has vanished. Forests and hills surrounded my city on three sides. Can't figure out where they, too, have disappeared! My entire town seems to have gone! I hope I haven't lost my way and reached a strange destination!'

'No, you're not in the wrong place,' he was told by the voice of the hydrogen bomb which would devastate Nagasaki on 9 August 1945. 'Now, you won't recognize Nagasaki either!'

The adeeb let out an agonized scream. He stuffed his ears with cotton wool and shut his eyes. Overcome by anxiety, the peon hurriedly shut the gates of the court.

But loud knocking ensued immediately. As the peon looked towards the adeeb in alarm, the latter opened his eyes and said, 'Let them in.'

Once again, an injured Hiroshima stood before them. Pus oozed from its wounds. The adeeb gaped at it and said, 'You're here again?'

'I had to return to show you my wounds. I have not been given the justice I deserve.'

'So, what is to be done now?'

'The scientists who made these devastating bombs and the politicians who put them to use, roam free even today. You must devise a suitable form of punishment for them; or else, their soaring ambitions will run amuck.'

The peon ordered each of these men to make an appearance in the court. America's President Roosevelt arrived, adjusting his three-piece suit. An arrogant Truman entered, knotting his tie. He was accompanied by Groves, the chief of the Manhattan Project, who tried to hold in his protruding paunch as he walked in. Atomic scientists like Oppenheimer, Fermi, Taylor, Arthur Compton, Conant and Zillard also made their appearance.

At the sight of them trooping into the court, Hiroshima could no longer contain itself and screamed, 'All of them are monsters! Murderers, every one of them! Enemies of human civilization and culture who deserve no forgiveness!' In an instant, Hiroshima had caught President Truman by the throat. Somehow, the peon succeeded in separating the two, but Truman's impeccable attire was soiled by the pus oozing from Hiroshima's gaping wounds.

The court, brimming with people, was festooned with the wings of all those butterflies that had perished during the first atomic test. Also in the court were corals and oysters, breathing their last. Singed sea anemone stood about as scarred mermaids fanned themselves with tulsi leaves.

'This is a straightforward case of mankind's callous extermination, because American President Truman had no ostensible reason or justification for the atomic attack! Truman, speak up! In the Mediterranean region, Mussolini had been killed. The Soviets had brought Berlin and Hitler to their knees. Hitler had made preparations for carrying out his joint suicide pact with his mistress Eva Braun. And Japan was ready to surrender. Why, then, did you order attacks on Japan using atomic and hydrogen bombs?'

'That was a military decision,' Truman replied.

'But your military command had chosen to attack the cities of Tokyo, Yokohama, Osaka, Kobe, Nagoya, Yawata and Kyoto...the same Kyoto where the imperial residence of Japan's emperor was located.'

'That was, indeed, a controversial issue,' Truman declared. 'After the death of President Roosevelt, I had become the President of an America embroiled in war...'

'You were a nine-day-old President, weren't you, when you made the crucial decision of attacking Japan with atomic weapons!'

'I was.'

'You needed the atomic bomb to counter the German offensive.

How was it that you decided to use it against Japan?'

'There were two reasons. Firstly, we did not want the Soviets
to assume control over a defeated Japan. Secondly, we wanted to
keep Japan under our control. That is why we had bombed Hiroshima
on 6 August. But on 8 August, Russia declared war on Japan and
attacked Manchuria. Dropping these bombs was a way of testing
their potential for destruction, curbing Russia and intimidating
Japan.'

'This potential could well have been tested in an ocean, on a
desert or on a mountain range.'

'I prefer not to interfere with military or paramilitary decisions.
And, yes, our first tests were conducted in the deserts of New
Mexico because...'

'Yes?'

'Because we had to gauge the exact magnitude of destruction
these bombs were capable of,' Edward Taylor, the inventor of the
hydrogen bomb, stepped forward to explain. 'In principle, I was
against this decision. I didn't want humans dying like insects and
grubs. But my opinions were of no consequence in the face of those
upheld by Oppenheimer and Graves. In fact, I had begun to regret
the horrifying possibilities of death that my invention had opened
up.'

'Why, in that case, did you invent the hydrogen bomb?'

'It was just a stage in the progressive march of pure science.
Science by itself is neither moral nor immoral. The question of its
morality or immorality arises when its relevance is determined in the
context of human welfare. Honourable adeeb, the core of my moral
being was shaken, when I learnt that these bombs would be used on
human habitations. I had bitterly cursed myself then.'

'President Truman, when you came to know of the awesome
destruction and havoc that these bombs could wreak, didn't your
conscience trouble you?'

Truman's glance was shifty. He remained silent.

'This inhuman decision was taken by these three monsters here!'
exclaimed the peon, pointing to Stimson, Truman's political advisor,
Graves, the director of the Los Alamos laboratory and director of the

Manhattan Project, and the scientist Oppenheimer. 'Honourable sir, like Hitler, Mussolini and Tojo, these three are not only war criminals, but also guilty of despicable crimes against humanity. Here's that demon, Stimson, who changed the course of scientific research for political expediency and told General Graves, "Our bombs symbolize political power. They should be used as quickly as possible against Japan, so that we can be sure of their destructive capability. They should be dropped over areas with a high density of population and especially those places where armament factories and workers' housing projects are located."'

General Graves looked at Oppenheimer out of the corner of his eye.

'And as for this scientist Robert Oppenheimer! He had written to a friend, "There are two things which afford me infinite pleasure—the science of physics and the desert! I always thought that there was no way to unite them, but today they appear before me as one—the miracle that is physics and the desert of Hiroshima stretching before my eyes!"'

'They are assassins, every one of them!'

'They are the enemies of mankind!'

'May worms consume them!'

'May their blood be transformed into rotting flesh!'

'These monsters should be sentenced to death by this court!' shouted Hiroshima, as Nagasaki came to stand by it.

'No,' the adeeb interjected, 'death would be a boon for these cruel and treacherous killers, for Yamraj's hell and the underworld of Hades would refuse entry to the spirits of these utterly corrupt men. Each one stands as a unique manifestation of the vilest of sins in the entire history of the universe. They symbolize sin at its most evil. In the chronicle of the atomic age, they will be remembered as the most demonic incarnation of violence. Their spirits will never rest in peace; they will never be free from the suffering of death. Even suicide will not absolve them of their sin. Ghosts are not known to lose their minds, but these three spirits will beat their breasts in a frenzy of lament till the end of time. The sound will forever echo in man's heart. And...and...' The adeeb was still speaking, when perspiration beaded his brow. He felt as if he was being throttled.

Startled, the peon quickly approached him and asked, 'What is it, sir?'

'Mahmood Ali, a terrible pain afflicts my heart!'

40

The few hearts that survive are only to be found in hospitals. The peon, Mahmood Ali, had the adeeb taken to one.

Three days later, the adeeb slowly regained consciousness in the ICCU. He imagined that he was lying on the soft sands of an island. As he gradually became alert to his surroundings, he noticed a picture on the wall in front of him. It depicted high-rise buildings in a township. They overlooked a plot of vacant land. On it stood a small shack. In the midst of these grand buildings, the shack looked like a half-burnt log of wood discarded in a cremation ground. As he became more attuned to his surroundings, the adeeb noticed an inverted bottle suspended from a stand on his left. He had been put on a drip.

The nursing matron's attention was drawn to him. She smiled and approached him. Touching him tenderly on the forehead, she observed, 'So you're awake now...that's good.'

'Where am I, Sister?' he asked.

'You're in the ICCU.'

'Oh...how long have I been here?'

'For the last three days.'

'What's there in that bottle, Sister?'

'Your blood pressure was very low; so, you were put on a drip.'

'Since when?'

'Last evening.'

'Since last evening? Oh...a drip...'

'Why, what is it?'

'In its place, you should've hung up a bottle of whiskey. My blood pressure would've become normal in half an hour.'

The nurse burst out laughing. The other nurses had never heard such loud laughter in the ICCU. It brought a smile to their lips.

'This patient will make a speedy recovery,' the matron informed her junior colleagues. 'He isn't worried about his heart.'

The adeeb was made to go through a number of tests in the ICCU. Only his wife was allowed to visit him every day for twenty minutes. Sometimes, his daughter Manu was allowed in for the same period of time. Let alone food, even water from outside the hospital premises was prohibited. Gayatri, however, occasionally managed to sneak in a chicken patty for him in her purse. The adeeb often remembered his grandchildren Anant and Minti. So, Alok would park his car right below the window of his hospital room and make the two children sit on the car's hood. Though they could not see their grandfather, they would wave out to him and send him their best wishes.

Having spent quite some time in the ICCU, the adeeb had come to realize that what he had been seeing on the wall facing his bed was not a picture after all, but an actual scene—a dilapidated shack that stood in a field over which loomed high-rise buildings. There was certainly one tiny change in the scene before him. Within the glass rectangle in front of him, the branch of a gulmohar tree—thrust against the windowpanes, no doubt by a gust of breeze—would occasionally wave its scarlet blossoms and disappear from view.

Laid up in hospital, he had taken to musing that once upon a time, the houses used to be small. The trees were tall and sheltered the houses in their shade. Now, the trees themselves were dwarfed by tall buildings and had learnt to live in their shade. However, the shack outside still enjoyed the shade of a tree...probably, a neem tree. He saw a woman pass by. She had a neem twig clenched between her teeth like a cheroot and carried some enamel utensils in her hands.

The nurse who was taking his blood pressure remarked, 'That's her...'

'Who?'

'The woman who lives in the shack,' the nurse replied, glancing at the heart monitor. 'She's a sweeper here. You were asking about her yesterday...'

'Sitting at your desk, you keep observing all our heartbeats,' the adeeb remarked.

A smile flickered across the nurse's lips as she asked, 'Shall I call her?'

'Call whom?'

'Kaushalya...the woman who lives in the shack...the one you want to meet.'

A few moments later, Kaushalya was standing by his bed.

'You seem much better today, Babu. Maybe they'll move you from the ICCU today and put you in an ordinary room. All I keep asking the good God is this—let everyone get well soon and go back where they belong.'

'Since when have you been working here?'

'Ever since Nanku joined the army.'

'Nanku?'

'That's my only son, Babu. Why did you send for me?'

'Oh, no particular reason...is that shack yours?'

'Yes, Babu, it is.' Kaushalya's reply was wary. 'Why would you want to know?' She looked at the adeeb suspiciously and declared, 'I'm not selling it by the way...no matter how much you offer for it, we aren't selling.'

'Kaushalya, I wasn't thinking of any business transaction. It was just a stray question...'

'Oh, no, Babu, not a stray question at all...whoever sets eyes on our shack, gets talking about buying it. They're willing to pay any price we quote, but I tell them off, making it very clear that our shack is not for sale. Once, a contractor had come in his huge car— the same fellow who has built all these massive buildings practically on top of us. His men started measuring out my land. We yelled at them. The next day, his goons arrived and threatened to throw us out. The third day the man turned up again...right here, as a patient in bed number four! The doctor said there was nothing wrong with him, but his lawyer insisted he'd had a massive heart attack. The doctors eventually gave in. The police were all over the place— inside as well as outside. Now, many people like him keep coming here...'

As the adeeb looked intently at Kaushalya, she continued, 'I even looked after him...prayed for him. One day, he asked, "Why do you work yourself to the bone here? Take a two-roomed flat and live an easy life. We'll even give you money over and above the flat. You can live comfortably without a care in the world." But I told him, Babu, that I would not sell my shack no matter what. And, the second point is—for all these years, the army has not given Nanku any leave. But one day, he'll come home. Then, what? What will he do if he finds the shack gone and his mother nowhere in sight? Am I right, Babu?'

'You're right, Kaushalya,' the adeeb replied in a voice choked with emotion.

'I may be working here now, but my heart is always there in that shack.'

The adeeb gazed at Kaushalya with great sadness. Then his gaze travelled to the shack beyond the wall of glass. At that moment, Sister called out to Kaushalya. As she was leaving, the branch with the gulmohar blossoms peeped in at the window again. Dushyant's words reverberated around his bed: *To live in the shade of my garden's gulmohar/To die for the gulmohar even in unknown alleys...*

The gulmohar branch peeped into the adeeb's room yet again. Perhaps, there had been a gust of breeze outside...

41

This time, the breeze that blew outdoors was laden with toxins. It leached the colour from the scarlet gulmohar flowers, turning them yellow. The adeeb was gazing beyond time, into the centuries gone by. It was the same breeze that had swept in from Ghazni in the eleventh century and demolished the Somnath Mandir. It had then blown from Somnath and demolished the Babri Masjid. The whirlwinds created by this poisonous breeze simply refused to die down.

In 1990, from the forecourt of the Somnath Mandir had started a tornado that left a trail of destruction in its wake as it passed through Ayodhya, Maharashtra, Uttar Pradesh, Karnataka and Andhra Pradesh before reaching Pokhran in 1998.

Buddha Purnima—11 May 1998. Three forty-five p.m. The arteries of the desert had burst open. The ground had trembled. Nine hundred feet below the surface, in the womb of Pokhran, three explosions had occurred. The wind had dropped as the temperature shot up to ten lakh degrees, matching the heat of the sun. Below the sands, hundreds of thousands of tons of rocky cliff had crumbled, melted and turned into clouds of vapour. A mile-long stretch of sand had risen like a gigantic mushroom cloud and lay suspended over the desert.

The adeeb had suffered another heart attack.

Then, another explosion had taken place in Chagai, Baluchistan. The wind had dropped. The arteries of the mountain had burst open. The temperature had risen to ten lakh degrees and Chagai had been reduced to hillocks of white ash.

It had been followed by another explosion at Pokhran.

Echoed by yet another at Chagai.

This time, the adeeb had suffered a massive heart attack.

The peon had rushed in. 'Sir, has it happened again...?'

'Yes, Mahmood Ali, the pain is far less intense this time, but my heart has been reduced to cinders.'

A gasping Salma had rushed in. 'Adeeb!' she had screamed. 'Tell me, please, what could have befallen my grandfather?' Noticing the adeeb's grave condition, she had quietened down.

Once again, he was moved to the ICCU. He had no idea how long he remained unconscious there. When he regained his senses, he had a strange dream in which the accursed, ever-restless spirit of Oppenheimer alternately beat its breast and roared with derisive laughter.

He opened his eyes. He was bathed in sweat. Salma was tenderly wiping his body. The nurse came in to give him a dose of medicine. Then, gently taking his hand in hers, Salma said, 'Could I tell you something?'

He could only gaze at her.

'These days, I have a strange dream,' she said.

He experienced an inexplicable flicker of anxiety, but blinked, as if gesturing for her to continue.

'In this oft-recurring dream, I see a spirit which laughs, then beats its breast...'

Staring at her, he hesitantly replied, 'It's the same dream, Salma. But its meaning seems to have altered...'

Before he could finish speaking, the collector of tears rushed in.

'Arrey, it's you! How are you?' the adeeb asked.

'I'm fine,' the man replied. 'If you remember...I had started collecting perspiration instead of tears. But now, instead of perspiration, I collect dreams...shattered fragments of dreams.'

'That's all very well, but where do you store these dreams?'

'There...at the place Prometheus has told me about—on the other side of the flaming forest, behind the mountain where the sun sets, in the abode of dreams...'

'It's good of you to do this.'

The adeeb was now lost in thought. When the nurse came to check his blood pressure, he said, 'I haven't seen Kaushalya.'

'She's gone looking for her son in the cantonment at Udhampur.'

'And her shack?'

'That's on the other side. You can't see it from here.' She noted his blood pressure, then remarked, 'We'll move you out of the ICCU and into a room after a while.'

Once he was moved, people turned up to see him. Wishes for his speedy recovery abounded. Gayatri began smuggling in chicken patties again.

Then the peon, Mahmood Ali, entered, accompanied by Prometheus. The adeeb looked on in amazement. Though chains no longer bound Prometheus, the vulture sitting on his shoulder was still busy gouging out his flesh and gulping it down.

'It's you...Prometheus!'

'Yes, adeeb, I am here to wish you a speedy recovery.'

'And your chains...the ones in which Zeus bound you?'

'My friend, I just could not bear the atomic attack on Hiroshima and Nagasaki. It infuriated me to a degree that generated a heat many times greater than the sun's. That was when Zeus's chains melted like wax! These gods cannot imagine what power the fury of mankind can have. And this vulture...this creature too will, one day, tire of gouging out my flesh. It cannot begin to fathom the depths of forbearance and tolerance of which the human race is capable. When this bird tires of consuming my flesh and eventually gives up, I shall bathe in the Nile. Then, I shall purify the waters of the Danube, the Ota in Hiroshima and the gulf of Nagasaki by bathing in them.'

Hiroshima and Nagasaki had also turned up to wish the adeeb well before they returned to Japan.

'Don't feel you are all alone,' the adeeb consoled them.

They expressed their gratitude. 'Now your collector of tears has also rendered to our eyes some dreams,' they told him. 'Who knows from how many dying eyes, he has salvaged such dreams.'

Then Montezuma took his leave.

'So, you too have chosen to go?' the adeeb asked him.

'No, my departure does not mean that I am returning to my land...I shall live here. This is the only civilization that has sustained its ancient peoples and cultures. It is only here that I will be able to survive...'

As evening spread across the sky, the peon entered with the nurse and announced, 'A lady wishes to see you for a couple of minutes.'

'A lady?' the adeeb asked in surprise.

'Yes, she was also a patient in the ICCU, like you are. She has been discharged today.'

'She was also here in the ICCU?' he repeated the words with a smile. 'That's interesting! It means that our hearts have been beating in unison. She's most welcome.'

As soon as the lady stepped in, a fragrance filled the room. The adeeb was stunned. He just could not believe his eyes.

'You!' he cried out in amazement.

'Yes, I'm here from Pakistan. My son is posted at the Pakistan High Commission here as the secretary of culture and information. I was desperate to see Hindustan. This time, when he came, he brought me along.'

The adeeb wanted to say something, many things. But he could not figure out what it was that held him back.

'When I arrived, I just travelled here and there for a whole month...'

'Did you...did you go...' the adeeb could not go on, his throat felt parched for words.

'I also went to Kanpur. The railway station is now so huge...it has changed so much...'

'It certainly is a great deal bigger now...but nothing else has changed,' the adeeb replied. Silently, he told himself, 'For me, a handkerchief still wafts down onto the platform there!'

'I suffered a heart attack when I returned from Kanpur. My son got me admitted here...'

'Vidya!' he wanted to call out loudly. 'Vidya!' But he restrained himself and all he asked was, 'And where is your son?'

'He has gone to pay the hospital bill. When he comes back, you will get to meet him. Your stories sometimes appeared in Pakistani magazines. I would read them and wonder if it was the same person...'

'The same person...?'

Pari smiled and said, 'I wonder if you received it...in the beginning, I even wrote you a letter...a very childish one.'

'I did get that letter.'

'That was, surely, destiny. Addresses have changed, changed so radically that leave alone the message, even my greetings would not have reached you...'

Her son arrived at this juncture and she introduced them to each other. 'This is Parvez, my son,' she said, 'and Parvez, here is the writer of the story I had made you read...'

'Adaab!'

'Adaab...'

As Pari rose from her chair, she accidentally dropped her handkerchief. To the adeeb, it seemed that the handkerchief had fallen once again to the ground. He gestured to it and said, 'Your kerchief...'

Pari picked it up, thanked him, bade him farewell and walked out with her son.

The adeeb could only look on. His words remained unspoken:
After Pokhran, all our peacocks either died or flew away to another
land. What happened to your honeybees in the date palms after
Chagai?

42

'...and so, honeybees and butterflies, peacocks, pigeons, sparrows,
kingfishers, bulbuls, khanjans, papihas and lalis shall never again
alight on our rooftops and houses,' the blind Kabir was saying. Then,
he picked up his ektara and began to sing, 'It's only a true believer
who understands the pain of others...'

He sang for a while, then picked up his white cane and set off.
From his shoulder hung a bag. From time to time, droplets of
muddy water dripped from it.

The adeeb gazed at him, perplexed. He quickened his pace and
caught up with him. Finally, he asked, 'Kabir, where are you
headed—Bandra Masjid or Mount Mary?'

'No, not there...this time, I'm embarking on a long journey—
first to Pokhran, then, to Chagai.'

Surprised, the adeeb was about to ask him the reason, when
Kabir, anticipating the question, continued, 'Certain people who
have completely lost their senses wish to use Pokhran as an arena for
testing strength and power. They are bent on distributing the toxic
ashes of atomic testing. Haven't you seen them in the newspapers—
those deranged expressions of people blinded by religion? Those
were the people who embarked on a rathyatra from Somnath. From
there, they had set out to demolish the Babri Masjid...'

'But how did you...? I mean...'

'You mean that I'm blind, don't you? Well, because of my
blindness, I can see everything so clearly.'

'But, what will you do there? What could you possibly hope to
achieve? I mean, what is your reason for wanting to go there?'

'I shall plant trees.'

'Trees?'

'Yes. Bodhivriksh...banyan trees. Banyan saplings are what I carry in my bag. Like Shiva, the roots of the banyan can absorb all poisons. At Pokhran, I shall plant the first bodhivriksh. The second one shall be planted in the Chagai Hills, once I have crossed the border. So, I'll be on my way.'

As the adeeb looked on, Kabir's white cane took the first step. His feet followed.

A Note on Shibli Nomani

In the course of reading this translated version of *Kitne Pakistan*, I had a feeling that I owe an explanation on one character who features prominently in the novel—the great nationalist and intellectual scholar Shibli Nomani. It is possible that in reading this, one may be inclined to think of Shibli Nomani as a bigoted zealot who supported Aurangzeb's Islamic zeal. It is incumbent on me to clarify that he was not. It was out of sheer intellectual honesty that he defended Aurangzeb and championed his cause in his writings. That is the reason why he is called to the court by the *adeeb*.

Kamleshwar

Translator's Acknowledgement

I would like to thank Kamleshwar, Javed M. Ansari, Anisur Rehman, and the University Grants Commission's Special Assistance Programme on Translation, Department of English, Jamia Millia Islamia, New Delhi.

Ameena Kazi Ansari